BALTIC THUNDER

An Alan Llewellyn Novel

Walt Breede

Baltic Thunder
by Walt Breede

Signalman Publishing
www.signalmanpublishing.com
email: info@signalmanpublishing.com
Tampa, Florida

Baltic Thunder is a work of fiction. Names, characters, most places and incidents either are the product of the author's imagination or are used fictitiously. Any resemblance to actual persons, living or dead, events or locales, is entirely coincidental. The reader may recognize some thinly disguised places. The author had the great good fortune to have lived for 27 years in the Commonwealth of Virginia and, in writing this work of fiction, did play a bit fast and loose with places, pubs and such in the name of telling a story.

ISBN: 978-1-940145-87-7

Signalman
Publishing

Dedication

This little novel is dedicated to the teachers, coaches and clergy of Archbishop Stepinac High School in White Plains, New York, during the late fifties, especially Reverend Monsignor John J. Mulroy, Father James H. Cashman, OSC, Brother Andrew Joseph, CFX, Brother Meinrad, CFX, Brother Isidor, CFX, Brother Leroy, CFX, Brother Lucas, CFX, Reverend Monsignor Stanley G. Mathews, Reverend Monsignor James M. McDermott, Reverend Joseph F. McGann, Reverend William J. McGann, Reverend Bernard J. McMahon, Mr. Raymond Morris, Reverend Harry Quinn, OSFS, Reverend John T. Ryan, CSV, Reverend Monsignor Jeremiah B. Sullivan, Mr. T. Joseph Sullivan, Mr. Joseph Torpy, Mr. Ignatius Volpe, Reverend Walter Murray, Reverend Thomas E. O'Keefe, Reverend John Lyons, Reverend Monsignor Francis J. Melican and Reverend Edward Kenrick.

WASHINGTON, D.C.
METROPOLITAN AREA

CAMP DAVID

BALTIMORE

SEVERN RIVER

MARYLAND

ANNAPOLIS
(U.S.N.A.)

PENTAGON

WASHINGTON D.C.

VIRGINIA

A. WASHINGTON
HIGH SCHOOL

PATUXENT
RIVER

CHESAPEAKE BAY

CHANCELLORSVILLE

CHESTERTOWN, VA

POTOMAC RIVER

RAPPAHANNOCK RIVER

NORTH SEA AND BALTIC SEA

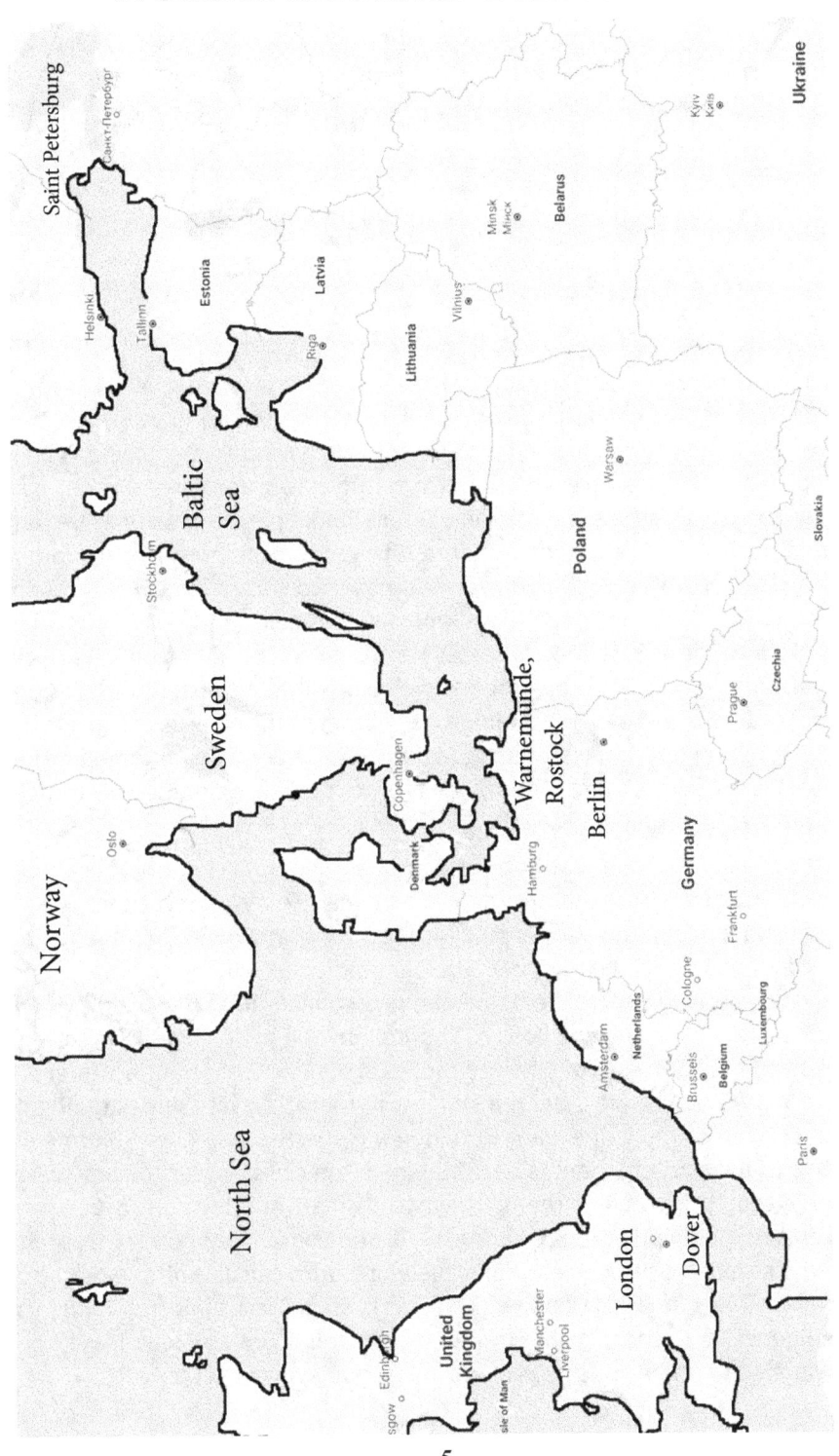

Prologue
Officer DiRienzo

Gerlach Community College
Gayles Ferry, Virginia
Late March

The night was cold and wet with a slashing wind out of the northeast. The icy rain whipped down, slant-wise. The young man circled the college parking lot in his battered Chevy Volt, its wipers slapping. His hair was black and his face appeared to be unshaven for several days, per the current hipster code. The only empty parking spaces were at the far end of the lot, a good one hundred fifty yards away from the academic building, Campbell Hall. Shit! He would have to walk all the way through the blowing rain. He parked and got out of the car and felt the icy rain slam into the left side of his face. He retrieved the rifle from the back seat. Tugging the operating rod handle back a little, he ensured that there was indeed a round in the chamber. The brass of the shell casing gleamed up at him in the dim light of the parking lot. There were nineteen more rounds in the magazine. Hefting the ten-pound rifle, he draped his trench coat over part of it and headed for the hall.

He knew that the first floor of Campbell Hall consisted of offices that were mostly closed and unoccupied at night. He also knew there was a faculty lounge that was open and a coffee pot keeping bitter coffee tepid. Occasionally, faculty members—usually adjuncts—hung out there for short periods. Less frequently, a campus cop like himself would pop in for a sip of the raunchy coffee. The bulk of the action during evenings was on the second floor—where the classrooms were. And the students. He knew because he'd been a student in room 218 last semester. Right at the top of the stairs. Sam Gardiner was the teacher. There had been twenty-four other students besides him in the class last term. They were privileged pricks, all of them. They were smart and lusted for lucrative careers in biomedical engineering, medicine and information technology. Why else come out on cold, rainy nights to learn calculus after working a full day? He had barely survived Calculus I with a C last semester. Tonight's students were most of his former classmates from Calculus I. He had watched them file in for class for the last two evening sessions.

He pulled open one of the heavy glass doors and savored the blast of warm air as he went in. He glanced at the clock on the wall by the stairwell. It read seven-twenty. Perfect! Gardiner's class would be going on break upstairs in ten or fifteen minutes. He mounted the stairs easily and silently.

Three pairs of upholstered chairs were clustered around the top of the stairs and they were all empty. Selecting a chair that faced the closest door to room 218, he sat. He kept the trench coat over the M-14 rifle, which he held across his knees. He looked at the clock: 7:22.

Gardiner's door opened at seven twenty-nine and Holly Ferguson was the first one out. The young man remembered her well. Holly, at age nineteen, was the youngest student in the class. She had light brown hair, blue eyes and a great smile. Plus a great figure. She recognized him immediately and beamed.

"Hey, Glenn!" she called.

He pulled the trench coat off the weapon, shouldered the rifle and leveled it at her chest.

"Die, bitch!" He snarled.

Then he pulled the trigger.

The rifle slammed. By the time the echo of that first shot died out, there were two more of his former fellow students out of the classroom and he shot them both. Stepping to the classroom door, he turned the selector switch to *auto* and emptied the rest of the magazine, making sure that he'd put at least two rounds into Gardiner.

The racket was hellish. The rifle roared repeatedly and intermittently. Three- or four-round bursts snapped into the classroom. Window glass shattered and people bled and screamed. When the firing ceased, there was only the sound of a couple of people whimpering and moaning. The young man turned and headed for the stairs. From the top step, he saw a uniformed security campus cop. He was pudgy and old but he had his Glock drawn. He raised it in a two-handed firing position.

"Drop the rifle and put your hands on your head!" Officer Gerry DiRienzo shouted.

The young man aimed the empty rifle at the cop and DiRienzo fired twice, hitting the young man in the midsection. The latter dropped the rifle and slammed back on the stairs, sliding down three or four steps before a foot caught in the banister railing, halting the slide of his body.

"Jesus!" whispered DiRienzo. He heard sirens.

"We're gonna need EMS here! Pronto!" he said into his mic.

"They're on the way," the dispatcher said. "Are you okay?

"Yeah. One shooter is down. I don't know if there are others. This one had an automatic rifle. And Christ knows what the situation is upstairs. Kids are screaming!"

"Don't go up there! Wait for backup! I say again, wait for backup!"

"Roger that," DiRienzo said at the bottom of the stairs. "I think the backup is here now. I think we need the medics more than the backups. All I'm hearing from upstairs is screaming and groaning."

"Wait till you've got the backup and they've secured the scene before you let the EMTs up."

"Roger."

Chapter One

Alan

1506 Prince Henry Street
Chestertown, Virginia
Late March

March is a month of huge contrasts in northern Virginia. Winter usually takes a few, last-gasp swipes at us. It rains a lot. There may be a couple of dumps of winter snow. It gets cold a bit. But then, towards the end of the month, the signs of spring start exploding all over the place. Daytime temperatures start bounding upwards. The dull, cold earth tones of winter start giving way to the bright pastel greens, yellows and pinks of budding springtime growth. This afternoon, we had several windows of our hundred-year-old Colonial on Prince Henry Street open and could hear birds trilling and warbling. It's a fabulous, miraculous time of year.

Trouble is, *I* wasn't really enjoying it all that much. I, being Alan Llewellyn, husband of Maria and father of fourteen-year-old Elizabeth. I, having shot a guy in the back and watching him explode in the woods behind Augustine Washington High School just a few short months ago. It wasn't an experience that led to pleasant dreams, much less unbroken, refreshing sleep. Even though the deed was morally necessary and in line of duty. If I hadn't pulled the trigger on the guy, he would have run into the high school cafeteria and pulled *his* trigger, blowing up a lot of kids and teachers along with himself. The fact that the guy I'd shot and killed was someone I'd known and liked didn't make dealing with the aftermath any easier. Nor did the fact that my Dash-Two, Darpley Roentgen Taylor— or Darps as he's known—and I had been able to keep the whole mess under wraps, more or less. My line of work is Director of the Bureau for International Affairs Studies (*BIAS*), a small, *sub rosa* intel fact-checking outfit. My boss, Jim Kehoe, President of the United States, knew that a terrorist had blown himself up when his bomb exploded prematurely on his way to the high school. The fact that a three-oh-eight caliber bullet fired by yours truly had initiated the explosion remained suppressed, at least as far as I knew.

I had arrived home on foot a few minutes before five-thirty. One of the great benefits of my job was that it was within easy walking distance from our Chestertown home. Things had morphed into near normalcy several weeks back, but I was still a bit screwed up. Today's news about the nut case shooting at a community college less than forty miles away didn't help. I decided to try and remedy things the best way I knew how. Drawing on the love of the women in my life. I found Maria, the primary love of my life, in the kitchen, where she was hard at work. Not fixing dinner, but doing her "day job," researching military history. She was working on a scholarly article on U.S. Navy aircraft carrier operations in World War II in the Atlantic.

"Hey, love," I said. I planted a smooch on her gorgeous forehead.

"How goes the war in the Atlantic?" I asked.

"It's over," she said, smiling. "For now, at least. I've had enough of it for today."

She closed her MacBook Pro and gathered up folders, pencils and other detritus of research and writing.

"Where's Elizabeth?" I asked, querying about the other love of my life, our lovely daughter.

"She's around somewhere," Maria said. "With Esmé."

Chapter Two

Sheila

Crystal City, Virginia
Late March

Vice Admiral Sheila Donegan, USN, Director of Naval Intelligence and Commander, Naval Intelligence Command let herself into her condo apartment. It was eight in the evening and she was exhausted, as usual at the end of her thirteen-hour workday. She popped off her medium heel uniform pumps, unbuttoned her uniform Navy-blue blouse and slipped it off her shoulders. She then went to her tiny liquor cabinet in the kitchen, pulled out a one-and-a-half-liter bottle of Dewar's scotch and poured herself a generous glassful after adding a small handful of ice cubes. Finally she collapsed on her small couch, grabbed the remote and clicked on the TV.

Admiral Donegan was a totally dedicated Naval officer. She had graduated from the Naval Academy close to the top of her class and had gone directly into Naval Intelligence. She had distinguished herself by graduating at the top of her class at the Navy-Marine Corps Intelligence Training Center (NMITC) at Dam Neck, Virginia. From there, her career had continued to take off. As a Lieutenant, she'd authored a forward-leaning and well-respected paper on the coordination among various Middle East and North African radical groups. As a Commander, she had a tour as the N-2 (Intelligence Officer) of the U. S. Sixth Fleet, during which she'd accurately predicted the darker side of the so-called Arab Spring. A few years later, as a Captain, she'd commanded NMITC and introduced reforms, which integrated Navy and Marine Corps intelligence collection and analysis efforts.

Her brief marriage to Lieutenant Bret Davenport, USN, ended tragically when his F/A-18 was brought down by rebel ground fire in Afghanistan. After the funeral, she decided to return to the use of her maiden name.

Now, at age 46, she was athletically slender and fit, five-foot-seven, had frosted light brown hair and nicely shaped features, which broke into smiles readily. Now, however, she was not smiling. A close look would have revealed the beginnings of crows' feet alongside her eyes and at the corners of her attractive mouth.

She was surprised that there was breaking news on the TV when she arrived home. In her office in the Pentagon, she had eight TV sets tuned to the major networks and cable news stations. When she'd left twenty-five minutes ago, she'd been on top of all the latest news. Now, however, she was behind the news curve. A breathless announcer was describing a scene of unbelievable carnage at a community college in Virginia. Her cell phone chirped. It was her office. She picked up the handset.

"Let me guess," she said. "You're calling about the shooting at Gerlach Community."

"Yes, Ma'am," Intelligence Specialist First Class (IS1) Porter said.

"I've got it on FOX now. Do you have anything to add?" she asked.

"No, Ma'am," Porter said. "Lone wolf shooter. Nineteen KIA, including the teacher. Six WIA. All students. Shooter was dropped by a campus cop. KIA too. Makes for a total of twenty dead."

"God bless the cop," Donegan said. "Do I need to come in?"

"No Ma'am. We'll track it from here. So far, it seems like a deranged college kid. No obvious terrorist connections," Porter answered. "So far, anyway."

"Okay," she said. "Call me if anything else develops."

"Aye, aye, Ma'am," Porter responded.

Admiral Donegan hung up the phone, leaned back on the couch and took another sip of scotch.

A loser/weirdo gets his hands on a gun and murders a bunch of people. Community college kids and a teacher, for God's sake. There's got to be a way to put an end to this crap, she thought.

Donegan had a niece in college. Not at Gerlach Community, thank the Lord.

Chapter Three

Sheila

Crystal City, Virginia and the Pentagon
Late March

Vice Admiral Donegan's alarm went off at five-thirty a.m. She built a cup of dark roast coffee in her one-cup coffee brewer. Then she turned on the TV to a local news channel that slid national and international news into their local broadcast in brief snippets. She retrieved the morning's copy of the Washington Post from outside her door.

ANOTHER MASS MURDER ON CAMPUS! screamed the front-page headline. ***Twenty Dead At Gayles Ferry Campus*** read the subhead. The story didn't add much to what she already knew. The shooter had been identified as one Wayne Wesley Holmes, a twenty-two-year old former Gerlach CC student who had lived with his mother. The slain teacher was an adjunct professor named Samuel Eliot Gardiner who taught evenings at the college. During the day, he was a popular mathematics teacher at Gayles Ferry High School.

Donegan sipped coffee and turned to the editorial page. The editorials were predictable, as were the op-ed pieces. Outrage. Frustration. Dump the Second Amendment! She sipped more coffee. She found herself starting to agree with the statistics-challenged editorial writers. *Good Lord! How much more of this slaughter do we have to put up with?* she thought.

She finished her coffee, glanced at the clock and headed for the shower. She needed to get to work. Forty-five minutes later she was heading north and west on the George Washington Parkway to the Pentagon. She arrived at her Pentagon office at five minutes after seven. She flipped through her message traffic, much of which was concerned with the massacre in Virginia. So far, it still seemed to be a homegrown atrocity as opposed to an international terrorist incident. Holmes, the dead shooter, was a dysfunctional loser from a dysfunctional fragmented family. He had attended a high school for socially dysfunctional kids, which he failed to complete. He attempted to enlist in the Army, lasted precisely twenty days before being discharged from boot camp and the Army for failure to comply with military regulations. His mom, divorced for fifteen years,

13

was a gun nut, collecting mostly military weapons. She had purchased the M-14 rifle that her son had used in the campus massacre legally on the Internet. After buying the rifle, she had modified it by adding a small switch, which would enable the weapon to be fired in the fully automatic mode. That modification was illegal. Charges were pending.

Most of the remainder of the morning's message traffic was centered in Syria, ISIS and an apparent Kurdish suicide bombing in Turkey. She flipped back to the messages about last night's campus killings. Nineteen community college students gunned down. Slaughtered. Dead. Her phone rang.

"It's the DNI's office calling," IS1 Porter drawled. "I think the old man wants to talk to you."

"Well, then," she said. "By all means put him through."

"Donegan," she said.

"Sheila," the Director of National Intelligence said.

She recognized the voice of Sam Braxton, the DNI, immediately. "How are you?" he asked.

"Kind of numb," she said. "That Gayles Ferry massacre has got me somewhat unglued."

"That's what I'm calling about, Sheila," Braxton said. "I know it's short notice, but could you possibly make lunch at noon today? My office, my treat? Just the two of us? We'll have you out of here by one fifteen. Promise."

Donegan glanced at her desk calendar. She had scheduled a ten-K run for eleven-thirty today. She suppressed a sigh.

"Yes sir. I'll be there at noon. Is there anything else I should know, prep-wise?"

"No, no. I think you already know everything you need to know for our little chat," Braxton said. "Shrimp cocktail plus a turkey sandwich on a croissant okay?"

"Yes sir. Sounds great. I'll see you at noon."

"Good. Can you come in civvies?" Braxton asked. "It's not a classified meeting, but I'd like to keep it off the skyline."

"Yes sir," Donegan said. "I have a change of clothes right here in the office."

"Good, good," Braxton said. "See you soon."

She elected to ride in her white Navy sedan, driven by her uniformed Marine Corps driver, Corporal McFarland, to the luncheon date. She had changed into a gray suit over a powder blue blouse. Civilian pumps—navy blue—encased her feet. She thought that taking her personal vehicle—with the three-star windshield sticker—might attract more attention than a Navy sedan carrying a civilian-clad passenger. Those white Navy sedans seemed to zoom around Washington and northern Virginia all day and every day and were part of the Washington scenery.

"I'll call you when I'm finished," she told McFarland. "I'm guessing it'll be right around thirteen fifteen."

She was hustled into the DNI's suite quickly. Braxton had stood up and was coming around his desk as she was shown into his office.

"Welcome, welcome Sheila. We'll have lunch in the next room. I'd like to keep things as comfortable as possible."

He pulled open a door to the right of his desk.

"Thanks, Sam," Donegan murmured, stepping through the door.

A small table was set for two. At the far end of the room, two comfortable-looking, overstuffed chairs flanked a coffee table.

"Would you care for a cocktail?" Braxton asked. "I'm having a scotch."

"That'll be fine for me," Donegan responded. "I'll just have to run an extra twenty minutes this evening."

A white-jacketed steward brought their drinks. Braxton held up his glass.

"Cheers, Sheila," he said.

"Cheers, Sam," she replied.

They sipped.

"Okay. I'm up," Braxton said, setting his glass down on the coffee table. "I invited you. Here's what I want to ask. What are your feelings about yesterday's horror show in Gayles Ferry?"

Sheila put her glass down on a napkin that the steward had left. "I'm appalled. And discouraged," she answered.

"I understand 'appalled'. But why 'discouraged'?" Braxton asked.

"Sam, how many more schools have to get shot up? How many students and teachers have to be slaughtered by some insane loser with a gun?"

"I have the same questions," he replied. "And some more. Like what needs to happen to correct this dreadful situation? And whatever needs to happen—*whatever*—who can and will make it happen? My questions at this point are rhetorical. Purely rhetorical."

"But your questions beg other questions," Donegan said. "Like what happens if the questions become real as opposed to rhetorical? And who is best suited to address and maybe answer them?"

Braxton picked up his glass without saying anything. He smiled briefly and sipped scotch. Donegan followed suit. As they put their glasses down, the same, white-jacketed steward entered with a tray. He placed two steaming shrimp cocktails on the table.

"Dry ice or hot shrimp?" Donegan asked, smiling.

"The former," Braxton said. "Bring your drink. Let's eat 'em while they're cold."

The rest of the luncheon conversation centered in current intelligence issues. The Soviet incursion into Syria. The future of the Assad regime in Syria. The Peoples' Republic of China's aims in East Asia and the South China Sea. No mention of the earlier "rhetorical questions."

Donegan politely refused the offer of wine with lunch, opting for sweet iced tea instead.

"I'm sure your afternoon is as full as mine, Sheila," Braxton said as they finished up small bowls of delicious chocolate-and-raspberry gelato. "I'm also sure that we're of like mind on the issue of schoolyard slaughters. I think I might try and get a somewhat larger group together to kick the 'rhetorical questions' around some more."

"Well, thanks for a delicious lunch," Donegan said. "And thanks for some intriguing food for thought as well."

She used her cell to call Corporal McFarland and told him that she would be at the door in three minutes. As she rode down in the elevator, she had to wonder what the purpose of the lunch was. And then later, as they got on the road on the way back to the Pentagon, she had to wonder some more about the reason for the lunch date. She thought she had a pretty good idea.

Chapter Four

Alan

I wandered around the old house in search of the girls. Elizabeth, our only daughter, has inherited a good chunk of her mom's beauty. At fourteen, she's on the cusp of becoming a beautiful young woman. Now nearly as tall as her mother, she has the same classical Roman features. Esmé is a classmate and friend of Elizabeth's. She's a short, slender girl with big brown eyes that always seem to look at me with an "I know what you're thinking, Mister Ell" expression. Which I found a bit unsettling. The girls were in the midst of their spring break from freshman year at All Saints Academy, a Pre-K-twelve Catholic school just outside Chestertown. I followed their voices into the family room where they were sitting on the floor. An old-looking, vaguely familiar, hardbound black book was on the floor between them. It had no dust jacket but it still looked like something that I'd seen before.

"Hi ladies!" I said. "What's up?"

"Hi Dad," and "Hi Mister Ell," they said.

Elizabeth picked up the black book.

"We're talking about an old book of yours, Dad," Elizabeth said. "I read it yesterday and Esmé read it today. We both finished it. Esmé finished it about fifteen minutes ago. I found it in the attic."

"Wow. You guys really read fast," I responded.

I looked a little closer. The only thing on the hard cover was a tiny gold logo—a torch. Probably the publisher's symbol. I picked up the book and opened the front cover and recognized the faded scrawl immediately. It was definitely mine: *A. Llewellyn – MIDN 3/c USN. Rm 5165 Bancroft Hall, U. S. Naval Academy.* I turned the page with my name on it and got the title page: *Seven Days in May*. I remembered it well. It was published in the early sixties and they made a movie of it a few years later. Rumor had it that President Kennedy pulled some Hollywood strings to ensure that they made the movie from the book. I think I read the book soon after it came out and then saw the movie a few years later. The book was a realistically spooky political thriller about the Joint Chiefs plotting a coup against the president. The authors were Fletcher Knebel and Charles W. Bailey II. If memory serves, Rod Serling of *Twilight Zone* TV fame wrote the screenplay for the film. Which followed the book's story pretty closely. I think I'd first read the book while on Youngster Cruise in the North Atlantic during the summer between my Plebe and Youngster years at Annapolis.

"Well, well," I said. "Have you developed a new interest in politics? And where did you find the book?"

"Yes, I think I have," Elizabeth said, taking the book and holding it in front of her chest. "This story is really fascinating. About a *coup d'état* attempt against the President of the United States. By the Joint Chiefs of Staff of all people! And I found the book in the attic. In a cardboard box full of dusty old books. Most of which had to do with electrical engineering or thermodynamics or other boring techno stuff like that. But this one really looked interesting. And it really was!"

She looked at me with a sly grin on her face.

"Well, no surprise there. I remember the book pretty well. They made it into a movie soon after it was published. The only surprises are that we still have the book and that you found it," I said. "You two oughta see if you can find the movie online."

"Hasn't your boss, President Kehoe, fired a General and some other big shots recently?" Esmé asked innocently.

Once again, I was amazed. I had no idea that these two girls gave a tinker's dam about flag officers' hirings and firings, let alone any sort of inside-the-beltway goings on.

"Well, yeah," I said. "That is if you count Dave Gamble. An Army three-star who was Director of the National Security Agency. Kehoe said it would be best for all concerned if he went over the side. I gather that NSA has been a little too vigorous in collecting stateside communications about U. S. citizens. Cell phone calls, text messages and social media content. Some fecal matter about that hit the fan in Congress and the press. Gamble had to walk the plank. And I think that Kehoe was spot-on in making that happen."

"Weren't there a couple of high-level civilians who walked the plank, too?" Esmé asked.

"Esmé, how do you *know* this stuff? And yes, he let two civilians go. One was his own national security advisor, Suzanne Palmer, a former high-level gal at State. She'd boasted in a college graduation speech that she could learn everything there was to know about any or all of the graduates at any time. That kind of suggested that the U. S. Government was reading everybody's mail. Not a great thing for a White House staffer to blab about in a public speech. Hence her speedy departure. The other one who went over the side was Phil Martinelli, director of the National Reconnaissance Office. He gave an interview to the L.A. Times in which he bragged about a new satellite reconnaissance capability which was developed under the auspices of the NRO. He boasted about it in fairly great detail. So both of them ran their mouths too much. And both of them should have known better."

Esmé nodded sagely and then looked at Elizabeth. She looked back at me and her eyebrows jumped a little.

"And now there are rumors swirling around in the media that Edwin Tanaka, Secretary of Education, is going to be fired," she said. "Because of some Federal mandate on education in the public schools that a lot of people don't like," she continued. "He's a retired Army General."

"I've heard those rumors, too, Esmé" I responded. "And you're right about his past. He's a retired General and a former Chief of Staff of the Army. But so what? So what if President Kehoe lets him go? Or doesn't?"

"Esmé thinks President Kehoe is *afraid* to fire General Tanaka. She says the president has made a lot of people in the government mad and if he fires General—er, Secretary—Tanaka, there could be some serious blowback. From within the government," my heretofore non-political daughter said.

Esmé and Elizabeth have been best friends for several years. And lately Esmé seems to have developed a nose for politics and especially political intrigue. Up until now, Elizabeth had not. But I guess times were starting to change on that score. Rapidly.

"Well first of all, I have no idea whether President Kehoe has even considered firing Tanaka," I said. "He doesn't confide with me about stuff like that. But why in heck would he be afraid of doing that anyway?"

"Seven Days in May," she said, holding up the old book. "With all these firings, he may see a conspiracy heading his way. Or maybe one is coming and he doesn't see it. May isn't that far away. And seven days are seven days. And those guys in the book—big-shot Washington insiders—Generals and Admirals—*were* apparently trying to throw the President out of office."

Good Lord, I thought. *Esmé's influences—and powerful imagination as well as her conspiracy theories—have been kicking in, big-time. A plot! To overthrow the President of the United States! What are these kids thinking of?*

"You guys need to remember that *Seven Days in May* is a novel," I said. "A work of fiction! From the days of the Kennedy administration and the Cold War. I don't have any inside scoop on what today's Joint Chiefs are thinking about, but I seriously doubt that they're plotting to remove the President. I think you and Esmé might have been eating too many Chinese fortune cookies."

Elizabeth didn't give me the eye roll. But she kept her eyes down and flared her nostrils a bit. More nuanced, more sinister. I won't swear to it, but I think Esmé grinned and gave me a little wink. Even more sinister.

Chapter Five
Sheila

Clifton Forge, Virginia
Early April

Vice Admiral Donegan felt the train beginning to slow. She recalled her tête-à-tête with Sam Braxton at their private lunch. She had to think that this gathering at his getaway in the hills of central Virginia had to do with "a larger group" to kick the "rhetorical questions" about the Gerlach slaughter around.

"Clifton Forge coming up!" The conductor's somewhat raspy voice announced.

Donegan watched out the window as thick forest gave way to small farms and then to residential dwellings and backyards. A light rain continued to streak the train's windows. She stood up to retrieve her overnight bag and a tubular fishing rod case from the luggage rack. She wore a navy-blue windbreaker over a Baltimore Ravens' long sleeved tee and a pair of slim cut black jeans. Her hair was pulled back in a short ponytail. As she alighted from the train, she spotted a parked Chrysler Town and Country van that looked familiar. The van had Virginia tags that Donegan recognized. A middle-aged man with a thin, white mustache climbed out of the driver's seat of the van. She recognized him as well. Pablo! Sam's driver and general factotum.

"Welcome, Admiral," the driver with the white mustache said, greeting the Director of Naval Intelligence respectfully. He opened a short, black umbrella and held it over Admiral Donegan. "I hope you don't mind waiting a tiny bit. Mister Nagle is due any minute. He just called on his mobile."

"No, of course not, Pablo," said Admiral Donegan. "That will give me a couple of minutes to load up my gear."

"Allow me to give you a hand, Ma'am," the driver said.

He picked up her small suitcase and headed toward the Chrysler. As he opened the rear door of the van, his phone dinged. He glanced at it.

"Ah, Mister Nagle has arrived," he said as he carefully placed Donegan's suitcase in the back of the Town and Country. He nodded toward a midnight-blue Cadillac that was moving carefully into a parking space two cars away. "As soon as we load his luggage, we'll be off to the cabin. There he is!"

A tall, slender man with dark hair dismounted from the Caddie and waved. Seconds later, Admiral Donegan, Pablo and Dick Nagle were exchanging handshakes in the wet parking lot as the train started to pull out of the station. Dick was the Deputy Director of the Central Intelligence Agency. He had spent most of his twenty-six-year career in the Directorate of Intelligence as an analyst.

"Good to see you, Dick," Donegan said. "Did you bring your fishing tackle?"

"Of course! There's no way I'd come out here to the mountains of Virginia and not bring my fishing gear.I understand that there's a well-stocked stream adjoining Sam's property."

He held up what looked to be a canvas, leather-trimmed briefcase.

"This is my travel tackle," he said with a smile. "An L. L. Bean kit. It has a six-piece rod that can be used with either a spinning reel or a fly reel. Both of which are included. How 'bout you?" he asked.

"Already in the van," Donegan answered. "Fly rod all the way, though."

"Well good luck with that," Nagle added, good-naturedly.

Pablo grabbed Nagle's medium-sized suitcase.

"The car's right this way, Mister Nagle," he said. "The cabin is about a twenty-five-minute drive from here."

"My guess is that the Chief is already there, waiting for us?" Nagle asked.

"Yes sir," Pablo said. "And Congresswoman DeWitt, Mr. McConnell and General Smalls are up there, too. Plus a new gentleman that I don't know."

"The Chief" was Sam Braxton, the Director of National Intelligence or DNI. Congresswoman Helen DeWitt was the current Speaker of the U. S. House of Representatives. Stuart McConnell was Deputy Director of the FBI and Lieutenant General Will Smalls was Vice Admiral Donegan's Army counterpart, the Army's Assistant Chief of Staff for Intelligence.

"We should arrive right in time for cocktails," Pablo said. "The place is near the top of a mountain. The Chief calls it 'the Hawk's Nest'."

The van headed away from the Amtrak station, its headlights boring through the gloom. A few minutes later they were out of Clifton Forge.

Chapter Six

Alan

1506 Prince Henry Street
Early April

I was looking through the mail at home a few minutes after my puzzling chat with Elizabeth and Esmé when a Baltic-North Cruise Line brochure caught my eye. They advertised a cut-rate cruise in the Baltic Sea in early June. The reason the rate was so low was probably because it was the first Baltic cruise of the summer. If we went any later, according to the flyer, the fares would jump by four hundred bucks. Per head. The early cruise schedule would have us underway on the first of June and put us back in England on the fifteenth. And then back in Virginia on the sixteenth. I thought that would work for me. I'd have to run it by the women. And then by my partners in intrigue at *BIAS*. Not to mention the President.

"Hey Elizabeth!" I called. Esmé had already left for home.

"What's up, Dad?"

"When's your last day of school?"

"Some time in early June," she said.

"Can you narrow it down a bit?" I asked.

"Sure. Let me check my agenda."

She scrabbled around in her backpack and pulled out a well-used, beat-up "agenda" that All Saints Academy issues to its upper school students for keeping track of assignments, homework, Holy Days of Obligation and regular holidays. She flipped pages.

"Here it is!" she said. "Last day is June sixth. But my last day is Monday, June second because I'm exempt from all my exams."

"Hmm. Perfect. Almost. You might have to miss your last day of school," I said.

"Definitely perfect," she said. "If I had to miss the last five or six days, that'd be even more than perfect!"

She pretends that she hates school. Actually, she loves it and does very well. Hence being exempt from all her exams. Her grades are all A's.

"What are you scheming about, Dad?" she asked, innocently.

"No scheming. Just a possible cruise for the Llewellyn family. In the Baltic Sea. In early June," I said, waving the brochure. "I'm guessing we'd have to leave on Friday, May thirtieth."

"The Baltic Sea. In June? Sounds chilly. I don't see much bikini time there. I'm guessing I won't come back with a tan."

"You might. The on-line brochure shows that M. S. *Nordschiff's* got two swimming pools. They're both outdoors but somewhat sheltered. And at that time of year, the days up there are really long. The sun hardly sets at all. And it's a great cruise."

I consulted the brochure.

"*Nordschiff* leaves from Dover, England. Goes to Copenhagen first, then to Warnemünde, Germany with a side trip to Berlin from there. I've always wanted to go to Berlin. My grandfather went to university there. Humboldt University of Berlin. And then the ship goes on to Tallinn, Estonia and Saint Petersburg. Two of Russia's greatest poets--Alexander Pushkin and Anna Akhmatova--wrote much of their poetry in Saint Petersburg. Plus, I've heard it's the most beautiful city in all of Russia. After that, *Nordschiff* takes us to two quick stops in Stockholm and Kiel. Then back to Dover. The Kiel stop includes a side trip to Hamburg as an option. And I've been thinking that I need a break. A change of scene. This sounds perfect."

Elizabeth surprised me. At fourteen, she's got amazing insight. And intuition. She walked over to my chair and draped an arm across my shoulders.

"I know you do, Dad. Mom and I were just talking about that. It's gotta be tough enough working on special assignments for the President of the United States. It's gotta be way worse when things get violent and people get killed."

I wasn't sure how much Maria or Elizabeth knew about the nasty details of some of my work at *BIAS* so I hemmed and hawed a little.

"You're wise beyond your years, Sweetie," I said.

"So let's go on a cruise," she said. "Baltic Sea, Alaska, Tahiti, wherever. As long as we can get away!"

"You sly vixen," I said with a grin, reaching around the chair back for an awkward hug. "Let's see how your mom feels about it."

Maria had segued from her role as an author and historian to family chef. She had garlic warming in olive oil and was slicing cherry tomatoes. The bouquet was fabulous, but then I'm partial to garlic and olive oil. She was seated at the kitchen table, and had black olives and basil ready for slicing and chopping. Cory, our two-year-old Labrador was stretched out under the table, watching us intently and waiting for stray fragments to drop. Our floors were always clean.

Elizabeth followed me into the kitchen. I can't swear to it, but I thought I caught sight of an exchange of conspiratorial eye signals between mother and daughter.

"What's up?" Maria asked.

"A cruise!" volunteered Elizabeth. "In the Baltic Sea. In June! Where the sun never sets!"

"Oh, I think it sets. Sunset's pretty late and it rises pretty early. But what have you two been conspiring about?"

Once again, I thought I might have espied coded eye signals between the two raven-haired, beautiful women, but I couldn't be sure. I handed the Baltic Sea Cruise brochure to Maria.

"No conspiracy. This just came in the mail this afternoon. Elizabeth was there when I opened it. We kicked it around a bit and now we're here to kick it around with you."

Chapter Seven

Litvinov

The George Washington Parkway
Arlington, Virginia
Early April

Colonel Valentin Litvinov, the Military Attaché for the Russian Federation, left his embassy office at 5:10 p.m. He was looking forward to a rare, free evening at home with his wife Natalya and their five-year old son, Sasha. But it was not to be. He noticed a small, chalked circle containing the numeral nineteen on the back of a "Stop" sign two blocks from his home. The chalked circle nineteen had a meaning.

"Meet at the usual place at seven p.m."

The message was from a source.

The rain started as Litvinov processed the message. The "usual place" was a parking pull-off on the northbound side of the George Washington Parkway just downstream from the Chain Bridge. He looked at his watch. The time was 5:25. There was a Starbucks just ahead. He pulled in, went inside and treated himself to a Grande Caramel Macchiato. Forty minutes later, he dumped his coffee detritus into the trashcan, headed for the coffee shop's exit and "the usual place."

By the time he left Starbucks, the rain was pounding heavily, fast, and loaded with steamy humidity. He pulled his silver-gray Buick cautiously into the parking overlook off the parkway and brought the big car to a careful stop facing the Potomac far below. The Buick sported Department of State Diplomat License tags with the letters "DYR" on the left sides of the plates. Russia. A two, seven and a zero were showing on the plates' right half but didn't tell the casual observer who was actually driving the car. A closely held guide, published by the State Department and issued to state and local police, would have told officers that the vehicle was licensed to one Colonel Valentin Sergeivich Litvinov, Military Attaché at the Russian Embassy. There were no other cars in the overlook even though it was only just shy of seven o'clock.

Two minutes later a Jeep Cherokee pulled into the overlook and parked alongside the Buick. The driver of the Jeep flashed his high beams twice where they reflected off the sheets of rain and the soaking-wet trees. Then he powered down the passenger-side window.

Litvinov opened his window.

"Shitty evening," said the man in the Jeep.

"Probably warmer here than in Moscow or Saint Petersburg," Litvinov responded. "Do you have anything for me?"

"Yes," said the man in the Jeep. "Indeed I do. Take this book. In it you'll find a list of the names and positions of some of the people involved. There are eight of them on this list. There may well be more. I don't know how serious or determined these guys are, but the fact that they're even thinking about somehow unseating a sitting president, much less talking about it, makes me take them seriously. Oh, and burn the fucking list once you've got it sent in. If they find it on you—which they won't—you'll only be PNG'd. If they trace it back to me, I'm toast. The slammer. Or worse."

"Don't worry. It will disappear very soon. What's the book?"

"*Seven Days in May.* You should read it. Quickly. And more importantly, forward it with the list."

Colonel Litvinov took the book and passed a business-sized envelope to the man in the Jeep. He recalled a previous conversation about some high-level scheming within the U. S. intelligence community.

"Thanks. We'll be in touch," he said.

The Jeep driver nodded, powered up his window and backed his four-wheel drive SUV out of the parking space. He then turned his vehicle and departed the little parking lot. Colonel Litvinov followed suit and headed his Buick cautiously through the pouring rain towards his residence in Great Falls.

Chapter Eight
Sheila

The Hawk's Nest, Clifton Forge
Virginia
Early April

"Welcome, welcome!" announced the Chief, Sam Braxton, from the porch of the large "cabin" as Pablo brought the van to a gentle halt at the foot of a rustic, wooden staircase.

The temperature must have been in the mid-thirties, Donegan guessed. There were occasional flying flakes of snow coming down and disappearing immediately after contact with the damp earth.

Braxton was a man of medium height and a bit chunky around the middle. His straight, brown hair was devoid of gray and was parted on the left side of his skull. The uniform brown color suggested the use of a men's hair coloring substance. It also appeared that he used some sort of gel to keep every hair permanently plastered in place. He wore black-rimmed glasses that appeared to magnify his brown eyes considerably. His age appeared to be somewhere within plus or minus five years of fifty. He was clean-shaven and today wore tan corduroy slacks and a long-sleeved Black Watch tartan shirt. Vice Admiral Donegan had felt tiny vibrations of suspicion about Braxton for as long as she'd known him. She never was able put her finger on what caused her little mental alarm bells to ring. And that went back to when she'd been a Lieutenant Commander and Braxton had been an Air Force Major. And an Intelligence officer. His military career seemed to have fizzled for some unknown reason and he retired as a major. Then he went back to work for the Air Force as a civilian and his career prospects took off. Now he was at the top of the U.S. Intelligence heap.

"Come on up. Pablo will take care of your luggage. Between his lovely wife, Carmen, and me, we should be able to put a glass in your hands in a minute or two."

Donegan and Nagel dutifully trotted up the steps and Pablo pulled the van around behind the house. The civies-clad Admiral and the CIA Deputy Director went through a front door that was ringed by shiny metallic tubing containing, Donegan thought, some sort of high-tech security sensors.

It probably detects weapons and explosives. Plus any sort of recording gadgetry, Donegan thought.

The front room took up the entire width of the building—a good forty-five or fifty feet, Donegan guessed. A wood fire blazed merrily in a huge stone fireplace at one end of the large room.

"Good evening, Madame Speaker," Nagle and Donegan said at the same time.

"Good evening. Nice to see you," the Congresswoman said.

"Hi Sheila, Dick," General Smalls said, standing and putting down a wine glass in one motion.

Congresswoman DeWitt wore a Kelly-green pullover, khaki slacks and highly polished penny loafers. She was a petite woman with steel-gray hair cut short in what would have been called a "D-A" fifty years ago.

General Smalls was tall and thin, maybe six-two or three. His hair was salt-and-pepper-colored and he wore it high and tight with barely enough to comb on top. He was dressed in a pale blue chambray shirt, faded jeans and western boots.

Stu McConnell, the Deputy Director of the FBI, was also tall and thin. His brown hair was cut medium-short and he was the only guest dressed more-or-less formally, sporting a blazer and a white shirt with a red tie.

"Everybody knows everybody. Except Roberto. Roberto Ironsides, perhaps," the Chief said, gesturing toward a slightly portly middle-aged man with a short, neatly trimmed beard and a balding head who had risen from a chair in the corner of the big room.

"Roberto is the CEO of *Algorithmics,* a consulting group that specializes in fixing damage to networks caused by viruses. Roberto himself is something of a notorious hacker in the cyber universe. World class. I'm told he can break into anywhere. On the few occasions when I've hired him for intelligence work, he's never disappointed."

The portly man smiled shyly and nodded modestly. The ceiling lights reflected brightly off the bald parts of his head. The other guests tittered politely and uncertainly.

"What are you guys drinking?" the Chief asked.

"Scotch and soda, please," Donegan murmured.

"Bombay Sapphire martini straight up. Lemon twist," Nagle said, as if he'd been here before. Braxton and Carmen, who had appeared magically, served Donegan and Nagle almost instantly.

"Anyone need a refill?" Braxton asked the room at large.

Heads shook in the negative.

"Okay. Cheers. And welcome." he said, lifting a glass. "Let's not beat about the bush. Probably several of you are wondering why we're here. For tomorrow's trout fishing, of course," he said with a chuckle. Everyone else in the big room chortled as well.

"But then, there's the Big Enchilada. For starters, you should know that this place is secure. Pablo and Carmen are cleared. You have my word that we're not being recorded. No one can listen, either. We've taken all the technical precautions.

"Last week's horror show at Gerlach CC is just the latest in an unending parade of mass killings by unhinged losers with easy access to guns.

"Any sane person—in this terrible milieu—knows that the Second Amendment to the U.S. Constitution must go. It dates back to when the United States had no armed forces to speak of. It is an amendment and needs to be amended. Like the eighteenth amendment. Prohibition. Here one year, gone five years later—when Americans figured out what a disaster it really was. I'm convinced that's what we have with the Second Amendment. A disaster. It may have made sense shortly after we had red-coated British soldiers sleeping in our houses and an overseas king having taxed our citizens to death, but that's not the case anymore. Not even close. Trouble is, our sitting president doesn't see it that way. There's no way that Kehoe will support the repeal of the Second Amendment. Much less modifying any other amendments to the Constitution.

"I've talked with most—if not all—of you individually and I think we're all agreed. Kehoe *must* go. *Must* go. For the sake of the country. And we can't wait till the next election. That would leave him in power for nearly two more years. That's two years too long. He's clinging to the Constitution like it was written last month instead of over two hundred years ago. Especially that Goddamned Second Amendment. The whole country—hugs excepted—desperately wants to get guns off the streets. We've had mass gun violence at a rate of approximately two shootings a month for the last six years. Way above the rates of other industrialized nations. This latest cop shooting in Massachusetts is one example. The horror show in Maryland where this sick bastard slaughtered his wife and children is another. And then, even closer to home, we had this nut job in Virginia murder an entire math class at Gerlach Community College. The Second Amendment keeps the guns on the street. The Second Amendment needs to be amended away. But that won't happen under this President. And then there's the First Amendment. Kehoe's totally opposed to sensible restraints on hateful speech. He came out with both barrels blazing when students at a Virginia university mounted a successful—SUCCESSFUL!—effort to shut down a scheduled speech by a conservative columnist. Because of the guy's opposition to abortion. By Kehoe's reckoning, college students—and others—favoring traditional marriage, for example, should be afforded the same speaking rights as those in favor of allowing the freedom of same-sex couples to wed. Not to mention the so-called pro-life crazies. And if that's not bad enough, he's got the gall to condemn a number of highly respected universities for putting sensible limits on irresponsible and hateful opinion- mongering in campus newspapers and speeches. He's a racist, homophobic, mean-spirited and anti-female bigot.

"Lately, rumor has it that he's created his own personal rogue intelligence production facility. He's cutting budgets all over the lot. Except for this sub-rosa mini-CIA. He's a threat to the country and to the American people. Hell, he's an enemy of the United States! An enemy for a president! Think about that! Ergo, he has to go. ASAP."

"Sam. I agree that Kehoe must go. ASAP, as you said. But I don't think tinkering with the First and Second Amendments to the Constitution goes far enough. We need a whole new Constitution. We're living in the twenty-first century, for God's sake! If we can pull off this power turnover, then we need to go all the way and hold a new Constitutional Convention," General Smalls said.

A couple of people in the room gasped. Others nodded in agreement.

"I'm not sure we want to go that far, General. It's one thing to arrange a 'power turnover' as you call it. It's another to shred the United States Constitution," Braxton said.

"I don't think that's all that radical an idea," Speaker DeWitt responded. "France has had, what, five constitutions? Since World War Two? And they're not exactly North Korea.

"And we can re-write it, preserving a lot of the original boilerplate and shredding some of the guts. The end result doesn't have to sound like some sort of Communist Manifesto. Actually, it can sound a lot like the original. With an amended First Amendment. And a disappearing Second Amendment."

"Okay, people. Our time is limited," Braxton answered. "Let's agree on two things. One, Kehoe has to go. The man is tearing the country apart. We need to engineer his departure from Sixteen Hundred Pennsylvania Avenue within, say, the next six months," Braxton said. "Shall we take a vote? All in favor?"

Everyone raised a hand. Braxton scrawled in his notebook.

"The second thing is building a new Constitutional Convention, if indeed that's what we want to do," he finished.

"And how do you propose to do both those things, Chief?" Admiral Donegan asked quietly.

The rest of the room was deathly silent.

"Well, I have a few ideas. But that's why we're all here. I'm hoping that some of you have some ideas as well. We'll kick them around and see if we can draft up a plan," Braxton replied. "And a one hundred eighty-day timeline."

He took a sip from his drink and the others followed suit.

"Show of hands on a new Constitution?" he prompted.

The result was the same. Unanimous.

"Okay. Dinner is about to be served. Some trout fishing for those so inclined tomorrow morning. I've mounted a marked-up, one-to-twenty-five thousand map in the den behind me for anglers' use. It has the stream and various hot spots annotated. Then we'll meet at eleven-thirty to kick things around some more over an early lunch."

Chapter Nine

Alan

1506 Prince Henry Street
Late April

After dinner, I sent Jim Kehoe, my boss and high school classmate and now President of the United States a non-urgent email.

> From: allewellyn@bias.gov
>
> To: keys@lisound.com
>
> Subj: Run and shoot
>
> Keys:
>
> Are you planning an off-the-skyline run anytime soon, on which I could join you and shoot the breeze? Nothing urgent. But we do need to chat.
>
> Loose

I heard back the next day.

> From: Hookes@LISound.com
>
> To: allewellyn@bias.gov
>
> Subj: Run and Shoot
>
> He's got a 5k run scheduled for the Yard at Annapolis Friday, May 9th at 10:45. {He's on a G-7 Conference Call right now. This is Michelle.) He says you're welcome to join. He's also scheduled to have lunch with the USNA Superintendent, VADM Kirkpatrick, at 12:15. I can easily add you to the official party for the lunch. You can ride w/ him on Marine One back and forth. You can even catch the chopper at Quantico and save some driving time/hassle. Let me know and Allison and I will set things up.
>
> Michelle

Allison was Kehoe's personal secretary. Michelle was Michelle Hookes, a "Special Assistant" to the President. She was a billionaire widow whose late husband had built and sold airplanes. After his somewhat early death, Michelle had an exciting career of her own. She had a very successful tour as U. S. Ambassador to Italy. After that, she semi-retired, giving an occasional speech to various, higher-level political/military groups as well as throwing a few A-list parties at her elegant Georgetown townhome. She'd caught the eye of President Kehoe at a talk she gave to the National War College after which he'd hired her.

Several months later, she'd become a target of a renegade cabal from the PRC Ministry of State Security. *BIAS*, in the person of yours truly, was able to successfully intervene, foiling the PRC assassination plot and saving her life in the bargain. Michelle and I had been fast friends ever since.

Kehoe preferred to keep me out of sight and thus out of mind. Other peoples' sight and minds, that is. When we ran together, we usually did so somewhere off the grid. Like within the privacy of the backside of the Marine Corps Base at Quantico. No public trots around the Tidal Basin or the National Mall in front of paparazzi and picture-snapping tourists. No jogging together in the public eye. But running in the Yard at Annapolis with a handful of Midshipmen was probably okay.

I wonder if he, like Maria and Elizabeth, noticed that I was a bit frayed around the edges. He's usually not all that solicitous. I emailed Michelle back and asked her to set things up for the Annapolis run, but to please leave me off the lunch list. I was confident that Allison would fill me in with the logistics details—i.e. when to catch the northbound chopper, ETR, etc. She did.

Chapter Ten

Litvinov

The Embassy of the Russian Federation
Washington, D.C.
Late April

Colonel Litvinov sat at his desk and lit a cigarette. A black-covered, hard-back book lay on his desktop, closed. A typed, one-page list lay beside the book. He had struggled through the book, in English. *Seven Days in May.* It was fiction, nonsense really. A ridiculous novel from the days of the Cold War. According to the story, the American Joint Chiefs of Staff—the leading military power brokers in Washington—wanted to remove the fictitious President from power. The issue had to do with a disagreement over a disarmament treaty with the old Soviet Union. In the book, a Marine Corps Colonel, serving as the Director of the Joint Staff, discovered the plot. He alerted the President and together the Marine Corps officer and the White House staff thwarted the scheme. Amazingly enough, in the story, none of the perpetrators was tossed into prison or made to disappear. They were all allowed to resign quietly—with their pensions presumably intact. According to the story, there was a little ruckus in the news media about the sudden resignations which died out quickly and that was that. *Only in America,* he thought.

He had found a full-length version of the movie *Seven Days in May,* amazingly enough on a Russian website. He watched the film twice. It seemed to follow the book's story line fairly closely. In so doing, it highlighted, in Litvinov's eyes, the absolute nonsense of the story.

He turned his attention to the single typed page alongside the book. This was the ticking bombshell. The A4 page contained a list of nine names, typed double-spaced. Litvinov recognized most of them. After all, serving as a military attaché was an intelligence assignment. The names he recognized were all from the American intelligence community. Military and civilian. Heading the list was Sam Braxton, the Director of National Intelligence. Litvinov's source for the list had also been the person who had given him the copy of the old novel. Without any attempt at an explanation. Did that mean that the people whose names were on the list were involved in plotting against the current American President?

It certainly looked that way.

He stubbed out his cigarette and glanced at his watch. Eleven forty. Valeriya almost always took an early lunch. She would most likely be in the canteen now. Valeriya was the personal secretary to the Ambassador. Litvinov hurriedly stowed the book and list in a lower desk drawer. He locked the desk with a key and dropped the key into a front pocket of his trousers. Grabbing his suit coat and pulling it on, he left his office hurriedly. He had the typical Russian paranoia about conspiracy.

"I'll be right back," he told his sergeant and hurried down to the cafeteria.

The lunchroom was packed already and it took Colonel Litvinov a few minutes before he was able to locate Valeriya. She was seated alone at a small table and sipped coffee as she paged slowly through a copy of *People* magazine. Litvinov wondered how the Ambassador was able to have the most beautiful woman on the large Embassy staff as his personal secretary. He took the seat across the table from her. She looked up him, puzzled.

"What's going on?" she asked.

"Emergency. I need fifteen minutes. Away from here. As soon as possible."

"I'll let you know within a half hour."

"Spasiba," he said. "Thanks."

He got up, gave her shoulder a gentle pat and returned to his office. He had just taken the steps to set up a clandestine meeting with his ambassador, His Excellency Viktor Malenkov. At least, a tentative meeting. He'd have to wait for word from Valeriya. And "clandestine" was the operative word.

Valeriya was his cutout to Malenkov. Litvinov had no idea what was going on with the American government or possible plotters. But he was keenly aware of a major struggle within his own government in Moscow. President Epifanov and the Mafiya appeared to be on one side. Foreign Minister Kirilenkov was on the other side and Ambassador Malenkov was in his pocket. And, since the Ambassador was his wife's cousin, he, Litvinov, was in *his* pocket.

Valerya walked into his office twenty minutes later, carrying a yellow post-it note. She handed it to him.

"Enjoy the rest of your day," she said with a wink and a smirk.

He read the note.

Cat House. 1515.

That meant the Big Cats Exhibit at the National Zoo at three-fifteen p.m. Today. Where the lions and tigers were.

He returned to his office, sat at his desk and took a yellow legal pad from a desk drawer and a pencil from another drawer. At the top of the page, he wrote: "7DIM" for the book's title. On the next line, he wrote "SB – DNI" and on the following line he scrawled "CW HDW SOTH," meaning "Sam Braxton – Director of National Intelligence" and "Congresswoman Helen DeWitt, Speaker of the House," respectively. He finished the abbreviated list, knowing that a sub-teen amateur code breaker with pimples could have it completely decoded in less than five minutes. But it would have to do for his purposes.

At ten till three, he re-donned his suit jacket, followed by a lightweight raincoat.

"I've a meeting. It's nearby, so I'll walk. I should be back by four-fifteen," he told the sergeant.

A light and chilly drizzle was falling. Litvinov regretted his earlier decision to follow the Americans' custom of not wearing a hat. He entered the zoo via the Connecticut Avenue entrance. He marveled at the absence of entrance fees at any of the Smithsonian Institution's attractions and took his time wandering downhill through the zoo and the light rain till he reached The Exhibit of the Great Cats. As he paused to regard two sleeping lions, a man wearing an orange-trimmed gray running suit jogged up to him and stopped.

"Right on time, Valentin" the man said. 'What's up?"

Litvinov opened a small umbrella before reaching into his pants pocket and pulling out a folded piece of paper, which he opened under the umbrella's shelter.

"'Seven Delta India Mike' equals 'Seven Days in May,' an American novel published in 1961," Litvinov said.

"'CW HDW SOTH' is 'Congresswoman Helen DeWitt, Speaker of the House.' You get the idea. I got a copy of the book and this list of names and positions from a source that has reported reliably in the past. My guess is that the list is incomplete. I report information—I don't analyze it. But this smells like a plot—especially if one reads the book."

"Both from the same source?" asked the man in the running suit.

"*Da*," Litvinov replied.

"You have the book?" the ambassador asked.

"I do. I've almost finished reading it."

"In English?"

"Yes. And it's a bitch," Litvinov said.

"Make me a copy," the ambassador said. "I'll have it translated."

The attaché gave a casual salute. "Yes sir," he said.

"Stay well and stay in touch. And get me that copy soonest," the ambassador said.

"Of course, Cousin," Litvinov replied.

Ambassador Malenkov turned and began jogging down the little hill through the gentle rain.

Chapter Eleven

Alan

The Yard

U.S. Naval Academy

Annapolis, Maryland

Late April

Allison, Kehoe's personal secretary, came through like she always did. In order to even get close to Allison, however, I had to get past an even more formidable potential adversary—Michelle. I did.

Invitations to Michelle's parties were to kill for because of the quality of the guest lists. I'd originally met Michelle in the aftermath of a very provocative speech of hers entitled "Thinking About Thinking About U. S. Foreign Policy." I somewhat jocularly referred to her as an "adversary" standing between Kehoe and the hordes that "needed" face time with him. For me, she was actually more of a facilitator than an adversary. If I needed to see Kehoe and it was at all physically possible, she'd make it happen. She insisted that I call her "Michelle," not "Ma'am"–*ever*. Today, I dialed her White House number, which I'd memorized.

"Michelle Hookes," she answered.

"Hi Michelle. It's Alan. Alan Llewellyn."

"Alan! What can I do for you?" she asked pleasantly.

"I wonder if you can put me in touch with Allison. I need her help in connecting with Cheetah during an up and coming trip to the Naval Academy." 'Cheetah' is Kehoe's Presidential Secret Service code name.

"I'm guessing this is the up and coming running trip? In about a week" she answered.

"Yes, Ma'am," I said stupidly.

"Alan, Alan, Alan!" she snorted. "How many times do I have to tell—"

"I know, I know," I interrupted. "You don't want middle-aged men calling you 'Ma'am.' Sorry—I forgot."

"You should know that by now," she said.

"Yes Michelle," I answered meekly "I do. Just a slip."

"You'll be hearing from Allison directly," she said.

"Thanks, Michelle."

I did.

Following Allison's directions, I caught the HMX-One[1] white top helicopter at MCAF[2] Quantico wearing running clothes. We landed on the south lawn of the White House and Kehoe came aboard almost immediately, followed by a clean-shaven young stud in running gear who, I figured, was Secret Service. About a half-dozen other folks got on the other chopper.

"*Cheetah's* ready to roll," the stud said into a tiny mike somewhere. And roll we did. Or rise we did.

"Loose, you old bastard," the President said slugging me playfully on the shoulder. "How's everything?"

"Pretty good, Keys," I said. "What prompted you to go for a run on the campus of my alma mater?"

"Jock, my Navy aide set it up," he answered. "Most of the Brigade of Midshipmen is gone on spring leave. It should be reasonably private, so it'll be fine for us to run together. A handful of Mids—a dozen or so--will run with us, but they're all cleared. How are Maria and Elizabeth?"

"They're great. And about the same size, now. Occasionally, I get this uneasy feeling that they are secretly conspiring about manipulating me. But that's probably just some sort of middle-aged paternal paranoia on my part."

"Right. Probably one of these days you'll catch some snarkiness from Maria that means she thinks Elizabeth and you are conspiring about manipulating her. Teenage daughters are funny that way. Masters—or mistresses—of manipulating and making parents do what they want. Manipulators extraordinaire. If I remember my sisters correctly."

The helicopter began a rapid descent. I saw the Severn River off to port. The helicopter flared and landed on a grassy practice field on the east side of the Yard.

"Don't worry about your stuff," Cheetah said. "We've got the use of a coaches' VIP suite. The crew will put our gear in the suite. We can shower and change there after our run. Take-off time for the return trip is thirteen thirty. From right here. I still don't know why you want to blow off a free

---

1   Marine Experimental Helicpter Squadron One
2   Marine Corps Air Facility

lunch, courtesy of Admiral Kirkpatrick, though."

"No major reason. Just trying to stay off the skyline," I said.

He nodded and led the way off the helicopter.

A small contingent of Midshipmen, male and female, was waiting for us—or for their Commander-in-Chief—on the road by the landing zone. They wore the Midshipmen PT attire of Navy-blue shorts and white t-shirts with blue trim. They also sported New Balance running shoes—all white. Gone, I guessed, were the days of every Mid being issued a pair of high-top sneakers—Keds, if memory serves. Nowadays, apparently, they all had expensive, high-performance running shoes.

The Mids here today were probably varsity athletes with competition scheduled soon meaning that they couldn't break loose for Spring Leave. Keys shook hands with all of them before we started running.

"Thanks for joining us for the run," he said to them. "I hope we're not too slow for you. This guy with the short haircut is Alan—he graduated from the Academy back in the day."

"Back in the day when there still was a thing called Plebe year," I said, grinning.

The Mids laughed good-naturedly and we took off at a relaxed, comfortable pace. The stud from the helicopter locked onto Kehoe from behind. There was an SUV ahead of us that, I suspected, contained armed Secret Service agents. I guessed that there was another, similar vehicle bringing up the rear. The weather was great as only days in Annapolis in May are—sunny and about seventy-seven degrees, no wind.

"Okay, Loose. What's up?" the Leader of the Free World asked, in a low voice.

"Um, I hate to say this, but I need a break," I said. "There were some details about us knocking down that suicide bombing plot in Virginia that you don't know about—and don't want to know. Bottom line, I need a short break and change of scene. I found a cruise that the Llewellyn family can afford. Baltic Sea in June. We'd get underway on June first. Back on the fifteenth. Baltic-North Line. The *M. S. Nordschiff.* Darps is well-prepared to cover at *BIAS.*"

We ran past the Naval Academy Sailing Center and headed upstream alongside the Severn River.

"The Baltic in June. Where will the *Nordschiff* stop?"

"We embark in Dover, south of London. Then we go on to Copenhagen, followed by Warnemünde, Germany—with an optional one-day, side trip to Berlin. Followed by port visits at Tallinn and then Saint Petersburg for a two-day stop. After Russia, there's Stockholm and Kiel. We'll leave Kiel, our last port of call, and return to Dover. There is a total of four "at sea" days, which are just what the doctor ordered for me. Walking or jogging the promenade deck in the Baltic Sea air. Working on my latest young adult mystery novel in the ship's library. Plus, I've always wanted to go to Berlin and Saint Petersburg. My grandfather lived in Berlin and attended Humboldt University there. And I've always worshipped Pushkin and Achmatova and their poetry. And I'll be able to spend time with the women in my life."

"Loose, you never cease to amaze me. But, sure. Go ahead and make your plans and go. You've definitely earned some vacation time. A little bird gave me some of the dirty details about the bombing attempt at Augustine Washington High School. Are you sure you don't need some professional intervention?" he asked.

"Wadda you mean? A shrink?" I asked, horrified.

"I don't know. Maybe a regular doc could decide whether a shrink might be able to help."

"No. Hell no. Let me try this change of scene thing in silence, enjoy the company of my two women and suck in some salty Baltic air. If, when I get back and I think I still have head issues, I'll talk to a doc and keep you posted. But I doubt that will be necessary."

"Fair enough," he said. We turned left around the western end of Worden Field, the Brigade of Midshipmen's super-green parade ground.

"After the ass whupping I've been taking in the press, I'm starting to think I might need a shrink myself," Kehoe said.

"Yeah," I said. "Your red-headed girlfriend at the Times wielded an especially poisonous pen Sunday."

"Not to mention Sunday's *Meet the Press* gang. They shat and spat all over me. Listening to those bastards, you'd think the First and Second Amendments to the Constitution were unconstitutional. And that ISIS was some sort of charitable, alms-giving organization."

We ran in silence past the "Captains' Row" of big houses overlooking Worden Field and the Severn.

"Who was the 'little bird'?" I asked, as we made the turn at the far end of the parade field.

"Someday when we're both retired, I might tell you," he answered.

Chapter Twelve

Alan

BIAS-Ripley Hall
Martha Washington University
Chestertown, Virginia
Early May

Upon my return from Annapolis, I drove directly from the Marine Corps Air Facility at Quantico, where the HMX-1 Chopper let me off, to *BIAS*. After arriving there, I spoke with Darps and Judy at some length about my up-and-coming vacation absence in the Baltic. Darps was still okay with everything and confirmed that he'd be there to cover. Judy was giving me the evil eye. Perhaps I overstated that, but she seemed to be watching me from under guarded lids.

Things had seemed to be pretty much under control at *BIAS*—the Bureau of International Advanced Studies. My place of work. I was the BMIC. Pronounced "Bimmick." The "Boss Man in Charge." Our shop supplied the occasional second opinion on Intelligence Community products that went to the desk of the President of the United States. He'd get a "paper" or an "estimate" and float it to *BIAS* where our little team of experts would give it a "sanity check." Surreptitiously. The reason was that President Kehoe had some serious suspicions about the quality or "purity" of the material of the intelligence he was getting from the Intelligence Community. *BIAS* wasn't a totally new idea. Kennedy had the Forty Committee. Subsequent presidents had the PFIAB—pronounced "piffy-ab" and standing for "President's Foreign Intelligence Advisory Board." *BIAS*, however, was off the grid. As in deeply hidden and highly classified. Plus, unlike the PFIAB, *BIAS* was very light in the brass department and fairly heavy in the smarts-and-knowledge department. The latter two "departments" don't necessarily walk hand-in-hand. My private suspicion is that the opposite is often true.

I hadn't said anything to daughter Elizabeth, but I suspected that one or two of the high-level firings she had alluded to in our earlier chat might have been due to some politically spun intel being tossed over Kehoe's transom.

"I have this suspicion that their info is becoming too politicized," Kehoe had said. "I'd like to believe that they're only trying to tell me what they think I want to hear—which is bad enough--but I think it may be a bit more sinister than that. One of the reasons for having Michelle around is that she has acutely sensitive antennae when it comes to political nuance. She can be an excellent truth-teller. I'm not suggesting that overseas evildoers are driving the Intel ship, but perhaps a few homegrown hotshots may be spinning intel judgments for their own political reasons."

That wouldn't surprise me one bit. I was growing more and more convinced that the scientific community had, in recent years, shed its vaunted neutral impartiality and adopted a shameless, nearly religious fervor about certain politically correct "scientific" views. Which were not really scientific at all. Ideology in spades trumping true science. Why not something similar with politics trashing solid intelligence? After all, moms and dads who said, sternly, "Always tell the truth," seemed to have largely faded from the scene.

At *BIAS*, we had the great good fortune to have two U. S. Secret Service Special Agents assigned. Mike Atwater and Luke Wallace. They were responsible for all facets of *BIAS* security—including personal security. This came after sneaky bastards of the Peoples' Republic of China Ministry of State Security started taking high-caliber pot shots at various USG functionaries, including yours truly (Okay, not so high-caliber) and the President's advisor, Michelle. Plus, the Secret Service had pipelines into the U. S. Intelligence Community that we—*BIAS*—did not. Not directly, at least. Every once in a while, when we needed sensitive stuff from CIA, NSA, or elsewhere in the Intelligence Community, Mike and Luke could be extremely helpful in going to the "big boys" and getting it.

We'd had a few minor—and not so minor--quibbles with the products of a couple of our big sister agencies—who weren't really sure we existed--and we were able to resolve most of them with minimal bloodletting—none on our side. We'd whisper into Kehoe's ear that he might consider raising such-and-such a question. And when he did, the Big Boys would go back to the drawing board and report back with something closer to the truth. So fine and dandy. Except I still wasn't sleeping all that well. Personal problem.

"Okay," I said to Darps and Judy. "*Cheetah* knows about the Llewellyn family vacation and has given it a thumbs-up. We're off on the evening of Friday, May thirtieth. I'll give you guys a bunch of phone numbers and our complete itinerary. *Inshallah*, you won't need to call. But if you do, fine.

I really need some sea air and a change of venue. But I don't need to be completely out of the loop, either."

I changed the subject from the Llewellyn family vacation plans to a few items on the *BIAS* horizon. I'd had a couple of hints from Kehoe that he was expecting a paper on the run-up to Lebanon's elections momentarily as well as an assessment of Turkey's support—or lack thereof--for U. S. efforts on crushing ISIS. He would expect *BIAS* to give him "sanity checks" on the Intel Community's papers. No problem. That's what we do. Darps agreed.

"Let's make sure we schedule a half day to shoot the shit about pending issue papers—and issues--before you hit the road," Darps said.

"Of course," I said. "How 'bout the Thursday a week before we leave? All day, if necessary?"

"May twenty-second? Morning? Or I can block the whole day in case we need it."

"Works for me," I said.

We all stood up. Darps left. Judy almost left and then did a quick *volte-face* and popped back into my face. I raised my eyebrows.

"Are you okay?" she asked.

"I'm fine," I said. "Why do you ask?"

"Because you don't seem fine," she said. "You come into work looking like you've been up all night. Looking like the proverbial dog's breakfast! You forget trivial stuff that you normally remember."

"Well, you're right. Sort of. I'm a bit off my game. That's why I'm taking a break on the Baltic Sea."

"I'm just wondering if you shouldn't be seeing a doctor and getting meds," she said. "Some anti-anxiety stuff like Xanax or Paxil."

"Jesus H. Christ! No! If some doc tells me that I need that stuff, I'll be out the door in a New York minute! Both doors actually! The doc's and that one right there," I said, pointing in the direction of the *BIAS* front door. "If I can't do this job without developing a dependency on some sort of prescription happy pills, then I'll just have to strike my colors and go back to the classroom."

"You'd be surprised at how many high-functioning adults take those anti-anxiety meds," Judy said. "Probably including a lot of teachers."

"Well, I'm not going to be one of them," I said. "But you should probably know that Kehoe kind of hinted at something similar. Not the meds. But a shrink."

"So I'm not being totally irrational," she said.

"Unless both you and Kehoe are," I said. "Totally irrational, that is. Give me a little time on the Baltic Sea."

Silently, I had to wonder if Judy wasn't one of those "high-functioning adults" popping anti-anxiety meds herself.

Actually, I did think I was getting better during the next few weeks. Even before getting to the Baltic. I started stretching out two or three runs a week, taking it slow, staying relaxed, and going farther. From three miles to four and then to five. It was tough at first but it tired me out the good way and helped with sleeping. I adjusted my bedtime to thirty minutes earlier and endeavored to not look like "the proverbial dog's breakfast" when Judy saw me first thing in the morning at work. Getting a decent night's sleep certainly helped with that. With not inconsiderable effort, I was able to tighten my focus on just about everything. It seemed to be working.

At home, we played around with packing/clothing schemes. The Baltic in early June could have anything from sleet and freezing rain to pretty sporty summer heat. I learned through Internet research that the Baltic is a pretty shallow sea and could go from flat calm to gut-wrenching waves in a couple of hours. But there was no way to dress for that. Just hope *M. S. Nordschiff* had plenty of Saltine crackers on board. I knew from experience that I was OK with rough seas, but I wasn't sure about my girls.

Judy was continuing to give me the shifty-eyed looks. But she seemed to be mellowing a bit and maybe was starting to think that I wasn't barking mad or on the verge of a major nervous breakdown.

I thought about a possible local Virginia fishing trip with Elizabeth. That would certainly do wonders for my jangled nerves. I glanced at the weather app on my phone for Waynesville, Virginia.

Tomorrow looked decent, fishing-wise. Occasional showers, but temps in the upper sixties. I wondered if Elizabeth was up for a bit of fly-fishing. Some of our best times together were times spent on trout streams.

Chapter Thirteen
Sheila

Algorithmics, Inc.
2288 Garrisonville Road
Stafford, Virginia
Late April

Vice Admiral Donegan drove herself, as she frequently did. She parked her Honda CR-V at a random space in the strip mall parking lot on Route six-ten. She dismounted from the vehicle and headed for a new-looking, two-story building constructed of bricks, concrete and espresso-tinted glass. She had come directly from work and wore her uniform. She felt that, this close to the Marine Corps base at Quantico, the uniform wouldn't attract undue attention.

En route to the building entrance, she observed four security cameras—two on light poles in the parking lot and two on the building itself. She let herself in and was greeted by a male receptionist seated at a desk. Behind the receptionist were two blue-uniformed security guards. One of the guards appeared to be monitoring a bank of several video monitors. Both of the guards were armed with automatic handguns and pepper spray. All three men sported high and tight haircuts.

"Good afternoon, Admiral. And welcome," the male receptionist said with a smile. "Steve, here will take you up to Roberto's office."

The blonde security guard smiled and stood.

"I'm Steve. I'll show you to where Roberto is waiting for you. Follow me, please, Admiral." He headed around a corner to an elevator and hit the "UP" button. The elevator doors hissed open immediately.
Well, thought Donegan. *Video coverage of the parking lot. No ID check. No sign-in. No clip-on ID tags. Probably facial recognition software. They recognized me before I got to the front door. Pretty impressive.*

The door hissed and thumped closed. Donegan felt the lift rise and stop, silently. After a couple of seconds, it opened.

"Right this way, Ma'am," Steve said, holding the elevator door and gesturing to their right. At the end of the short corridor, there was a dark hardwood door flanked by a key-code entry lock. Steve reached around Donegan, punched in a code and inserted his forefinger in a socket just below the keypad. The door clicked open.

"After you, Admiral," the security guard said. Donegan entered an office suite, followed by the guard.

"He knows we're here, now. Just step..."

A door popped open and Roberto Ironsides stepped out, holding out his hand.

"Admiral! Great to see you! Welcome to *Algorithmics*! Please come in."

Donegan had learned that Braxton and Ironsides had scheduled the meeting a week ago. They had told her that they had deliberately scheduled it for a Friday afternoon when much of Washington was hurriedly scurrying out of town for the weekend. All communications about the meeting had been via coded text messages over throwaway mobile phones. The code had been developed by *Algorithmics*, which had installed it on all the mobile phones before distributing them. It was automatic. One could type in "I love you" as a message and then hit *SEND*. "I love you" would be transformed immediately into something like "AXH$# DKLMN %THB5," which would appear on the recipient's screen verbatim. After the recipient—who had a code-enabled phone—pressed *TALK*, followed by a code-after-prompt, he or she would see "I love you." No one else would see the message unless they had one of the special phones and the message had been addressed to him or her as well.

Roberto opened the door from which he'd emerged and held it for Donegan.

"Have a seat, Admiral. Anywhere but Speaker DeWitts's chair. We're saving it for her—she should be here momentarily."

Donegan entered a conference room. It featured a standard conference table, a flat-screen video monitor at one end and a laptop on the table. There were several empty chairs. Seated around the table were the DNI, Sam Braxton, Lieutenant General Smalls, the Army's Assistant Chief of Staff for Intelligence and the Deputy Directors of the Central Intelligence Agency and Federal Bureau of Investigation, Dick Nagle and Stu McConnell, respectively..

"Good afternoon, Madam Speaker," Ironsides announced as the door popped open and "Steve" held the door for Congresswoman DeWitt. "Your seat is right there to your left. There's a name tag."

Everyone else in the room stood in respect for the arrival of the

Speaker of the House. Congresswoman DeWitt, clad in a gray business suit with white chalk stripes over a white blouse and wearing burgundy heels, waggled her fingers and said, "Hello, everyone!" and stepped to her chair. Ironsides marched to a podium at one end of the oblong conference table.

"Let's start with a doomsday scenario," he said. "Probably seven out of ten people associated with the U.S. Government know that the biggest fear of any potential PRC-USA confrontation is that of China launching a nuke directly vertical—straight up into space." His first power point slide showed a photo-like artist's rendition of a Chinese ballistic missile leaving its launch pad atop a great gout of flame. His second slide showed the missile much higher, still spouting fire and flying vertically. The third slide showed a digitally enhanced photo of a missile warhead exploding in flight.

"This—a thermonuclear event—would occur approximately a hundred fifty kilometers above the earth's surface. The altitude is one of the two main variables in the equation. The other is the warhead's payload. The result is an enormous electromagnetic pulse or EMP. And the result of that," he paused and showed a slide of a blacked-out earth against a pink sky. "Would be a total shutdown of virtually all satellites. Communications, weather, navigation, reconnaissance—the works. Plus all ground-bound communications. Not to mention computers. All fried. And the Chinese could shuffle the deck. Maybe cause multiple nuclear detonations at different times and altitudes. Shut down electrical grids. Cause modern automobiles to fail. The possibilities are endless and awful. Obviously, everyone hopes that this never happens. And maybe it won't—we don't think the PRC has hardened their own systems sufficiently to protect them from themselves. Much less a retaliatory strike. And the U. S. does have some hardened systems that can survive an EMP and can retaliate.

"But then there are the wild cards. North Korea. Maybe Iran. Maybe Pakistan or India, depending on how their politics swing."

He paused and changed to another slide, this one showing two young men and two young women seated before a large console containing two large, flat screens and a myriad of numerical readouts and dials.

"The reason I bring this up—you're probably very knowledgeable about what the PRC is up to and capable of. But we at *Algorithmice* have developed a computer-based system that selectively replicates the effects of various forms of an EMP."

"You mean some sort of a *virus* that shuts stuff down?" Donegan asked.

"Sort of. *Algorithmics* has developed a little package that can shut down most military C4I systems the U. S. Government uses. Plus several civilian applications. Permanently or temporarily. And we don't need to shut down very much else in the process. We have a little video that we'd like to show you."

Donegan felt a frisson of something akin to fear at the notion of a civilian contractor—even a U. S. civilian cleared contractor—doing top-secret work on a project that could use the U. S. Military as a target.

Chapter Fourteen
Alan & Elizabeth

Chestertown & Waynesville

Virginia

Early May

When I got home, Maria's car was gone from its usual parking place in the driveway, so I parked in front of the house. Then I went inside, hunted for and found Elizabeth.

"Do you think we might find a trout or two in Goose Creek? Tomorrow?" I queried.

"I thought you'd never ask!" she responded. "I've been dropping hints all over the place! For the past two or three weeks!"

Goose Creek was a small stream that emptied into the Rapidan River not too far north and west of Chestertown. Rainbow and brown trout inhabited its cold waters, courtesy of the Virginia Department of Game and Inland Fisheries.

"Yeah, I think I've noticed. But the weather has been really lousy. Until today and tomorrow," I said.

"That's never stopped you before," she said. "But whatever. Tomorrow?"

"Tomorrow," I confirmed. "Leave at six? Be on the water by seven? Weather's supposed to turn a bit foul again. Drizzly. But not too cold. Temps in the upper sixties. Trout should be hungry."

"Fabulous!" she grinned and gave me a hug around the neck that did wonders for my morale. "But I'll need a note for school the next day."

"No problem," I said. "We'll use the 'Elizabeth missed school yesterday because she was feeling out of sorts' note."

I told Maria of our plans over cocktails and she also thought trout fishing with Elizabeth was a great idea.

When I awoke the next day, it was still pretty dark and I could hear gentle raindrops hitting the roof. I picked up my watch and examined it through bleary eyes. It read zero-five-thirteen. I figured I could walk Cory and be back in time to wake up Elizabeth by five-forty-five. We could hit the road by six as planned. I jumped out of the rack and pulled on a pair

51

of jeans and a sweatshirt that I'd staged the night before. Socks and shoes followed. I splashed cold water on my face in the bathroom and brushed my teeth. Then I sneaked down the stairs, started a cup of coffee brewing and shrugged into a waterproof Navy windbreaker. I headed outside with Cory in tow. The rain was gentle and seemed warm. I thought we were good to go for some trout fishing in the foothills of the Blue Ridge.

Elizabeth powered down a bowl of Cheerios while I toasted an English muffin and sipped coffee. We were backing out the driveway by six-oh-two. We hit a favorite, tiny parking place on the bank of Goose Creek at six-fifty-five as it was just starting to get light.

We had tried taking Cory fishing with us. Once. It was a total disaster. She must have had duck-hunting Lab genes in her ancestry. We couldn't keep her out of the water. That tended to drive the trout into hiding. We ended up incarcerating her in the truck by which time the trout were hugging the creek bottom on a hunger strike. So no more trout fishing trips for Cory.

We had rigged our fly rods the night before with small wet flies and yarn strike indicators about six inches above the leaders. The latter were short, due to the predicted cloudy water. We slithered into our waders and headed for the nearby bank of Goose Creek.

"Be careful," I said. "It looks like the creek is running pretty hard. Don't go past knee-deep."

"I know, Daddy. I know."

She waded into the creek, which was flowing fast and was coffee-colored from the runoff. I went about thirty yards downstream, waded in and made a short cast. I saw my strike indicator twitch but I wasn't quick enough to set the hook. Then I heard Elizabeth holler.

"Got one!" she yelled.

I saw her rod, bowed and throbbing, as she retrieved line and a hooked, fighting trout. Seconds later she had it at her knees, an olive-and-shocking pink rainbow that looked to be about fifteen inches long.

"Catch and release?" she asked, knowing the answer.

"Of course," I said.

She worked the fly gently out of the trout's lower jaw and we both watched as the fish sped away.

"First one of the season, Dad," she said proudly.

The second and third trout of the season were Elizabeth's as well, courtesy of missed strikes by her old man. Two more rainbows about the same size as the first. Fifteen or sixteen inches. Broad-shouldered trout that must have weighed between two and a half and three pounds apiece. The next trout was Dear Old Dad's, however, and it felt like a crazed crocodile on the line. It stripped off line down to the backing twice and then began to tire. It must have been five or six minutes before I had the fish in front of my shins. It was a slab-sided Brown, copper-colored with black and a few blood-red spots. The fly—a size 10 Wooly Booger—was barely hanging from its jaw. I unhooked the trout easily with my thumb and forefinger, moved him fore and aft in the current and suddenly he shot away like a tiny attack sub scooting out of the Sea of O. But he was anything but tiny for an East Coast trout.

The rain was falling with a bit more authority, but it was still warm. Suddenly I was tired. I sloshed out of the creek and flopped down under a dripping gum tree where I watched Elizabeth play and land another rainbow. She held the fish up with both hands so I could see it before she released it. I photographed her and the trout with my phone without getting up. The picture looked pretty good nonetheless. Then she sloshed out of the creek and flopped down on the wet ground alongside me.

"I'm hungry," she said.

"I'm whupped," I said. "And starved. Let's peel off the waders and head down the road to Momma's Diner for some unhealthy breakfast."

"Sounds good to me. But that was some really good fishing," she said, shucking off her waders.

"Yes, it was," I said. "And that was the first German brown trout that I've ever caught. In my whole life," I said, as I peeled my waders off. "Who's going to get our shoes?"

We got home a little before eleven-thirty. I was pouring a fresh cup of coffee using our new K-cup gizmo when my left pocket chimed. A text. From President Kehoe.

Chapter Fifteen

Alan

1506 Prince Henry Street
Early May

I turned the phone over and checked the screen. It took me by surprise.

Loose,

We need to shoot the shit - soonest.

Like today. And it has to be way off the skyline.

HMX-1 can get me wherever

I need to go. Any ideas about where?

The "when" is today. ASAP.

Keys

That was fairly clear. The Man wanted us to meet. Today. But not in the public eye. I thought about Camp David and rejected the idea immediately. A shitload of reasons—mainly bunches of heliborne and vehicular traffic descending unexpectedly on Camp David on a weekend would send off all kinds of alarms. I figured our meeting place had to be the backside of the base. Quantico. I texted him back.

Keys,

LZ Alligator, west side of Quantico. Should be out of sight and out of mind unless the Marines have something going on out there. The guys in HMX-One know where Alligator is and whether it's clear or not. And let me know the time. I'll be there as long as the Marines let me in. Loose

I launched the text. HMX-One was Marine Experimental Helicopter Squadron One. One of whose missions was transporting the President of the United States and his or her family members from and to various locations stateside and overseas. Where the distances and runways were too short for the eighty-ninth Military Airlift Wing's Boeing Seven-Forty-Seven Air Force One. Or where LZ restrictions necessitate a helo. Less than two minutes later, my mobile sounded its sonar ring tone.

Allison, Kehoe's personal assistant, was calling. I answered.

"Hi Allison. I understand he called earlier. I'm back and at his beck and call."

"Just a sec, Alan," she said.

A line clicked open.

"Alan, you worthless weasel! You went fly-fishing for trout this morning! And I'm sitting here pushing papers around and putting up with nutzo visitors," the President snarled into the phone.

"Yes sir! Not only that. I landed a brown trout that must have been eighteen inches long and weighed in at about four pounds. Elizabeth landed and released four hefty rainbows! But you're the one who makes the big bucks!"

"You rat bastard!" the president growled, gleefully, using a phrase that had become immensely popular with us during our teenage years in Clancyville, New York. "But we need to talk. Soon. And off the skyline."

"Yes sir. I got that from the text," I said. "How about somewhere on the west side of the base? Today?"

"Okay. I got your text reply. Let's go with LZ Alligator in ninety minutes. Does that work for you?"

"Yes sir. Ninety minutes. At LZ Alligator. As long as the Marines will let me go there."

"No sweat, GI. We'll take care of that. Just be there."

I glanced at my watch. Eleven o'clock. I would be at LZ Alligator on the far side of Quantico a few minutes before 12:30.

"Okay, Sir. Adios," I said.

"See you soon," the President said.

"Yes sir. An hour and a half," I said.

Chapter Sixteen

Alan

LZ Alligator
Marine Corps Base
Quantico, Virginia
Early May

I arrived at the back entrance of the base at twelve-fifteen. There were a half-dozen Marines at the gate and they were spread out tactically and looked to be heavily armed. A Staff Sergeant checked my ID card, flashed it in front of a gizmo that looked like the gadgets that UPS delivery guys carried, saluted and said "Sir, you're good to go. You can park at the LZ. Three miles dead ahead on your right."

"Thanks, Staff Sergeant," I said, returning his salute, which felt awkward, sitting and wearing civilian clothes to boot.

I had no sooner parked the Explorer and climbed out of it when I heard the helicopters approaching. Armed Marines were scattered around the periphery of the semi-open field that made up LZ Alligator's outer perimeter. Two white-top VH-sixties were snaking rapidly down into the LZ. Fortunately, the morning rain had quit but the skies were still gray. I guessed that Kehoe was in the lead bird. My guess was wrong. He emerged from the second chopper, wearing his work clothes—a blue suit, a white shirt and a red tie. I guessed that the Secret Service had him rotate between the lead chopper and the dash-two randomly for security purposes.

We shook hands and he continued to walk away from the two choppers. Neither of the birds cut their engines.

"Let's get a little bit farther away so we don't have to scream at each other," he said.

We walked about another fifty meters. And then he stopped and turned to me.

"This is really close-held stuff," he said. "I had a sudden request for an "unofficial" visit from the Russian Ambassador, Viktor Malenkov. This morning. While you and Elizabeth were fly-fishing for trout," he said with a slight grimace.

"It was weird for a number of reasons," he continued. "One, they—the foreign ambassadors—never request immediate appointments. Normally, I'd get a heads-up, either from the Office of the President of Russia or, through State channels, from the Ministry of Foreign Affairs via their embassy. But not this time. Malenkov came directly to me. Seemingly on his own.

"Two. The message was totally off the books. Nothing in writing. He said he'd had intelligence that there was a quote—potential *coup d'état* against me—brewing. Here. In Washington. Unquote.

"Three. He claimed he'd mentioned the report to the Russian Foreign Minister Kirilinkov by secure phone and the Minister advised him—the Ambassador—to pass along the report to me. So he did. What thinkest thee about that?"

"Jesus Christ," I said. "Methinks I smell a rat."

"Here's what I think," Kehoe said. "First of all, from what I've seen and heard, President Epifanov is not in the loop. That's strange, but it fits with other intelligence we have that suggests there's a schism of some sort at the top of the Russian government. President Epifanov is on one side, along with a handful of *Mafiya*-connected oligarchs and a shitload of money. Kirilinkov, the Foreign Minister, may well be on the other side. Our intelligence suggests that he's just as nationalistic as Epifanov but nowhere near as crooked when it comes to money and oligarchs. Secondly, *BIAS* needs to sniff around and see if there's any substance to what the Russians are saying. Or whether they're just jacking us around and blowing smoke up my ass."

"That means that the restraints on *BIAS* collecting in CONUS have to come off," I said.

"I know," he said. "They're already off. By Top Secret Executive Order. Which I signed two hours ago. *BIAS* should have it by secure FAX by now. This is a super-fucking tightly-held operation. My hope is that it will end up quickly. And quietly. Then we'll go back to the original rules of the game. Business as usual. And I'll cancel and burn that goddamned executive order."

"Jesus Christ," I said again. "Did Malenkov give you any details? Like names?"

"Just one. Ironsides. Roberto."

"American or Foreign? Sounds like he could be either one," I said. "I certainly have never heard of Roberto Ironsides."

"I had never heard of him, either. I guess we don't read *Forbes* or *The Economist* enough. But he is American. I put the Secret Service on him and they told me that he's the president and CEO of a small corporation called *Algorithmics, Incorporated*, a highly successful bunch of consultants who check into—and usually solve—customers' knotty IT problems. Usually caused by viruses. He's also a major-league hacker, well known in 'hacker circles' which I didn't know existed either. At least in this country. I thought they were all in China and Russia. According to Michelle, his politics are of the progressive persuasion, but she doesn't know of any big-time political connections or activities. Or money moving. She also said that there are rumors that *Algorithmics Inc.* has a dark side, a super-secret shop run by Ironsides personally. Supposedly, it has a dozen or so geeks that can go where no one else can go when it comes to networks," the President added.

"And he's the only guy named?" I asked.

"Yes," Kehoe answered. "According to the Russians."

"Well, that begs the question. Who the hell else is on the list?"

"No shit," he muttered. "That's a major league sticking point. The rest of the goddamned list."

"Not to mention who's running the show?" I added. "Could that be Ironsides?"

"I don't think so," Kehoe responded. "According to the Secret Service, he's very much an *Eminence Grise* who generally prefers to remain in the background. Also, somewhere during our chat, Malenkov used the phrase 'within the government' when he referred to the putsch. Ironsides isn't in the government."

"Um, Jim. Shouldn't the Secret Service be the ones carrying the ball on this? I mean they're the guys charged with protecting you."

"Yes," he said. "And they're the best on God's green earth when it comes to preserving Presidential health and safety. Protection from snipers, poison, suicide bombers, nut jobs and the like. But an insider political coup? That's like entering a shadow world where nobody knows what the rules are. I have spoken with Jack Irving of the FBI. I've told him about what the Russian Ambassador told me. I also told him I would be tasking other Intelligence Community assets to look at the problem. Without mentioning *BIAS* by name. He didn't say much of anything.

That's why I want *BIAS* to take a more penetrating and focused look at this thread. I can guarantee that you guys will have the full support of the White House and the Secret Service in your efforts."

"Okay. But in order to make that happen, I've got to cut some *BIAS* people in on what you just told me. Darps and Judy at a minimum," I said. "And, since you sent them that FAX to *BIAS*, they're probably cut in already."

"Yeah, I know. Just keep the sourcing out of it when you talk to your people. No mention of the Russian Ambassador or Foreign Minister. Also, there's the other issue at work here. The split in the Russian hierarchy. My guess is that Minister Kirilenkov and Ambassador Malenkov are jumping off the reservation on this."

"How about generic Russian sources? No names?" I asked. "Can I tell my people 'Russians' or 'Russian sources' without naming names or positions?"

"Okay. 'Generic Russians' is fine. That's what I told Jack Irving. Generic Russians. And I'm guessing that the Bureau will put a big, fat magnifying glass on the Russian Ambassador. And probably the rest of the embassy staff as well. Not to mention various other Russians around the country."

"I can't think of anything else right now," I said, weakly.

"And I gotta run," he said.

We shook hands and he turned and jogged to his helicopter. The second one. Thirty seconds after he disappeared into the hatch, there was no sign of the choppers. And I was standing in LZ Alligator looking skyward and feeling dazed and dumb.

I pawed at my mobile and thumbed in Darps' mobile number.

"Yo," he answered.

"Wilderness in an hour," I said. "We need to shoot the shit. Urgently."

I couldn't remember the last time I'd used the word "urgently." In a sentence. Maybe never. In my whole life. Like catching a big brown trout.

Chapter Seventeen

Alan

The Wilderness Battlefield, Virginia
Mid-May

"**W**ilderness" was the little farmhouse annex that Darps and I used as a safe house. It was on a real farm near the site of the Battle of the Wilderness in which the Union and Confederate Armies slaughtered each other inconclusively late in the Civil War. To get to it, I had to go past a country funeral home. It sat alone among pastures, complete with a handful of horses. One of which must have pulled the old-fashioned hearse that was parked outside the funeral parlor. The hearse was black and narrow, had glass or Plexiglas sides inside of which hung partially drawn purple curtains. A pair of black shafts, which went on either side of the horse, and four wooden, spoked wheels rounded out the hearse. A weathered wooden sign stood by the side of the road.

Warren B. Gillis – Funeral Home and Crematory – Est. 1957.

I wished I'd had the chance to see a country funeral with the horse-drawn hearse, but it never happened.

Our place was a crummy little dump, but it was free from prying eyes and/or ears, as far as we knew. It had feeble heat in winter, a single window air conditioner for summer, a coffee maker and a crappy old TV. The battered fridge in the kitchen made ice the old-fashioned way—we filled up plastic ice-cube trays at the sink and stashed them in the tiny freezer till they froze many hours later. Darps had a half-gallon of Dewar's stashed in a cupboard for "emergencies." To put the homemade ice to good use every once in a while.

I arrived there in just under the agreed-upon sixty minutes. Darps was already there as evidenced by his silver Saab convertible parked in the driveway behind the house. The late spring Virginia heat and humidity had begun sneaking in. Sweat popped out on my torso as I parked the Explorer alongside the Saab and let myself in. The TV was on, tuned to a Yankees game. Darps had just started the coffeemaker brewing and it smelled good.

"Ahoy, Shipmate!" I said. "I do believe we have a shitstorm on our hands."

"Do I need to break out the scotch?" he asked.

"Let's start with coffee. I'll tell you what *Cheetah* told me. And then we can decide if we need to spike the coffee."

"Okay," he said. He pulled two mugs from the cabinet over the sink and poured us coffee. "So what's up?"

"A possible coup. Or putsch. Against the President. *Our* President. Not to mention the Constitution," I said.

"Jesus H. Christ," he growled. "Do you know what you're saying? Or are you pulling my leg?"

"Yes," I said. "I know what I'm saying. And no, I'm not pulling your leg. I'm playing back what *Cheetah* told me an hour ago. And he was playing back what he learned from Russian sources."

"Russian? Well that just makes the whole situation more screwed up than ever! The Russians! Holy mackerel!"

"There's more," I said. "He wants us—*BIAS*—to take a look at it. He signed a classified executive order giving us the okay to collect here in CONUS."

"So that was what that mysterious FAX was about! Judy called me about it a little while ago but said she couldn't get into details," Darps muttered.

"Yeah," I said. "I'm not sure where to start. He's also spoken with Jack Irving at the FBI. I think we should let that string play out by itself. Meantime, on our side, we probably need some serious brainstorming, for one thing. There's the aforementioned Russian thread. And there's at least one American thread. A huge one. And maybe more. For starters."

"Yeah. But before we go any further, we definitely need a few more brains on board," he said. "Sammy, for one. Probably Ashleigh as well."

He was referring to Sammy Chen, our China analyst, who had mega brainpower to bring to bear on any tough issues—China-related or not. And Ashleigh MacDonald, our in-house lawyer, who was also loaded up with smarts.

"Yeah, you're right. Plus Judy. Not to mention Anastasia. Then there's Mike and Luke. And they are probably already witting via Secret Service channels. Kehoe has already used the Secret Service to spook out info about the one name he got from the Russians—an American by the name of Roberto Ironsides. But we've got to hold everything very close. I don't want any of us blabbing about a possible Constitutional crisis in the middle of a Virginia college campus. Or any place else, for that matter. So I'm thinking that we need to establish a new compartment—SCI-wise."

"Did *Cheetah* give you any timelines?" Darps asked.

"No. He gave me precious goddam little. He did give me the Ironsides name. He's some sort of IT superstar. Neither of us had ever heard of him. The Secret Service took a look at him and learned about his off-the-record reputation as an über-hacker. He owns and runs a company called *Algorithmics* that reportedly is a cutting-edge technology exploration and repair firm. They have done some black work for some elements of the U. S. Intelligence Community. His politics reportedly lean toward the left, but he's not particularly active politically. At least so far. Michelle knows a little bit about him, but apparently not much—nothing damaging. That's all."

We sipped coffee.

"We need to get the inner circle together. First thing tomorrow. I know tomorrow's Sunday but I don't think we can afford to fuck around with this. Let's start with Judy and Sammy. We can start kicking things around. Then we can bring Ashleigh and Anastasia in first thing Monday. Plus Luke and Mike."

Anastasia was our Russian principal analyst. She had been born in Russia, had come to the states as a thirteen-year-old when she'd been adopted and learned English with lightening quickness. She then blazed through high school; a baccalaureate degree followed by a quickie M.A. and then a Ph.D. at Columbia.

She was petite, had light caramel-colored hair, which she usually wore in a ponytail, and large brown eyes. She looked about fifteen. And she had a mind like a steel trap. Sammy had met her back in the past when the two of them had been temporarily recruited to the same study group. He, in turn, recruited her shortly after he came to *BIAS*.

"Do we need to keep a line open with Jack Irving and the FBI?" Darps asked.

"Yes. Definitely. But carefully. I've no idea whether or not the FBI is involved in the plot or not, but we probably want to play things close to the vest. But, yeah, we need to stay in touch," I answered.

Chapter Eighteen

Alan

BIAS

Chestertown, Virginia

Late May

We actually got rolling early Sunday morning. I walked to seven o'clock Mass and strolled over to *BIAS* from church. Sammy and Judy were both working away when Darps and I arrived at the *BIAS* building at seven-fifty-five. We had a fairly useful sit-down during which Darps and I outlined what Cheetah had told me yesterday. We talked in general terms about what our approach should be. We all agreed that we needed to clamber up the learning curve as fast and as high as possible. Who was talking to the Russians? And which Russian or Russians? Why did the Russians come to us? Was there any way in which we could effect a penetration at *Algorithmics* and see what Ironsides was up to? We agreed to have a larger, lengthier meeting first thing tomorrow and adjourned a few minutes before noon.

After locking up and setting the alarms, I cornered Judy under an ancient oak tree out front with a question.

"What do you think about a new compartment for this stuff? As in SCI?" I asked.

"Not only yes, but hell yes!" she answered. "A coup plot against the President is pretty dicey stuff." That settled it.

On Monday morning, I checked the computer login as soon as I got in. Ashleigh and Anastasia were already aboard as were Judy and Darps. Luke arrived three minutes later and Mike arrived two minutes after that. Might as well bring everybody in and get rolling right away, I thought.

"Meeting in the Sensitive Compartmented Information Facility—SCIF— in ten minutes," I told them. "Room twenty-two-fifteen. Hot stuff."

Even though we didn't use our SCIF that often-- Judy, Darps and I were pretty much the only users. Up till now, that is. It was where SCI material, protected by code words, had to be stored and the only place where SCI could be discussed. Communications into and out of the SCIF were severely restricted. Only personnel with SCI-Code-Word clearances were allowed in.

The worker bees nodded and started gathering up pencils, notebooks and iPhones.

"No phones in the SCIF," Judy reminded them.

We started our meeting at eight-oh-three.

"Okay. We'll begin with establishing a new SCI compartment. '*Thunder.*' That's our new code word. As of now, no one else beyond those of us here is cleared for Thunder. Unless and until I say so in writing. Judy, please prepare the NDA's and other paperwork for us to sign before we quit. As well as the other necessary paperwork for squaring things with the White House."

"NDA's" were Non-Disclosure Agreements. They are bigger deals in the government than they are in private industry. Out in the civilian world, you can get admonished, scolded or even fired for violating an NDA. In the government, you can be prosecuted in federal court and end up in jail for years for a violation. If you're a government contractor and violate a signed NDA, you're treated pretty much like a government employee. That's why Edward Snowden is still living in Russia.

BIAS had a presidentially decreed fast track to establish SCI compartments. So that's what we did. We used the fast track.

"Okay. We're in the compartment. Make sure we have that White House FAX marked appropriately. Notify them formally and in writing about the new compartment. And ensure that all *Thunder* documentation is appropriately registered, marked, numbered and stored in the SCIF.

"I met with *Cheetah* Saturday afternoon. He has some pretty solid indications that there is a *coup d'état* effort brewing against his presidency and by extension, against the Constitution of the United States. His info claims that this plot is cooking somewhere within the U. S. Government.

"He knew of only one name—Roberto Ironsides. Who, incidentally, is *not* part of the Government. The Secret Service has determined that Ironsides is a super-hacker who runs a somewhat spooky IT firm, *Algorithmics, Incorporated.* They have done some black contracts for elements of the U.S. Intelligence Community in the past. Michelle Hookes says he's somewhat left-leaning but not particularly active politically. At least not so far. If he's indeed involved in a coup plot against the President, then that puts him over the edge and into a huge left wing, disloyal political cauldron. As of now, there are no other names. That's a major gap. There has got to be a number of high-level U.S. Government weasels involved in this plot. Something like this doesn't get started among a bunch of GS-

7's or Third-Class Petty Officers. If it indeed exists, there has got to be a bunch of high rollers involved. And there's got to be a list of the bastards' names. Somewhere.

"And if that's not enough, *Cheetah* told me that his info came from Russian sources."

I stopped and took a swig of water from a plastic bottle. Everyone in the little room except for Darps looked stunned. I thought I heard a couple of gasps.

"Alan," Anastasia interjected. "Let me see if I've got this straight. Somehow, *Russian* sources got word to President Kehoe that there's some sort of coup against him cooking within the U. S. Government?"

"That's it in a nutshell," I said.

"Did Epifanov call him up on the Presidential hotline and tell him: "Jimmy, old chap. Some of your people are working on a plot to throw you out on your ass?" Sammy asked.

I laughed.

"It was a bit more complicated than that," I said. "But the sourcing is a delicate issue and a pretty murky one at that. About all I can say at this point is that (a.) the source is Russian, and (b.) there is something strange going on in the Russian government. And, oh yeah, (c.) the source for this info has no direct connection to *BIAS*. Kehoe does have the FBI sniffing the U. S. side of things. Jack Irving is fully briefed. I'm not sure that I am, so I don't know what they—the FBI—are up to."

"How weird!" Anastasia said. "I mean I know that there seems to be some sort of power struggle going on in Moscow. There have even been some vague reports about that in the Western news media. Including our own. But for them—the Russians--tipping off the highest levels of the U. S. Government about something similar going on here in the States is pretty bizarre."

"I agree," I said. "And I think we're done for now. We've established Thunder. I've outlined our problem. I'll be getting back to you after I've digested all this and decided how we need to attack it. I'd be grateful if you all gave some thought as to how we might best deal with the problem as well."

I think my *BIAS* teammates appreciated my aversion to long-winded meetings. As I watched bodies scurry out of the SCIF, a little worry popped up in my fevered brain. Would this issue kill our family's Baltic vacation?

Chapter Nineteen
Sheila

Stafford, Virginia
Late April

The text message announcing an "emergency" meeting of "the group" at the *Algorithmics* office complex at Stafford came in at a few minutes after four. The meeting was scheduled for seventeen-thirty.

It was 1610 when Vice Admiral Donegan left her Pentagon office. Stafford was a bit of a haul—maybe forty-five miles. At this time of day, the traffic could be fierce. And it was. She arrived at the parking lot at *Algorithmics* at seventeen-twenty-five.

She was admitted immediately and plopped down at an empty chair, reflecting that this was the second "emergency" meeting in a week. Once again, Roberto Ironsides led off the meeting.

"Sorry, all. I didn't want to keep you here all that late on last Friday for a number of reasons. Security being the primary one. The longer a gathering like ours lasts, the more attention it attracts. Because of the personalities involved. And that's the last thing we want. Attention. Also, I didn't want to destroy the entirety of everyone's Friday evening. I think Washington Friday evenings are rather special. Both for those of us with families and those without. I conferred with Sam and we decided to do the 'Part Two' of the meeting this evening. And I promise you it'll be quick.

"I mentioned a video of a demonstration of our little disruption capability and we'll watch that this evening.

"The video was shot at Fort Sill, Oklahoma, the home of the U. S. Army Field Artillery School and the hub of field artillery doctrine and training for the Army and the Marine Corps. It is right outside the city of Lawton, Oklahoma, which is about eighty-five miles southwest of Oklahoma City and is a very active base—please don't mistake it for some sleepy garrison encampment. There is a lot of troop movement in and out of Fort Sill and a lot of artillery training goes on there. The Army's formal schools as well as Active and Reserve units of the Army and the Marines go full bore year around. A lot of ammo goes "boom" there just about every day. This video was shot last Wednesday evening. The video cam was located on

Mount Scott, just north of Fort Sill and Lawton.

"Mount Scott is part of the Wichita Mountains National Wildlife Area and is open to the public. The peak is about twenty-four hundred feet above sea level, which puts it about thirteen hundred feet above most of Fort Sill. There is a road to the top that is open to the public. A team of three *Algorithmics* employees drove to the summit just before dark and set up the video cam. Let's run the video."

The room lights dimmed and an image of many widely scattered pinpricks of light popped up on the big screen.

"This is the main post at Fort Sill at twenty-one-twenty-nine hundred hours on Wednesday, twenty-five April. There is a little bit tighter fringe of bright lights at the top of the screen that are lights of homes and retail outlets off post in Lawton. You can see the time stamp running on the lower right-hand corner of the video."

Ironsides paused.

"There!" he snapped.

The lights on Fort Sill went out. Almost all of them. And all the lights at Post Army Airfield. Gone. A very few pairs of moving headlights and taillights from vehicles stayed on. All the lights in Lawton at the top of the screen stayed on.

"That outage was controlled from downstairs in this building. Watch the time stamp. The few moving lights are from headlights and taillights of older-model cars. Like pre-nineteen-ninety-five."

The time stamp on the video ran from twenty-one-thirty to twenty-one-thirty-one in darkness and silence and then, after a long minute, it flipped over to twenty-one-thirty-two at which time the lights on Fort Sill all snapped on.

"We turned the lights back on right here as well," Ironsides said. "That was the plan. Now let's take a look at a little message traffic."

He clicked the mouse and a slide appeared.

```
PRECEDENCE: FLASH
CLASSIFICATION: TOP SECRET
FM: CG AAFAC FORT SILL
TO: CG TRADOC
INFO: CJCS, CSA
SUBJ: C4 ANOMALY (TS)
```

```
1. (TS) ENTIRE COMMAND AND ASSOCIATED ACTIVITIES
(INCL HQS, FACILITIES, REYNOLDS ARMY HOSPITAL,
POST ARMY AIRFIELD, FAMIY HOUSING, COMMS, TV,
ETC.) EXPERIENCED A TWO-MINUTE TOTAL OUTAGE OF
ELECTRICAL POWER, ELECTRONIC COMMS AND COMPUTING
CAPABILITY STARTING AT 2130S TILL 2132S AT WHICH
TIME EVERYTHING WAS RESTORED.
2. (U) CIVILIAN POWER IN LAWTON APPEARED TO
REMAIN UNINTERRUPTED.
3. (U) INVESTIGATION UNDERWAY. MORE TO FOLLOW.
     BROWN SENDS
     CLASSIFICATION: TOP SECRET
```

Murmurs of "Holy shit" and "Good grief" hissed through the room as he moved to a new slide.

"Here's another," Ironsides said, clicking the mouse again.

```
PRECEDENCE: FLASH
CLASSIFICATION: TOP SECRET
FM: WHCA
TO: CG AAFAC FORT SILL
INFO: SECDEF WASH DC
      CJCS, CSA
      CG TRADOC
SUBJ: C4 ANOMALY AT FORT SILL (TS)
REF: CG AAFAC FORT SILL (TS) MSG 26APR0345Z.
1. (TS) WHAT THE HELL IS GOING ON WITH THE QUOTE
ANOMALY UNQUOTE?
2. (S) ADVISE SOONEST RE INVESTIGATION RESULTS.
     COOPER SENDS
     CLASSIFICATION: TOP SECRET
```

"Good Lord!" Donegan sputtered. "The White House Communications Agency just poked their nose into the 'anomaly'!"

"No shit!" Braxton added. "A shutdown like that is pretty damned important and it grabbed White House attention. Charlie Cooper is a Marine Corps Brigadier General in charge of the White House Communications Agency. But he speaks for the President. Does anyone out there know that the quote anomaly unquote came from here?"

"No!" said Ironsides emphatically. "And if that changes, we could all end up in the slammer. If we're lucky. So this is one thing that we will all take with us to our graves."

He paused.

"This capability is the war-stopper," he said.

The inhales of breath were audible.

"I don't think I need to spell it out. We have the capability to shut down everything. And start it up again five, ten, or fifteen minutes later. Except next time it'll not be limited to a few grid squares in the middle of Oklahoma."

Braxton stood up and added, "With a brand-new President of the United States and a new chain of command after the shutdown," he said in a somber voice. "President DeWitt. As the Speaker of the U. S. House of Representatives, she is next in line of succession after the departure of Kehoe and Syd Girtler, the sitting President and Vice President. Both of whom will be arrested and detained in Fort Leavenworth Federal Prison. While everything is shut down. That will be a fifteen-minute operation, according to current plans. Girtler's replacement as VP will be Dave Gamble."

"How on earth do we engineer *that*?" Donegan asked.

"President DeWitt appoints him," Braxton said. "The Twenty-fifth Amendment to the Constitution says: 'Whenever there is a vacancy in the office of the Vice President, the President shall nominate a Vice President who shall take office upon confirmation by a majority vote of both Houses of Congress.'"

The meeting ended several minutes later.

Driving back to her Crystal City condo, Donegan felt several major pangs of uneasiness. About the enormity of what they were preparing to do. Shutting down campus and schoolyard mass murder was a good thing. Shutting down the whole freaking government and locking up duly elected representatives of the American people was a hell of a price— even for a good thing. Civilian contractors having such easy, unfettered access to the Top Secret military command, control, communications and intelligence infrastructure was another thorn in her side. Braxton and Gamble were bona fide Government employees. But Ironsides was a total civilian—a contractor. And he apparently had total control over all U.S. Military C4I systems. A fact that Donegan found extremely unsettling. At best.

Chapter Twenty

Sheila

The C and O Canal
Washington, D.C.
Mid-May

"Admiral Donegan calling for Director Braxton" said Petty Officer Porter. He nodded at the Admiral and she picked up her phone just as Braxton came on the line.

"Hi Sheila," he said heartily. "To what do I owe the pleasure?"

"I know you're a runner, Sam," Donegan began. "I am too, even though my pace is one befitting my advanced age. But I was wondering if you'd be up to three or four dignified miles on the C&O Canal Towpath around lunchtime. It's a beautiful day."

"How does four miles in forty minutes sound?" Braxton asked. "I could meet you on the Key Bridge any time after eleven-thirty."

"Perfect!" she said. "How does eleven-forty-five at the middle of the bridge sound? We can run upstream on the towpath for twenty minutes and turn around and come back. And not worry about distance at all."

"Works for me. See you at the middle of Key Bridge at eleven-forty-five," Braxton said and hung up.

Donegan hung up as well. She looked at the ceiling of her comfortable office and wondered how this little meeting would work out.

"Porter. Line up the vehicle for a short run to the Key Bridge at eleven-thirty-five. I'm meeting the DNI on the bridge for a run up the towpath."

"Aye, aye Ma'am," Porter responded.

Then she turned to her email. It was mostly inane drivel.

Two and a half hours later, she alighted from her Navy vehicle and headed across the Key Bridge toward Georgetown. She wore a NAVY TRACK ball cap, a blue-trimmed, white t-shirt with a small USNA logo and Navy running shorts. Halfway across the bridge, she made sure she wasn't blocking anyone, halted and began stretching, first her left quad and then the right. Three seconds into her right quad, she spotted Braxton jogging across the bridge from Virginia. Dropping her ankle, she waved and caught his eye.

"Hi, Sheila!" he said. "You're right. It is a beautiful day!"

"Hi Sam. Thanks for joining me. Let's get on the towpath and head west for twenty minutes."

"Just as long as we keep it dignified," Braxton said. "I don't want to collapse or throw up two miles up the river."

"I couldn't agree more," Donegan said. "It's too nice a day to spoil it with pain or vomiting."

The two scrambled down the dirt path alongside the bridge and turned right on the towpath, running parallel to the canal and the Potomac below. They ran easily, loping along at a comfortable pace, without saying anything, for several minutes.

"Okay, Sheila. I'm guessing you want to talk about something," Braxton said finally. "If I'm guessing wrong, no big deal. We'll just enjoy the day and a pleasant run. But . . ."

"No, no, you're right, Sam. There are a couple of things I'd like to air out with you. And I didn't want to wait for our next formal meeting, much less flap my jaws in some office in D.C. or Virginia."

"Okay. Understand. Shoot," Braxton said.

"Okay. First of all, we've spoken about locking up the two big guns in Leavenworth."

Donegan was speaking about Kehoe and Girtler. She felt certain that Braxton knew of whom she was talking.

"I assume we're talking about some sort of a court martial," she added.

"Actually, it's a little more complicated than that," Braxton said. "Kehoe being the Commander-in-Chief of the Armed Forces. We're establishing a Special Military Tribunal made up of a handful of retired Flag Officers. Three or four stars. All services. There will be an equal number of retired Cabinet secretaries. We'll have a Trial Counsel—a retired Marine Corps Major General. Ditto for the Defense Counsel. Except he's Air Force. I was planning to brief the plan at one of the group's meetings. Soon."

"And what will the charges be?" she asked.

"Treason," he said.

"My God," she said.

"What's the matter?" he asked. "I hope you're not having second thoughts."

"No, no. It's not that," she said, looking at her watch. "This is a good place—and time—to turn around."

The two turned and headed back toward Georgetown. "What is the basis of their treason?" she asked.

"Betrayal of their oaths to preserve, protect and defend the Constitution of the United States. Dereliction of their sworn duty to protect the citizenry. We have two dozen witnesses lined up already."

"It's just that what you're talking about will be such a huge spectacle," Sheila responded. "The President and Vice President of the United States being tried for treason. At a 'special tribunal.' I just wish we could make those two guys go away. Just disappear."

"I'm sure some of our comrades-in-arms from some overseas countries would make things happen that way," Braxton said. "But here and now, in the good ole U.S.A., we've got to give the developments at least a thin veneer of legal respectability."

"I'm sure you're right," Donegan said.

"How comfortable are you with Ironsides?" she asked after a few minutes.

"Totally. He's got virtually all the top tickets, clearance-wise. Has had for years."

"I understand that. But seeing a *contractor* having total control over all military C4I systems gives me the heebie-jeebies."

"Roberto's okay. He's cleared for just about everything. He's got the full trust and confidence of the United States Government," Braxton assured her.

"What if this 'special tribunal' comes up with a finding of not guilty?" Donegan asked,

"Won't happen," Braxton replied. "The case will be airtight. They'll be guilty. You can count on that. There is one more thing, however. The Russians. NSA says they have indications that they may know something. About what we're planning."

"Good grief," she said. "Any details?"

"Not yet. None. I'm worried about leaks."

They stopped at the Key Bridge. Both had worked up a healthy sweat.

"Thanks for the run—and for the chat," Sheila said as they shook hands.

"Thank you. Let's have lunch next week. I'll call you."

Sheila jogged away in her clammy running gear. It had started to dry out but still smelled like a cage at the zoo.

As she ran slowly toward the Pentagon, she mentally flipped through her tiny network of special contacts within Naval intelligence that were witting of her membership in "the group" and failed to come up with a single credible candidate for leaking anything about the group's plans or activities to the Russians. There were one or two who might be capable of going to NCIS or the FBI. But not the Russians, she thought. Anyway, none was witting about exactly what the group was planning.

On the other hand, she had to worry about herself. Like the famous whore in Venice, she was now at least thinking seriously about working both sides of the canal.

Chapter Twenty-One
Sheila

The Army-Navy Club
901 17th Street, NW
Washington, D. C.
Thursday
Mid-June

"I'm not sure this is the best place for us to meet," Vice Admiral Donegan said as she seated herself. Her misgivings were mixed. On one hand, she was genuinely concerned about meeting openly with the "other" DNI. On the other hand, her partially compromised position with "the group" added to her unease.

"I think it's fine," Sam Braxton responded as he sat down. "What could be more natural than the Directors of National and Naval Intelligence than to meet for lunch at the Army-Navy Club?"

"Probably the two of us meeting for lunch in a mess that was cleared for classified discussions in your building or mine," Donegan replied. "But I guess we're not attracting too much attention."

She wore a tan suit over a royal blue blouse and dark blue pumps. When the waiter took their drink orders, they both asked for sweet iced tea.

"I'm planning on getting the group together on Friday. Probably at Great Falls again. But I wanted to bounce a couple of things off you first," Braxton said.

The waiter appeared with the iced tea.

"Would you like a few minutes more?" he asked, eyeing their untouched menus.

"Umm, yes please," Braxton mumbled, picking up his menu and opening it.

Donegan ordered a blackened grouper sandwich with a side of coleslaw and Braxton chose a chopped Cobb salad. The waiter collected their menus and left.

"There's still a leak," he said, softly. "The Russians seem to have at least a hint of what's in the works."

Donegan raised her eyebrows.

"Good Lord," she whispered. "You mean *our* works?"

Braxton nodded as he chewed a dainty mouthful of chopped salad.

"If they know what's going on, who else does?" Donegan continued.

"Exactly. That's why we're meeting Friday. To look at the calendar. We're going have to move things up. If we're going to make them happen at all."

Their waiter showed up with two pitchers and topped up their water and iced tea glasses. They murmured their thanks.

"There's also some weird political stuff going on in Moscow," Braxton said after another bite of salad.

"I've seen those reports. I don't think any of that stuff is weirder than what's going on here," Donegan observed.

"I don't think anything could be weirder than what's happening here," agreed Braxton.

Donegan put her fork down with her sandwich half-eaten and dabbed at her lips with her napkin. Braxton looked at her.

"Sandwich not good?" he asked.

"It's fine," she said. "Excellent. But for some reason, I'm suddenly full."

She took a sip of iced tea.

Five minutes later, they had the waiter box up Donegan's sandwich and split the tab. They paid with separate credit cards and left.

"See you Friday," Braxton said.

"Yes. Friday," she mumbled as Corporal McFarland pulled up in the white Navy sedan.

Chapter Twenty-Two

Sheila

Crystal City
Early June

Vice Admiral Donegan let herself into her apartment. She made sure the door was locked, retrieved her phone from her purse and collapsed on the couch and went to the address book on her phone. She went to the D's. "Donegan, Bobby. LCDR USN. OpNav." Followed by a trio of phone numbers. Bobby was her younger brother. He lived in North Arlington with his wife and their five-year-old daughter, Gillian.

She poked in the numbers for his mobile, hoping to get him rather than family members.

After two rings, he answered. "Donegan."

"Bobby. It's Sheila," she said.

"Hi Sheila. How are you?" he asked.

"I'm not sure," she said. "Is there some place where we can meet privately? Like now? I have to talk to you about something absolutely *critical* that needs to stay off the air. Totally."

"I hear what you're saying, Sheila. Critical. Now. Off the air. Umm, how about Indigo Landing? Not the restaurant itself. That's too high viz if you want to stay off the skyline. It's on the Potomac just south of Alexandria. There are a couple of benches and picnic tables outside their parking lot. We can keep a pretty low profile there. If we're in civvies. I can get there in thirty minutes."

"Okay. I know the place. I'll meet you there in a half an hour. Find a seat and I'll find you."

"Okay. I'm wearing a black t-shirt and blue jeans. I'll try and find a table fairly close to the parking lot."

Donegan changed into sweats and running shoes. She found an Orioles ball cap through which she pulled her short ponytail. Finally, she donned a large pair of sunglasses.

Thirty-two minutes later, she jogged into the Indigo Landing parking lot and immediately spotted her brother. He was sitting on a weathered bench, reading a copy of *Field and Stream*. She hurried to his side and sat down.

"Hey, bro," she said. "Sorry I'm sweating."

"Hi, Sheel," he answered. "Not to worry. What's up?"

"Um, I know that this sounds crazy. But do you have any direct White House connections?"

"Jesus Christ, Sheel," Bobby said. "You're the three-star. I'm just a lowly Lieutenant Commander. You're a helluva lot closer to that flagpole than I've ever been. Or ever will be, for that matter."

"Don't sell yourself short. I have some pretty high-up connections, but somehow they all stop somewhere short of the White House. I just was wondering if you know somebody that has a direct connection there. Like an old shipmate, maybe."

"What kind of connections?" Bobby asked.

"All the way to the top."

"Sweet Jesus."

"This is really serious," the Admiral said. "I have a message that needs to go to the President himself. And I'd hate for some minion—even a high-level minion—to shortstop the message and have that result in a total disaster."

"Can you tell me any more than that? Like what sort of disaster are we talking about?" Bobby asked.

"Not sitting here," she said. She looked around the periphery of the parking lot, her eyes settling on the turgid Potomac. "Wanna walk a bit? Or jog?"

They both stood up and headed for the jogging-and-biking trail that ran more or less parallel to the river.

"Okay," she said as they headed downstream into a deserted section of the trail. "There's a plot. Against the Government. Against the President himself."

She paused to take a breath.

"I've been involved in it. But I can't stay involved. I need to get out. I need to get word of the plot to the President. I realize that it's career suicide for me and I suppose I could well end up in Leavenworth, but I don't care. I've got to shut it down."

"Good Lord", Bobby muttered. "It strikes me that there's no good answer or no good result lurking anywhere in this rat's nest. Isn't there some way you can get an anonymous tip to the White House?"

"I don't think that'll work, Brother Dear," the Admiral replied. "I think they get anonymous tips all the time. Rather low credibility. I say again. Do you have a pipeline into the White House?"

"My first reaction is 'no.' But then, maybe I do. At least indirectly. I have an Academy classmate. Smartest guy in the class. Went into submarines after graduation and then got out of the Navy. Ran a hot shot-consulting outfit and then dropped off the radar. Word on the street is that he went to work for the President as part of some sort of super-secret intel fact-checking group. And that's all shithouse rumors. I don't know anything for sure. That's all, folks!"

"Can you hook me up with him?" Sheila asked.

"I dunno," Bobby answered. "Give me a day or two to see if I can run him down."

He gave her a gentle punch on the shoulder. "I'll get back to you."

"As quickly as you can," said his big sister. "I'm deadly serious about this—this scheme or plot or whatever the hell it is."

The two siblings turned and headed back to the Indigo Landing parking lot, arm in arm.

"Talk to you soon, Sheel," Bobby said.

"I hope so," said his big sister.

The two siblings hugged. If asked, both would have agreed that there was an element of desperation in the hugs. That bothered both of them.

Chapter Twenty-Three

Alan

1506 Prince Henry Street

Mid-May

"What's the matter?" Maria asked as we climbed into bed.

"Who said something's the matter?" I asked, disingenuously. She saw through my pathetic attempted subterfuge immediately.

"I did," she said. "You're clinging to the ceiling like a bat in a dark cave. Something is really wrong. What is it?"

"Okay. You're right. I feel like I'm stretched between the horns of a huge freaking dilemma. We have this Baltic cruise scheduled. End of the month. My idea. Kind of a cure for the ugly after effects of that terrorist attack on Washington High School. Everybody, from Kehoe on down, signed off on the trip. You and Elizabeth loved the idea. Lord knows, I did. Then we got wind of a red-hot intelligence problem that may involve some parts of the U.S. Government. He—Kehoe—tasked *BIAS* to take a look at the quote issue unquote. So I'm wondering if we need to cancel or postpone our cruise. The idea troubles me greatly. To say the least."

"Hmm," she muttered. She turned toward me and put her right arm around my shoulders.

"Your call," she said. "The Baltic Sea will be there for a while. If we need to delay, we need to delay. No big deal."

"But if we delay, the cruise costs us twelve hundred dollars more."

"We can afford that. Might have to have more hot dog and mac-and-cheese combos in the dinner diet, but we won't starve."

"I'm not crazy about that. I'm okay with the mac and cheese and the hot dogs—as long as the latter are Nathan's. But I worry that, if we delay the cruise, I'll end up staying here and working the problem and plan on going on the cruise later, the problem could continue hanging over our heads. And then summer ends and Elizabeth goes back to school. And if we're not careful, the cruise goes down the toilet."

"Well," she said. "You're an intelligence professional. Get together with your boss and try and figure what the timelines look like. Maybe it might be smarter to go cruising on the Baltic right away and then be back as things here really start to heat up."

"You're really smart, Lover," I murmured, squeezing her tightly. "Except I'm not really an intelligence professional. I'm just an ex-Naval officer and former high school teacher."

"You're working intelligence for the President of the United States. That makes you a *de facto* intelligence professional," she said.

She kissed me and grabbed me where she knew I love to be grabbed and things went south from there. So to speak. In a great way. Somewhere in the back of my mind, I planned to talk to Kehoe tomorrow.

Chapter Twenty-Four

Alan

BIAS
Chestertown, Virginia
Late May

The next day started well. I felt like my rough edges had been smoothed off by spending a fair amount of time in Maria's arms.

I arrived at the *BIAS* building at seven-twenty-five. Judy was already there and was busy unlocking the building and silencing the alarms.

"Anything new?" she asked.

"Not that I know of," I said. "I'm going to ask *Cheetah* if I should cancel our cruise."

"Here's a thought," she said, looking me straight in the eye. "Ask him to *approve* you going on the cruise. Keep it on the positive side. And then go. That's what he'll tell you to do. Go on the cruise. But if you ask him if you should cancel, he might start to think about it and then say 'yes.' Or 'maybe.' You don't want to have to look either of those options in the face," she said.

"At this point, I'm not sure what I want."

"At this point, you want to get your ass out on the Baltic Sea cruise with Maria and Elizabeth," she said.

I couldn't argue with her. Women rule my life.

Two minutes later, I was poking up an email.

From: ALlewellyn@BIAS.gov

To: Keys@LISound.com

Subj: Cruise

Keys,

In view of current concerns, am wondering about the Llewellyn family Baltic cruise. My position now is not to change anything and go as planned as we discussed. My gut feeling is that we can still sneak it (the cruise) in before the shit starts hitting the fan around here. Our first week or two of effort at BIAS will be nearly all research anyway. I've already turned the troops loose on that. They can do it without me. By the time they're done, I'll be home.

What thinkest thee?

Loose

I heard back almost immediately.

From: Keys@LISound.com

To: ALlewellyn@BIAS.com

Subj: Baltic

Loose, Go! By all means! We'll be in touch as necessary.

Keys.

Okay. The trip was still on. I called Maria and told her. She sounded delighted.

"I'll text Elizabeth—during her lunch period—and let her know! She'll be ecstatic!"

I felt good. But there was a microscopic little cyclone blowing around the back of my brain. I thought it might have been tied to Kehoe's choice of words. "We'll be in touch . . ."

"You were right," I said to Judy a few minutes later. "The cruise is still on, per *Cheetah*. Now we need to do a little plotting and scheming. Or maybe I should say 'planning'."

"Okay. What do you want to do? And when?"

"Meet with you, Darps, Sammy, Ashleigh, Mike, Luke and Anastasia," I said, ticking off the names on my fingers. "Tomorrow. As soon as you can set it up. Let's plan for a minimum of ninety minutes," I said.

She jotted some arcane symbols on her steno pad and said, "I'll let you know."

Chapter Twenty-Five
Sheila

Crystal City
Early June

The thunder started to rumble just as Admiral Donegan left the Pentagon at seventeen-thirty. By the time she arrived at her parking place at the Crystal City condos, the raindrops were pounding her Honda like marbles flying out of the sky. She decided that an outdoor run was out of the question. A workout in the condo complex gym would be head-clearing and dry. And safe from lightning strikes. At six-fifteen on a Friday evening, she knew that the gym should be nearly empty.

She changed quickly into workout clothes, grabbed a towel and headed for the elevators and the gym. There was one other person working out—a girl on a treadmill. CNN was on the wall-mounted TV.

"Feel free to change the channel," the girl said. "I wasn't paying much attention."

"CNN is fine with me," Sheila said. She felt like her mind was going a thousand miles an hour and she wouldn't be able to concentrate on the TV unless something truly cataclysmic got her attention. She programmed an elliptical trainer for a forty-minute workout—ten minutes slow and flat, twenty minutes medium-fast and hilly and ten minutes slow and easy. She started on the slow and flat phase and tried to escape from her conflicting emotions. On one hand, it was a relief to have told Bobby what she had been doing and what she planned to do—or at least try to do. She was part of a conspiracy to overthrow the President and Vice President of the United States. And now she was trying to blow the whistle on the conspiracy and the conspirators. Which action could put her in a federal prison for a helluva long time.

Her participation in the conspiracy would certainly kill her naval career. Or worse. Hence her anxiety on top of her relief. She felt better when the forty minutes of the workout were up. She hoped Bobby would call soon. She needed to start thinking about hiring a lawyer—soon.

She let herself into her apartment, thinking of a frozen pizza and some eye-glazing TV. The phone rang. The landline. The Caller ID said "B.

DONEGAN."

She picked up. "Hey, Bro," she said.

"Hey Sheel," he said. "Can we meet downstairs?"

"Here?" she asked.

"Yeah," he said.

"Now? I mean are you here?"

"Yup. I'm in my car trying to stay dry. Across from your main entrance."

"Why don't you come up here? It's plenty dry."

"Off the grid and all that stuff," he said. "I don't think it would be wise for me to be seen hip-hopping up to your condo. Probably isn't wise to be seen sitting here, for that matter."

"I'll be down in two minutes," she said.

A minute and forty seconds later, she popped out the front door into the rain. Wearing a sweaty t-shirt and running shorts. What the hell! Bobby was her brother. He'd seen her looking worse. She opened an umbrella. Headlights flashed on a car across the parking lot. She trotted through the rain to the car, which she recognized as Bobby's VW *Tiguan*. She opened the passenger side door and climbed in, awkwardly folding her dripping umbrella.

"What's up?" she asked.

"The guy that I told you about—Darpley Roentgen Taylor—Darps, as he's known—would like to meet you at J. Bryan's pub in Chestertown, Virginia. Two hundred Hapsburg Street. Tomorrow. At seventeen hundred. Don't wear your uniform. He said that the more you resemble a quote-civilian swine-unquote, the better."

She grinned for the first time in the last forty-eight hours.

"I think I like this guy," She said. "'Civilian swine' indeed."

"Wait till you meet him before you decide that you like him," Bobby said. "He's a bit on the eccentric side to say the least. 'Weird' is probably a better descriptor. But if anyone that I know can get you into Sixteen Hundred, he can. But he is very determined to stay off the air. No email, no phones, no text messages. Just face-to-face at J. Bryan's. Hell, I had to meet him at an I-95 rest stop to talk to him—he wouldn't even talk to me on the phone."

"I think his caution works for me as well. Christ knows who's listening these days. Staying off the air is good," she said.

"You bet, Sheel," Bobby said. "And by the way, you know where our house is. Feel free to drop by any time. Gillian is so proud that her old man has a big sister who's an admiral."

"I hope it won't be too bad a blow if her old man's big sister has to trade in her admiral's uniform for an orange jump suit."

Chapter Twenty-Six

Sheila

J. Bryan's Pub

Chestertown, Virginia

Early May

Vice Admiral Donegan walked into J. Bryan's on Hapsburg Street in Chestertown at 1650. She felt like she was skulking. A three-star Admiral is accustomed to the spotlight. Now she felt like she was hiding under a rock. She was doing her best to look like a "civilian swine." She wore slim LL Bean jeans and a Carolina Panthers long-sleeve t-shirt. High-mileage running shoes were on her feet. She hoped she wouldn't be refused admission for a dress code violation. She wasn't.

She found a small table against the back wall from where she could watch the front door. A waitress appeared at her table.

"What can I get you, Dear?" she asked.

"A glass of pinot grigio, please," Sheila replied. She glanced at her watch. Sixteen-fifty-five. Two minutes later, the waitress returned with a generous glass of wine. At the same moment, a man entered the pub. He removed a brown fedora, revealing a bald head. He had a neatly trimmed Van Dyke beard and moustache—not a scraggly hipster special that seemed to be so much in vogue these days. He glanced warily around the pub and his gaze settled on Donegan. It had to be Darpley. Or Darps. Bobby's Naval Academy classmate. She gave him a brief wave and the hint of a smile and he strode over to her table.

"Admiral?" he asked softly.

"Sheila," she said. "Bobby's sister. Let's keep things informal. Darps? Please have a seat."

The waitress reappeared.

"Can I get you anything, sir?"

"Sure. A pint of Guinness, please. And a plate of wings to share."

"A dozen? Or two?" the waitress asked.

Darps glanced at Donegan who raised her hands defensively.

"Two or three will probably do for me," the Admiral said. "Wings that is."

"Can we do a half dozen?" Darps asked.

"Yes sir."

A young couple that looked Irish suddenly appeared on the tiny stage in the back corner of the pub. A bright light came on.

"Conroy and Conroy, brother and sister, directly from County Galway!" announced an amplified male voice with a brogue.

The brother carried an accordion and the sister carried a fiddle. They immediately broke into a raucous version of *A Jug of Punch*, upping the noise level in the pub and making Sheila feel more comfortable about talking.

Darps turned to Sheila as the waitress left.

"My classmate and your brother, Bobby, said you had some information that you felt was extremely important and needed to get into some high-level hands," he said.

"Yes," she said. "The highest level hands. The information directly affects the health and well-being of the owner of those hands."

The waitress returned with Darps' pint and the small plate of wings. He waited until she left and leaned over the table.

"So what are we talking about here?" he whispered.

Sheila picked up a chicken wing, sloshed it in blue cheese dressing and took a bite.

She took a deep breath.

"A coup. From within the United States Government. Against the President," she whispered.

"Sweet Christ," Darps muttered. He paused, looked away for an instant. He looked back into Donegan's eyes. "I probably wouldn't tell you this if you weren't a Vice Admiral in the United States Navy. But I have to tell you that this is not the first chunk of info that we've heard about something like this. We got a cryptic message from other, non-U.S. sources that something similar to this was afoot. We only got one American name supposedly connected to the plot. One. And it wasn't yours, by the way. A civilian—not a government guy. We didn't get any names of American conspirators who are part of the government."

"If you had, my name would probably have been on the list," Donegan said.

Darps snorted involuntarily as he tried to sip Guinness.

"I'm guessing there's more to this story than what you're willing to tell me," he said.

"I'm not so sure I need to tell you any more," Donegan whispered. "Remember, I said that I need to get the info to the President, himself."

Darps sipped Guinness. Donegan took a hummingbird-sized sip of wine.

"Not to put too fine a point on things," Darps said. "But you didn't say precisely that."

"Sorry. When I said 'the highest-level hands,' I was implying the President."

"I get that. Now."

He paused and nibbled on a chicken wing after dragging it through the blue cheese dressing.

"We need a way to communicate. I'm not in a position where I can say, 'Sure; The President will see you at zero nine hundred tomorrow,' or anything close to that. Your office is in the Pentagon, right?"

"Yes."

Darps took another sip of Guinness.

"Do you have an assigned parking spot?" he asked.

"Yes and no. I have an assigned area. For flag and general officers. It's in North Parking, close to the building."

"What kind of car do you drive?" Darps asked.

"Honda. CR-V. Silver," she said. "Virginia tags. SD-YCH. Blue Navy three-star sticker on the windshield."

"I'm thinking. We could use your car as a dead drop. Take an empty manila folder with you in your vehicle the next time you leave home or work. Keep it in your car. On the front seat. If you need to see me, put the folder on the dashboard. Just forward of the steering wheel. I'll swing by the Pentagon every morning and check your car on my way to work. I have a Pentagon car pass and Government ID. I can come by your condo's parking lot on Saturday and Sunday mornings. In any case, if the folder is on the dashboard, we'll meet in the long-term lot at Reagan National at eighteen-thirty that day."

"Suppose you need to see me?" Sheila asked.

"I'll leave a purple post-it note stuck to your driver's side window. One of those skinny little sticky notes. Same meeting arrangement. Eighteen-thirty at Reagan National, long-term. Same day. My ride is a silver Saab convertible."

"Umm, sometimes I work late--like past eighteen-thirty. What then?"

"If you're gonna be working late, check your car sometime between seventeen hundred and seventeen thirty. If I've left the skinny sticky note, try to bail out from work early enough to make the eighteen-thirty meet. If you can't make it, you can't make it. We'll just try again the following day."

"Sounds good," she said and finished off her pinot grigio.

"Umm," Darps mumbled. "We also need loop closers. If I get your message—the folder on the dashboard—I'll give your cell a one-ring hang-up call sometime during the day. You do the same if you get my purple sticky note, call. For confirmation. If there's no call it means the connection failed. We start over from scratch the next morning."

"Sounds good. One-ring, hang-up calls to confirm. Umm, this was my meeting, my treat," she said, taking out a wallet and placing a twenty and a ten on the table.

"Well thank you," Darps said. "I'm sure you'll be hearing from me. Soon."

The two exchanged phone numbers and left the pub.

Chapter Twenty-Seven

Alan

Our vital *BIAS* staff meeting did not happen as planned. A big fat fly flew directly into the ointment. It all started with a text from Darps yesterday evening just before Maria and I were sitting down for cocktails.

> Importantissimo! Meet me at first
> parking Lot in PWFP @ 0700. Tomorrow!

"PWFP" meant Prince William Forest Park. A woodsy park adjoining the Quantico base. I'm guessing that Darps didn't want to use up time going out west to the ranch at the Wilderness and that he had picked up a super critical nugget of some sort. I pulled into the Park at zero-six-fifty-eight. National Park guys were opening the gates. As soon as they let me in I went to the first parking lot that was on the right and pulled into a random space. The lot was empty. I cut the ignition and Darps's silver Saab poked into the parking lot and parked alongside my battered Explorer. We both climbed out of our vehicles.

"I've got coffee. And bagels. From Einstein Brothers," he announced. "Let's find a picnic table."

We did.

"Okay, Shipmate. Here goes," he said after we'd opened the coffee cups and unwrapped the bagels.

"As you know, I had this chat with Vice Admiral Donegan last evening. The DNI. She's the older sister of our classmate, Bob Donegan. That's how we made the connection. Through Bob. He called and I met him off-line. He set up the meet with his sister, the Admiral. I went, we met in Chestertown and we talked.

"She wants to meet with Kehoe. Himself. About a plot. Against him. From within the government. Our government. Sound familiar? She may well be a part of the conspiracy herself. And I think she wants to blow the whistle on it. She thinks she sees imprisonment at Leavenworth in her future. But she still wants to go forward with this. So she's definitely serious. And I think rational. Her conversation with me was quite guarded. She definitely wants to talk to Cheetah himself. Face-to-face. She wants to keep her name out of the mix as much and for as long as possible. I think she thinks that if she tells a minion—like me, or even you, for example—what's really happening with the plot, the word might not get to the man. Or might get filtered—and thus distorted—somehow."

"If she's involved in the plot, then she must know who all else is involved. She must know the whole fucking list." I said, half to myself.

"Yeah. But I see us sitting betwixt the devil and the deep blue sea," Darps said. "She could (a.) be telling the total, unvarnished truth or, (b.) be totally insane. Or (c.) both. In which case she might walk into the White House with a bomb strapped to her. Or a poison fountain pen in her bra. Or whatever. *Cheetah* is put in danger. On the other hand, if we take no chances and keep her away from *Cheetah*, then the plotters could well pull off their coup and the country is screwed in another way."

"Well that's not our call," I said. "I'm going to tell *Cheetah* what we have and leave the decision on whether or not he sees the Admiral up to him and the Secret Service. And I'm going to have to give him her name. Maybe he can fix her up with an appointment with Michelle," I added.

"I'm not sure that'll work. I doubt that this Admiral will be satisfied with seeing some White House staffer instead of the Prez himself," he said, getting to his feet. We dumped our coffee-and-bagel leftovers in a trashcan and clambered into our vehicles. We both wasted no time in heading off to Ripley Hall. Once there, I reached for the red, secure phone to the White House.

"Site Alfa. Staff Sergeant Thompson," said a voice.

"This is *BIAS* Six," I said. "I need to speak with *Cheetah*."

"Roger, sir. Wait one."

About forty or fifty seconds later, *Cheetah* came on the line.

"What's up, Loose?"

"I think we stumbled onto a hook into the plot," I said. "She's a U.S. military flag officer. She wants to talk to you. Directly."

"You're not telling me much. Who is this woman? What's her involvement in the plot? What the hell is going on?"

"Do you have any space in your schedule in which we—you and I—could talk face to face for a couple of minutes? Like today? I think I've said all I can say on the phone—even this phone—plus I don't know a hell of a lot more than what I just told you."

"Can you be here at seventeen hundred? I hate to stick you with rush-hour traffic, but that's the best I can do."

"I'll see you at seventeen hundred," I said, hoping that seventeen hundred wouldn't be too late.

Chapter Twenty-Eight
The DNI

Algorithmics, Inc.
Stafford, Virginia
Late May

Braxton dialed Ironsides, from Washington.

"Are you at your office, Rob?"

"Yes sir."

"Don't go anywhere. I'll be there in forty-five minutes."

"Yes sir. See you in forty-five."

Both men hung up.

"Have the car brought around," Braxton told his secretary. "Now, please. I'm going to *Algorithmics*. Should be back by noon. Twelve-thirty at the latest. I'll have the mobile and the iPad."

He grabbed his devices and his jacket and left.

He had lain awake throughout much of the night, thinking about his recent interaction with Donegan. And became increasingly uneasy about her. If anyone could be on the cusp of selling out the operation, it had to be her. She was kind of itchy-twitchy about the idea of publicly trying Kehoe and Girtler for treason. She seemed kind of squirrely about Ironsides, a civilian contractor, having the power to shut down U.S. Government—especially U.S. military—C4I systems. Around four this morning, he decided that Donegan had to go. Hence the call to Ironsides and the trip to Stafford.

Steve, the blond, uniformed security guard, was at the *Algorithmics* front door when Sam's Lincoln pulled up at nine forty-two.

"Good morning, Mister Director. And welcome," he said as he held open the front door. "I'll park your car."

"Thanks, Steve," Braxton said. "Don't go anywhere. We may well need you soon."

Roberto was waiting for him at the front desk.

"Morning, Sam," he said, shaking the Director's hand.

"Hi Roberto."

Both men headed toward the elevator in silence. Both knew that something was afoot. And it had to be very sensitive and had to be closely held.

"Coffee?" Ironsides asked as he held his office door for Braxton.

"Please. I was up for more than half the fucking night," Braxton replied.

Roberto popped his head outside his office.

"Two black coffees, please, Sarah," he said.

He and Sam sat down. Sarah appeared with the coffee almost instantly. She closed the door softly on her way out.

"Okay. What gives, Sam?" Ironsides asked.

"Donegan," Braxton answered. "The Admiral."

Ironsides let out a deep sigh.

"I'm not surprised. I've suspected that there was a problem with her that I couldn't put my finger on for the last two or three weeks. But what is it?"

"I'm extremely worried that she's having severe and profound second thoughts about our mission. That she may be thinking seriously about blowing the whistle on what we're trying to do."

"Ergo, she's got to go," Ironsides muttered.

"Ergo, exactly. She's got to go. And that's what I'm here to discuss. Her departure."

"That's a big deal. She's a three-star Admiral. We make her disappear; NCIS, the FBI and the DC Metro Police Department will be all over it. Plus the Secret Service and maybe the Park Police. And Christ knows who else. It's not like offing some dirt bag druggie. She's the big leagues. Director of Naval Intelligence. And her loss will get big league attention."

"I know, I know," Braxton said. "We've got to make her disappearance from earth appear completely random."

"Not an easy thing to do. She leads a pretty structured life. She's single. A widow, actually. Hubby was a fighter pilot. Got shot down over Afghanistan. Killed."

"She *is* a fairly serious runner," Braxton said, almost to himself.

"Where does she run?" Ironsides asked.

"All over town," Braxton replied. "The mall, Georgetown, West Potomac

Park, the C&O Canal, wherever."

"When you say 'the C&O Canal,' I assume you mean the towpath?" Roberto queried.

"Yeah. The towpath. Not the water. From Georgetown, heading west. And then back into town."

Ironsides picked up a phone.

"Send Steve up," he said. And hung up.

"Does she run on the towpath on specific days?" he asked.

"Actually, I think she does. I think she runs the towpath on Wednesdays unless some big meeting or TAD[3] interfere," Braxton said. "In fact, I ran with her once on the towpath recently. At her invitation. And it was a Wednesday."

Steve, the blond-haired security guard from downstairs, tapped on the door and opened it.

"C'mon in, Steve," Ironsides said. "We might have a special assignment for you. Have a seat."

Steve took off his hat and sat.

"Uh, it's about Vice Admiral Donegan," Ironsides began. "We're worried that she's worried. To the point where she might be thinking seriously about blowing the whistle on our plan."

"I think I'm starting to understand," Steve said. "She needs to be taken down?"

Neither Ironsides nor Braxton said anything, but both men nodded. Thirty seconds passed in silence. Then Braxton spoke up.

"It's got to be totally anonymous. Random." "Nothing can tie her demise to us," Ironsides whispered hoarsely.

"She jogs on her lunch hour. At various places. But she seems to favor a run up the C&O Canal Towpath on Wednesdays," Braxton said.

"How far does she go?" Steve asked. "And at what time?"

"She usually starts at the Key Bridge, usually goes anywhere from two to three miles upstream and then turns around," Braxton answered. "She almost always goes during lunch, leaving her office around eleven-thirty or eleven-forty-five. A Navy car drops her at the Key Bridge. She usually jogs back to the Pentagon, returning fifty or fifty-five minutes later. And she usually runs alone. But not always."

3   Temporary Additional Duty, A short trip out of town.

"Hmm. There's lotsa woods along the towpath. Should be plenty of sniper shot opportunities. With plenty of easy getaway routes. You say the word and I'll get to work on it," Steve said.

Several seconds of silence ensued.

"Word," said Ironsides. "And quickly."

"It'll take some homework. Surveillance. Of her and her running times and routes. Cover and concealment, all that stuff," Steve said.

"Okay. Understand. Just limit the number of people who are witting to no more than two or three. You plus two others. Max."

Chapter Twenty-Nine

Alan

BIAS

Chestertown

Late May

We finally started our meeting in the SCIF at ten. A day late. But everybody was there.

The Power Point slides were marked TOP SECRET - THUNDER top and bottom. We didn't print up any extra copies of them either. Judy opened the meeting by advising everyone that the meeting was classified Top Secret, code-word Thunder. Then I took over and clicked up a newly made slide. It read:

TOP SECRET
THUNDER

(1)   (TS/Th) **FIRST SHOT:** Apparent/Probable coup d'état attempt against President Kehoe from w/in USG. Planning reportedly is in progress.

(2)   (TS/Th) **SOURCE OF INFO:** Government of Russia (GOR) (Unofficial). Reliability – Questionable. Access – Unknown.

(3)   (TS/Th) **POSSIBLE INVOLVEMENT:** USG Intelligence Community members, current and former; possibly including non-USG civilian contractor Roberto Ironsides of *Algorithmics, Inc.* (Named by Russian source.)

(4)   (TS/Th) **TIMELINE(S):** Unknown.

(5)   (TS/Th) **NEW STUFF:** Late contact (day before yesterday evening) with an active duty U. S. flag officer suggests he/she may be involved in plot against *Cheetah*. The officer wants to speak to Kehoe directly. Request is in the works via *BIAS*. We're awaiting a response from the White House.

I interrupted myself.

"I spoke with *Cheetah* in person Saturday and he seems to be taking the threat seriously. But he doesn't know anything. Hence, of course, he tasked *BIAS* to take a look at things. Needless to say, this is HEE-YUGE!

"He also gave some rather vague instructions to the Director of the FBI to poke around and see what they could find out about a plot within the U. S. Government. And he cautioned the Director against quote leaking *anything* unquote via 'chums' or 'pals' at the New York Times. Or Rolling Stone. Or anyone or anything else for that matter. Personally, I'm not at all certain that, as aa member of the U. S. Intelligence Community, the FBI's hands are clean on this conspiracy or whatever you want to call it.

"As you all know, he unhooked the restriction on *BIAS* collecting stateside, for starters. A one-time, THUNDER-only basis. Darps's meeting with the flag officer in question resulted from the decision to drop the restrictions on stateside collection. Then there are other issues associated with that officer. About things like personal loyalty, his/her oath as an officer and the enormity of the plot. But I'm just speculating. We've passed the request for the flag officer to meet with *Cheetah* up the line and we'll see what happens. So we're going forward in that direction. Here's the plan as it stands now."

I clicked the mouse and the next slide popped up.

TOP SECRET

THUNDER

- (TS/Th) Request for unnamed flag officer meeting with President Kehoe pending. Any additional info we have is fragmentary and is based on morsels that *Cheetah* shared with me.
- (TS/Th) Research I. Centered on NSA. Action: Secret Service. Mike and Luke. Everything and anything on *Algorithmics, Inc.* and its CEO, Roberto Ironsides. Especially communications w/ U. S. Government sources.
- (TS/Th) Research II. Action: Ashleigh. Open-source. Ditto, above.
- (TS/Th) Research III. Action: Anastasia. All-source. Extraordinary Russian connections w/ USG. Official and/or unofficial. Stuff that is out of the mainstream. Coordinate w/ USSS, particularly on NSA take.
- (TS/Th) Research IV. Action: Sammy. All-source. Any and all connections between Russians and *Algorithmics*.
- (U) *BIAS* Timeline: Twenty-one days.

TOP SECRET

THUNDER

I started to run my mouth again. "First of all, let's stipulate, like the lawyers say, that our first two to three weeks will be focused on research. Hence our twenty-one day timeline. Unless we turn over an anthill that dictates we speed everything up. Let's take the bullets one at a time," I said.

The next slide showed the original slide with the first bullet highlighted and the others dimmed.

"The *Cheetah* meeting with the American flag officer is out of our hands now. We just have to see what he decides and if he does meet with him/her, what comes out of that meeting."

I flicked to the next slide.

"On the next bullet, I want Mike and Luke to use the Secret Service-NSA channel to gather any and all collection NSA has about *Algorithmics*, their CEO, Roberto Ironsides, connections with the Government of Russia and any connections either one or both have with elements of the U. S. Intelligence Community. Anything in the past twelve months and anything ongoing.

Special Agent Mike Atwater, U.S. Secret Service, waved a meaty hand over the table.

"*Algorithmics* reportedly has had black contracts with a number of elements of the U. S. Intelligence Community in the past," he said. "So I think we need to nail those down and see if there are any lingering connections. There's no doubt in my feeble mind that those bastards at NSA will try to stonewall us. In that case, we'll need to trot out POTUS security issues and beat them over the head with them. If they continue to stonewall, we'll go to *Cheetah* himself if we have to.

"And here's where it gets really squirrelly," he continued. "At this point, as with the FBI, we don't know whether NSA has a foot in part of this cabal or not. Or if one or more individuals within the Agency or Bureau are involved. So, once we start floating queries their way, we may be letting a very large cat out of the bag. But I think we have to take that chance," he concluded, nodding at me.

I nodded back and picked up the bait.

"I realize this is dicey territory, but I'm confident that you and your Secret Service colleagues up the road can do it with discretion. If some of the Washingtonians are skittish, I'm confident that *Cheetah* will be happy to clarify things for them. But, for obvious reasons, I'd like to hold that option out as a last resort."

Mike shoved his hand in the air again.

"We start asking questions, other people are going to start asking more questions," he said.

"I understand that," I said. "You guys—the Secret Service--are charged with the safety and security of the President. Make sure you keep any and all requests for info about this stuff wrapped up in issues of Presidential security. That shouldn't be too hard. After all, a coup against the President, by definition, threatens his safety."

"Good point," Mike answered.

"On the other hand," I continued. "If they—NSA and the FBI—start to think that you or we are sniffing around their possible involvement in a plot aimed at a takedown of the president, then everything could come crashing down on our heads. To say the least. So we need to tread very softly. And very carefully."

I looked around the room. Everyone looked like they understood.

"Third bullet," I said. "That's you, Ashleigh."

I changed slides to one with the third bullet highlighted.

"Go after the same stuff. *Algorithmics*, Ironsides, any and all connections with the government and especially with the Intel Community. You're doing open-source exploitation. Press, Internet, cable news, whatever. Special attention to Sunday morning talk shows. Which you need to take with the proverbial pinch of salt. Feel free to coordinate with Luke and Mike on what they get from NSA. Highlight any and all contradictions and agreements between what you get and what they get."

"Especially the contradictions," Darps murmured.

"Bullet number four," I continued. "Anastasia. Everything Russian connected to us. The U.S. Government. The Intelligence Community especially. We don't give a rat's ass at this point about Russian wheat sales to China or natural gas sales to Poland. What we do care about is any kind of communications—particularly back channel communications--between Russia and elements of the USG."

I hesitated and took a sip of water.

"Fifth bullet," I said. "Sammy. Yours. All-source. A powerful, focused look at the Russian-*Algorithmics*-U.S. Government network. If there is such a thing. With a special eye on Ironsides. Anything you can get your hands on. Legally.

"Any questions?"

"Legally? Really?" Sammy asked.

"You know what I mean," I said.

There was a babble of chatter and several questions. I tried to field them clearly and truthfully. Finally things settled down.

"Thanks, everyone," I said. "Keep Judy's '*Thunder*' caveat in mind. But everyone needs to remember that there's a list somewhere out there. A list of names. Names of conspirators. American conspirators. We need that damned list. Big time. We also need to know if there is some sort of U. S. Government "nest" where this coup activity is centered or whether it's widespread and scattered throughout the Government.

"That does it for now. Except for Darps and Ashleigh."

"Before you go," interjected Judy. "The top five drawers of safe number six are for Thunder material. Safe number six only has five drawers. So that makes it simple. The NDA's are all typed up. So don't leave today without seeing me to sign off on them."

A few seconds later, everyone was gone except Ashleigh, Darps and yours truly. I sat down and gestured for Ashleigh and Darps to do likewise.

"I'm sure I told you that *Cheetah* pulled off the restrictions on *BIAS*'s collecting in CONUS. Neither he nor I got very far into the details. But I'm considering asking him to go through his military aides and get to our U. S. military Foreign Liaison Officers to get you two—and Annie, as well as a companion for Ashleigh, if you like—invited to a few Washington social functions. Mainly military stuff for starters and then, hopefully, some other embassy stuff here in D. C. When the invitations come, pick and choose, go to functions you select, meet people and listen. Your cover will be very shallow. We'll have consultants' business cards printed up that you can pass around. I'm certainly not asking you guys to try to recruit anybody—just keep your ears open and troll. Especially for any tidbits regarding extracurricular contacts between our Russian brethren and our own American brethren, intel-wise. And anything that's floating out there about *Algorithmics* and/or their boss, Roberto Ironsides. Just come in the next morning and write up a summary of what you heard. If anything. And we—the U. S. Government--will reimburse your expenses. Mainly travel. I don't need to buy you expensive new wardrobes. Let alone hundred bucks-a-bottle champagne for hostess gifts. But gas money and parking fees are OK. Or taxis, for that matter."

Both Ashleigh and Darps chuckled a bit but still looked a bit uncomfortable. Neither said anything.

"What?" I asked.

"Um," Darps said. "I guess I don't mind going to a few—emphasis on the few—Washington social affairs. I can't answer for Annie. I'll have to talk with her about it."

"Of course, I said. "I asked the two of you—you, Darps and you, Ashleigh--because I thought you would be most comfortable in the role. Or roles. And you are excellent observers."

"Um," Ashleigh said. "I'd be lying if I'd said this doesn't make me a little nervous. I'm not really a big-time party animal. And I'm fine with going alone—er, unescorted. I guess I'm between boyfriends now."

"I understand," I said. "But, as I said, you're an excellent observer. I'll try to get the invitations tailored to occasional, medium-sized gatherings. Neither huge galas nor intimate tête-à-têtes. You and Darps can coordinate with each other, attend some of the same functions—or different ones-- and then compare notes. It may be a total waste of time, but I'd feel like we were missing the boat if we didn't wade in and see if we could pick up something relevant around Washington. The stakes are pretty damned high. And it goes without saying—we need to know who the conspirators are. If there even *are* conspirators."

"Won't we be duplicating the efforts of other U. S. intelligence community members?" Ashleigh asked.

"Perhaps," I said. "But probably not. The FBI is witting and somewhat tuned in. As is the U. S. Secret Service. But their involvement is at the margins. *Cheetah* tasked us—*BIAS*—with looking at a conspiracy within the U. S. Government. I don't think anyone else—the conspirators themselves excepted—in the Government knows of the plot. Let alone being out there trying to smoke out information about it."

"What is it exactly we're trying to hear?" Darps asked.

"Sorry," I said. "I should have made that clear at the start. First of all, you're listening for any hint of a possible action against the President and/or the Vice-President of the United States. From within the U. S. Government. And you probably won't hear the tiniest morsel about that. Unless it comes from one or more of our fellow Americans. Who, I'm guessing in all likelihood won't be at many of the social functions you'll be attending. At least not in great numbers. Indications are that the plot—if there even is a plot—is homegrown—made in the U.S.A. I still don't know what to make out of this latest U. S. flag officer connection. But then again, there is that pesky Russian connection. So the other thing you're listening for is any hint of an unofficial connection between Russian intelligence and U.S. intelligence. One or two Russki military attaches meeting some American spook for a beer or Russian diplomats making golf or tennis dates with Americans. That sort of thing. Which can easily and usually are totally above board and legit. But which could warrant a second, closer look.

"We probably need to sit down for an hour or two and shoot the breeze about this in some detail. And I need some more prep time before we do. So I'll have to get back to you."

"Hmm," muttered Darps. "This sounds like a pretty high stakes game."

"No kidding, Shipmate," I said. "It's way off the table from where we've been playing heretofore."

Chapter Thirty
The DNI

The Hawk's Nest
Blue Ridge Mountains
Virginia
Late May

Bacon and sausage sizzled in two large cast-iron skillets on the huge stainless-steel kitchen stove. In the great room, Carmen circulated with a tray of drinks—Bloody Maries and Mimosas. Buttery late-spring sunlight streamed through the large windows of the Hawk's Nest.

"Pablo is ready to take omelet orders even as we speak," Braxton announced over the chatter. "Enjoy your brunch and we'll brief the plan that has emerged--with considerable help from everybody here--in about forty-five minutes."

"The only good Bloody Mary is one which you can see through," said Dick Nagle, the CIA Deputy Director, to Braxton. "I think this one makes the cut," he added, holding up his glass and stirring the drink with a celery stalk.

"I aim to please," Braxton said. "Heavy on the Stoli, light on the Mr. & Mrs. T. By the way, that was a nice rainbow you snagged this morning."

"It was a helluva lot of fun," Nagle said. "But I have to wonder where our beautiful Admiral is."

"She called in last night. Said she was off her feed. I've been having some wobbly thoughts about her and her commitment to this effort. Shall we try and scare up an omelet," Braxton said, changing the subject--twice.

"Let's try and mark our places with our drinks and then go after the omelets," Nagle said.

They placed their drinks on a table, dropped their napkins on their chairs and headed for the kitchen, plates in hand.

Braxton felt torn. He had just blabbed to Nagle, without meaning to, about his doubts about Donegan.

Thirty-five minutes later, Pablo had started picking up plates and silverware and Carmen circulated around the great room with two pots of coffee—regular and decaf.

Braxton stood up.

"Here are the bare bones of the plan," he said. "Feel free to take notes, but I'm asking everyone to drop their notes in the shredder bag by the front door on their way out. Memory is fine, but we don't want any paper about this floating around."

Now, I guess we'll see what's up, Nagel thought, silently. He sipped black coffee, nervously.

"I've tentatively scheduled E-Day for the twenty-third of October, a Thursday," Braxton said. "Kehoe has a long weekend scheduled for Martha's Vineyard, beginning Wednesday evening the twenty-second." he punched a remote and a fifty-inch TV set at the end of the room lit up. He keyed the remote again and a slide popped up on the screen. It read:

EXECUTION DAY MINUS ONE (E-DAY-1)

Movement to Contact

Algorithmics: C4I Warm-Up

Targets Review

10-man FBI detachment moved to Thorncroft Inn, Vineyard Haven.

Main Characters In Place: (Speaker DeWitt, DDCIA Dick Nagle. Willard Hotel, D. C.)

Braxton keyed the remote and a second slide popped up on the screen.

Invitation to TV news personality, Christopher Marks, for "Special Announcement" in Speaker's Office for tomorrow, E-Day, at 0715, delivered by messenger.

He punched the remote again and a third slide appeared, followed by two more.

DAY TWO

Execution Day (E-Day)

0700: Algorithmics Shuts down all NCA comms/ systems as well as FOXNEWS and amateur radio.

0715: Speaker DeWitt and Dick Nagle arrive at Speaker's Office with FBI camera crew.

0715 (± 5 min.): TV News Personality Christopher Marks arrives in Speaker's Office.

0715: 10-man FBI detachment moves to Gallagher Cottage on Martha's Vineyard. Takes CHEETAH into custody.

0715: 5-man FBI detachment moves to Joint Base Andrews in Camp Springs, Maryland to take CHIPMUNK into custody (He will be there for a 0720-tee time at the base golf course.)

0723: FBI Helos (2) transport CHEETAH and CHIPMUNK to JOINT BASE CAPE COD, MA for further transport to Fort Leavenworth, KS.

0729: Algorithmics reconnects NCA, commercial and amateur comms.

0729: CJSCOTUS administers Oath of Office to PRESIDENT DeWitt.

0730 PRESIDENT DeWitt makes formal announcement over nationwide TV and Radio that former President Kehoe has been formally relieved of his duties as President and has been transferred to the U. S. Army Medical Center at Fort Leavenworth, KS.

She also announces that former Vice President Girdler has been relieved and is being transferred to the Reynolds Army hospital at Fort Sill, Oklahoma. He is expected to be charged with obstructing justice for trying to cover up a serious mental illness suffered by President Kehoe.

Finally, President DeWitt announces that she has appointed Richard Nagle as Vice President of the U.S., pending Congressional approval.

0900: Repeat foregoing announcement. Hold semi-open press conference w/ Q's and A's.

1500: Ditto

"Okay. That's the bare bones of the plan. It obviously needs a lot of fleshing out. That's why we're here. To get a leg up on the fleshing out part. Sorry for the horrible mixing of metaphors.

"Oh, and by the way, NSA intercepted a couple of text messages between Kehoe and this guy Llewellyn a couple of days ago. Recall that Llewellyn is the one who's heading up Kehoe's secret little intel agency. They were to meet at Quantico—in the woods. Nobody else. Unscheduled. You've got to wonder what in hell that was about. I don't know about you all, but it makes me a bit nervous. To say the least."

Two and a half hours later, an Amtrak train, the eastbound Cardinal, squealed into Clifton Forge Station, arriving from White Sulphur Springs, West Virginia. Two and a half minutes later, the train rolled out with a half-dozen more Washington-bound passengers.

Chapter Thirty-One
Ashleigh

In front of Union Station

Washington, D.C.

Late May

Five and a half hours later, the eastbound Cardinal rolled into Washington's Union Station. Four and a half minutes after that, Ashleigh MacDonald of *BIAS* jogged past the main entrance to the station and ran into a clutch of exiting passengers, a couple of whom she recognized. Congresswoman Helen DeWitt (D, NY), Speaker of the House, for one, seemed to lead the little group out of the station. Madame Speaker wore a gray suit over a white blouse. Ashleigh was pretty sure she recognized another, younger-looking woman who also looked familiar. Palmer? White House staff? She wore a navy skirt and a bright yellow golf shirt. Both women—Palmer—if indeed it was her--and DeWitt--wore black flats on their feet. Madame Speaker climbed into a waiting limo. Three or four other faces in the group looked vaguely familiar, but she couldn't tie names to them. The others were all male. McConnell, deputy director of the FBI? She wasn't sure and continued on her run, as the little group appeared to disperse.

Sweet Lord, she thought. *That's a funny group to be together coming out of Union Station on a Sunday afternoon.*

She continued running to her Connecticut Avenue apartment. She fished inside the belt of her running shorts for her key card and let herself in. She heard the door lock click behind her. Still wearing her wet running gear, she called Darps at his home in Alexandria. He picked up on the second ring.

"Hi, Ashleigh. What's up?"

"We need to talk. ASAP."

"Your place or mine?"

"How 'bout halfway between? Union Station?"

"Perfect. Know where *Uno*, the pizzeria in the station, is?"

"Yeah. I can be there in thirty minutes if that works for you."

"I'll see you at *Uno's* in half an hour," Darps said.

She stripped out of her clammy running gear and took a superfast shower. After toweling off briskly and applying a couple of swipes of deodorant, she pulled on dry, clean running clothes, including a warm-up jacket and pants. She put on clean, dry socks and a dry pair of running shoes. She tucked her wallet into a pants pocket and grabbed her key card. Three minutes later, she was outside, heading for the *National Zoo* Metro station.

Thirteen minutes later, she was stepping off the Metro at Union Station. She was starting to feel misgivings as she made her way to the Pizzeria. Perhaps she was making too big a deal out of a coincidence. She felt better when she spotted Darps, sitting at a tiny table, looking professorial over a glass of red wine.

"Hi," she said, plopping herself into the chair opposite Darps.

"Hi, Ashleigh," he said, half-standing. "Glass of wine?"

"Sure. Chianti would be nice."

Darps flagged down a waiter, ordered the wine, sat and gazed into Ashleigh's eyes.

"I think I might have seen some of the people on the list," she said.

The waiter brought her wine and placed it on a tiny napkin on the tiny table.

Darps raised his eyebrows and took a sip of his wine.

"I was here a little less than an hour ago," she began, glancing at her watch. "Here at Union Station. Outside. Running. Past the main entrance to the station. Then who pops out of the station doors? Madame Speaker DeWitt. Plus I think Suzanne Palmer, the erstwhile National Security Advisor. Plus a couple of other faces that looked familiar. Guys. I just can't tie names to the faces. Maybe McConnell from the FBI. But there were three or four faces that I'm pretty sure I've seen before. Intelligence Community faces."

"Uh, okay. So what?" Darps asked.

"Um. Sunday afternoon. A small group of high-level Intel insiders disembarking from an Amtrak train together here in D.C. I just have a problem imagining that they were all playing the slots together up in Atlantic City. They must have been off somewhere doing something. Together. Maybe they were plotting. That's it."

"You're right," Darps agreed. "They could—emphasis on 'could'—be the nucleus of 'the list.' It's a helluva long shot, but I think I'll give Alan a heads-up nonetheless."

He took a mobile phone from a jacket pocket.

"You're going to *phone* him about that?" Ashleigh whispered.

"I'll text him. Obscurely. To make sure he's there first thing tomorrow morning. I don't think there's anything he—or we—can do tonight. But he needs to be there first thing in the morning. How about something like this? Quote. Two of our eyes feasted on some interesting somebodies. Could be break-through stuff. See you at zero-eight-hundred. Question mark. Unquote."

"Sounds good to me," Ashleigh said. "Pretty vague but pretty heavy at the same time."

Darps poked his phone numerous times and sat back.

"There we go. I'll plan on seeing you first thing in the a.m. at Ripley Hall. With Alan. You might want to jot down times and names from the Union Station gaggle this afternoon. And name 'possibilities' for the faces whose names you're unsure of. And think about where we might want to go from there."

Darps laid a twenty on the tiny table and stood up.

"Thanks for your alertness on this, Ashleigh. It may well indeed be a breakthrough. See you in the morning."

Their waiter swooped down to pick up the twenty.

"Could I order a small pizza to go?" Ashleigh asked him.

"Of course, Miss. What would you like?"

"A small, thin-crust Chicago pizza. With pepperoni and sausage."

"That'll be fifteen, ninety-nine," he said. "Should be ready in fifteen minutes."

Ashleigh dug out a twenty and handed it to the young man.

"We're good to go," she said.

She sat back in her uncomfortable chair and looked at the ceiling and thought. Congresswoman Helen DeWitt, Speaker of the House. Suzanne Palmer-—maybe--fired National Security Advisor. McConnell of the FBI? Three or four shadowy faces that she thought she recognized but didn't have names for.

When she got home, she immediately sat down with a yellow legal pad and jotted down "Approx. 5:30 p.m. Sunday." Under that heading, she scrawled "Helen DeWitt, "Suzanne Palmer?? Stuart McConnell? Et al???"

There was nothing worth watching on TV so she put a couple of CD's of Boccherini guitar quintets on the stereo and sat down with her Chicago pizza, a glass of merlot and a library edition of *Back Channel* by Stephen L. Parker. The book was a fascinating novel about an African American college girl that got caught up in the Cuban Missile Crisis in nineteen-sixty-two. Ashleigh forgot all about the familiar faces she'd seen outside Union Station.

Chapter Thirty-Two

Alan

BIAS

Chestertown, Virginia

Late May

I arrived at *BIAS* a little early, beating Judy by about fifteen minutes. That always irritates her for some obscure reason which is something I usually try to avoid doing. I've learned over the recent several months that keeping her happy makes for a much smoother running ship. But this morning, what the hell. Time was running short.

After she arrived, I chatted her up with small talk while I drew a cup of coffee and endeavored to not resemble a dog's breakfast and I think I more or less succeeded. She wasn't giving me the shifty look under the guarded lids any more.

"You've got kind of a weird email in your in-box," she said. "For some reason, the sender CC'd me—I have no idea why. Much less who the sender is. Much, much less what the hell it means."

"Hmm. Lemme check it out," I mumbled, starting to feel like the dog's breakfast. Booting up my desktop, I immediately went to my email.

FM: XRAY@bling.com

TO: ALlewellyn@BIAS.gov

CC: JPalladino@BIAS.gov

SUBJ: The List

The Russians have it. One or two of them may be willing to trade.

Cheers,

X

"Do you have any idea what the hell that means?" I asked Judy after stepping across to her office.

"None," she said. "I already told you that. What list is this person talking about? And who the hell is 'XRAY'?"

"We should be able to answer your second question with Mike and/or Luke and their NSA connections," I said. "But I have no idea what list he or she is talking about."

Actually I did have a glimmer of an idea. But only a glimmer.

I went back to my desk, still a bit puzzled. Every once in a while, *BIAS*—even though our very existence is classified--gets an out-of-left-field tidbit that seems to have no connection to the real world and I suspected this was one of those. But I wasn't all that sure.

Luke came in a few minutes later and I showed him the email.

"Any thoughts on who the hell 'XRAY' might be?"

"Not the slightest," he said. "But maybe our NSA buddies can figure it out. I'll be glad to give that a shot."

"Please be my guest. I had the same thought. I'll forward the email to you. Go for it," I answered.

Twenty-five minutes later, he was back standing in my office door, looking perplexed and puzzled.

"It's crazy," he said. "I called NSA secure. They say there's some sort of digital fog hiding *'XRAY@bling.com'* and they can't identify him or her. At least not right away. They can't locate him or her either. Which is really spooky. My buddy says they'll kick it upstairs and get back to me."

"You're right. That's very spooky, indeed," I said. "Make a short memo summarizing that and stick it in the *Thunder* file. I'm not sure that's where it belongs, but just in case. I don't suppose you know anything about quote the list unquote?" I left the sentence hanging.

"No. And I asked my NSA buddy about that too and he told me he'd check into that and get back to me." Luke held up his hands in a semi-hopeless gesture and left.

I forwarded the email to Darps, Sammy and Ashleigh with an "any thoughts?" query.

Less than two minutes later, Ashleigh was standing in my doorway, wide-eyed.

"It's the names of the conspirators!" she said softly yet firmly. "The names of the people who are plotting the coup against the President. That's the list. It has to be!"

"Come in, have a seat and talk to me," I said.

She did.

"Is Darps in yet?" she asked, glancing over her right shoulder toward the door.

I poked keys on my computer.

"No. Not yet. Wait! He just punched in. He's here. Why do you ask?"

"He and I are both supposed to meet with you in—uh—ten minutes," she said.

That's when Darps appeared at my door.

"Grab yourself a cup of coffee, Shipmate," I said. "You too, Ashleigh. And then maybe you two can tell me what the hell's going on. Let's go to the SCIF."

Minutes later, they were both seated with steaming mugs of coffee. I had topped off my cup and it was steaming too.

"Okay. Who goes first?" I asked.

"Okay. I'll go first, since we already started discussing the eerie email," Ashleigh said.

"What 'eerie email'?" Darps asked.

I swiveled the SCIF monitor about ninety degrees so Darps could see it.

"This one," I said. "As you can see, I just sent it to you. Luke had NSA take a look at it and it seems it's wrapped up in some sort of digital fog. So we don't know who the hell XRAY is or what list he's talking about."

"I think I can help a little bit," Ashleigh said. "The so-called 'list' he mentions has *got* to be the list of conspirators. Or at least a partial list, anyway. And somehow, he or she—XRAY—knows that the Russians have a copy. That's for starters."

"And pray tell how do you know that?" I asked, somewhat skeptically.

"Pure intuition," she said. "Two words clicked together the second I read that email. 'List' and 'Russians.'"

"You said that *Cheetah* got the word about the plot from the Russians," she said, following up. "The spooky email—the one from 'XRAY' this morning—must mean that the Russians have the list of the conspirators. Which makes perfect sense. That's it," she said. "End of story. Sorry it's not more interesting."

"Well, then, who the hell is XRAY and what is bling.com?

"I have no idea," she said. "At this point, it might not matter. But the fact that *someone*—with connections to the Russians—thinks they know who the conspirators are—is important!"

"I agree," I said. "I'm going to get the team together and float this with them. With us, actually. At this point, I've no idea where we can go with this, other than waiting for word from NSA. And winding up Anastasia to go after the Russians. The only trouble with that is that Anastasia is one person and there's a shitload of Russians running around D. C. and New York. And San Francisco and God knows where else.

"What else?" I continued.

"Union Station. Yesterday," Darps muttered, nodding toward Ashleigh.

"This is totally anecdotal," Ashleigh said. "But it still may be important. I was running yesterday afternoon. Ran past Union Station right around five-thirty. Just as I approached the main entrance, a cluster of people came out, more or less together. Intelligence people. Congresswoman DeWitt, Speaker of the House and former Chairman of the HPSCI."

She pronounced the acronym "hip-see." She meant the House Permanent Select Committee on Intelligence.

"I think Suzanne Palmer, former National Security Advisor to the President was there as well. I'm pretty sure I recognized her. Plus—maybe—Stuart McConnell, FBI Deputy. That's a guess. But an educated one. There were three or four other guys who looked vaguely familiar. But I couldn't tie names to their faces."

"Okay. Let's get a couple of analysts on this. Find out what trains were arriving at Union Station between five and six yesterday for starters. Find out what, if anything, in the public domain gives us any info on the recent travel plans of Speaker DeWitt and McConnell. Check Palmer, too. She's a private citizen now, so she probably doesn't advertise her travel plans, but it's worth a look. Then, let's see if you can ID any of the 'familiar faces' you saw. And let's see if any other prominent members of the Intelligence Community did some traveling that might be tied in with Madame Speaker, McConnell and Palmer."

Chapter Thirty-Three

Alan

BIAS
Chestertown
Late May

Luke appeared at my door.

"Guy upstairs at NSA just got back to us, Boss," he said.

"Tell me more," I said.

"Okay. Here goes. XRAY is somebody at *Algorithmics.com*. My guess would be Ironsides himself. That's for starters."

"Pretty damned good," I said. "Keep going."

He did.

"Digital fog is some sort of *Algorithmics* contrivance used to mask addresses of email senders. It was cooked up in-house at Algorithmics a coupla months ago. As of now, it's as good as a signature attesting that the email in question came from Algorithmics. According to NSA, nobody else has the program to pull that shit off. Except them—NSA. And if they were doing it, they wouldn't tell us."

"So where are we with this hairball?" I asked.

"I'm not finished," Luke said.

"Sorry," I said. "Pray continue."

"Okay. Here goes. I'm pretty damned sure that 'X-Ray' has got to be Roberto Ironsides. Nobody at NSA will sign off to that effect, but my contact says he'll bet his ass, hat and poncho liner that X-Ray is Ironsides. And that quote the list unquote is the list of conspirators. U. S conspirators. Who are conspiring against the President. And, as he says in his email, the Ruskies have it. And maybe one or two of them would be willing to trade. For something. That's all, sports fans."

"Well, holy shit. Methinks I sense a breakthrough," I said.

"It sounds like your buddies at NSA are all over *BIAS* and our efforts to smoke out the plot against the President," I added.

"I don't think so," Luke responded. "My guy is witting, but he gives the impression that nobody else at NSA is. He kind of duped out a lot of the hard intel himself. And what he passed along to me, he did in person face-to-face. We met in a gas station just off the BW Parkway."

Chapter Thirty-Four

Alan

BIAS and the Wilderness, Virginia
Late May

By Wednesday, we had Ashleigh's hunch and Luke's bombshell thoroughly digested. Both of which I was inclined to embrace as likely to be true. Plus, we had been able to confirm that Speaker DeWitt, Nagle, Stuart McConnell and Suzanne Palmer had gone to Clifton Forge, Virginia on Saturday from where they'd returned the next day. Madame Speaker, Palmer and Stuart McConnell via Amtrak. Nagle by private vehicle. We also had somewhat "iffy" indications that Lieutenant General Will Smalls, the Army's Assistant Chief of Staff for intelligence and Retired Army Lieutenant General Dave Gamble, former Director of the National Security Agency had joined the party. Also traveling via Amtrak. Together. Returning on Sunday. A day in the country. I figured it was time for a classified email to the boss. *Cheetah*. I thought some more and didn't feel we had enough ammo to start taking serious pot shots at high-level government officials, much less accusing them of plotting treason. In writing. So I scaled back my email to a plain vanilla sitrep with no speculation about names and faces.

TOP SECRET
THUNDER

FM: ALlewellyn@BIAS.gov

TO: Keys@lisound.com

SUBJ: SPOOKY MORSEL (U)

ATT: email XRAY@bling.com Sent by: XRAY On 04 May 4:42 AM

1. (TS/THUNDER) WE (*BIAS* – JUDY AND I) GOT THIS WEIRD EMAIL (ATTACHED.) I TOSSED IT TO THE TROOPS FOR THEIR REACTION AND ONE OF MY SHARPEST KNIVES OPINED THAT QUOTE THE LIST UNQUOTE MUST BE THE LIST OF THE NAMES OF THE AMERICAN CONSPIRATORS.

2. (TS/THUNDER) WE CHECKED W/ NSA AND GOT ZILCH

INITIALLY ON XRAY AND BLING. LATER, WE GOT SOME
SERIOUS GUESSWORK FROM NSA THAT XRAY WAS A BIG
WHEEL AT ALGORITHMICS. YOUR RUSSIAN SOURCING AND
XRAY'S STATEMENT THAT "THE LIST—THE RUSSIANS HAVE IT"
LED MY ANALYST TO HER CONCLUSION—WHICH I SUPPORT
WHOLEHEARTEDLY.

3. (TS/THUNDER) WE NEED TO TREAD CAREFULLY HERE.
ANOTHER SOURCE SUGGESTED THAT THE SPOOKY EMAIL
MIGHT HAVE ORIGINATED AT ALGORITHMICS AND XRAY
MIGHT BE THE BOSS MAN. ANY THOUGHTS?

LOOSE.

TOP SECRET

THUNDER

I received his answer in just under an hour.

**I think your knife is very sharp indeed. See where the
conjecture/conclusion lead,** he said in an UNCLAS text message.

I decided I needed to stretch my legs a bit, so I went topside to see
Darps. He looked up as I popped into his office. I jerked a thumb toward
the west.

"Now?" he asked.

I nodded and said, "I'll drive."

Twenty-five minutes later, after a quick detour by Einstein Bros' Bagels,
we arrived at our little dump on the farm near the Wilderness.

"Okay, Podnah, what's going on?" he queried as he unlocked the back
door of our little hovel.

"Let me get this gizmo going," I said, unzipping my laptop bag. "You get
the coffee going, unwrap the bagels and I'll show you."

A few minutes later, I had my laptop up and running and I checked into
my email. Darps was pouring steaming coffee into our mugs. The coffee-
and-bagels combo smelled good.

"Remember this? From Monday?" I asked after a sip of coffee.

I showed him the XRAY email.

"Hell, yes. I don't think we ever figured out where it came from," he
said.

"You're right," I answered. "I handed the email over to Luke for checking out with NSA and got zilch at first. His source said there was some sort of digital fog around XRAY and Bling and he couldn't crack it at his level. He kicked it upstairs, presumably to bigger guns and/or bigger computers, and said he'd get back to us."

"There's got to be more," he said. "Otherwise, we wouldn't be here. What gives?"

"You're right," I said. "There's a ton more. One of the big guns at NSA got back to Luke and suggested—way off-line—that 'Bling' is actually Algorithmics and that XRay is probably Ironsides himself. Ashleigh is convinced that the list the XRAY-guy is referring to is the list of conspirators. American conspirators. Against the President and the Constitution. And I'm inclined to believe she's right."

Darps steepled his fingers and looked at the ceiling.

"For what it's worth, I also think she's probably right as well. I'm not sure about the Xray-Bling-Ironsides connection. And I just wish I had some huge bright idea about how to smoke out the names on that list," he muttered. "But I'm comin' up empty."

"I'm in the same boat," I said. "All I can think of is pushing Anastasia a little harder, ditto for Mike and Luke with their NSA contacts and finally, pushing you and Ashleigh into the D.C. social scene."

"I was afraid you'd say something like that," Darps answered. "I think you've aleady started that. I received an invite in yesterday's mail to a cocktail party being hosted by the Inter-American Defense College at Fort McNair next Wednesday. I'll plan on going. Annie is happy to go as well. I'm guessing that a lot of our Latin American comrades will be there, but I'm not so sure about our Russian comrades. And I have serious doubts about anything popping to the surface about the plot."

"I'd bet that the Russians and the Chinese will be there—trolling. It's a uniform affair—so you can spot our Russ friends fairly easily. You don't need to engage—just get close enough to listen a little. How's your Russian?"

"Pretty bad, but serviceable," he said. "My Spanish is okay too, but not all that great. I took Russian at the Academy for three years and did a foreign exchange cruise with the Russian Navy. The *Nastoychivyy*. A destroyer. I'm pretty rusty. And I'm not confident that I'll hear anything useful."

"Well, you never know," I said. "Go, practice your Russian and Spanish a little, have a drink and listen. If you hear anything, write it up."

Chapter Thirty-Five

The DNI

1724 River Road

Occoquan, Virginia

Late May

Sam Braxton sat alone in a restaurant on the south shore of Occoquan Creek in Occoquan, Virginia. There were four other patrons that he could see. A waitress came and he ordered a glass of pinot grigio and a tuna sandwich with chips. When the waitress left, he took out his *Algorithmics*-supplied secure mobile phone and punched in a message, which was instantly coded. He had copied the message from a three-by-five card on which he'd drafted the note in English to make sure he had it right. He observed wryly that he had originally included Vice Admiral Donegan among the addees but then had deleted her. The benefits and the curses of technology!

TO: MADAME SPEAKER DEWITT, IRONSIDES, LTG SMALLS, LTG GAMBLE, PALMER AND MCCONNELL. CHANGE OF VENUE. NEXT MTG SCHEDULED FOR FRIDAY 16 MAY 1330, AT CHASE COTTAGE, 75 CLINTON STREET, OXFORD, MD. PURPOSE: SOLIDIFICATION OF PLANS AND TIMELINES. LIGHT SNACKS AND DRINKS WILL BE SERVED. PARKING IS SKETCHY—COME EARLY AND EXPECT TO WALK A BLOCK OR TWO. PLAN ON FINISHING BY 1730 LATEST.

BRAXTON.

He pocketed the phone and tore the three-by-five card into narrow strips. Leaving his linen napkin on his chair, he went to the men's room where he paid brief homage to one of a pair of urinals. Then he went to a sink, took the torn-up index card from his jacket pocket, dropped the torn strips into the sink and washed his hands thoroughly. He pulled a paper towel from the dispenser over the sink and dried his hands. In one quick motion, he scooped up the soggy card strips from the sink into the paper towel, crumpled the whole wad together and dropped it into the trashcan alongside the door as he headed back to his table. He noted with satisfaction that his wine had arrived.

Chapter Thirty-Six
Sheila

```
The Pentagon
Washington, D. C.
Late May
```

Vice Admiral Donegan's vague feeling of uneasiness began as she started her fifteen-minute drive to work. It intensified during her walk from North Parking to her secure Pentagon office. Once inside at her desk, she clicked through her message traffic, her unease shot up some more.

There was *nothing*—nothing at all—absolutely zilch from Sam Braxton. Nothing about "The Group." No meetings. No cryptic messages. Nothing. She'd heard nothing from the DNI in over a week. She was starting to worry that either her conversation with Bobby or her chat with Darps at J. Bryan's Pub or both had been compromised.

Surely not, she thought. If either one or the other had been, NCIS would have been waiting outside her office door this morning with handcuffs. Or there would have been a "Papa Sierra Mike![4]" message from the CNO. Unless the conversations had somehow been leaked to Braxton and company. She stood up and strode to her office door.

"Say, Porter," she said.

"Yes ma'am," he said, starting to rise from his chair.

"Carry on, carry on," she said motioning him to stay seated. "Do you think you can get a copy of the DNI's schedule? For today?"

"Yes Ma'am. No problem. I'll call over and have them fax or email it. Should be here in a few minutes."

"Okay. But don't make a big deal out of it. Keep things low-key."

"Aye, aye, Ma'am."

Four minutes later, she sat at her "classified" terminal and looked at the DNI's schedule. It was marked **SECRET (NOFORN)**. The activities were, for the most part, mundane. A SIGINT Committee meeting at the Intelligence Community Headquarters building on F Street at zero-nine-hundred. Lunch with two SSCI staffers at a Capitol Hill watering hole

---

4   PSM = Please see me.

at eleven-thirty. Then the shot out of left field: "1430: Meeting. Chase Cottage. Oxford. Finis 1730."

She had no idea where or what "Chase Cottage" was. Oxford? Oxford, Maryland? On the Eastern Shore? Wherever the hell it was, she wasn't invited. She was now convinced that she was being cut out of the pack.

"Porter. Do you know what 'Chase Cottage' is? This says it's in Oxford. Does that mean Oxford, Maryland?"

"Don't know, Ma'am. But I'm pretty sure the DNI has a safe house in Oxford, Maryland," Porter answered.

Donegan glanced at her watch. It was seven thirty-five. She wondered if Darps had come through the parking lot yet. She grabbed her Navy cover.

"Porter, I'm going to run down to my car and retrieve something. Be right back."

"I can run down and get it, whatever it is, Admiral," Porter said.

"I don't think Vice Admirals should have First Class Petty Officers fetching their PMS medicine," she said with a thin smile.

Porter collapsed into his chair.

"Aye, Ma'am," he said weakly.

Once at the car, she moved the manila folder from floor in front of the passenger seat and put it on the dashboard, just forward of the steering wheel. She re-locked her car, and took a small bottle of Ibuprofen from her purse before heading back to her office.

On the way up, she resolved to write a letter to Bobby—with instructions to get it to Darps if anything happened to her. She would leave it in a prominent spot in her apartment. If anything should happen to her in the immediate future, *someone* would find the letter and get it to Bobby. She decided that the letter needed to be written ASAP. Instead of running during lunch hour, she would drive home and put the letter together.

Chapter Thirty-Seven
Sheila

The Pentagon
Washington, D. C.
Late May

"Porter, I'm going to run home for a quick sandwich. I'll be back by thirteen hundred and I've got my cell," Admiral Donegan announced as she stepped out of the office at eleven-thirty.

At her apartment, she threw a quickie bologna and mustard sandwich together, poured a glass of low-fat chocolate milk and sat down with her laptop.

May xx, 20xx

Bobby Dearest,

If you're reading this, it means I've gone to my eternal reward—probably because of the conspiracy in which I've been involved and which you and I discussed. Either that or I've been locked up. I don't recall exactly what I told you and/or Darps, but here's a summary. Please feel free to share this letter with Darps and whoever else who might prove helpful in preventing a total national disaster.

Point One. There is an active conspiracy within the US Intelligence Community aimed at overthrowing the US Government, including the President and Vice President.

Point Two: The conspiracy is headed by the DNI, Sam Braxton. He is assisted by Roberto Ironsides, Chairman and CEO of *Algorithmics*, Inc. *Algorithmics* is involved in the technical side of the plot in ways that I've only got a vague idea, but they do involve temporarily shutting down all government C4I systems!

Point Three: Others involved in the plot are Congresswoman and Speaker of the House, Helen DeWitt, Dick Nagel of the CIA, Stuart McConnell of the FBI, LtGen Will Smalls, ACSI, Army and Suzanne Palmer, formerly of the White House Staff.

Point Four: There are some indications that the White House is suspicious about the plot. And that is making Braxton nervous. *I* may be making Braxton nervous. I think that's why he's cutting me out of the pack and has moved the execution timeline ahead from October to June, this year.

Point Five. Plans call for arresting Kehoe as well as VP Girtler and trying them both for treason. Speaker DeWitt is third in line of Presidential succession and is to be the new President and Nagle will replace Girtler as Vice.

Time is short. I have to run. Perhaps I'll have more time later. But now I'm due back at work.

Love to you and your wonderful family,

Sheila

Admiral Donegan folded the letter and tucked it into a legal-sized envelope. She addressed the latter to: LCDR Robert Donegan, USN with the notation "To be delivered to LCDR Donegan in case of my death."

She deposited the letter on her dresser in her bedroom before returning to her office at the Pentagon.

Chapter Thirty-Eight

Alan

1506 Prince Henry Street

Late May

Things around the ranch at 1506 Prince Henry continued to go reasonably well. Until this morning. The shit hit the fan at about seven-twenty a.m. That was when I walked outside to head off to work and someone opened up on me with an automatic weapon. I saw the muzzle flashes and hit the deck, rolling quickly behind the big beech tree in the middle of our front yard. I tucked my legs under me to keep most of my body parts behind the tree, pulled out the Beretta M9 that I usually carry and searched the street. I saw the guy immediately. He wasn't even trying to conceal himself but was standing alongside a parked silver-gray Dodge Charger, dressed in blue warm-ups and holding an H&K MP-5. I cranked off a round and the machine pistol went flying and the asshole went down.

I got up and started running toward him and he got up, slithered into the Dodge and headed east with a squeal of rubber. He must have left the motor running while he got out and shot at me. I cranked off another round with no visible effect. Then he and his car were gone. I hoped that my second bullet hadn't entered anyone's house and holstered the Beretta. I didn't get a good enough look at him to get a coherent description—he did have blond hair and a high-and-tight haircut.

Maria and Elizabeth couldn't have missed the gunfire. At least some of the shots that snapped past me must have hit the house. I dashed for the front entrance.

"Everybody okay?" I shouted as I blew through the door.

I heaved a huge sigh of relief as I heard two familiar female voices answering. From the cellar stairs.

"We're Okay," they said, in unison.

"All clear!" I hollered. "The asshole is gone but possibly bleeding."

"Watch your language!" Maria snarled, protectively. "Have you called the police?" she asked as she trotted up the stairs, followed by Elizabeth who was understandably wide-eyed.

"No," I said. "I think I'll start with Luke or Mike. See what they recommend."

I pulled out my mobile and speed-dialed Luke.

"Yo, Alan, What's up?" he answered.

"Some turd opened fire on me with an automatic weapon just as I left the house a few minutes ago. I hit the deck and returned fire and separated him from his weapon. But he still got away. In a silver-gray Dodge Charger. I didn't get a tag number and haven't called the cops."

"I'll call the cops. Then I'll come by your place and will be there when the cops arrive. Which they will. Did you retrieve the shooter's weapon? Or did he take it with him?"

"No, to both questions. My guess is that it's still lying in the street. I'll run out and get it."

"Nah. Leave it for the cops. Stay put and I'll be there in about six minutes."

He was true to his word. He was there in just under five minutes. The cops arrived two minutes later, a police cruiser at first, followed by another cop car and then an unmarked. Luke must have called them from his car on his way here. Once he got here, he sent us Llewellyns upstairs and went to the door to deal with the police.

The cops picked up the MP-5 from the street after drawing a crude outline of the weapon in yellow chalk on the pavement. They strung yellow crime scene tape around our front yard and part of the street. They also policed up several cartridge cases and placed little plastic markers at each location at which they'd retrieved a shell casing. I was willing to bet that one or two of the cartridge cases were mine. I'm not sure what Luke said to the cops since I stayed upstairs with Maria and Elizabeth. I heard a couple of phrases like "under United States Secret Service protection," "highest classification level," and of course the ubiquitous "national security" catchall. Whatever, it seemed to work. In the middle of everything, Mike showed up in another unmarked car and I watched from our bedroom window as he showed his Secret Service credentials. The next thing I saw was the cops handing over the bagged MP-5 and the several Baggies with cartridge cases to Luke and another cop taking down the yellow tape. Mike and the plainclothes cop signed a few papers.

As the last cop cars pulled away, another unmarked vehicle with D.C. tags pulled in and stopped in front of the house. Two people in civilian clothes climbed out—a Caucasian male and an Asian female, both appearing to be in their mid-twenties, both wearing rather drab gray suits. Both of them carried bulky, stainless-steel briefcases.

Luke came upstairs while Mike stayed outside with the newcomers.

"These guys are our crime scene techs. They're really good and they'll suck up any and all info from the scene. The local cops are happy to wash their hands of the whole thing," Luke said. "Our guys here are going to work right away. The Public Affairs Office in D. C. is spinning up a release that says you're a special assistant to the President and thus have Secret Service protection. They'll refuse to speculate on the identity or motive of the shooter."

"That's good," I said. "Because I have no fucking idea who the asshole was or where he was from."

Both Maria and our daughter pursed their lips at the use of vile language by the Old Man who, truth be told, was probably still stressed and in a mild state of shock.

Out in the street, the male tech had begun stringing yellow crime scene tape around a larger chunk of territory than the locals had encircled. It included a good-sized piece of our front yard plus more than half the street in front of our house. Two more SUV's with D. C. tags showed up and a total of five people jumped out. Two men and three women. One of the female techs—the Asian woman--turned on blue flashing lights in the unmarked car and sat sideways on the front seat while she pulled on a pair of clear plastic booties. Then she climbed across the yellow tape and proceeded to mince along the area in a most methodical way. She had a digital camera attached to a strap around her neck and a mobile phone in her right hand. She walked twenty-two steps south, turned and took a step and then walked twenty-two steps north. She paused to use the camera a number of times and appeared to speak into her mobile on numerous occasions. Her progress was quite slow and methodical. Her male partner had retrieved what appeared to be a small portable vacuum cleaner from the car and began following the Asian woman at a slight distance. He had ear buds in both ears. He stopped occasionally and ran his little vacuum cleaner over the terrain—either our grass, the concrete sidewalk or the macadam roadway. The other technicians busied themselves with various gizmos.

I don't know how long it took the seven Secret Service techs to work the crime scene and vacuum up whatever they needed. I called the *BIAS* office and talked to Darps and Judy. I told them I'd be taking Elizabeth to school and then I'd be in. Luke said he didn't know how much time the techs would need to clear the crime scene, but it might not be till tomorrow.

"So whiskey-tango-foxtrot?" I asked Luke.

"You know as much as I do," he said. "But we should get a full report tomorrow. Or the day after."

I fixed myself a salami and Swiss sandwich on marbled rye and poured myself a glass of low-fat chocolate milk. I grabbed an apple from the basket on the counter.

"Ladies? Luke?" I asked. "Anyone want a salami sandwich?"

"Not I," said Maria. "I'm not hungry."

"Me, neither," Elizabeth added.

"Thanks but I already had breakfast," Luke said.

"Well this has got to do for breakfast and lunch for me," I said. "I'll finish this off, drive Elizabeth to school and head in to Ripley Hall."

"I'll be right behind you," Luke said. "Can't be too careful till we find out what the hell's going on. Mike'll stay here, with Maria and the techs, at least for a while."

Chapter Thirty-Nine

Alan

1506 Prince Henry Street

Late May

I got home at five-twenty. The temperature was still in the eighties and the sun was pretty high. Summer was not far off. I'd mowed the lawn on Saturday and today was Wednesday and the grass was already looking like I needed to mow it again.

Just as I was reaching for the front door, it popped open and I was face-to-face with Elizabeth, Esmé, and Cory who was all-awag.

"Girls exercising dog or the other way around?" I asked, giving Cory a scritch behind the ears.

"Does it really matter, Mr. El?" Esmé asked.

"I suspect it doesn't," I replied. "Any new conspiracy theories?"

Esmé raised her eyebrows and immediately reached for her backpack.

"Wait'll you see this, Dad!" Elizabeth said with a sly chuckle.

Esmé was unfolding a piece of copier paper that appeared to contain a photocopy of a newspaper article.

"Check this out," she said, shoving the paper toward me.

I noticed that someone had scrawled *"The Daily Lawtonian – April 30"* in ballpoint cursive above the copied headline, which read: **MYSTERIOUS NIGHTTIME POWER OUTAGE AT SILL.**

"My brother is a soldier and is stationed at Fort Sill and he knows I love conspiracies, so he sent me this," she said. "It's from the local newspaper."

I looked at the article again. Underneath the headline there was a subhead: **SILL SPOX SEZ ARMY CHECKING WITH NASA.** That little blurb was followed by the name of the Staff Writer, which in turn was followed by the text of the article.

A curious "anomaly" hit electricity, communications, and computers for two minutes Wednesday night at Fort Sill.

At 8:31 CDT all electrical connections on post were interrupted; at exactly 8:33, they were all restored. During the time period, electricity and local communications in Lawton were not interrupted. Fort Sill spokesperson, Major Sandra Anderson, said that Sill officials are in contact with NASA to see if some sort of space-based anomaly could have precipitated the outage.

"What do you think about that, Mister El?" Esmé asked.

"Probably way above my pay grade," I said, lamely. "But it *is* interesting."

"Do you see anything connecting the quote Fort Sill anomaly unquote with some sort of Washington funny business?" the sly little chick asked innocently.

"No," I said. But I crossed my fingers behind my back as I said that. There seemed to be a bunch of loose ends waving around in the breeze and I just wasn't sure.

"Cory and I are going to walk Esmé home. Wanna come along, Dad?" Elizabeth asked.

"You bet," I said. "Lemme tell Mom."

I stuck my head in the door and hollered that I was going with Elizabeth and Cory and would be back with them in twenty minutes.

The three of us gabbed about the mysterious power outage at Fort Sill all the way to Esmé's house and then Elizabeth and I continued the chatter, as we turned for home in the delightful May gloaming.

We crossed the threshold at five-fifty, ten minutes before cocktail time. I decided to check my "home" email and I did. The most recent was from Baltic North Lines.

"Holy cow!" I half-shouted.

Both black-haired women jumped into the family room and chirped, "What's up?" simultaneously.

"Because we made reservations for three on the cruise and made them before May fifteenth, we automatically get to bring a fourth guest! Free! Let me read this email again and make sure I've got this right," I mumbled.

I read it again.

"I got it right. We can have another guest at no charge except tips and extra charges on board Nordschiff!"

I looked at Maria and Elizabeth. My parents still lived in Clancyville, New

York. They go to the Caymans for two weeks every February but beyond that, they don't go anywhere. And they stay together. So one parent or the other joining us on the cruise was totally out of the question.

Maria's parents had both gone on to their eternal rewards years ago. Elizabeth's eyes were flashing.

"Esmé?" she croaked.

"Let me talk to her mother first—before you mention it to Esmé," Maria said. "I wouldn't want to get Esmé's hopes up and then have her parents nix the idea for some good reason or other that we don't know about. That would cause a huge and unnecessary disappointment."

"I'll say," Elizabeth said.

Chapter Forty

Litvinov

The two Russians met at the cathouse. The Ambassador wore sweaty running clothes. Litvinov wore a civilian suit and a white shirt and tie. The two tigers were asleep. In an adjacent compound, two lions were pacing.

"I'm thinking it is time for us to leak some more information to Kehoe. I don't want those American pricks to succeed in overthrowing him," said the ambassador. He wore wearing a Georgetown T-shirt and was sweating mightily. The temperature was in the upper eighties.

"If I may, Excellency," Colonel Litvinov responded. "I'm pretty sure Epifanov *does* want those pricks to succeed. He wants the American Government to be de-stabilized. What better way than for President Kehoe to be thrown out on his arse?"

Litvinov shrugged off the suit jacket and placed it over his right shoulder. He was sweating, but not nearly as profusely as his ambassador.

"Christ it's hot. No wonder the tigers are sleeping. Think about it," he said quietly. "If two or three of the plotters suddenly get fired—or even arrested—what will Epifanov and his toadies in Moscow think? They'll think—or know—that Kehoe and his minions tumbled to the details of the plot. And then, suspicion zooms in on the Russian Embassy in Washington for spilling the beans. Yourself and myself. At best, we get posted to some pesthole like Kathmandu or Djibouti. At worst . . ." he held up his right hand in the shape of a pistol aimed his forefinger at his temple and cocked his thumb. Twice.

"*Da, da*. You're right. We have to wait until just before things start to happen. Or until the Americans have figured it out for themselves."

"Speaking of which, I met Michelle Hookes, Kehoe's trusted old lady advisor at our Revolutionary Day reception last November. She's quite charming—I chatted with her for a few minutes. I also saw her at another reception a few days ago at the Interamerican Defense College. There was also a civilian American couple and an unescorted American civilian female that I'd not seen before. Later, I tried to look them up and found only one of them. Darpley Roentgen Taylor, a former Naval officer. A woman, presumably his wife, accompanied him. No one from our embassy who attended the reception recognized the lone, unescorted woman. We did manage to get a copy of the guest list. There was one "Ashleigh MacDonald" from the U.S.A. on the list. She's apparently a consultant with Ashland Associates, a tiny software firm in Ashland, Virginia. I'm guessing that the unaccompanied young woman was her. Maybe we can use one of them as a vehicle to get the info to Kehoe when the time comes."

"Hmm. New faces are always interesting. Did you report them to Moscow?"

"I reported the contact with Michelle Hookes. But I did not report the new faces."

"Why not?"

"I think that would be obvious, Cousin," Litvinov answered. "If their presence on the scene could mean that the Americans are starting to smell a rat about their plot and we bring that to Moscow's attention, we could bring *us* to Moscow's attention. Epifanov's attention. And I don't think we want that. At least not now."

"I like the way you think, Cousin," Ambassador Malenkov said, chuckling. "Like one of the more sinister Dostoevsky characters. I have to run. We'll talk soon."

He gave a little salute and broke into a jog heading downhill from the cathouse toward the Rock Creek Park exit. Colonel Litvinov began the uphill hike to the Connecticut Avenue gate.

Chapter Forty-One
The DNI

Gravelly Point Park
Arlington, Virginia
Late May

Gravelly Point Park is a small plot of National Park Service real estate to the immediate north of Ronald Reagan National Airport. Most park aficionados go there to experience the jet noise and the proximity of speeding airliners landing or taking off at Reagan National. If the wind is out of the south, the big jets land to the south, roaring over the park with their landing gear down. If the wind blows out of the north, the planes shriek over the park northward on their takeoffs under full power. Either way, the big jets look like they are close enough to touch. Either way, there is a lot of noise. And that was why Sam Braxton picked it for the site of an emergency meeting of "the group." He watched as various members of the group—minus Vice Admiral Donegan--grabbed the last few free parking spaces in the tiny Gravelly Point Parking lot.

The thundering roar of an arriving jet, passing overhead, momentarily cut off any possibility of conversation. The outside temperature hovered around eighty-five, Fahrenheit.

Sam Braxton sat at a weathered, wooden picnic table alongside another equally dilapidated table. He wore a nondescript, tan ball cap and large, dark sunglasses. An orange-and-white, flowered Hawaiian shirt over tan chinos rounded out his wardrobe. There were two large picnic coolers on the vacant table. Congresswoman DeWitt and Roberto Ironsides had joined Braxton. Madame Speaker wore a red Washington Nationals cap and a pair of large sunglasses plus a red polo shirt and a blue denim skirt. Ironsides also had a large pair of sunglasses perched on his prominent nose. His uniform of the day included a Yankees ball cap, a dark blue shirt with sailboats outlined in white and faded tan chinos. Dick Nagle ambled up and took a place at the occupied table. He sported a pale, blue Oxford shirt with a yellow tie and navy-blue pants over black tasseled loafers. Stu McConnell wore a gray FBI suit.

"Hello, everyone," Sam said, slipping into a weathered picnic bench.

"I'm sorry to call a meeting on such short notice," Braxton said, just as another jet roared low overhead. "There's bottled water and iced tea in the coolers. Help yourself.

"I picked this spot because it's close and probably impossible to bug."

He smiled thinly as another jet thundered overhead.

"Some strange developments have popped up. Very strange," he said. "It appears that the Russian Government has suspicions about our little plan. At least some people at NSA seem to think so.

"On top of that, we have indications that the Russian Ambassador to Washington has had at least one unscheduled meeting with our President. We have no idea what they discussed. Although I have suspicions."

He looked over his shoulder. A two-engine jet was lined up on final approach, still far enough away to be relatively quiet. When Braxton turned back to the picnic table, he started to say, "There have also been..." at which time, the engines of the inbound Boeing seven fifty-seven roared over the park.

"Rumors," he began again. "...rumors that Kehoe is getting some sketchy information about our plan and that said information is coming from Russian sources. I need each and every one of you to review your contacts with your subordinates and consider whether any of them might be leaking information to the Russians. What in the name of God might be a valid motivation for that I can't even begin to fathom. If some do-gooder wanted to blow the plan out of the water for political or ideological reasons, why not just pick up the phone and call the FBI? Why screw around with the Russians?"

"Um, Sam. There's another issue floating out there," Nagle said. "It may or may not be related to the Russians."

"What's that, Dick?" Braxton asked.

"There are reports that someone shot at Alan Llewellyn a few days ago. With an automatic weapon. When he came out of his house in Chestertown at seven twenty in the morning. He wasn't hit and the shooter got away. But left his weapon behind. Was that us? Quote. Firing one across his bow? Unquote?"

"No. Definitely not us. We don't have the resources to send shooters to Chestertown to try and gun down the likes of Alan Llewellyn."

"Hmm. If we have the resources to totally shut down Fort Sill, Oklahoma, one would think that sending a shooter to Chestertown to take a potshot or two at Llewellyn wouldn't be that big a deal."

"Dick, Dick! I didn't realize you were a conspiracy theorist! There is a total of sixty-four people who work in the *Algorithmics* building in Stafford plus a dozen more like us in D. C., Government officers or civil servants. Software engineers, programmers, network specialists, bureaucrats, *et cetera*. But absolutely no assassins."

Nagle thought about the heavily armed security guards at *Algorithmics* in Stafford—just north of Chestertown—but said nothing. Were they part of Braxton's total of sixty-four? What he had begun to think of as his "misgivings monster" was beginning to rear its ugly head again. The notion of shooting at Americans was deeply unsettling. And he wondered where Sheila Donegan was.

Chapter Forty-Two

Alan

1506 Prince Henry Street
Late May

When I walked home Friday evening, three things became obvious to me. First thing, I realized that summer was truly on its way to the Old Dominion and was nearly here. My "business casual" attire of polo shirt and khakis felt vastly preferable to a suit-and-tie combo. But I was still starting to work up a healthy sweat. The second thing was that my cell chirped from my pants pocket. I pulled the phone out. The screen said "MARIA – HOME" and showed our landline number.

"Hi," I said.

"Hi." It was indeed Maria. "Are you still planning on picking up sandwiches?"

"You bet," I said. "*Panini*, actually. I'm on my way to Federico's even as we speak."

"Good. I got you in time. We'll have an extra mouth to feed this evening."

"Esmé?"

"Right the first time."

"Good. I'll throw in an order of fried calamari along with the extra *Panino*."

"Sounds good. *Ciao*," she said.

The third thought was that the Baltic Sea cruise was closing in on the Llewellyn family. Which was a good thing. But I knew that there was something else.

Fifteen minutes later, I walked into the kitchen with a large, white shopping bag that exuded a drool-inducing bouquet and just had time to plant a kiss on Maria's lovely lips when I was assaulted by a short but strong female tornado. Esmé threw her arms around my neck, nearly knocking me and the panini to the floor in the process.

"Thank you, thank you, thank you!" she squealed.

"God help us, child! What the hey?"

"The cruise, you silly man!" she said and hugged me harder.

Maria and Elizabeth were laughing. I guessed that Maria had spoken with Esmé's mom and that, one way or another, the cruise invitation had been tendered. And, I guess, accepted.

"Well, let's catch our breath over drinks and calamari," I said.

I poured apple juice for the girls and sherry for Maria; I splashed a not-so-wee dram of Scotch over a small handful of cubes for the Old Man.

"Here's to another Friday," I intoned, holding up my glass.

"Here's to the cruise in the Baltic," Esmé echoed, holding up her apple juice.

I opened the box of calamari and de-lidded a little container of marinara sauce. I squeezed the juice of half a lemon over the pile of fried squid. Everybody munched and sipped for a bit and Esmé put down her glass.

"Have you had time to think about that power outage at Fort Sill, Mister El?" she asked.

I put my glass down, too. "Not much," I said, truthfully. "How about you?"

"Actually, I have," she said. "And here's what I came up with. Three possibilities. One. Some sort of weird space thingy caused the outage like the Army chick at Fort Sill said. Two. Some sort of super-secret test that the good guys were doing caused it. Or maybe still are doing. Three. Some sort of super-secret test that bad people are doing caused it. Evil doers. That's it. And I don't put much stock in number one."

"Hmm. Interesting," I said and took a sip of scotch. "Three possibilities; one of them is innocent and the other two are sinister to varying degrees. And you don't think the innocent one is credible."

"That pretty much sums it up. Can you come up with other possibilities?" she asked.

"Well Esmé, what do think of this? A total accident. Totally innocent."

"What? Like some kid fooling around with a science kit in his basement? I don't think so. This is way too sophisticated. Whatever it was, it only affected stuff on post at Fort Sill. Not outside the fence in Lawton. Or elsewhere in Oklahoma. At least not that we know of. And it turned Fort Sill's stuff off for *exactly* two minutes. On the dot. That sounds deliberate as well as sophisticated to me. Not like some sort of random accident or some kid fooling around, Mister El."

"Good points, kiddo. It's certainly something to think about. Um, do you still happen to have that copy of the Lawton newspaper article about the outage?"

"Sure do. Wanna look at it again?"

"Actually, I'd like to make a copy of it," I said a little sheepishly.

Chapter Forty-Three

Litvinov

It was seven-fifteen Saturday morning when Colonel Litvinov's landline in the bedroom of his residence in Great Falls shrilled.

"God's teeth!" he muttered, groping for the phone.

"Allo!" he barked. He had not yet mastered the smooth American "Hello" when answering the phone when awakened from a sound sleep.

"Good morning to you as well," purred the sultry voice of Valerya, the Ambassador's personal secretary. More importantly, Valerya was his primary connection to the Ambassador himself.

"It's nice to start the day to the sound of your lovely voice," Litvinov mumbled, mindful of his wife's sleeping form beside him. "What's happening on this particular Saturday morning?"

"Do you know where Gravelly Point Park is?" Valerya asked.

"Just north of Reagan National?" he said, tentatively.

"That's it," she answered. "Right off the northern end of the main runway. You are to be there in thirty minutes. Your cousin is leaving right now on a run. He says it will take him thirty minutes to run to the park from here."

Litvinov wondered where "here" was. He doubted it was the Embassy. Valerya's phone call came across as "Unknown." He suspected that his cousin was boffing his secretary.

"I'll be there in twenty-nine minutes," he said, "*Das vidanya*." He hung up the phone and climbed stiffly out of bed.

Twenty-five minutes later, Colonel Litvinov pulled his Buick into the small parking lot at Gravelly Point just as a US Airways A320 lifted off Runway One and roared over the Park. *Wind must be out of the north,* he mused as he climbed out of the Buick and glanced at his watch. He looked northward towards the Fourteenth Street Bridge and saw a tall, slender figure with dark hair running south. It was too far to tell who it was from his looks, but his gait gave him away—His Excellency Viktor

Malenkov, Litvinov's wife's cousin. The ambassador. Litvinov stepped away from the car and waved. The dark-haired figure waved back and cut across the grass toward Litvinov's parking place. He arrived just as another outbound jet—this one a United Boeing Seven-Thirty-Seven—thundered over the park.

"Top of the morning to you, as our Irish friends like to say," the ambassador said, pulling a water bottle from a holder on his belt. "This is a great place for conversations if you don't want anyone to listen in." He slugged down several swallows of water.

"And as long as you don't mind the frequent interruptions," Litvinov added.

"I had that book—*Seven Days in May*—translated. Then I read it. What absolute balderdash!" the ambassador said.

"I couldn't agree with you more," Litvinov replied. "Total tommyrot. But I don't really think the source gave it to me to suggest something identical was happening now. With the Joint Chiefs rebelling over a USA-USSR treaty that they didn't like. Ridiculous! Rather, I think, he—the source—is implying that some sort of conspiracy may be underway *somewhere* within the American government. And its goal *could* be to unseat Kehoe. And finally, those names on the list are connected to it."

"I agree. And I only gave Kehoe one name from the list. The civilian. Ironsides."

"Once again, I'm an intelligence collector, not an analyst," Litvinov said. "But it strikes me that Ironsides' name is--at worst--the second most important one on the list. And I think you did the right thing in holding back the other names."

"That wasn't my choice. Our esteemed Foreign Minister—Kirilinkov himself—directed me to float Ironsides' name to Kehoe and withhold the others. But, new subject—"

Another jet cleared the end of Runway One and thundered over the park.

"Do you know," the ambassador continued as the jet noise faded, "an individual named Alan Llewellyn? An American. I think he's a former naval officer."

"Not off the top of my head. But I can check the files," Litvinov answered.

"Please do that. I've already checked ours and the latest entry was in ninety-two when he supposedly left the Navy," the ambassador said. "He may have some connection with this so- called plot. One way or another."

"Okay, cousin-in-law. Got it. Anything else?"

"*Nyet*. But this guy—Llewellyn—might be worth taking a look at," the ambassador said. He looked up, waved and started to run as another jet roared overhead.

"See you soon," he said. But Colonel Litvinov couldn't hear him.

Chapter Forty-Four

Alan

BIAS
Chestertown, Virginia
Late May

I was sitting in the SCIF with the Thunder inner circle—Darps, Judy, Sammy, Ashleigh, Anastasia, Mike and Luke. We had a laptop set up with our SCI television set and I'd decided for once to use Power Point.

"Okay. Here's what we know—or suspect," I said. I flicked on the first slide. It filled the screen.

**TOP SECRET
THUNDER**

- GOR to USG pipeline. Coup plot?

- R. Ironsides of *Algorithmics*, Inc. Involved?

- Madame Speaker DeWitt, VADM Donegan, CIA DDIR Nagle, FBI DDIR McConnell, Former APNSA Suzanne Palmer traveled more than once to Clifton Forge, VA April-May.

- Sam Braxton owns a part-time, pretty posh residence just outside Clifton Forge.

- There are high-level tensions/strains within GOR.

**THUNDER
TOP SECRET**

I let the round table absorb the bullets for a minute and then started to talk:

"We know that *Cheetah* has some sort of pipeline to the Russians and that the Russians are telling him that there's some sort of coup against him—Kehoe—brewing somewhere in the U.S. Government.

"We know that the Russians say that Roberto Ironsides of *Algorithmics, Inc.* is involved in the plot somehow.

"We know that several high-level members of the Intelligence Community, including former Chairwoman of the House Permanent Select Committee on Intelligence and current Speaker of the House, the Deputy Director of the FBI as well as the former National Security Advisor to the President rode the Amtrak *Cardinal* between Clifton Forge, Virginia to Washington D. C. a little over three weeks ago. We think that Nagle went by private vehicle.

"We know that Sam Braxton, the Director of National Intelligence has some sort of fancy mountain chalet just outside of Clifton Forge.

"Finally, we know that there's some sort of pissing contest going on at the highest levels of the Russian government. We do *not* know of any connection between said pissing contest and the alleged coup plot within the U. S. Government. Or if there's any connection between the Russian pissing contest or their information coming our way. It wouldn't astound me if the Russians were cooking up the story of a plot for a coup within the U.S. Government as a means of dragging USG attention away from the problems in Moscow. Disinformation. Their stock-in-trade. Amen. Have I left anything out?" I asked.

"I don't think so," Ashleigh said slowly. "But I think that some of that info that we know might give us a 'tentative roster' of the evildoers."

"Bingo, you sly vixen," I said and clicked the mouse button for the next slide.

TOP SECRET
THUNDER

TENTATIVE List of Conspirators (TS/TH)

- Samuel J. Braxton, DNI (TS/TH)
- Congresswoman Helen M. DeWitt, MC (NY54) (TS/TH)
- Vice Admiral Sheila V. Donegan, USN (COMNAVINTCOM) (TS/TH)
- Suzanne M. Parker (Fmr APNSA) (TS/TH)
- Roberto S. Ironsides (Chrm/CEO, *Algorithmics, Inc.*)(TS/TH)

THUNDER
TOP SECRET

"I can't emphasize enough how tightly held this list must stay, let alone its tentative nature. No leaks whatsoever! Think of it as a red-hot, in-house, code-word protected work-in-progress and that's all--till we decide otherwise. If *ANY* name or names on the list get out and they turn out to be *NOT* on a valid list of conspirators, and the release is somehow tied to us, we are totally, totally screwed. *BIAS* will be discredited and quite probably shut down, Kehoe will be political dead meat and all of us will be lucky to get jobs servicing Porta-Johns. Some of us may find work making license plates.

"Finally, on a happier note, here's something coming in from deep left field. It's unclassified as it's clipped from a newspaper—the 6 May edition of the *Daily Lawtonian* of Lawton, Oklahoma," I said as I clicked the mouse for the next slide. The photocopy of the *Lawtonian* article came up.

"Run your eyes over it and see if it pushes any of your buttons."

Silence ensued for about thirty seconds as people read and digested the newspaper article.

"*Algorithmics*?" asked Ashleigh.

"Well, well!" I half whispered. I thought of Esmé's three possibilities for the cause of the "Sill Anomaly." Possibility Number Three—"...Secret test that bad people are doing," came pretty close to what Ashleigh had just said. And vice versa.

Chapter Forty-Five

Alan

```
The Battlefield Park
Chestertown, Virginia
Late May
```

Battlefield Park in Chestertown is one of my favorite places to run. It is a splendidly wooded remnant of the fiery hellhole that was the middle of Chestertown halfway through the Civil War. Trouble is, many other folks also number the park among their favorite places to run. At least if the number of runners there is any indication. Of late, I'd not run in the park as I try to avoid crowds when I take Cory on a run and I'd been doing that a lot recently. Today, Elizabeth—slightly traumatized at the idea of leaving her dog with Esmé's parents for our upcoming two-week cruise— had taken her on a long walk. So I ran down to Battlefield Park alone and joined the throng of runners through the stately grounds.

My first thoughts were about my meeting with my *BIAS* buddies about the THUNDER issue. The plot against the President. I thought that we had everything in place. A research effort, checking out the possible Russian connections. A hard look at Roberto Ironsides. Then, the red hot "list": the travelers to Braxton's chalet outside Clifton Forge-Congresswoman DeWitt, Nagle, Deputy Dog at CIA, McConnell, Deputy at the FBI and Suzanne Palmer, the wicked witch of the East. Let alone the DNI himself. Vice Admiral Donegan remained a major league question mark.

I thought about it. We had no information that would prompt an arrest of anyone, much less stand up in court. The *BIAS* troops were doing the spadework, digging through any and all available information on the cast of characters.

Then, there was the issue of the Llewellyn family vacation. With Esmé joining us. I was still wondering if I should pull the plug on that. We were scheduled to leave the day after tomorrow. I turned around the loop on the road through the Battlefield and headed back west. *Hell no,* I decided. *If Kehoe wants me to cancel, he'll tell me. He hasn't told me. So we'll go.*

Chapter Forty-Six

Alan

The Atlantic Ocean
Friday - Saturday
Late May

We got away on time. The hired limo hauled us swiftly from Prince Henry Street to Dulles. Thank the Lord our flight got away on time as well. Our places were the center row of four seats in the Boeing Triple Seven. Maria and I had the two left seats and Elizabeth and Esmé had the two to our immediate right. I treated myself to a double Bloody Mary before a light dinner of a pork cutlet and a pseudo-Caesar salad—*sans* anchovies--and a tiny roll. I watched an old re-run of *Cider House Rules* in which Michael Caine famously said to the boys in the orphanage, "Good night, you Princes of Maine and Kings of New England!" And then I got up and visited the loo for which I had to stand in line. When I got back to our seats, the three women were sound asleep. I, on the other hand, may have dozed off for a few minutes here and there throughout the night, but spent most of the time trying to read and watching the GPS track of our flight on the monitor. I dislike the prospect of public sleeping and possible public drooling. I got up and walked around a couple of times. When breakfast finally came, it consisted of a tiny slab of French toast with a quarter-sized sausage patty. Tasty but tiny. The coffee and orange juice, on the other hand, hit the spot.

Maria, Elizabeth, Esmé and I joined about fifty thousand or so of our nearest and dearest friends for customs and immigration at Heathrow. After we slogged through the process, we stepped outside the quarantine area. A woman with short, blond hair wearing a navy-blue suit and a white blouse that came in a few inches south of a Navy uniform held a sign that said *Baltic North Line Guests*.

"Will you get us to our hotel?" I asked.

"I believe so. Your names, please?"

"Llewellyn," I said. "There are four of us."

She consulted an iPad.

"Yes sir, Mr. Llewellyn. Grosvenor House on Park Lane. Sailing on

Nordschiff on Monday. We'll get you to the hotel now and to the ship in Dover on Monday morning."

"Sounds good," I said.

"Just wait here for a few minutes till I collect four more passengers. Then we'll go to the bus."

I have to admit that her bright Danish accent perked me up nicely.

We joined her and the other passengers and went to the bus. The latter was a short-cut version. The English weather was gray. Or grey. We got to Grosvenor House in about forty-five minutes. Maria, Elizabeth and Esmé plumped down on what appeared to be comfortable lobby furniture whilst I staggered over to the desk to check in.

"Good morning, Mr. Llewellyn," said the clerk with a smile as I handed him our passports and a credit card. "I believe there's a message for you," he said.

He turned around, found a pink telephone memo slip and handed it to me.

"Someone called you about twenty minutes ago."

"Thanks," I said, puzzled. I looked at the note.

Please call Captain Van Horn, U. S. Naval Attaché, at [44](20) 7499-9000 at your earliest convenience.

"I'm afraid you're a bit early for check in, Mr. Llewellyn," the clerk said. "Your rooms are not ready yet. Our guest checkout time is twelve noon and official check-in time is three o'clock. But I'm sure we can get you and your family into a couple of rooms well before that. And if you'd like to leave your luggage with us, we can secure it till your rooms are ready. Meantime, you can have breakfast and use the phone as necessary. There's a house phone at the table across the way. Just press "O" for an outside line, then dial the number on your note. I'm pretty sure it's the American Embassy."

We finished the check-in paperwork and he took our bags.

"I'll send someone to come and get you when your rooms are available, sir," he said.

I walked across the lobby to the three women. They looked amazingly fresh and pretty for having had such a hard night. But then, maybe my night had been a bit rougher than theirs.

"Do you ladies fancy an English breakfast?" I asked. "Our rooms aren't ready yet. And I do have to call the American Embassy. The Naval Attaché left a message. This morning."

"Saturday?" Maria asked. "That's a little strange. But yes, I'd love to try an English breakfast. I've heard so much about them. And the breakfast on the plane was a bit spare."

"Maybe if we have a big English breakfast and our room is ready soon, we can sleep through lunch," Elizabeth observed.

"Works for me," Esmé added.

"Okay, let's get seats in the restaurant, order breakfast and then I'll call the embassy."

We ordered "Full English Breakfasts" all around for twenty-five pounds a pop. That was a little under a hundred forty dollars for the four of us. For breakfast! Excluding tip! Yikes! I was starting to wonder about the efficacy of this trip in assuaging my PTSD.

I went back into the lobby, found the phone and dialed.

"Office of the Naval Attaché. Petty Officer Rantz," a polite female voice answered.

"Good morning. My name is Llewellyn and I just arrived in London from the States. There was a note here at the hotel to call Captain Van Horn."

"Yes sir. I'll switch you right over to the Captain."

"Good morning, Mr. Llewellyn. Captain Bob Van Horn, here. Welcome to London."

"Thank you, Sir," I said. "How can I help you?"

"I'm not sure what's going on, but I'm supposed to invite you to the embassy. This morning. For something urgent that won't take long. That's about all I know. I can send a car and Petty Officer Rantz to your hotel. She's a Yeoman First and she'll have her Navy ID. But she'll be wearing civvies. We're only about five minutes away. You probably won't be gone from the hotel for more than a half hour."

I calculated for a microsecond.

"How does this sound, Skipper? We've just ordered breakfast and our rooms aren't ready. When I can get my wife and daughter and our young guest fed and safely to our rooms, I'll call Rantz and she can come and get me. Maybe in an hour or so?"

"Sounds good. But if it looks like it's going to be much more than an hour, give me a call back and we can adjust. I got the idea that some higher-up in D. C. really wants to talk to you soonest."

"Yes sir. I'll call Rantz within an hour. And I'll be there soon thereafter."

"Tell her your room number when you call. I'll have her come up to your room and get you. And please bring your passport."

"Aye, aye sir," I said. "Thank you."

I had to wonder what the hell that was about.

I rejoined Maria, Elizabeth and Esmé at the breakfast table. A waitress showed up with a huge tray. She placed before each of us a large plate containing scrambled eggs, English bacon, sausage, potatoes, fried tomato slices, fried mushrooms and toast that looked like it had been fried with the bacon and sausage.

"Would you care for tea or coffee?" she asked.

Maria, Esmé, Maria and Elizabeth all requested tea. I asked for coffee.

"So what's up with the embassy phone call?" Maria asked. "I'm surprised that they're open on a Saturday."

"They're probably not open, but even so, there are probably a lot of people working there. The Naval Attaché wants me to come in. They're sending a car," I said.

"For what?" Maria asked, suspicion dripping from her voice.

"I don't know," I said lamely. "I have no idea. He couldn't talk about it on the phone. He did say it wouldn't take long."

All four of us leaned into our breakfast. It was scrumptious. We ate like starving wolves in the middle of an Alaskan winter.

As we were finishing up, a bellhop showed up at our table.

"Mr. and Mrs. Llewellyn?" he asked.

"Yes," I said. "That's us."

"Your rooms are ready, sir," he said.

"Okay. Give me a minute to settle our bill here and we'll go with you."

"Yes sir," he said. He made some sort of signal and our waitress showed up with our tab. I signed it, adding a tip and we pushed back from the table. Six minutes later, we were in our rooms, Numbers Four-Twenty and Four Twenty-Two, adjacent. I tipped the bellhop. He didn't seem to mind that it was dollars. I hadn't been able to get pounds yet.

I telephoned the embassy. Petty Officer Rantz said she'd be at the hotel within ten minutes. Maria dug into her suitcase and disappeared into the loo, emerging wearing nightwear. The two girls disappeared into Room Four Twenty-Two.

"I take it you guys are going to snooze a little," I said. "Even though you seemed to sleep all the way across the Atlantic."

"Airplane sleep isn't all that great," Maria said. "I'm going to try and catch up."

"I'm guessing that the girls are planning the same thing," I said

There was a knock at the door.

Chapter Forty-Seven

Alan

London

Late May

I went to the spy-hole. There was a young, attractive woman outside the door. She held what appeared to be an active-duty Navy ID card in front of her right shoulder.

"I'm Petty Officer Rantz, sir. From the Naval Attaché's Office at the Embassy," she said.

I believed her and opened the door.

"Hi. I'm Alan Llewellyn," I said, holding out my hand.

She shook it.

"Hi Mr. Llewellyn. I have a government vehicle downstairs waiting to take us to the embassy. It's pretty close. The car will bring you back here when you're done. Which I'm told will be soon."

"Do you know what this is about?" I asked. Mess Deck petty officers invariably know more than anyone else about what is really going on. On board ship. My guess is that the same axiom holds true for embassies and naval attaché offices as well.

"No sir. I think it might involve special communications, but I don't know for sure."

See what I mean. She knew.

I turned back into the bedroom.

"Bye, Love," I said to Maria. I was pretty sure she was already asleep.

I made sure I had my key card and passport and left. I followed Petty Officer Rantz to the elevators. She wore a pale blue, short-sleeved blouse and a khaki skirt, which stopped just above her knees. The knees looked fine from behind, as did the rest of her legs. We caught the elevator down to the lobby together.

There was an unmarked black Ford Expedition with a civilian driver waiting outside in the hotel's horseshoe drive. Petty Officer Rantz hopped into the shotgun seat--on the driver's left--and I got in back. Two or three minutes later, we were at the American Embassy, an edifice that looked to be only slightly smaller than the U. S. Capitol.

"Right this way, sir," she said and I followed.

She led me through extensive security. I had to empty my pockets, go through a metal detector and show my passport to an armed Marine Lance Corporal. I followed Petty Officer Rantz to a comfortable office with American and U. S. Navy flags and an impossibly young-looking guy dressed in civvies and sitting behind a desk that held a hand-carved wooden sign that read "CAPT Robert Van Horn, USN" over carved Naval Aviator wings. My guess was that it had been carved in the Philippines.

"Good morning, sir," I said.

The captain stood and smiled.

"Hi, Mr. Llewellyn," he said. "I'm not sure what's going on, but somebody in Washington wants to chat with you. Secure. I'll take you upstairs to the comm center and I gather they'll put you in a little booth and patch your call through. I do need to eyeball your passport, first."

He did. Five minutes later, I was sitting in a little room with a table on which rested a modern-looking phone with an attached handset. A skinny young man wearing silver-rimmed glasses and a wispy mustache invited me to pick up the handset.

"Just pick up the receiver. Like a regular phone. You'll hear a few beeps while I make the connection. Then you can talk and listen," he said.

Captain Van Horn put a legal pad and a pair of pencils on the table.

"In case you need them," he said. "Greg, here, will bring you back down to our office when you're done and then Rantz will escort you back to your hotel."

I sat and picked up the handset. Greg and Captain Van Horn left and closed the door. I heard several beeps and then a familiar voice.

"Hello. Mr. Llewellyn? Alan?"

Michelle Hookes. Special Counselor to the President.

Shortly before the abortive assassination attempt on her, the White House (read President Jim Kehoe) had hired her as a special advisor. From what I heard she was worth every penny of her very sporty salary which she didn't really need.

"Ma'am. You're up early! It's gotta be zero-six thirty there. Saturday morning."

"How many times do I have to tell you to call me Michelle?" she snapped. "I feel old enough as it is without middle-aged men calling me 'ma'am'! And yes, I usually do try to sneak a couple of extra hours sleep on weekends. But there's been a serious new development. In *Thunder*. It affects you. And I thought you should know about that, you being the headman at *BIAS*. And because of where you are and where you're headed, The President is asking you to make a pickup. He's spending a couple of days at Camp David, by the way."

Jim Kehoe, President of the U. S., was somewhat notorious for avoiding the posh vacation spots many of his predecessors seemed to favor-— Martha's Vineyard, Newport, Palm Beach, and the like. When he wanted to get out of Washington he had Marine One haul his ass out to Camp David. It was beautiful, quiet and way off the skyline.

"Uh oh," I said. "Pickup? I'm not sure I like the sound of that. Remember, I went on this cruise to get a little R and R."

I didn't tell her that I felt a silent thrill of something inside me awakening.

"I know, I know. This shouldn't be all that rough. More like quick and easy, Alan."

I wasn't sure I believed her. But what the hell. A task was a task. A mission was a mission. Hence my little frisson of excitement.

"Okay, Michelle. Lay it on me," I said.

"I don't have a lot of details. What President Kehoe needs you to do is pick up a document in Saint Petersburg. A port that *Nordschiff* is scheduled to visit. It's a super critical, extremely sensitive piece of paper that can't be transmitted through standard Russia-USA channels."

"Good Lord," I mumbled. "What are the details?"

"Well, as I said, it's *Thunder*-related. I really don't know anything else," she said. "I'm informed that you'll get more detailed instructions between now and your arrival in Saint Petersburg."

"That's it?" I asked. "I'm starting to get those 'drop through the wormhole' feelings. Like I'm tumbling into a parallel universe! And I don't want to spend my vacation days crawling through the sewers of Saint Petersburg"

"I know it's a bit on the surreal side," she said. "*Cheetah* knows that, too. And I'm pretty sure you won't have to visit any sewers."

"Surreal? No kidding. But I guess I'll take it one day at a time. Any idea where or when I'll be contacted?"

"None. The ball's in the Russians' court. I suggest you enjoy the cruise with Maria and Elizabeth and her friend and see what happens."

"Okay, Michelle. That's what I'll do. Anything else?" I asked.

"Nope. That's it."

"Mission orders. That's what I like. No micromanaging."

"Do I detect a tiny note of sarcasm in your voice?" she asked.

"No ma'am! You know me better than that."

"I know I do. That's why I asked the question. And don't call me 'ma'am'!"

"Sorry, Michelle. Bye and stay well."

Petty Officer Rantz walked me out to the Expedition and then rode with me back to the Grosvenor House. For some reason, the dull, achy glumness I'd been feeling for the past several weeks seemed to have dissipated. I felt curiously upbeat and invigorated, especially for someone who'd just stayed up all night. I joshed and flirted harmlessly with Petty Officer Rantz all the way back to the hotel.

It was high noon when Rantz dropped me at Grosvenor House. I went up to Room Four Twenty and used the key card. The room was dark. I could see a female shape racked out in the gloom. I sneaked into the room and traded my passport for my Kindle Fire and sneaked back out, closing the door silently. The woman in my life was trading food for sleep. My guess was that our daughter and her best buddy were doing the same thing in the adjacent stateroom. I listened at their door for a few seconds and heard nothing but silence. I guess that teenage girls didn't snore. I decided to take the opposite tack and trade food for sleep. I went back downstairs, ordered a steak sandwich, a salad and a bottle of Stella. And even though I was in the middle of London, the beer was nice and cold.

Chapter Forty-Eight
Alan

The North Sea
Early June

The same cute Danish girl with the short blond hair and the slight Nordic accent herded us *Nordschiff* passengers onto what could have been the same short bus that we'd taken from Heathrow. After several minutes of stop-and-go driving through the traffic of downtown London, the bus ramped up and we headed south on a major highway. All four of us feasted our eyes on what we could see of England's lush countryside. Green, rolling hills, the occasional dairy cattle or sheep farm, farmhouses and villages. And an interesting mixture of English and metric measurement systems on the road signs. Interesting to an ex-math teacher like me, at least. "Speed limit 60 mph" on one sign and "Dover - 40 Km" on another. We arrived at Dover two hours after leaving the hotel. *Nordschiff* was ready for us. We boarded and were photographed. We collected room keys—magnetic cards that showed our photos, names, and stateroom number and allowed us to charge drinks, refreshments and services. Not to mention re-boarding the ship at ports of call. When we got to our staterooms, our bags were already there.

I flopped into a chair. At that point, I didn't care what happened. I hadn't got any messages from any Russians. I just wanted *Nordschiff* to let go her lines, get underway and start steaming northeast.

Maria, always efficient, quickly unpacked and stowed clothes in a dresser and a closet. Elizabeth and Esmé took their luggage into their interior stateroom across the passageway. I watched the goings on in a semi-daze.

We heard multiple deep-throated blasts from the ship's whistle.

"Attention *Nordschiff* passengers," a slightly accented baritone voice blared over the intercom. "We will be getting underway in fifteen minutes. In thirty-five minutes, passengers will be asked to report to your lifeboat stations which are posted on the inside of your stateroom doors."

Seconds later, Elizabeth popped her head into our room. "Let's go see the white cliffs of Dover!" she said excitedly.

Even though I was whipsawed, I couldn't resist the lure of the white cliffs or our daughter's enthusiasm. All four of us went to the Promenade Deck and watched as lines were retrieved and the big ship moved sideways as if by magic away from the pier. Back in my good old Navy days, the gray ships—frigates, destroyers and cruisers—didn't have the benefit of thrusters that could move the ship sideways. Sneaking away from a pier or snuggling close to one depended on the skills of the Officer of the Deck, the helmsman and the lee helmsman. Not to mention the snipes in the engine room. Or the tides and currents. But enough of the old fart reminiscences. We got away from the pier quickly and smoothly.

Minutes later, I snapped a digital picture of the grinning women with the white cliffs of Dover looming behind them like a row of giant, almost-white teeth.

We made it through the lifeboat drill and returned to our staterooms. I unpacked my bag and found space for my clothes. The four of us sat and hung out for about an hour and then wandered up to the Explorers' Lounge, a cocktail lounge *cum* library with nice big windows. We could see a narrow strip of bluish land sliding by on the port side horizon. It must have been England or Scotland. A string quartet of pretty young women was playing Haydn stuff. The women wielded two violins, a viola and a cello. I noticed that their sheet music was on iPads, rather than on paper. I ordered drinks—apple juice for the girls, pinot grigio for Maria and a Bombay Sapphire martini *pour moi*.

"What's 'pinot grigio' Mr. El?" Esmé asked.

"It's a dry, slightly fruity Italian white wine," I said.

"Since we're outside the United States, why don't I try a glass of that?" she asked looking innocent and impish at the same time.

"Try me again in about seven years," I said.

Esmé wrinkled her nose.

Our waitress was an attractive young woman named Tamara, according to her nametag. She was quite personable. When I ordered a second round, I asked her about the musicians who had continued to play and play very well.

"They're Russian," she said. "Most of this crew—other than the officers and sailors—are Filipino. I am. The officers are Danish. My husband, Eduardo, is a chef on the Lido deck. He's Filipino, too. But the bands are always from Central Europe. Poland, Hungary or Russia. These girls are Russian."

"Interesting," I said. "They're very good."

"I think they've spent most of their lives studying music," she said.

The women played. Extremely well. They were dressed identically in black dresses with minimal gold trim. Three of the four of them had rather long, caramel-colored hair; the fourth had jet-black hair cascading over her shoulders. Their features were exquisite. As was their music. I wondered if young women had to be beautiful to get into music schools in Russia.

After around forty minutes, we made our way below to the dining room. We enjoyed a meal of lamb chops, roasted potatoes and salad. Our dining companions were a Canadian couple from Ottawa named Scott. They were delightful. The woman, Priscilla, taught English literature at a private girls' prep school in Ottawa. Her husband, Charles, was a banker. We enjoyed peach cobbler for dessert and passed on coffee.

The two Llewellyn women and our short fellow traveler were still awake when I gave up and hit the rack. We had a king-sized bed in each of the two staterooms. I hit the port side of our king and fell asleep immediately. The women could have gone to the casino and gambled away the entire family fortune, tiny as it is, and I wouldn't have been any the wiser.

I awoke when a fair amount of sunlight boomed under the blinds. It was 5:30 am. I pulled on a pair of sweats and laced up Adidas shoes over Nike socks. When I got to the Promenade deck, the sun was well up. There was a bunch of people walking. Their average age must have been between fifty-five and sixty. I joined them and jogged on the outside.

By the time I got back to the stateroom a few minutes before seven, there was a printout of an International New York Times news summary in the little mailbox outside the room. I grabbed it and let myself in. Maria was sitting up on the starboard side of our bed.

"Should we shake for who has the shower first?" I asked.

"I think not," Maria said. "Women have priority."

"But women should be awakened by women, I said. "How 'bout I shower while you wake up the girls." Maria picked up the telephone and punched buttons.

"Breakfast in thirty minutes, girls," she said and hung up the phone. "I'll grab the shower."

So much for patriarchal authority.

"Okay. Just don't use up all the hot water."

I sat down and started reading the news. Allah be praised, there was a crossword puzzle. And a Sudoku for Maria. Life is good.

Today on the cruise schedule was listed as "At sea." Late tomorrow morning we were scheduled to tie up in Copenhagen. Spending today underway with nothing to do suited me just fine.

Meantime, there was breakfast. After showers *et cetera,* the four of us went up to the Lido deck where they had a splendid breakfast buffet. I had smoked salmon and a bagel with creamed cheese, capers, sliced tomatoes, chopped hardboiled eggs and raw purple onion rings, washed down by orange juice and coffee. The girls had French toast--hefty slabs the size of roof shingles unlike the tiny slivers that they had served us on the airplane--along with healthy bunches of sausage links. Maria had tomato juice and tea. Elizabeth and Esmé had milk.

Outside, the day was sunny and the sea was dead calm. *Nordschiff* ploughed through the flat sea with powerful authority.

"What are you going to do today, Dad?" Elizabeth asked.

"Write some," I said. I write young adult novels as an avocation. Have yet to sell any via the traditional publishing route, but did self-publish one with the help of a shipmate who owns a self-publishing outlet. I keep hoping for a call from an interested agent. Meantime I keep plugging away with new stories. They keep my mind active and involved in something other than intelligence work for the President. Plus they're fun, even though the royalty checks are paltry. Especially during these days of eBooks. My most recent royalty check was for seventy-one cents. That's right—zero dollars and seventy-one cents.

"I think I'll take the laptop up to the Explorer's Lounge, get a fancy cup of coffee and pound the keys for a bit. I'll probably walk or jog some more before dinner. What about you guys?" I asked.

The two girls looked at each other for a second. Elizabeth pointed over her shoulder to the pool.

"I think we'll try the pool and the sun. It looks like a beautiful day."

We looked at Maria.

"I'm going to do some easy walking on the Promenade Deck and then find a deck chair and start a new Robert Crais novel. I loaded up ten novels on my Kindle before we left, so I'm really ready for these 'At sea' days," Maria said.

"How 'bout we all meet poolside for lunch?" I suggested. "I think they serve burgers and sandwiches out there by the pool. Noon? If it's too crowded or too cold, we can always come inside."

We went back to the staterooms and then scattered. I wandered up to the Explorer's Lounge, got myself a caramel macchiato with cream and found a place to park my MacBook Pro. I started work on an adventure novel featuring a twelve-year-old girl named Sarah Mansfield. I'd written two other "Sarah stories" in the past year and I felt like the fictional Sarah and I had become good friends of long standing. I placed the start of this story in Bedford Village, New York. It was fun, jumping into the story. Sarah was a smart girl two years younger than Elizabeth. Her mom was a cop. A detective. Every once in a while, Sarah was able to figure out a way to help her mom solve a knotty mystery.

I worked on the story till around eleven-thirty. I trundled the laptop back down to our stateroom, changed into swimming trunks, a Navy t-shirt and flip-flops and headed for the pool. My darling daughter appeared to be asleep on a poolside chaise, clad in a bikini that would have easily fit in my wallet if it were folded up. Esmé sported huge sunglasses and a bikini that was even tinier than Elizabeth's. Of course, she, herself is tinier than Elizabeth. She perched on an adjacent chaise reading from her Kindle. I jumped into the pool and swam a few laps. I saw Maria enter the pool deck and I made for the nearest ladder.

"*Ciao, Bell*a," I said, dripping.

"What do they have for lunch?" she asked, cutting to the chase.

"Hamburgers, hotdogs and pizza," I said. "BLT's, salads and fries as well."

"I'm starving. I'd love a BLT with fries and a Coke."

"Let me see what the sleeping beauties want and we'll join you and I'll order us lunch. I think I need to get in one of the lines. Why don't you find us a table?"

Elizabeth had awakened and was wrapping herself in some sort of *Nordschiff* bathrobe. Esmé closed her Kindle, slipped on a similar robe and followed Elizabeth to the table where Maria was seated. I took orders. We had a pleasant, leisurely lunch in the intense Baltic summer sun as *Nordschiff* powered through the flat sea. Everybody seemed to agree that a post-lunch nap sounded good. I think the last nap I'd taken was when an afternoon parade was cancelled at Annapolis due to thunderstorms and I was a sleep-deprived Midshipman. If I remember correctly, all Midshipmen were sleep-deprived. All the time.

Things picked up after the nap. I went walking on the Promenade Deck starting a little after four. The North Sea skies had turned a bit gray. The sea was no longer dead-flat calm like it had been this morning; there was a little swell running which we could barely feel on *Nordschiff*. But feel it we could. I could see the level of the horizon oscillating slowly up and down beyond the ship's railing. The Promenade deck was marked in kilometers. I walked and jogged seven clicks in just under an hour. A little over four miles.

We arrived at the Explorer's Lounge at the same time the Russian quartet entered, carrying their instruments. This evening, they all wore white long-sleeved blouses and black skirts that came down to just above their knees. They sat down. One of the violinists looked me squarely in the eye for about three seconds and then turned to her iPad. I'd like to think it was because of my drop-dead good looks, but I knew better.

After about fifty-five minutes, they stopped playing and stood up. Break time, I guessed. I ordered a second cocktail from Tamara and then I stood up. I excused myself to the ladies.

"I'm off to the head," I told them.

I entered the Men's' and strode across toward the urinals. I heard the door open behind me and an accented female voice called my name.

"Mistair Loo-vellyn!"

I turned. It was the Russian violinist who had stared at me earlier. She held her violin and bow in one hand.

"We need to talk," she said, in accented English.

"*Here?*" I asked, incredulous.

She was a bit short--around five-one or two--that made her kind of cute. Her facial features were cute as well. There was nothing wrong with her figure or what I could see of her legs, either.

She smiled.

"No. Of course not," she said. "We finish playing for the evening at nine o'clock. I'll meet you on the Promenade Deck aft at nine-fifteen. Come alone. We'll walk and talk. It won't take long."

Then she spun on her heel and left the men's head. I stepped over to the urinals wondering what the hell.

I finished my business in the head and decided not to mention anything about my visit from the female Russian violinist therein to Maria and the girls. At least not here in the Explorer's Lounge. I finished my drink mostly in silence and we went below to dinner. We ended up with the same Canadian couple as the night before. Priscilla, the English teacher, was an avid Jane Austen fan. As was my dearly beloved, Maria. Charles, Priscilla's husband, and I didn't have much of a chance to get words in edgewise. But he did seem to be a nice guy. I was a lifetime Yankees fan. He was an ardent Blue Jays fan and hated the Yankees malevolently. He was still an OK guy.

After dinner, Maria, the two girls and I repaired to our staterooms. It was seven forty-five.

"There's a showing of *Emma* in the theatre, starting at eight," Maria said, continuing with the Jane Austin theme. "The Gwyneth Paltrow version. I'm going to meet Priscilla and watch it."

"We're going too," said Elizabeth. "Unless it's toxically boring. Then we'll go to the casino."

"Arghh," I said. "I don't think Baltic-North will serve you booze until you're twenty-one. I'm not sure about gambling."

"We'll figure things out," she said. "Maybe we'll both love *Emma* and just stay at the movie with Mom."

"Okay. Let me tell you guys what I'm doing. Remember before dinner when I went to the head at the time the string quartet took a break?"

They all nodded.

"Well, one of the Russian violinists followed me into the head. She knew my name. She said I'm to meet her on the Promenade Deck at nine-fifteen. Tonight. To 'walk and talk'. I'm guessing she's a Russian contact that Michelle alluded to when I spoke with her back at the embassy in London."

"Good Lord," Maria said.

"She followed you into the *men's room?*" Elizabeth croaked in disbelief.

"No big deal," I said, even though the gender-neutral bathroom craze hadn't really flared up as yet. But maybe the craze was alive and well in Europe. After all, I could remember visiting a cavernous mens' head in a railroad station in Germany and was mildly astonished when an elderly woman swabbed the deck around my shoes while I was taking a leak. But that was twenty-some odd years ago.

"And I'm not particularly worried. The sun is still up at nine-fifteen at this latitude. And she's kind of small. I don't think she'll try and throw my ass over the side."

I noticed that Elizabeth's eyes had widened even more as I related all this to Maria.

"Dad," she said.

"Yes, sweetheart," I said.

"I've got an idea. Esmé and I can sneak on to the Promenade Deck a little before nine-fifteen. We can hide inside the doors for the after stairwell. Then, we'll follow you at a safe distance. If the Russian chick tries to throw you overboard, we can run up and kick her butt."

I laughed.

"Not a bad idea," I said. "I think both of you are bigger than the Russian violinist. Even Esmé. You should be able to kick her butt easily. And if all she and I do is walk and talk as I expect, you can follow quietly at a safe distance. Keep an eye on us in case things suddenly go south."

I was thinking that this strategy would keep the two girls out of the casino and away from lowlifes who might want to buy them booze and bankroll a few turns of the roulette wheel. And whatever else lowlifes might have in mind for teenage girls in the casino. At least for a while.

I looked at my watch.

"It's nearly eight," I said. "If you two want to catch *Emma*, you'd better head up to the theater now."

They did.

I sat down to read. Till ten after nine.

I walked up the ladder to the Promenade Deck and stepped outside. It was only about thirty meters to the aftermost part of the deck. The sun was fairly low and behind us, turning *Nordschiff*'s wake into a golden flame. The air was pleasantly fresh and salty. I walked aft and leaned against the railing, facing forward. Less than a minute later, a figure I recognized emerged from one of the after starboard doors.

"Good evening, Mr. Llewellyn. Again," she said.

"Good evening," I said. "But I don't know your name."

"I'm Veronika," she said, holding out her hand.

We shook.

"Call me Alan," I said.

"Shall we walk?" she asked. "Our contract with Baltic-North stipulates that we are not permitted to interact with the passengers. Except with our music. So we have to make this quick. Or I'll get in trouble."

"Okay, Veronika. Let's walk. You talk."

"In Saint Petersburg, *Nordschiff* offers a waterborne tour of the city on both days that you'll be there. Sunday and Monday morning. You will need to sign up for one of those tours. It does not matter which. Before your tour, you'll also need to buy some rubles. Probably about two thousand, five hundred rubles. That's about forty dollars, U. S. You can do that on board any time after we tie up in Tallinn. I'm told that the U. S. Government will reimburse you for the rubles. The Russian bankers will come aboard Nordschiff in Tallinn to trade currency.

"In Saint Petersburg, the last stop on the tour of the city is a gift shop. In the gift shop, you'll find a salesgirl named Natasha. Or, more probably, she'll find you. She'll be wearing a nametag so you'll recognize her easily. You'll ask her for a copy of the book *The Poems of Anna Akhmatova*. It costs about twelve hundred rubles. You'll tell her 'I'll pay cash. In rubles,' and she'll fetch you a copy of the book. You pay her and that's that. When you go through Russian customs to get back on board *Nordschiff*, you can tell them that you bought the book and show it to the customs inspector. It'll be in a plastic gift shop bag with a legitimate receipt."

"I've got it, Veronika," I said. "Water tour. Gift shop. Natasha. *Poems of Anna Akhmatova.* Cash. Rubles. But I do have a question."

"Yes?"

"How does a book of poetry convert to a document?"

"I've no idea. The book contains a little more than three dozen poems. On the left-hand pages, the verses are in Russian. On the facing pages, there is the same poem translated into English. My guess is that one or more of the English versions contains the encoded document, but I'm not sure," she said. "For all I know, it could be the Russian versions, but I really have no idea."

"Okay. I'm sure that whoever collects the book will know how to figure it out."

"There will also be a piece of paper in the book with a lot of numbers on it," she added.

"Makes sense," I said. "Especially if they're using the book as a code."

"Good night, Mr. Llewellyn."

"Good night, Veronika," I said, pronouncing her name the Russian way.

Vair-own-EE-kah.

She disappeared through the forward ladder well doors and I continued on around the Promenade Deck. Glancing over my shoulder, I saw two slender young women about forty meters aft. One tall, the other short. Elizabeth and Esmé. It was good and fun to know that I was in capable hands. I headed around the bow and back aft toward our stateroom. I made my way to the doors to the ladder well leading to our room and then to the stateroom. The two girls showed up at the door a couple of minutes after I let myself in. They were giggling as I let them into the stateroom.

"Isn't she a little young for you, Dad?" my smart-assed daughter asked. Esmé continued to chortle quietly.

"If you must know, she had a message. That I was expecting," I said. "Official business."

"Can we go to the casino, Dad?" Elizabeth asked. "The movie was pretty boring."

I looked at my watch.

"It's just about over, anyway, I think," I said. "The movie."

"All the more reason to go to the casino," she said.

"As long as you don't lose more than twenty bucks and are back here by ten-thirty. And don't let any dirt bags buy you booze."

"Ten thirty?" she yelped. "That's only an hour away!"

"You're right," I said. "Spot on. See you in an hour."

She snorted and the two girls stamped out of the room.

I settled in with my book and ten minutes later Maria was letting herself in with her key card.

"I *love* that movie," she said. "Paltrow is absolutely fantastic! Did you make your connection?"

"I did," I said, holding a forefinger to my lips.

"Where's Elizabeth?" she asked, skillfully changing the subject.

"Up in the casino. With Esmé," I said. "At least I assume she's with Esmé. I feel better when I know that the two of them are together."

"Did you give them a curfew?" Maria asked.

"Yes," I said. "They should be back here in about forty minutes."

Chapter Forty-Nine
Alan

The North Sea
Early June

Elizabeth and Esmé knocked on our stateroom door at ten-thirty on the dot. Maria opened the door.

"You'll be glad to know," Elizabeth announced. "I won twenty-five Euros. On the slot machines. Esmé won twenty."

"Did any dirt bags try to buy you girls booze?" I asked.

"One guy offered to buy us 'a drink'. We drank Diet Cokes," she said. "But he wasn't a dirt bag. He was nice, clean-cut and spoke with a slight accent. He asked me to blow on his dice, but I said 'no'."

"How old was this maggot?" I asked.

"I'm not sure. Mid-twenties, maybe."

I began pondering putting the casino off limits to the girls when *Nordschiff's* incredibly loud whistle blasted a deafening total of six times. Then, all three of us felt the deck tilt as the big ship turned sharply to starboard.

All three women looked at me.

"If memory serves, six blasts of the ship's whistle meant that someone had gone overboard. If I remember correctly, that's a U. S Navy Man Overboard distress code meaning the same thing for all ships. *Man Overboard*. I don't know for sure. But I'm guessing that someone has gone over the side of *Nordschiff* and we are now trying to go back and find the poor bastard. Someone must have seen it happen and reported it. I'm guessing that whoever went overboard went off the starboard side and that's why the ship turned to starboard."

I pointed with my thumb out the window. Our stateroom was on the starboard side.

"To swing the screws—er, propellers--away from the poor blighter in the water," I continued. "That's kind of standard procedure. As is the turn back to port to head back to where the man overboard should be. That's what we're starting to feel now."

"Good Lord!" Maria said. "Who would fall over the side of a Baltic North Lines cruise ship in the North Sea at ten-thirty at night?"

"My guess is someone who had sucked in too much booze," I said. "I'm guessing that's the usual narrative on cruise ships."

"So someone gets drunk and then dives over the side?" Elizabeth asked, an expression of disbelief on her face.

"I don't know, sweetheart. Could be. My guess is that someone had too many drinks and then tried to sit on a rail, maybe take a selfie, and fell overboard. But I don't know. Maybe they were trying to do a photo of a *Titanic* scene or whatever. Once, in the South China Sea, we had a Marine deliberately jump into the ocean off U.S.S. Iwo Jima. He was severely depressed. The good news is that it was broad daylight and we got him back. But we'll probably never know about this incident."

I stood up.

"I think I'll go topside and see if I can see anything," I said.

"I'll go with you, Dad," Elizabeth said.

"Me, too. If it's okay," Esmé added.

Maria said, "I'll depend on the three of you for a report. I'm exhausted. I'm going to crawl into bed and read for a few minutes. If I'm asleep when you come back, save it for the morning."

The two girls and I went up, the two of them in the lead and the Old Man following, to the Promenade Deck. We walked forward. There were a couple of dozen people clustered up there. Powerful searchlights shone down on the surface of the sea from the area of *Nordschiff's* bridge. A lifeboat with four crewmembers was zigzagging in the ocean slowly off the port bow. They had a strong, hand-held light shining onto the surface. One of the sailors had a handheld radio. Another sailor held a life ring. I could hear traces of voices, both from the handheld and from the ship. They were obviously looking for someone who had gone into the sea. *Nordschiff* had hove to. The big ship was dead in the water.

"They're looking for someone. Who must have gone overboard," I said.

"That's horrible," Elizabeth said, squeezing my hand. "Here, in the North Sea. In the dark. What time is it, anyway?"

I punched the night light on my watch.

"Ten fifty-seven," I said.

"Yikes," Elizabeth said. "I doubt they'll ever find the poor soul."

The last time I'd heard someone use the expression "poor soul" was when my grandmother used it about thirty years ago at a friend's funeral. I wondered if expressions like that were passed through Welsh genes.

We watched and waited for a half hour, holding hands the whole time. Then the lifeboat came back to *Nordschiff* and hooked up. Most of the searchlights shut down. The lifeboat started to rise.

"I guess they're giving up the search," I said.

I think Elizabeth gave a little sob. I know she squeezed my hand again. Harder, this time.

"Sorry you had to experience this, ladies," I said, inadequately. I held the hands of both of them.

"Sorry for you, too, Dad," Elizabeth said, sniffling. "This was supposed to be a fun, relaxing cruise for you."

Chapter Fifty

Alan

Copenhagen
Early June

We were at breakfast in the cafeteria up on the Lido Deck at about eight-forty the next morning. I'd treated myself to bacon and scrambled eggs, liberally dosed with Tabasco, with a side of a buttered English muffin with orange marmalade on top. Plus OJ and coffee. The women went for pancakes and sausage. Maria and Esmé had OJ and tea and Elizabeth had apple juice. Elizabeth had related what we had seen last night from the Promenade Deck to her mom down below in our stateroom as we were getting dressed. We were about ten minutes into noshing our breakfast when an announcement with a faint Danish accent came over the PA system.

"Attention *Nordschiff* passengers. Our arrival in Copenhagen is delayed thirty minutes. Our arrival time at the pier will now be eleven-thirty a.m. Tour companies have been advised. We had a delay in our transit from Dover last night of a little over an hour and we've been able to make up over half that. Our departure time from Copenhagen remains at seven pm this evening."

We Llewellyns and Esmé had signed up for a bus tour of Copenhagen that included a lunch stop in Tivoli Gardens. We found our tour bus at eleven forty-five. We made several stops and were amazed at how many Danes were getting around their capital city on bicycles, even though the weather was drizzly and the vehicular traffic was pretty heavy. I took a few pictures, some with one or the other of the three beautiful women, some with all three, and all with some sort of picturesque Scandinavian buildings in the background. Elizabeth took probably ten times as many pics as I did. We both took pictures of the Little Mermaid statue. At lunch, we all had Danish open-faced sandwiches that were to die for. The young ladies washed their sandwiches down with Coke, which cost almost as much as the sandwiches. Maria had mineral water that cost close to the tab for my bottle of beer. We got back to the ship at five-thirty, took our time getting cleaned up and went to the Explorers' Lounge at about six-fifteen. There was no chamber music, no string quartet. Only a broadcast

171

CD of Antillean Dances by Wim Statius Muller.

I thought that Tamara looked a bit stricken as she took our drink orders.

When she returned with the drinks, I asked, "Are the Russian girls ashore in Copenhagen?"

She bent over and whispered, "Haven't you heard?"

"Heard what?" I asked, stupidly.

"One of them fell overboard last night. The ship launched a boat and tried to find her, but couldn't. The other girls are not playing tonight."

"Mother of God," Maria whispered. Elizabeth just gasped. Esmé pursed her lips.

"Do they know any details?" I asked.

"They may but I don't," Tamara answered. "The rumor is that a passenger saw her from his balcony as she fell and reported the emergency to the bridge. There were Danish police and Danish Navy officers as well as German Navy personnel on board all day. Also some Russians from their embassy in Copenhagen. Supposedly, Royal Danish Air Force helicopters and Naval surface units were to start searching again at dawn. But the sea temperature is around fifteen degrees. She certainly couldn't survive all night in the ocean."

"Good Lord," I said. "That's about sixty degrees Fahrenheit. We heard the ship's whistle a few minutes after ten-thirty. The girls and I went up to the Promenade Deck and saw the boat in the water and the lights and figured someone had gone overboard. But we had no idea it was one of the Russian girls."

I wondered if it was Veronika.

"Do you know which of the girls it was?" I asked.

"They say it was the one called 'Ronny'," Tamara said. "One of the two violin players."

"Good Lord," I repeated. "That sounds like it could be a nickname for Veronika—the girl I spoke with about an hour and a half before we heard the 'man overboard' whistle."

"I think it must have been her. One of the Filipina girls said she'd heard her name was Veronika. Even though everyone called her Ronny."

Imelda straightened up and darted off to wait on another table. I took a deep pull at my drink. So far, this Baltic cruise wasn't really easing my PTSD. Not an iota. It wasn't a joy ride for my girls, either. Both Elizabeth and Esmé looked like they were in a state of shock. I made a decision.

"Let's go down to the Promenade Deck and stop there and talk outside for a few minutes. Then we'll go below for dinner. What say?"

The women stood up. We rode the elevator to the Promenade Deck. The sky was cloudy but it was still broad daylight. The drizzle had stopped. Guys were scurrying around on the pier. *Nordschiff* was making preparations for getting underway.

"Okay, here's what Michelle Hookes told me in London. And it's not for sharing. That's why I had to go in to the embassy to take the call. And why we're having this chat outside now. It's highly classified. There *is* a strong Russian connection. Somehow, the Russians seem to have learned of a coup attempt by members of the U.S. Government against President Kehoe and have informed Kehoe. He-Kehoe-tasked us—*BIAS*—to smoke out whatever details we could. We have mined a few morsels. Now, the White House is expecting a document from the Russians. About which I know next to nothing—other than it has to do with this coup attempt. And it can't be sent through 'normal channels,' whatever the hell that means. Some info is flowing in from the Russians. They want to pass something to the President. And it looks like I'm the conduit. Next move is up to the Russians. And the Russians just made their move. With that violinist last night. She and I talked for a couple of minutes yesterday evening. You guys must have seen us," I said, nodding toward Elizabeth and Esmé. They nodded back.

"Her name is—or was—Veronika. She told me to pick up a book in a gift shop in Saint Petersburg. The gift shop is part of a city tour sponsored by the ship. From a saleswoman named Natasha. That conversation was finished by about nine-twenty or so last night. Then, a little after ten-thirty, she—Veronika—apparently went over the side. When I spoke with her yesterday evening, she was neither under the influence of alcohol nor did she seem the least bit upset or depressed, much less suicidal. Ergo, I'm guessing she was pushed or thrown over the side. To her death. My guess is that her death has something to do with her contact with me."

"Does that mean we're in danger?" Maria asked.

"Possibly. Possibly," I said. "I think it would be good for us—the Llewellyns plus Esmé—to stick together. All the time. Yesterday, we went our separate ways—one to a deck chair, two girls to the pool, me to the Explorer's Lounge. Then last night, we split up again after dinner. From now on, let's stay together. We can take turns picking what to do and where to do it. But whatever we decide, we'll do it together. Plus, whenever we're in our staterooms, we need to be locked in."

All three women seemed to agree with that. Of the three, Esmé was the only one who looked excited in a positive way. I could swear that I saw a faint hint of a grin lurking in her eyes and at the corners of her mouth. We went to the dining room and joined Priscilla and John for dinner.

Nordschiff got underway as our waiter served the entree, veal cutlets that we could—and did--cut with our forks. Elizabeth and Esmé had their heads together. I spoke up to John and Priscilla Scott.

"Have you heard the rumor? About someone falling overboard?" I asked.

"We have not, but we were wondering," John said. "We heard the ship's horn blasting away last night and felt her making a couple of sharp turns. I thought that maybe another vessel had gotten in our way. And *Nordschiff* was swerving to avoid a collision. Today, we were ashore all day in Copenhagen. And heard nothing about anyone going overboard. We just got back on board an hour ago."

"Any idea who went overboard?" Priscilla asked.

"A waitress in the Explorers' Lounge said it was one of the Russian girls in the string quartet that usually plays there in the evenings," I said carefully. "They weren't playing this evening," I added.

"Good Lord! The poor thing. That's horrible, if it's true," Priscilla observed.

"As of now, the part about the Russian musician is only a mess-deck rumor. But we're pretty sure *someone* went overboard. After hearing the ship's whistle, Elizabeth, Esmé and I went topside. The ship had hove to and had searchlights on and a boat in the water. They definitely seemed to be looking for someone."

Chapter Fifty-One

Alan

Berlin
Early June

Nordschiff was scheduled to arrive at Warnemünde, Germany at 5:45 am. We had arranged to go on an all-day tour of Berlin and had to be on the pier at seven for a quick bus transfer to Rostock. There, we'd board a train for the two-and-a-half hour train trip to Berlin. On the Lido Deck, they'd start serving breakfast at six. I could get out of the rack at five fifty-five and make it to breakfast at six; the ladies needed a bit more prep time. So we went to our staterooms, read for a while and zonked out pretty early. At least Maria and I did. I put in a wake-up call for five-fifteen.

I didn't have the best sleep of my life, to say the least. Since arriving in London, I'd been sleeping pretty well. But tonight, my mind was racing. If Veronika got pushed or thrown over the side an hour after talking to me, that was very damned unsettling. It probably meant that there was someone aboard *Nordschiff* who didn't want me to complete my mission. Such as it was. And was willing to kill a Russian girl to prevent it. Or at least delay it.

I had a second cup of coffee at our early breakfast in the hope that it would dispel the grogginess caused by a restless night.

On the train from Rostock to Berlin, I had a pleasant surprise. The trip was entirely within the former German Democratic Republic or what used to be called Communist East Germany. I guess I'd expected wall-to-wall blast furnaces and dumpy communist apartments. Was I ever wrong! We traveled through lush farmland, populated with well-fed cattle. The rich, green pastureland was punctuated with occasional villages and the frequent green tracts of forest.

We arrived in Berlin a little before ten. Our bus tour of the city was somewhat rushed but well done. We saw Checkpoint Charlie, remnants of the Berlin Wall and Humboldt University of Berlin, which my mom's father attended. We stopped at the Brandenburg Gate, crowded with tourists in the summer sunshine. Took a bunch of pictures. An early afternoon lunch and additional sightseeing on our own followed the morning bus tour. I thought I'd use at least some of that free time to make contact with my buddies at *BIAS*.

My chance to contact *BIAS* seemed to appear after lunch. It was a little after two. We'd had lunch at—of all places—a pizza joint, called *"12 Apostel."* And the pizza was good! Not quite New York good, but close. After we left, we walked to the Holocaust Memorial, a somber, sprawling cluster of gray, granite rectangular prisms of varying sizes, ranging from as small as a child's coffin to the size of a small graveyard chapel. It was deathly quiet. I think I could see the back of the American Embassy from where I sat. I thought about going there and trying to make a secure phonecall to *Cheetah*, but that would probably attract God knows how much unwanted attention and take too much time as well. We were due back at the bus in less than an hour. I pushed buttons on my phone for Darps' mobile.

"Yo, Shipmate," he said.

"Hey," I said. "Did anybody up the road clue you into our latest little adventure? Over here?"

"Yeah. Michelle called and sort of explained. It sounded very what-iffy."

"Well it's not what-iffy any more. Two nights ago, the guys from the other side made contact. Actually, it was a girl, a Russian. With instructions. For me to pick up a document in Saint Petersburg. An hour or so after she talked to me, she went over the side of the ship. Out in the middle of the North Sea.

"My guess is that it was no accident. There could be a connection between her message to me and her so-called accident. The ship made a rescue attempt but they never found her. I suppose it could have been a coincidence, but you know what I think about coincidences," I said.

"Christ on a bike," Darps muttered. "I'll get word up the road and I'm sure somebody—either from there or from here—will get back to you if there's any change or mid-course corrections."

"Okay, Shipmate. We get underway for Tallinn at twenty-one-hundred tonight. We tie up there at zero-seven-hundred tomorrow morning. It's fourteen-hundred here now. Cell phone service may be spotty."

"I'm sure, between here and up the road, we'll be able to reach you if we need to. One way or the other. Stay safe."

We rang off.

Chapter Fifty-One
The DNI

Roberto Ironsides's mobile phone buzzed. Caller ID revealed it was Braxton, the DNI. Ironsides picked up immediately.

"Hi, Sam. What's up?"

"Things are starting to blow up. We need to execute the plan very soon, if not immediately."

"Can you tell me more?"

"No, not now. But we need to meet off-line. Soonest."

"Okay," Ironsides said. "Where are you now?"

"At my office. I can be at your place in forty-five minutes."

"I'm thinking that we should meet somewhere other than my office," Ironsides observed.

"Yeah. You've got that right," Braxton answered. "There's a high school near your office. North Stafford High School. Just a mile or so east of your building. It's Sunday. There shouldn't be anyone there. Maybe a couple of teachers, but they'll be indoors and won't see us. Let's meet behind the school building in fifty minutes. At two fifteen. I'll be driving my Volvo."

"Okay. Roger that," said Ironsides. "See you in five-zero minutes."

He grazed through a stack of email for the next thirty minutes, and then stood up.

"I'm going out for a quick meet, Sarah," Ironsides told his secretary. Sarah was wearing cargo shorts, flip-flops and a red tank top in honor of Sunday. Her overtime was pretty robust as was her figure in the tank top. "I should be back in less than an hour." Ironsides said. "I'll call if it's gonna be longer."

He left, climbed into his Honda Pilot and headed east on Route six-ten. He turned into the deserted North Stafford campus, pulled around to the rear of the school building and spotted Braxton's blue Volvo immediately. He drove to it and parked alongside. Braxton climbed out immediately, jerked open the passenger door of Ironsides' Honda and sat down.

"I think we have a major fucking problem staring us in the face," he said.

"The Russians?" Ironsides asked.

"Bigger. And closer to home."

"Uh oh. That sounds bad," Ironsides responded. "Donegan?"

"It is. It's Donegan. I think she's on the verge of spilling her guts about the whole plan."

"Holy Christ. What makes you think that?"

"A bunch of things. She's a bit squirrely about the shooting attempt on Llewellyn. She's more than a bit squirrely about publicly trying Kehoe and Girtler for treason. She's showing signs of instability. I'm afraid she may be ready to bolt.

"Also, for what it's worth, NSA has picked up a couple of phonecons between her and her brother, a Navy Lieutenant Commander. She hasn't spoken with him for nearly three years but spoke with him twice in the last week."

"Okay. That's it. She has to go. I'll get Steve and his shooters to take her out. They should have all their 'homework' done by now."

"And no fiddle fucking around like you did with Llewellyn. This job needs a rifle. A kill shot. One shot and done."

"Okay. What kind of timelines are we talking about?" asked Ironsides.

"ASAP," Braxton. "As soon as you can make it happen. She needs to be taken down. Soonest."

"Okay. It'll probably take several days." Ironsides glanced at his wristwatch. "No more than three to five unless she leaves town."

"Soonest," Braxton said, again.

Chapter Fifty-Two

Alan

Berlin

Early June

"Stay safe," Darps's words echoed in my brain for a few seconds as I watched Maria and the two girls turn around and head back toward me.

"Hi again, ladies. I think we should head for the bus," I said.

"That's what we thought," Elizabeth said.

I think all four of us took a few seconds to look over the acres of the massive, gray stone blocks commemorating the Holocaust. In Berlin. In silence. Solemn silence.

Then we headed for the bus.

We were nearly there and had the bus in view when I spotted a thirty-ish man approaching us. He had nearly white blond hair, wore a green polo shirt, khakis, and white jogging shoes. He carried a walking stick, but he wasn't much more than thirty and he wasn't limping.

"Move over—to the right!" I hissed, pushing my wife's left shoulder to the right into our daughter and her girlfriend. I lurched to the left as the blond-haired guy jabbed at my knee with his cane. He missed. I let him have it with a left hook to the ear that staggered him.

"*Sukin sin!*" he hissed in Russian. "Son of a bitch!"

He poked ineffectually at my right leg with the cane and I spun around and let him have it again, this time with a right to the mouth. He went down, bleeding and dropping his stick. Drops of clear liquid dripped from the tip of the cane, which looked like it had a skinny basketball needle protruding from the end of its tapered wooden tip.

I looked up. Mercifully, the Llewellyn women and Esmé were fine and almost to our bus. I followed them to the bus and got on behind them, pushing Maria in the ass. Jakob, our German-Jewish tour guide looked at me, wide-eyed.

"Jakob," I said. "I think that guy on the sidewalk is a Russian. And I think he tried to poison me with that fucking walking cane. He was trying to

179

stab me in the knee."

Jakop did a quick, eyeball headcount of the bus and then, to his credit, gave instructions to the driver and our bus pulled away from the curb. I could see that the blond Russian was sitting up on the sidewalk behind us. Jakob was chattering into his cell phone in German. My German is pretty rudimentary, but I would have understood my own name if I'd heard it. Thanks be to God, I had not.

Fifteen minutes later, we were on the train. Three minutes after boarding, the train was sliding and clacking through the suburbs of Berlin and out into the countryside. And I started to relax. A little.

"Alan, what the hell was all that about?" Maria asked, in a semi-whisper.

"I don't know, Sweetheart. I don't understand anything about what's going on here. But I think that bastard was trying to poison me," I said. "Somebody doesn't want me to get the Russian stuff and deliver it to the White House. Poor Veronika got tossed over the side of the *Nordschiff* for trying to facilitate that. Then, the bastards—whoever they are--tried to jab me in the knee with a poison-tipped cane."

"Good Lord," she whispered. "Are you sure?"

"Honey, at this point I'm not sure of anything. But that blond-haired prick sure as hell looked like he was trying to jab my knee or thigh with his cane. The cane had a needle tip. He called me a son of a bitch in Russian after I hit him. And I don't think I was imagining the drops of liquid leaking from the tip of the cane after he dropped it."

The more I thought about things, the worse it got. I had no idea who the hell the evildoers were, but whoever they were, they had "assets"--i.e., dirt-bag thugs—on board *Nordschiff*—which they'd apparently used to pitch Veronika overboard. They also had assets in Berlin--the white-haired blond guy who tried to stab me with the poison cane. In a few hours time, we'd be steaming for Tallinn and after that, Saint Petersburg. If the bad guys were in fact Russians, then their numbers were about to rise and then spike. Which was bad news for us. But that didn't really make sense. If the Russians were trying to communicate sensitive stuff to the highest levels of the U. S. Government, why the hell would other Russians try to prevent that from happening? Obviously, I didn't know enough to understand the game plan. One thing I did know. There wasn't any place where we could assume we'd be out of harm's way--not here on the train, not on board *Nordschiff*, and not in Tallinn. And certainly not in Saint Petersburg.

We were back on board *Nordschiff* by about six-thirty, feeling a bit bushed and bedraggled. We went to the staterooms to freshen up.

I reminded the girls to make sure to lock their door and immediately locked ours.

"I think we've been pretty good about keeping these doors locked most of the time. Let's make sure they're locked whenever one or more of us is in here—always," I said. "And I think we need to stay with the 'stick together rule' pretty much all the time, too," I added.

Suddenly, there was a double knock at the door, which startled both of us.

"Mister Llewellyn, I'm Captain Hans Bergkamp, *Nordschiff*'s Executive Officer. We need to talk," a lightly Danish accented voice said through the door.

I looked through the spy hole. I saw a tall guy with a white shirt and navy-blue epaulettes with four gold stripes. He had blond hair streaked with a bit of gray and sparkling blue eyes. He was clean-shaven. I opened the door.

"Yes, sir," I said. All those years of wearing the blue suit still had their lasting effect.

"Would you be so kind as to accompany me to the ship's communications center, Mister Llewellyn?" he asked. "There is a special message for you that we're not at liberty to carry through the ship."

"Yes sir," I said. "Do you have any idea how long this will take?"

"Not long," he said. "Probably no more than five or ten minutes or so."

"Okay," I said, realizing I was breaking our family stick-together rule. I turned toward Maria.

"I'm going to the comm center with the captain," I said. "I should be back in ten minutes or so. Make sure to lock up."

I stepped outside and closed the door.

The Danish Officer said, "I'm sorry to bother you with this, but it seems there is a special communiqué from Washington for you. It came through Copenhagen to us. Via the Danish Navy."

We shook hands.

"I'm Alan Llewellyn, sir. I was a Lieutenant Commander in the United States Navy, once upon a time. Now I'm a civilian research guy on vacation."

"Okay, Mr. Llewellyn. The communications center is up four levels. Just follow me."

I followed the Danish officer to an elevator. We raced up and the Captain led me off the lift, through a short passageway and into a darkened compartment, not unlike the comm center on a U. S. warship. There were several people in front of computer monitors and two men wearing headsets. I couldn't tell if they were sailors or civilians. An officer with three stripes on her shoulder boards seemed to be in charge.

A brief exchange in Danish ensued.

"Okay, Mr. Llewellyn. Have a seat at this table, please. Here is the message for you."

Captain Bergkamp held out a chair. I sat. The three-striper handed me a folder. I took it.

I opened the folder.

TOP SECRET FOR BIAS/ALAN LLEWELLYN/OB DANISH MS NORDSCHIFF.

RPV ON TRACK YOU AND FAMILY ON BOARD NORDSCHIFF

24/7 COMMENCING 2100Z 05JUN. COMMS AND RECON PKGS ONBOARD AND ACTIVE. INTERFACE YOUR MOBILE 5403548876 ACTIVE.

TOP SECRET

RPV meant, "Remotely piloted vehicle." A drone. 2100Z meant nine P. M., Greenwich Mean Time. Midnight here. 05 June was today. So the drone would be on station at midnight tonight, local time. "Comms" and "recon" no doubt meant communications and reconnaissance capabilities. The drone and my mobile phone were synched. Apparently *BIAS* and the White House were keeping an eye on us.

I stood up.

"Thank you, Captain," I said, handing him the folder. "That helps a lot."

"You're welcome, Mr. Llewellyn," we'll run this through the shredder immediately."

"Thank you again, sir," I said. We shook hands. "I can find my way back."

I knew that Captain Bergkamp had read the message. As had the Commander in charge of the *Nordschiff*'s comm center. As had the communicator manning the apparatus that the message came in on. And Captain Bergkamp had no doubt informed his boss, the skipper of *Nordschiff*. I had to trust the Danes. I did.

When I got back to our stateroom, it was seven-oh-five p.m. I glanced out the cabin's generous porthole. It was still broad daylight. Busloads of Nordschiff passengers were still returning to the pier from various Berlin tours.

"We've got company," I said to my girlfriend. "Or soon will have. The good kind. A U.S. drone. It'll keep an eye on the ship and enhance communications back to *BIAS*. Starting at midnight tonight. Let's go to the Explorers' Lounge for drinks and then go to dinner."

"Well, I guess that's good news," she said. She reached for the phone to alert the girls.

Chapter Fifty-Three

Alan

The Baltic Sea
Early June

We dined alone that evening. I don't know about our Canadian friends, but the elder Llewellyns were a bit knocked out from a long and busy day even if Elizabeth and Esmé were not. Dinner was chicken cacciatore with mushrooms and fettuccine. Tired as we were, all four of us scarfed up the dinner like starving dogs in a smokehouse. After dinner, we went to the Explorers' Lounge where the ladies had ginger ales and I savored a Remy Martin. The three female Russian string instrumentalists were back, playing Schubert. Veronika was missing, not surprising in light of what we'd heard. The other violinist, definitely red-eyed, looked like she'd been crying.

Before we finished our drinks, we could feel *Nordschiff* start to vibrate slightly and then begin to glide away from the pier. The lights of Warnemünde and Rostock started to slip away. By the time we returned to our staterooms, the ship was well out in the Baltic and the sea was dark. Pitch dark. Despite all the angst of the day, I slept the sleep of the just. According to the women the next morning, they did as well.

Chapter Fifty-Four

Alan

The Baltic Sea
Early June

The next day, Friday, was another "at sea" day. This one made me a bit uneasy. I had little in the way of clues about shit-birds prowling about the decks of *Nordschiff* bent on doing harm to members of the extended Llewellyn family. But I did worry about that eventuality.

"Would you like to join me for a pre-breakfast walk?" I asked Maria at seven-fifteen a.m. "'A turn about the decks', as the Brits might say. See if we can see anything?"

"That would be delightful," she said. "Let me ask the girls. Or should I say 'tell the girls'?"

Surprisingly, they said yes. Cheerily.

By seven-thirty we were off. *Nordschiff* was slicing through a flat blue sea. The sun was well up and it was a bright, clear morning. The sea was calm and smelled salty-good. We could see land off in the distance to port. I guessed it was Sweden. I also wondered about our "friend," the drone. Scanning the Baltic skies, I could see nothing. Not that I should. Too high, too far and too quiet. But I guessed it was out there. I wondered if it was keeping an eye on any on-board dirt bags. My guess was that there was some sort of electronics package that was Hoovering up any and all electronic emissions from *Nordschiff* and its environs. Hopefully including cell phone conversations by the dirt bags. Seven-thirty in the morning here in the eastern Baltic meant it was eleven-thirty last night back in Virginia and DC--probably not a great time for a comm check. I'd try later in the day.

"My stomach is growling," Elizabeth said.

"One more lap," I said.

Elizabeth snorted and Esmé rolled her eyes and we reversed direction and made another circuit of the Promenade Deck. I didn't say anything to Maria and the two girls, but I thought I noticed a guy, right after we changed direction, about fifty meters ahead of us. He darted quickly into a door leading to an inside ladder well. Could have been an innocent

185

morning walker. Or possibly, a mal-intentioned dirt bag. Then we went to the staterooms for showers and then up to the Lido for breakfast.

Maria had tomato juice, raisin bran and tea, Elizabeth had OJ, pancakes and sausage, Esmé had the same except she substituted French toast for the pancakes and I had SOS—creamed beef on toast, shit on a shingle in Navy parlance-and coffee. It was the first time since I'd left the Navy that I'd had SOS and it hit the spot.

At a few minutes after eight, right after we'd returned to the staterooms, my cell rang. It was Darps. I answered, "Hi there, Shipmate," and sat down on the couch.

"Your situation in the Baltic--plus your assignment--have got various folks' knickers in a knot," Darps said.

"Well no shit! That would include my own. Remember, I took this trip for R & R, to draw down my PTSD. Now I've got some Russian girl thrown overboard and killed after contacting me and some Russian asshole trying to poison me in Berlin. And I'm concerned about the safety of my wife and daughter and my neighbor's kid, who came along for the ride, to say the least."

"Understand. You're due in Tallinn tomorrow, Saint Petersburg the day after. A security team will pick you up before you arrive in Russia. I can't get into details on this line, but you and the women will have protection," he said. "Between now and the teams' arrival, you all need to stick together and keep your eyes open."

"What about when we get there?"

"You're to quote carry out your instructions, unquote. That's from the Old Man himself. Plus, you will have the protection. A team will be in place before you get to Russia and will remain in place for the duration."

Which had to have meant Kehoe himself was insisting on my "carrying out my instructions."

"Okay," I said. "I've got it. Anything else?"

"Nah," he said. "Stay safe. I wish it were the two of us on this gig, rather than you, Maria, Elizabeth and what's her face."

"Esmé is her name. But remember our little journey started out as a family vacation. This mission was a late add-on."

"I know, I know," he said. "But you were still in London when you got the mission. Far be it from me to second guess our boss, but if I'd gotten into the loop a little earlier, we could have made some major-league adjustments."

"If you're hinting that we could have sent Maria, Elizabeth and Esmé home from London, that would have gone over like the proverbial turd in the punch bowl."

"Yeah, you're right. But I probably could have come up with something a bit more creative than just sending them home. But that's water over the dam. Or under the bridge. So, for now, keep your head down and your eyes open."

We ended the call and I went across the passageway and knocked on the girls' door.

"C'mon over for a quick-and-dirty meeting," I said.

A couple of minutes later, I was closeted with the three beautiful women.

"I just spoke with Darps and there is some good news. Washington is sending over a security team for added protection for us by the time we get to Saint Petersburg," I said.

"Does that mean Washington is suddenly more worried about our situation, Mr. El?" Esmé asked.

"Well yes and no," I answered lamely. "I think they're reacting to what I've been telling them about what's been happening here. Now, changing the subject, what can we do together today? Any great ideas?"

"There's a presentation at nine-thirty this morning in the ship's theater on digital photography. I think I'd like to sit in on that," Maria said. "There's a Canon Rebel T6 digital camera on sale in the ship's store. I might treat myself."

"Sounds good to me," I said. "How long does the presentation last?"

"Till eleven,"

"What do you guys think?" I asked Esmé and Elizabeth.

"Works for me," Elizabeth said. "I've been taking a ton of pix. Maybe it would help if I knew what I was doing."

"Okay. Sounds good. We'll learn about taking pictures with our phones and digital cameras. Afterwards, how about having lunch in the Pinnacle Grill instead of up on the Lido?" I asked. "Just for a change of scene." I didn't say anything about trying to keep the dirt bags off balance, but the thought was in the back of my mind.

The women liked the idea. Especially Esmé. She had heard "a rumor" of a scrumptious and huge shrimp cocktail that was served at lunchtime in the Pinnacle.

"We could take a post-lunch nap and then hit the gym for an hour or so," Maria added. "Then maybe a relaxing swim topside as long as it's not too cold outside."

"Hmm. I'm thinking we'll sleep well tonight," I said.

"Nothing wrong with that," Maria said.

"We're docking in Tallinn tomorrow morning," Elizabeth added.

"Yeah," I said. "I'm looking forward to it," I added, crossing my fingers behind my back. Actually, I was a bit worried about what might be waiting for us on the streets of Tallinn.

We farted around with *Nordschiff*'s New York Times news summary and our Kindles till it was time to head for the digital camera class up in the theater.

Chapter Fifty-Five

Alan

Tallinn, Estonia

Early June

Friday night was not a great night for sleeping, even though I'd had a boatload of exercise. At least not for *my* sleeping. I guess it was okay for Maria and presumably for the two girls as well. Maria snored gently throughout the large chunks of the night through which I remained awake. Gentle, lady-like snores--not the toilet-flushing roars of my old Bancroft Hall roommates. But I stayed awake a lot for some reason and tried to avoid the tossing and turning and thrashing. I tried to limit my shifts from my left side to the right side and vise-versa to once every fifteen minutes. I watched the bedside clock. Whenever I got to sixteen or seventeen minutes before a flip, I considered it a small victory of sorts. Sometime after two-thirty, I must have dozed off.

When I awoke, light was washing in through the blinds and the bedside alarm clock read five-twenty-five. I visited the loo, got a drink of water and climbed back into the rack. I tried to go back to sleep but realized quickly that there was no more sleep in my immediate future. I stared at the overhead for a few minutes and then plopped my feet back on the deck.

A peek out the porthole showed that Nordschiff was nosing her way into an industrial area in which other ships were berthed. In the background was a cluster of rooftops with a sprinkling of church steeples nestled against wooded hills. Tallinn!

I glanced over my shoulder. Maria was still sleeping. I popped open our cabin door and listened at the door across the passageway. Nothing. I guessed from the lack of any noise, the two girls were also in the Land of Nod. Unless, God forbid, they were still up in the casino. But I wasn't really worried. They were two good girls, although every once in a while, tiny *frissons* of doubt about Esmé waltzed unbidden into my mind. Silently, I pulled on sweats, grabbed the Adidas shoes and socks and headed for the Promenade Deck. There were walkers already there, striding energetically. I sat down on a deck chair, pulled on the socks and shoes and joined the other walkers. The Baltic summer air was crisp. *Nordschiff* was gliding along very slowly as she entered an area with quays on both sides, some of which had ships tied up. Most of the ships looked like large, seagoing ferries.

By the time I'd walked for forty minutes, *Nordschiff* was securely tied up pier-side. Even though the morning was cool, I'd still managed to work up a sweat. I returned to our stateroom. Maria was kneeling on the rack in her pajamas, peering out through the porthole. I marveled at the exquisite excellence of her pajama-clad derriere.

"Okay!" I said. "This time the old man gets the shower first. Since he's ready and you're not."

Maria dove under the covers and rolled over and closed her eyes. I figured I could take my time in the shower. I wasn't worried about the hot water supply.

I emerged in a cloud of steam after the shower and a quick shave, clad in a Nordschiff terry cloth robe. Maria skittered into the loo with another white Nordschiff robe over her arm. I got into khakis and a polo shirt, checked outside the stateroom and found the International New York Times news summary in the little mailbox.

I tapped on the door across the passageway.

"We're up!" came the response.

"Breakfast in thirty minutes!" I said to the closed door.

Returning to our room, I grazed through the news stories, attacked the crossword and was finishing it off when Maria completed her morning ablutions and the two girls scrabbled at our door. The four of us went aloft to the Lido breakfast buffet. I'm not sure about my girlfriends, but I was starving. I went to the omelet station and ordered up a ham, cheese and mushroom four-egg bomb. I added OJ, toast and black coffee to my tray and found Maria, Esmé and Elizabeth whose trays were nearly as heavily laden as mine. Breakfast hit the spot!

By the time we had finished breakfast, *Nordschiff* had passengers going ashore in Tallinn, which we had planned on exploring on our own. Which we did. Being careful to stay together and keep our eyes peeled. We had to cross a fairly large and wide-open port area before going through a gate in an eight-foot chain link fence. There was no immigration or customs check. Once through, we were in the city. I wasn't sure which made me edgier—the wide-open port area or the narrow, crooked streets of Tallinn. Esmé loved the "fairy-tale look" of the place and Elizabeth took a ton of pictures. We had lunch in a Greek restaurant with outside tables. In Estonia! Globalization at work! Or maybe it was just the EU—a major subset of globalization. That Saturday turned out to be another uneventful—but enjoyable—day. We were back aboard by five and *M. S. Nordschiff* was underway right on time at six-thirty. There had been no threat—bombs or poison or anything else—on the beach. At all. Leading to an attitude of semi-complacence. Always dangerous.

We had dinner with our Canadian friends, the Scotts, back on board. Esmé and Elizabeth had ascertained that there was a showing of *The Matrix* scheduled for eight o'clock that evening. Maria and I agreed to attend the showing, which did not make a huge hit with the girls. But I was serious about the need for the Llewellyn family and our adopted daughter sticking together. So we did. I fell asleep four or five times during the movie and paid for that slackness with a few sharp elbows delivered to my rib cage by the lovely Maria.

"You were starting to snore," she whispered.

"Tough night, last night," I whispered back.

After the movie, Maria and I accompanied the two girls to the Casino. They all hit the slots while I had a beer at the bar. The beer cost me eight Euros plus a tip. Approximately eleven bucks. The women won sixty Euros from the slots. Life isn't fair.

Chapter Fifty-Six

Alan

Saint Petersburg
Early June

Usually I don't have two bad nights in a row. Since I had tossed and turned till two-thirty a.m. the night before last, last night I was asleep by the time my head was three inches above the pillow and dropping. I don't think I moved again till the northern sunshine beamed into our stateroom underneath the blinds at five till five. I got up, went to the loo and got a glass of water.

As I came out of the head I heard a soft tapping at the door. A familiar voice said "Alan? You awake?"

Luke!

I stumbled across the stateroom and opened the door.

"If you can come up to the promenade deck, I've managed to scrounge a thermos of coffee and a couple of paper cups," he whispered. "We can shoot the shit. Probably be best if you threw some clothes on rather than come up in your skivvies. You'll freeze your ass off if you don't. It's pretty chilly up there."

"I don't want to leave the girls alone," I muttered.

"Not to worry," he whispered back. "There's Agent Ally McNulty, United States Secret Service, three doors down. She's good and she's got your girls under observation. She'll take good care of them."

"Let me get some sweats and flip-flops," I said.

Once we were "up there," Luke poured me a paper cup of coffee. Steam exploded from the cup into the chill morning air and into my cold nostrils. The bouquet was fabulous, especially given the damp northern air sliding by *Nordschiff* and my early exit from the warm rack. The first sip of coffee was exquisite.

"Thanks for this," I said. "It's perfect on a chilly morning in the Baltic. By the way, what the hell are you doing here and now?"

"Working," Luke said. "We came out on the pilot boat two hours ago. You probably know all about pilot boat stuff from your Navy days."

"Yeah. When a beast like *Nordschiff* comes into a port like Saint Petersburg, the port requires that the ship take on a skilled, licensed and local pilot. The pilot helps the conning officer get the ship to its slot at the pier or anchorage or whatever. The port supplies a boat to bring the pilot aboard. For a fee, of course. You hitched a ride on the pilot boat."

"You got it. For an additional fee, of course. There are five of us. Two two-person teams. One male and one female per team. McNulty is my partner. Mike, from our office at *BIAS*, has the other team, along with Emma Reedy from the White House Detail. We all have staterooms close to yours. We'll keep you covered, twenty-four, seven. Twelve-hour shifts. Mine started at zero-five-hundred. With Ally. We'll make sure we have you guys covered when you go ashore, as well."

"Well that's a huge relief!" I said and took another sip of the hot and fragrant coffee. "But I thought you said there were five of you."

"I did indeed," he said, smiling thinly.

"So whiskey-tango-foxtrot?" I asked.

Luke glanced at his watch and looked up. As did I. A woman appeared.

Judy!

"Well, Judy!" I said, delighted. "What are you doing here in the Gulf of Finland?"

"Helping your wife. Looking after your daughter and her friend, Esmé. And, last but not least, looking after you and these cowboys," she said.

"Well thank the Lord," I said, giving her a huge hug. "I always feel like I'm less of a loose cannon when you're around. And that sly dog Darps--I see his hairy hands all over this."

"You're pretty close to being absolutely right. And I guess that's a good thing," she said. "But remember, I'm here to provide an extra layer of security for Maria, Elizabeth and Esmé."

"That works for me," I said, fervently. "But I never thought of you as 'security.' *Per se.*"

"Look at it this way. Another pair of eyeballs equals more security," said Luke.

"Yeah," I said. "I know that. That's why we're where we are with *BIAS*. But somehow, I feel like I've strayed from the fold on this gig. This is totally operational. Not just more eyeballs. But I'm delighted to have Judy along to give us a hand and maybe keep us in line."

Walt Breede

I tried to bring Luke and Judy completely up to date on the past few days as a couple of tugs—and presumably, the pilot, nudged *Nordschiff* toward her Saint Petersburg berth.

A little later, *Nordschiff* tied up at the pier. Maria, the girls and I had already signed up for today's boat tour of Saint Petersburg back when we booked the cruise. But I needed to buy some rubles. When we finished breakfast, we wandered down to the Purser's Office outside of which uniformed Russians were selling Russian currency. I bought a hundred dollars worth which got me a little bit less than six thousand rubles which should handle the poetry book and maybe a couple of souvenirs. It was nine-thirty. The tour was scheduled for ten.

Chapter Fifty-Seven

Alan

Saint Petersburg

Early June

Our boat tour of Saint Petersburg was fantastic. I had no idea that the city was such a picturesque, waterborne metropolis. Rivers and canals dominated the cityscape—a boat tour was the only way to see the place. Built by Peter the Great on the delta of the River Neva, it is actually a city on many islands. The buildings were very elegant and European and seemed to avoid the usual Communist dreariness one sees in so many Russian cities. The rivers and canals lent an exotic flavor to the Baltic cityscape. Our tour guide was a young woman named Larisa who spoke excellent English, occasionally broken up with short pauses as if she needed to stop and concentrate. She worked hard and came through very well.

We stopped and disembarked, as planned, at the Cathedral of Our Savior on the Spilled Blood. Said blood was that of Tsar Aleksandr II, slain at the site by a rebel group. Aleksandr III, his son, had the cathedral built in his father's honor. An on-site gift shop happily slurped up tourists' rubles. Our "adopted" daughter, Esmé, and we Llewellyns stayed together— which wasn't easy with the crushing crowds. I looked for books. Suddenly, a young woman in a white sweater and a blue skirt popped up in front of us. Her nametag said *Natasha* in Cyrillic as well as Latin characters.

"May I help you?" she asked in English.

"Yes," I said. "I'm looking for a book titled *"The Poems of Anna Akhmatova."*

"I can help you with that," she said with a captivating smile.

"Good," I said. "I can pay in cash. In rubles."

"Very good," she said. "Wait here. I'll be right back."

She was right back, carrying a hardcover book with a profile photo of an aristocratic-looking woman on the dustcover. The title, in English, read *"The Poems of Anna Akhmatova."*

"Perfect," I said. "What do I owe you?"

"One thousand, two hundred fifty rubles," she said. "Since you're paying in cash, Mr. Llewellyn," she said, startling me a bit. I didn't remember telling her my name. But then, according to the dear departed Veronika, Natasha was expecting me.

"Sounds good, Natasha," I said, handing her fifteen hundred Rubles.

"I'll be right back with your book and your change, Mr. Llewellyn," she said.

Natasha was as good as her word. She reappeared almost instantly with a plastic bag imprinted with the gift shop's logo—a line drawing of the cathedral--and a small handful of currency.

"Here's your book and your change," she announced. "The receipt is in the bag with the book. And there's an important piece of paper folded in between the book and its dustcover." She flashed me her incredible smile.

"Uh oh," I mumbled. "Suppose some guy at customs finds that?"

"Not to worry. That won't happen," she said. "The book will be in this Cathedral Gift Shop bag. The legitimate receipt will be in the bag with the book. No one will give it a second look."

She handed me the bag.

"*Spasiba,*" I said. "Thanks."

"You're welcome," she said.

Maria, Elizabeth and Esmé picked up a couple of trinkets--a replica of a coin from Tsarist Russia, a hand-painted dish showing the cathedral of Saint Isaac, and a skinny book, ostensibly containing the poems of Yuri Zhivago.

When we returned to the pier, a scowling, uniformed customs official glanced at our purchases and waved us through.

Back in our stateroom, I suddenly felt exhausted. It was four-thirty p.m. I collapsed on the starboard side of the king-sized bed and muttered, "See you in an hour or so." I popped my forearm across my eyes and went to sleep.

I opened my eyes at five forty-five. Maria was reading. I climbed out of the bed, went to the loo and washed my hands and face.

"Sorry about crashing on you," I said. "Anything new from Luke, Judy or anybody else?"

"Luke popped in," Maria said. "He said there were a couple of quote dirt bags unquote following us while we were on the boat tour and ashore, but the Secret Service detail--or somebody—seemed to scare them off. So they kept their distance. He said there appeared to be a Russian FSB[5] team involved as well and that perhaps, they, the FSB Russians, scared off the dirt bag Russians. Everything seems to be secure here on board. Mike and what's her name—Emma—have the watch now. On us. No doubt Judy is hovering around somewhere."

Elizabeth and Esmé, who were sitting on the little sofa in our cabin, watched the Llewellyn parents intently during this little exchange.

"Well, I'm awake and refreshed," I said. "Let's head up to the Explorers' Lounge for an aperitif and then to dinner," I said.

"Sounds good to me." Maria said.

"It'll be interesting to see if the Russian girls are playing," Esmé said.

We went out the door and headed for the elevators. Before we left, I took the poetry book in its bag and flipped it open. There was indeed a piece of paper folded into fourths between the dust jacket and the book itself. I took it out and unfolded it. It contained groups of five numbers, each group separated by a comma. Each group of five numbers with its comma was separated from the next by what appeared to be a five-space gap. I stowed the book and the paper in my suitcase, which I stashed in one of the built-in closets. That wouldn't provide much protection in the event of even a semi-serious search, but it would park the book out of sight of curious room stewards and maids.

In the Explorer's Lounge, the Russian string quartet was still, unsurprisingly, a Russian trio. The women looked elegant in Burgundy skirts and white blouses. The music was elegant as well—the elder Bach, I thought. The women appeared expressionless—no signs of tears or red-rimmed eyes. Everything seemed to be under control. We enjoyed the drinks and the music and went below for dinner. It was swordfish steaks and they were exquisite. The side dishes were white spring asparagus and escalloped potatoes. Also exquisite.

After dinner, we repaired to the Explorers' Lounge. Maria ordered a Drambui, I a cognac and Elizabeth a Sprite. Esmé raised her eyebrows at me when I ordered the cognac.

"We're way, way outside the United States," she said. "How 'bout I try a cognac?"

"I'm pretty sure you wouldn't like it," I said. "Nice try, in any case. Remember what I said about a seven-year wait. But a Sprite or a Coke will work," I said.

She wrinkled her nose at me. Again.

Judy showed up right after Tamara served the drinks.

"Hi, Llewellyns," she said. "May I join you?"

"Of course," Maria and I said together as Elizabeth stood and pulled another chair over to our table.

Chapter Fifty-Eight
Alan

Saint Petersburg
Early June

"I have some word from our nation's capital," Judy said, quietly.

"From the President himself. It was a text, but it was from the man himself. Not Hookes. Not from *Chipmunk*. *Cheetah* himself. It says, quote, Loose needs to deliver Russ message to me personally. No cutouts. Unquote."

"Jesus Christ," I said, choking on the words as I glanced at the girls. Elizabeth pursed her lips in silent disapproval at my use of the Lord's name in vain; Esmé appeared to be suppressing a grin.

"I'm wondering why the hell he didn't text me," I growled.

"My guess is security," Judy said. "He's probably trying to minimize electronic contact with you."

"I have to wonder what the hell is in that Russian message that makes it so damned sensitive," I muttered, half to myself.

"My next guess is that we'll never know until maybe after you deliver the darned thing," she said.

Judy refused our offers to buy her a drink.

"Thanks, but I just don't feel like one right now," she said. "My internal clocks are still all messed up. I think I'll run off to bed."

"Are you going ashore in Saint Petersburg tomorrow?" I asked.

"No," she answered. "No visa and I'm not signed up for any tours. How about you guys?"

"Nope," I said. "We have visas but no real reason to go ashore again tomorrow. We enjoyed a wonderful boat tour of the city today. But, given the circumstances, I think we'd be best off if we stayed aboard. The ship gets under way just after lunch, anyway."

Judy left. Maria and I looked each other in the eye. I swiveled around and caught Tamara's eye and gave her a "two" sign with my two fingers. A minute later, she placed a Drambui in front of Maria and another cognac in front of me. I signed the chit and picked up the snifter.

"After all, we're on a cruise," I said.

"Yes. But we may be playing in the danger zone now," Maria said.

Chapter Fifty-Nine

Alan

The Baltic Sea
Early June

The Llewellyn family and our adopted daughter "sort of" slept in, wandering up to the Lido for breakfast around eight-thirty. We took a leisurely, six-lap walk on the Promenade Deck after breakfast.

We lazed around throughout the remainder of the morning. We all agreed that yesterday's Saint Petersburg tour had sufficed. We'd had a nice overview of the beautiful city. True, there was a ton more to do and see, but then there was the issue of the evildoers and our port visit was scheduled to end no later than two-o'clock when *Nordschiff* was due to get underway.

We went together to the Explorers' Lounge where Maria and I worked on our laptops. Elizabeth and Esmé joined us and I bought the two of them Cappuccini. They seemed content to slurp the *caffe*, shoot the shit and giggle for a while.

We were able to meet the members of the protective detail whom we didn't already know just before lunch. Ally, Luke's partner, was a tall, slender woman in her early thirties with short, blond hair. Mike, of course, was an old friend from *BIAS* whom we occasionally referred to as Luke's "white twin." He was a male, needless to say, with broad shoulders and a thick neck—*a la* an NFL linebacker. Emma, his partner, was also tall and slender and also had short hair. But it was jet black and she had vaguely almond-shaped eyes that were almost as black as her hair.

Around eleven in the morning, I decided to make a slight adjustment. I retrieved *The Poems of Anna Achmatova* from the suitcase in the closet. I then went on-line and found a ship's Directory and a listing and a number for the ship's Executive Officer, Captain Bergkamp. I punched in the numbers.

"Bergkamp," answered a familiar masculine voice.

"Good morning, Captain. This is Alan Llewellyn," I announced. "I wonder if we could have a word."

"Ja, of course," he said. "Would my office be okay?"

"Yes sir!" I responded. "Right away?"

"That would be fine, Mister Llewellyn."

"Thank you, sir," I said. "I'll be there in a few minutes."

I stuck the book—still in its gift shop bag—under my arm and left the stateroom, heading for Bergkamp's office. I arrived there in a few minutes and knocked.

"Come in," a voice responded.

"Good morning, sir," I said. "I just learned that this book has become an 'object of interest' to certain parties. I wondered if the ship had a safe in which we could store it securely."

"But surely, your stateroom has a safe, Mr. Llewellyn," he said.

"Yes sir, it does, but I'm led to believe that it might not be sufficiently secure. I was wondering if *Nordschiff* might be able to provide enhanced security."

"I'm sure we can," he responded. "You say it's a book? Just a book?"

"Just a book," I said. "In Russian and English."

His eyes narrowed slightly when he heard the word "Russian."

"I'll have the ship's communications officer clear the combination off the safe in your stateroom. Then you can set the new combination and only you will have it. No one else. In an emergency, of course, technicians from the ship's crew would be able to access the safe, but not without a lot of fuss and to-do. I think that's the best we can do."

"That's fine, sir," I said. "Thanks."

I wasn't one hundred percent satisfied with his "solution," but any port in a storm.

We were finishing lunch when *Nordschiff* got underway. Tomorrow was another "at sea" day on the cruise itinerary; we were due to tie up in Stockholm at seven-thirty Wednesday morning.

After lunch, two guys with Nordschiff ID badges showed up at our stateroom to zero out the combination on our stateroom safe.

"You're good to go, Herr Llewellyn," one of the guys said. "All you need to do is punch in three two-digit numbers. Press "enter" after each set of two. Press "enter" twice after the third set and you'll be all set."

After the two guys left, I followed the locksmith's instruct1ons. Entered "nine, four," followed by "enter," "eight three," followed by "enter," again, finally "zero four," followed by "enter" twice. I tried the lock. It worked. I locked up the Achmatova book in the safe and felt a little bit better about it. Not too much better, but a little bit better.

We enjoyed Tuesday at sea. Luke came by our lunch table and told us that a *Nordschiff* security officer had advised him that five Russians had disembarked at Saint Petersburg yesterday. They seemed to agree that their departure resulted in a lower threat level on board *Nordschiff*—at least for the time being.

When we walked on the Promenade Deck, I kept my eyes peeled for suspicious-looking dirt bags and saw none. No guys slipping into or out of ladder-well doors or hanging about. I did catch sight of Ally with the short, blond hair. Keeping an eye on us. Which made me feel good.

Maria and I accompanied Elizabeth and Esmé to the pool after lunch. Maria made sure that the girls slathered the sunscreen on each other.

"But Mom—that's like putting on a bikini and going into a darkened closet and closing the door!" Elizabeth whined.

"Not true, Sweetie," her mother responded. "You can still get a nice, even tan and not roast your skin into melanoma."

Elizabeth snorted in defeat and spread the sunscreen around with her hands with a little help from Esmé.

Maria and I opened our laptops at a small table in the shade. I noticed Mike taking a seat at a table across the pool and Emma flaking out on a beach chair not far from the girls. She was wearing a pale blue bikini and she slathered on sunscreen as well. The overall impression was quite good. The pale blue worked well on the lightly tanned and oiled skin. She placed a medium-sized, pink beach bag on her table. I guessed her weapon was there. Our protection was in place.

Chapter Sixty
The DNI

Great Falls Park

McLean, Virginia

Early June

Dick Nagle's email from Braxton had arrived on his home computer just before he left his house for Langley at six forty-five a. m. The email appeared to be addressed to all members of "the Group" except Vice Admiral Donegan. He had to wonder about that.

The subject line read "Code Purple." That meant emergency meeting. And that no doubt meant short-fuze. Like now. The text was indeed short and cryptic:

MTG 1730 TODAY @ OVERLOOK #3, GFP, MCLEAN.

When Nagle arrived at seventeen-twenty-five, Braxton was there. So was Ironsides. As were Nagle, CIA, McConnell, FBI, Smalls, Army Intel, and Suzanne Palmer, former--fired--National Security Advisor to the President. Among the missing were Congresswoman Helen DeWitt, Speaker of the House, and, of course, Donegan.

"We've got a problem, folks!" Braxton, raising his voice so he could be heard above the roar of the tons of water crashing over the rocks behind him. He continued, "NSA has found the name 'A. Llewellyn' and the phrase 'Baltic-North' in some Russian chatter. They also picked up the phrase 'USG plot' several times in the same chatter. Nobody's connected a bunch of dots that we know of, but that stuff has got me worried. We found that Alan Llewellyn, who is rumored to be the director of *BIAS*, Kehoe's rogue little intel service, is on a cruise on board *M. S. Nordschiff* with his family. *Nordschiff* is the flagship of the Baltic-North line, a Danish cruise line that operates in northern European waters during the summer. Why in the name of Christ the Russians should be chattering about that in some of the same traffic in which they're talking about a 'USG plot' is a huge goddam mystery to me. I think that all of us need to take a long, hard look at our respective organizations and examine them for possible leaks."

"I'm guessing that these 'long, hard looks' are to be surreptitious, Chief," said Nagle.

"Thank you and yes, Dick. I don't think it would be smart to crank up any heavy counterintelligence artillery to try and smoke out a leak. Our efforts need to stay under the radar. Our contacts have been so closely held that that shouldn't be difficult."

"Does that stuff have anything to do with Admiral Donegan's absence from the last couple of meetings?" Nagle asked.

"Umm, no. I don't think so," Braxton replied. "My understanding is that she has some sort of family emergency. Obviously, getting her replaced at this stage of the operation would be a very dicey business, to say the least. We have to proceed with utmost--*utmost*—-caution. Which is exactly what we're doing."

Braxton entertained two more questions and adjourned the meeting.

Chapter Sixty-One

Alan

Stockholm
Mid-June

We arrived in Stockholm on time. The weather was warm and sunny. We had signed up earlier for another boat tour, on which we saw much of the Stockholm archipelago and enjoyed the fine weather. I was amazed at how much of Stockholm was scattered over a bunch of islands. The Secret Service was always in the shadows. Except at lunchtime when they jumped out of the shadows.

Maria, Elizabeth, Esmé and I had just disembarked from our tour boat for a one-hour lunch break and sat down at a lovely outdoor table at the *Strandbryggan* restaurant. We ordered (I think) Swedish open-face sandwiches, mineral water and beer when an attractive blonde woman approached. She looked Swedish. But she wasn't. She was Emma, Mike's Secret Service partner.

"Hi," she said. "I'm Emma. We met the day before yesterday. Mind if I sit down?"

I remembered her features and the short blond ponytail. There was a fifth chair at the table. I half-stood.

"Of course we remember you Emma. And please," I said. "Have a seat. Join us."

I pulled out the extra chair.

"Thank you," she said. She sat down and leaned in over the table.

"I think we have a problem," she began. "I don't want to alarm anybody, but we need to get all four of you back aboard *Nordschiff* soonest."

"But we've just ordered lunch," I said.

"We'll take care of lunch," Emma said. "We'll pay the tab plus a twenty-five percent tip. There are bigger fish to fry than whatever you're having for lunch. That's why you guys need to get back to the ship ASAP. I have a cab waiting for you."

Thinking this was a classic case of the necessity to act and hold the questions for later, I stood up and gestured Maria and the two teenagers to do the same.

"Where's the taxi?" I asked.

"Right there," she said, nodding to her left. "He's waiting for you. He's been cleared and paid. And tipped. All you need to do is ride with him to the pier where *Nordschiff* is tied up and get aboard."

A shiny black cab with a lighted "Taxi" sign on the roof and a yellow price sign *320 Kr* in the back window seemed to be waiting for us. We went for it and piled into the front and back seats.

"Nordschiff, please," I stammered. "The cruise ship."

"Yes sir. I know," the driver said in perfect English and we left. Quickly.

At the pier, I thought about padding the tip with my somewhat meager stash of Swedish Kroner; I glanced at the meter and mentally calculated a twenty-percent tip. I took out my wallet,

"No, sir," he said. "Everything's been taken care of. Including the gratuity."

I should have known. Emma was correct. Everything was taken care of. The CIA Station Chief at the U. S. Embassy, Stockholm, must have a small fleet of taxis on retainer. Either that or the Secret Service troops on board *M. S. Nordschiff* had a bountiful expense account.

After the rapid taxi ride, we boarded quickly enough and went directly to our staterooms. Actually, all four of us converged on Maria's and my stateroom.

"You gotta wonder what the hell all that was about," I muttered.

Maria just raised her eyebrows.

"Do you think they're still serving lunch on the Lido?" she asked. "I'm starving."

"They serve till three. We're good. Let's go," I said.

"Give us a couple of minutes for the loo, Dad," Elizabeth said.

"Of course," I said.

Ten minutes later, we were grazing through a mercifully shortened buffet line. I gathered up a small pile of chicken wings, a salad and a couple of hard rolls. I added a bottle of Carlsberg beer. Elizabeth had a bowl of chili plus a little pile of cheddar cheese and tortilla chips and Maria had a big Cobb salad. Esmé had a bacon cheeseburger and fries. She also had a Sprite and Elizabeth had an iced tea.

"I still have to wonder what the hell was happening on the beach," I muttered.

"I guess you mean 'ashore in Stockholm' when you say 'on the beach'," Esmé said.

"Yes, Ma'am," I said. "I have to wonder what was going on that made the Secret Service want to hustle us back aboard *Nordschiff*."

I was also concerned that apparently there had been a lot of stuff going on around us in Stockholm--stuff that I had failed to notice.

"Maybe we're about to find out," Maria said. "Here comes Luke."

"Hi guys," he said. "Mind if I sit?"

He sat without waiting for an answer.

"Want to grab some lunch?" I asked.

"No thanks, I had a sandwich about an hour ago. Just thought I'd update you."

Here? Now?" I asked.

Luke looked around. The Lido was nearly empty. Probably because it was late and a lot of passengers were ashore.

"Sure. Here goes. A three-man team--make that a three-person team. Two guys and a woman—all Russians-were apparently following you guys. We think we detected traces of Polonium-two-ten in their immediate vicinity. So we decided to get you back aboard ship. No Polonium here."

"Polonium? Good Lord!" I said. "That stuff is really lethal."

"Precisely," Luke said. "That's why you are back on board the ship. We're not totally sure that those bastards were intending to poison you guys, but why take a chance? Especially after the Polonium-two-ten showed up in their vicinity. The Germans think they may have tried to use it on you back in Berlin."

Luke also confirmed that our lunch tab in Stockholm had been taken care of. And that was that. Polonium! Good Lord!

After lunch, the Llewellyn family and guest went back to the old folks' stateroom and read for about a half an hour. I think we all started getting restless at about the same time.

"What say we hit the gym?" I asked. "Lots of folks are ashore. We can probably have the place to ourselves."

"Sounds good to me," Maria said, standing up.

Ten minutes later, the four of us walked into an empty gym. CNN International was on the two flat-screen television sets bolted to the bulkheads. The news broadcast was covering unrest in Venezuela. Maria climbed aboard a bike, Elizabeth manned an elliptical trainer, and Esmé and I started farting around with the weights on a weight machine. Forty-five minutes later, we staggered out, a bit on the tired, sweaty and sore side.

"Ladies first on the showers," I said. "You're up. I'm taking my book up to the Promenade Deck to read and let the sweat dry off. I'll be back in a half an hour. Lock the doors when I leave. I'm sure one of the Secret Service team members will be on watch."

I wasn't crazy about leaving the ladies, but we did have Secret Service protection, so I went up two decks and found an empty deck chair. A couple of minutes later, Luke found another chair about twenty feet from mine. No one else was in sight. I guessed his partner, Emma, was guarding the girls. A glance at my watch told me it was five after three. Nine-oh-five in the morning in Virginia. Time to check out the comms package on the drone. I dialed Darps's mobile.

"Hey, Shipmate!" he said, sounding like he was on the next deck chair. "How are things in—let's see, if this is Wednesday, you must be in Stockholm. How are things in beautiful Sweden?"

"A little crazy. We—the Llewellyn family plus guest—just got yanked back aboard ship from a tour of Stockholm because of a nasty-sounding threat."

"Yeah, I got a text from Luke a few minutes ago."

"So, Shipmate," I said. "Tell me this. Why in hell can't I just give the fucking package to Luke or Mike and let one of them jump on a jet for D.C. and let the Llewellyn family enjoy what remains of our so-called vacation?"

"Because, Shipmate, our boss, *Cheetah*, says that the package is so fucking radioactive that he and the Foreign Minister of Russia agree that access to it must be limited almost to zero. That means no hands other than yours handle the thing until you slip it into *Cheetah's* hot little hands. When you get back here."

I sighed and remained silent for several seconds.

"Okay. So what's the story with the Russian Foreign Minister? How come *Cheetah* isn't dealing with his Russ counterpart—the President—directly?"

"Some sort of Russian pissing contest. The Russ ambassador reports to the Minister of Foreign Affairs. Who reports to the President. Unless he doesn't want to. So there's some sort of disconnect in the communications between the Foreign Minister and the President of Russia. That's where we are."

"Sweet Jesus," I muttered. "I have to wonder what in God's name is in that book."

"I have no idea and I'm sure your protective detail has no clue, either," Darps said.

"I'm wondering if I should jump ship here in Stockholm and hustle back," I said, talking as much to myself as to Darps. "There may not be enough time to do that here in Sweden, but we could probably disembark in Kiel and fly back to CONUS from Hamburg. With the fucking book. Tomorrow."

"The vibes I'm getting at this end are that the time isn't as crucial as the security and restricted access. In other words, you should finish your cruise and return on schedule," Darps said. "Just keep the book totally under wraps until you get it to the White House. Or Camp David."

"Beautiful. That leaves the Llewellyn family—and our temporarily adopted daughter--on the skyline for various dirt bags to take potshots at."

"True. And I'm sorry about that. And more importantly, *Cheetah* is truly concerned and hopes that you, Maria, Elizabeth and what's her name keep your heads down. But look at the bright side. You have a phalanx of Secret Service studs protecting you and your family. That kind of demonstrates that *Cheetah* is serious about your safety. Not to mention Judy. Whose presence means that we at *BIAS* are equally serious."

"That makes me feel better. A little better," I said.

We finished the confab by agreeing that the drone comms link seemed to be working well and that we'd stay in touch. I still had to admit to myself that I was more than just a bit uneasy with the current state of affairs.

I looked at my watch. Twenty minutes had passed. The women probably were not yet completely bathed and dressed. I opened my Kindle Fire and closed it again. The Swedish afternoon was too beautiful for reading a mystery. Ten minutes later, I stood up and headed below to the stateroom.

Chapter Sixty-Two

Alan

.

```
Stockholm and the Baltic Sea
          Mid-June
```

Before I even opened the door, I detected the bouquet of some sort of nice-smelling, feminine spritz. The women had transformed themselves from sweaty gym rats to real-life visions of feminine grace. I noticed that our only daughter had put on lip-gloss, no doubt under her mother's tutelage. That started me thinking about moving to Switzerland, near a girls' school with high stone walls topped with glass shards. Fuming about the lip gloss would be a zero-sum game for me. Or worse. So I held my tongue and mumbled something lame like, "You guys smell nice and look nice, too."

I grabbed some underwear and jumped into the head, hoping to transform myself from a male gym rat into something more civilized. The shower and shampoo helped and the deodorant no doubt helped some more. I donned a blue Oxford shirt and a fresh pair of khakis plus loafers and we were ready for the Explorers' Lounge.

The female Russian trio was playing Vivaldi. They appeared serious but dry-eyed. Tamara showed up tableside. Elizabeth ordered a glass of apricot nectar and Esmé ordered a V-8. Maria and I ordered Ketel One Martinis, cold and straight up. Tamara put a bowl of mixed nuts on our table, followed by a folded scrap of paper. She spun around and left before I had a chance to ask her anything. I unfolded the scrap on the tabletop. There was a brief message.

Be very careful in Hamburg!!!

And that was it. I didn't know from whom it had come. Tamara? The Russian girls? My guardian angel? I had no clue. Mike and Emma were seated at a window-side table off to our left, but they didn't seem to be paying any attention to the note or me. Tamara chose then to show up with our drinks.

"How has your day been?" she asked.

"So-so," I said.

"Did you see Stockholm?" she asked.

"Some of it," I said. "From a boat. It's all islands."

"I love Stockholm," she said. "It's my favorite city. But I only come in the summer. Maybe if I came in the dead of winter, I'd change my mind."

I was pretty sure that Baltic North ships spent their winter seasons plying the warmer waters of the Mediterranean and so they didn't get to experience the glories of Stockholm in the winter.

Tamara turned on her heel and left. I still had no idea about the cryptic note about Hamburg. I needed to talk with Luke. Or someone.

I finished the martini. And waved to Tamara. Some guy back in my callow youth--I'm thinking it might have been Maria's dad--gave me a philosophical morsel when he said "Martinis are like breasts on a woman--one is not enough and three are too many." I ordered my second. Maria stayed put with one. But then, she no doubt has a different philosophical perspective than that of her father and her husband.

Nordschiff sidled away from the pier as we went below for dinner. We could hardly feel the motion.

Chapter Sixty-Three

Alan

The Baltic Sea
Mid-June

The night wrapped its arms around *Nordschiff* as she headed south-southwest diagonally across the Baltic, picking up speed. Maria and I watched the nineteen-sixties film *The Condemned of Altona*, starring Sophia Loren, Maximillian Schell and Frederic March. The dark film is based on a play by Jean-Paul Sartre. Altona is a borough of Hamburg, which, I figured, was why *Nordschiff* was showing the Italian film in the ship's theater the night before we tied up in Kiel to visit Hamburg. Elizabeth and Esmé had gone to the casino. Mike was in the row behind us at the movies and Emma was keeping an eye on the two girls. I'd told Elizabeth again not to lose any more than twenty-five bucks and to avoid any and all dirt bags.

When the movie ended in a thoroughly depressing fashion, Maria and I immediately headed for the Explorers' Lounge. Mike, of course, followed us. I spotted Judy sitting by herself and I sidled to her table and asked if we could join her.

"Of course," she said. "I was actually waiting for you two."

"You were wise to opt out of the movie," Maria told her. "It was very well done but horribly dark. Very depressing."

We sat. Tamara was still on waitress duty, but the Russian string trio was gone. A Dave Brubeck album was playing on the Explorer's excellent sound system. Maria and I both ordered double cognacs after sitting through the moroseness of *The Condemned.*

"Let's chat about tomorrow," Judy said.

"We've signed up for a tour of Hamburg," I said. "The bus leaves the pier at seven-thirty in the morning. Gets into town a bit before nine and then takes us on a tour of the city for an hour or so. Then we get off the bus and get on a boat for a half-hour tour of the Alster Lake.

"After the boat tour, we're turned loose for lunch on our own and then meet the bus in front of the Four Seasons at two. We should be back at the pier in Kiel at about three-fifteen."

213

"I'm pretty sure Mike and Luke have all that info. I'm also pretty sure that they're both a bit skittish about your day in Hamburg, for some reason," Judy said. "I'm not sure why. Would you mind if I accompanied you guys on your tour and to lunch in Hamburg?"

"You're more than welcome, Judy," I said. "But wouldn't that set the cat amongst Luke's and Mike's pigeons? According to them, it could be a bit on the risky side."

"I know. But another pair of eyes with you guys might be helpful."

We agreed to meet for breakfast on the Lido between six-forty-five and seven. Judy would try to sign up for the bus-and-boat tour on line.

Tamara brought our hefty cognacs and we used the first swigs to try to block out the horrors of *Altona*. Elizabeth chose that moment to show up with her buddy.

"See," she said, talking to Esmé. "I *told* you they'd be here! Hi Mom and Dad. Guess what! I won forty Euros on the slots!"

Maybe if I turned her loose on the slots, she could have her first year of college paid for by the end of the cruise. My guardian angel jabbed me in the ear and I limited my response to "Nice job. How did you do, Esmé?"

"I lost my twenty-five dollar limit in the first fifteen minutes," she said. "I'm not as lucky as Elizabeth."

"In the long run, you, Elizabeth, and all the rest of us are all just as lucky—or unlucky. And the ship's casino is luckier," I said. "The ship keeps the casino open because it makes money. Always."

I glanced at my watch. Ten-thirty.

"I think it's time for the Llewellyns to hit the rack," I said. "We've got to get up at six-fifteen for our Hamburg tour."

"I should go to bed as well. I can't lose any more money or I'll be in trouble. According to my parents, I'm supposed to play by Llewellyn rules during this cruise anyway," Esmé said.

We all stood up, said good night and headed for the staterooms.

Mike followed us.

As we reached our door, Maria and the girls went into the staterooms. Mike stopped me and said "You really need to think some more about bagging that tour of Hamburg tomorrow."

I closed the door, gently and faced Mike in the passageway.

"Bullshit," I said softly. "We booked this cruise for a family vacation.

And I'll be dammed if I'm going to cancel parts of the cruise because of some Russian assholes making threats. We're reasonably good at keeping our eyes open. And we have you guys—the U. S. Secret Service, for God's sake—on our side. We should be fine."

"Somehow I figured you'd say something like that," Mike said, with a wry grin. "But let the record show that the Secret Service recommends that you cancel your tour and stay aboard ship tomorrow."

"Mike. You disappoint me," I said. "You're recommending that we get under the covers and hide. Like craven dogs. And screw up our vacation in the bargain."

"Well, yeah. But you know that the Secret Service always has the security of those under its protection first in mind. As we do here. With you. And your family. And what's-her-face. There will be other vacation opportunities," he said.

"Esmé is her name. And who knows when us Llewellyns—and Esmé—will have another shot at Hamburg?" I asked, somewhat rhetorically.

"Suit yourself, Alan," he said. "Sleep well."

I let myself into the stateroom. The only light on was from a small lamp on the little desk. Maria seemed to be fast asleep or nearly so. I went into the head, washed up and brushed my teeth. I changed into my sleepwear--a Navy t-shirt and a pair of Navy soccer shorts and climbed into the rack alongside Maria. I was asleep in minutes.

Chapter Sixty-Four
Sheila

The C & O Canal Towpath
Washington, D. C.
Mid-June

Vice Admiral Donegan paged through her message traffic on her computer. There was a lot of "stuff" there. ISIS had just claimed responsibility for a suicide bombing in Dacca that had claimed twenty-seven lives—twenty-two Bengalis and five foreigners, including one American. An Israeli soldier had been stabbed to death at a checkpoint near Hebron; the Palestinian perpetrator had been shot dead by IDF troops. The Royal Navy had just launched their newest nuclear fleet submarine, HMS Ambush. The Peoples' Republic of China continued to "enlarge" several of the Paracel and Spratley Islands in the South China Sea.

But there was nothing—absolutely nothing—either from the DNI or from brother Bobby or his spooky friend, Darps. Much less anything from the White House. She glanced at the time/date slug on her computer screen: Fri zero-seven-eleven.

It was time to send a message to Darps. That she needed to see him. She hoped he hadn't been through North Parking yet as she grabbed her cover from the coat rack and stood up.

"I'll be right back," she said to Porter. Before he had a chance to answer, she was gone. Once in the parking lot, she unlocked her Honda and moved the manila folder to the top of the dashboard in front of the steering wheel. She hoped she wasn't too late and returned to her office.

By eleven-thirty, she had heard from Darps. A one-ring hang-up on her cell. Which meant that he'd got her message and would meet her at eighteen-thirty at the long-term parking lot at Reagan National. There was nothing else. From anywhere. She decided to go for a run. Today was Wednesday. The C & O Canal towpath would be perfect. She changed into her Navy running gear in the head, laced up her shoes and told IS1 Porter, "I'll be back in about fifty-five minutes." The time was eleven-forty. She had her Navy sedan drop her off where the Key Bridge met M Street.

She was about a half mile west of the Key Bridge and following the Potomac upstream when the .375 H & H Magnum round launched from across the river crashed into her chest, completely destroying her heart and lungs and knocking her body into the bushes on the north side of the trail. She experienced an instant of flashing pain and then nothing. In that instant a massive gout of her blood began sinking into the dry earth around the weeds.

By twelve-forty-five, Porter had started getting nervous. At twelve-fifty-five, he dialed the Admiral's mobile and got her voice mail. At twelve-fifty-six, he popped into Lieutenant Davis's office.

"I think we've got a missing Admiral, Sir," he told the Lieutenant.

"Whadda you mean?" asked Davis.

"She went for a run about eleven-forty. Said she'd be back in fifty-five minutes. That would make her ETR twelve thirty-five. It's now twelve fifty-five. She's twenty minutes late and her cell went right to voice mail when I tried to phone her."

"Holy Christ," the Lieutenant said. "When did you call?"

"About two minutes ago, Sir."

Lieutenant Davis grabbed his cell from his desk and punched in a speed-dial number.

"Shit. Her phone's still going to voice mail," Davis said. "Is the Commander here?"

"No sir. He's working out."

"Did he go running with the Admiral?"

"No sir. He left about ten minutes before she did. Said he was going to the Pentagon. You're SOPA[6]," Porter said.

"Well I guess I'll have to be the one to call NCIS," Davis said, reaching for his desk phone.

"This is Lieutenant Davis, Naval Intelligence. Our Admiral, Vice Admiral Donegan, left for a run over an hour ago. Said she'd be back in fifty-five minutes. She's not back and her cell goes right to voice mail. We're concerned, to say the least."

The Lieutenant listened for a couple of minutes, which seemed a long time to IS1 Porter.

"Uh oh," he said. "I'll be here."

---

6   Senior Officer Present Afloat.

He hung up the phone.

"NCIS says they're monitoring Metro Police radio traffic about a shooting on the C&O Towpath. Victim was a female. Apparently Navy from the looks of her running gear. Sounds like it could be our Admiral," Davis said.

"'Shooting?'" Porter repeated. "Fatal?" he asked.

"They didn't say. They're sending a couple of people over here right now. It doesn't sound good," Davis said. He looked like he'd aged eight or ten years since Porter had arrived at his office.

IS1 Porter heard voices from outside Lieutenant Davis's office. The receptionist, Marian, popped her head in the door.

"There are two NCIS agents here to see you, Lieutenant," she said.

"Okay. I'm expecting them," Davis said. "Send 'em in. Porter, have a seat. You should be here for this."

A man and a woman wearing civvies entered Davis's office.

"Hi lieutenant," the woman said. "I'm Special Agent Susan McCallum. I spoke with you on the phone a few minutes ago. This is Special Agent Chuck Evans. I think we have bad news."

"Okay. Have a seat and let's get the bad news out on the table," Davis said. "This is Petty Officer Porter. He works in Admiral Donegan's office. He's been trying to track the Admiral down."

"According to the MPD, a female runner was shot and killed with a high-powered rifle while running on the C&O Canal Towpath around noon. She was wearing Navy running gear. The MPD cops notified us, we went to the scene and determined that the victim apparently was Vice Admiral Donegan."

"Jesus Christ. Have you notified the CNO[7]?" Davis asked.

"Yes sir, We were doing that when you called us. The ID still isn't confirmed, but we're pretty sure it's her. Chuck here has met her a few times. He went to the crime scene and saw the body."

"It's her unless she has a twin sister," Evans said.

Marian popped her head in the office.

"CNO's office on line one," she said.

Chapter Sixty-Five

Alan

Kiel-Hamburg
Mid-June

A glance at my watch after I awoke on Thursday told me it was five-fifteen. I went to the foot of the bed, pulled back the blinds a little and saw that the sky was already Baltic gray. *Nordschiff* was gliding slowly through a crowded port. Kiel! Even at 5:15am, Kiel was a busy harbor.

I visited the head, sloshed mouthwash around to lose the morning monster mouth and ran a brush through my short hair. Maria was still blissfully in the arms of Morpheus when I emerged so I donned sweat gear quietly and followed up with running shoes. I paused to put an ear against the door of the girls' stateroom—heard nothing—and headed for the Promenade Deck. Luke picked me up before I got to the ladder well.

"Top o' the mornin', Alan," he said, smiling.

"Fancy meeting you in the here and now," I responded.

"I know, I know," he said. "Protection can be a pain in the ass. Just ask our boss. But I've got some bad news. Real bad. Let's get out of this passageway."

Seconds later we stepped out onto the Promenade Deck.

"It's Admiral Donegan. Naval Intelligence. Assassinated. By a sniper. While she was running on the C&O Towpath."

"Good Christ," I started to say. "Dead?"

"As the proverbial doornail. Didn't have a chance. High velocity round right in the chest."

That was when my mobile chimed. I took it out. Darps.

"Yo," I said. "I think I just heard what you're about to tell me."

"Donegan?" he asked.

"Yeah!" I said. "That's fucking terrible! Does Bobby know?"

"Yeah. The CNO's office was going to tell him. I told them I'd do it. Bobby is our shipmate. So I told him. One of the hardest things I've ever done."

"Okay," I said. "God bless you. And him. Luke just told me a couple of minutes ago. Give me an hour or two to get my arms around this and I'll call you back."

"Roger that. Except wait a few hours—it's eleven-thirty at night here and I've got to hit the rack."

"Okay," I said. "I'll call you around eight, your time. Now try and get a few zees"

I pressed the button to end the call.

"Sounds like you know all we know which isn't much," Luke said, "No shooter, no suspect. But I'm going to ask you again to pull the plug on that tour of Hamburg today. We have info--admittedly sketchy--that renegade Russians are running loose in Germany and could be a serious threat to you and your family. That, plus this assassination of Admiral Donegan, has got us nervous as the proverbial cat covering up shit. To say the least. And the word is that they really want that damned book you picked up in Saint Petersburg. Along with the piece of paper that goes with it."

"Okay Luke. Normally, I'd tell you to take your advice and stick it where then sun doesn't shine. But Donegan getting whacked sheds a whole new light on everything. So, much as I hate the idea, I will pull the plug on today's outing. Wanna walk with me?" I asked.

"I'd love to, but I'd best drop back behind you a bit," he said.

"Okay. Actually that makes me feel better. I've got to think about the ramifications of the Donegan murder. Later I'll call Darps back. Maybe meantime I'll need to chat with you, Mike and Judy. This murder puts a whole new light on our situation here. Anyhow, I'm going walking for forty minutes and Inshallah you'll have my back."

I set off at a brisk walk, heading clockwise. It was fascinating observing the port of Kiel as *Nordschiff* continued in a stately fashion farther into the busy harbor. The news about Donegan was very unsettling. To say the least.

By the time I'd finished three miles and worked up a decent sweat, *Nordschiff* was made fast to a pier and gangways were being adjusted. I headed back to our stateroom. There was a two-page copy of the International New York Times news summary in our mailbox. My gal was up and showered and was drying her hair.

"Are the weasels up?" I asked.

"Yup," she said. "Unless they went back to bed after I called them."

I opened our door, stepped down the passageway and planted my right ear against the girls' door. I got an earful of morning TV and female chatter. All was well. Here. I popped back into our stateroom. Thirty seconds later, I was standing under a hot shower. I shaved under the shower and managed to avoid slicing myself with the razor. Then I jumped into some clothes. I paused briefly to tap on the girls' door and we headed for the Lido and breakfast.

We strode into the buffet at six-fifty and I looked around and immediately spotted Judy hovering over a cup of something steamy.

"There's Judy," I said to the ladies, unnecessarily.

We walked over to her table.

"May we join you?" I asked.

"Of course," she said. "I was waiting for you. Having a cup of tea and growing hungry."

"You've heard about Admiral Donegan?" I asked.

"Yes. It's horrible," she said. "Absolutely horrible."

"In more ways than we know," I answered. "Umm, this is as good a time as any to pass the word to everyone. We're staying aboard today. No Hamburg tour. Vice Admiral Donegan was murdered yesterday. While she was running. At lunchtime in D. C. Apparently by a sniper."

"What's that got to do with us in Hamburg?" Maria asked.

"Lots," I said. "She is—was—directly connected to my little side-job on this cruise. The fact that someone murdered her back in D. C. makes the stakes in the game we're playing here a lot higher. Plus, the Secret Service got word of some bad-ass Russians prowling around and they strongly recommend that we stay aboard."

"Rats," said Esmé. "I was hoping to see some of those notorious Hamburg whorehouses."

"Esmé, you are a piece of work," I said. "Besides, they don't let anyone under eighteen on the street where the whorehouses are," I continued.

"I'm just trying to round out my education, Mister El," she retorted. "Anyway, I'm starved."

"In that case, let's hit the chow line," I said.

We did.

Chapter Sixty-Six

Alan

Thursday
Kiel
Mid-June

"Okay," I announced as the last morsels of breakfast began to disappear. "I've got to sit down and brainstorm this awful development--Admiral Donegan's murder. I'm going to allow myself a few hours after which I'm going to call Darps. Like I promised him I would. I can do the brainstorming in the stateroom or the Explorers' Lounge. Anyone who wants to join me is welcome. We'll just have to coordinate with Mike and Luke. Any takers?"

"Yup!" Esmé piped up, raising her hand. "Count me in. I love a mystery."

I thought about that for a couple of seconds, wondering if Esmé's parents would appreciate me involving their fourteen-year-old daughter in a real-world murder mystery. But then, she was already involved since she was traveling with the Llewellyn family. Besides the murder took place thousands of miles away from us.

"Good," I said. "Anybody else?"

"Of course," Judy said. "It sounds like it's related to what we do at *BIAS*, so please count me in. I don't know whether I'll be able to add anything to the brainstorming process, but I should know what and how you're thinking."

"I was hoping you'd say something like that."

We squared things with the Secret Service. Maria and Elizabeth decided to hang out in our stateroom together, reading news, doing sudokos or whatever for an hour. Then, they'd swim and bask before meeting us on the Lido for lunch at noon.

Once Judy, Esmé and I settled into a far corner of the Explorers' Lounge, I opened the brainstorming session.

"Here goes," I said, to get the ball rolling. "Several weeks ago, *Cheetah* heard from a Russian source that there was a coup plot brewing against him somewhere in the U. S. Government. He tasked *BIAS* to look into

222

that. He—President Kehoe—removed the normal restrictions on *BIAS* stateside collection activities. We went to work. That much you know," I said, nodding at Judy.

"About a week and a half ago, Vice Admiral Donegan contacted *BIAS* without actually knowing it. She asked her brother, Bobby, a Lieutenant Commander who works in OPNAV—and a Naval Academy classmate of Darps and myself--if he had a conduit into the White House. She intimated that there was a plot within the U. S Government against the President and that she was a part of it. She was willing to fall on her sword to blow the whistle on the plot, even if it meant that she'd end up in Leavenworth. She felt she needed to speak directly to the President. He, Bobby, referred her to Darps. She and Darps had a semi-clandestine meeting in which she spilled a few of the beans and asked for a meeting with Kehoe. Darps told her he'd see what he could do and then told me and I advised *Cheetah*. He said he'd think about it. At that point, we didn't know if Donegan was a nut case and could be a physical threat to the President or was a hot link to a real-live plot. About which we'd had a fair bit of corroborating info from the Russians. Then, we Llewellyns left on this cruise. With Kehoe's blessing, I might add. The call I got at the embassy in London came from the White House and tasked me with picking up some info from some Russians in Saint Petersburg. And you guys know all the rest, leading up to this morning's bad-horrible-news."

"Um—what about the so-called 'Fort Sill Anomaly,' Mister El?" Esmé interjected.

"What about it?" I rejoined.

"Well, it came about in the middle of all this, time-wise. Somebody, or something apparently shut down virtually all things electronic on Fort Sill, Oklahoma, for exactly two minutes. At the same time, right outside the fence in beautiful downtown Lawton, everything stayed up and running. Seems to me, if there is a coup against the government brewing, that Fort Sill business could well be connected to it."

"Hmm. Excellent point, Esmé. Here's what I'm going to tell Darps when I call him.

"First, send flowers to the appropriate funeral home for Admiral Donegan. From Bobby Donegan's Naval Academy classmates and the Admiral's shipmates, Darps and myself. No mention of *BIAS*. I'll also tell him to send Sammy or Ashleigh or both to the funeral to pay respects and to eyeball the mourners.

"Second, monitor MPD and NCIS progress on the murder investigation.

"Third—and this is a new one, thanks very much to you, Esmé—see if *BIAS* can spook out any more information on the Fort Sill anomaly, including any possible connections to the plot against Kehoe. Any other news bits from papers besides the *Lawtonian*.

"Fourth, and finally, I'll tell him that I'll summarize all the nasty blips on the radar that have popped up during our cruise so far. I should have that finished up and sent to Darps at *BIAS* within the next five-to-six hours or so."

Chapter Sixty-Seven

Alan

Kiel

Mid-June

Nordschiff has two swimming pools. The smaller forward pool was deserted. On top of that, the weather seemed to be turning sour. Lowering, gray clouds and a damp chill were settling in. Luke and I found a table with a couple of chairs by the vacant forward pool.

"Okay," Luke said. "That ambush of Vice Admiral Donegan on the Towpath has got a lot of folks climbing the walls."

"No shit," I mumbled. "Do we have any idea who's behind it?"

"No clue," Luke said. "All they know is that the shooter used an extremely powerful rifle. It basically blew away her chest. There was a thought of flying you and the women—-and the book--out of Flughafen Hamburg commercial, but there's not enough time. The last flight leaves in just under an hour. By the time we get you booked, pack you up and get you from here in Kiel to the airport in Hamburg, that last flight will be long gone. Even if we requested a delay at "the highest levels," it would be too long a delay. They thought of launching a jet from the eighty-ninth Military Airlift Wing to pick you and the family and the book up in Hamburg and flying you all back to CONUS. To Andrews."

The eighty-ninth MAW is the unit that mans and flies Air Force One and a whole fleet of other aircraft that moves other U. S. Government big shots from place to place. Usually ending up at Joint Base Andrews right outside D. C.

"But that has time constraints as well," he continued. "It would take them eight hours to scramble a special jet and the crew and another eight hours to fly it here. That puts it here at zero-eight-hundred tomorrow. *Nordschiff* sails at seven this evening. Waiting for the jet puts you and the family—and the book—bare-assed naked in Kiel or Hamburg for thirteen fucking hours, waiting for the eighty-ninth. Unsat."

"So that leads me back to my original question," I said. "Whiskey-tango-foxtrot?"

"We stay on *Nordschiff*," he said. "As far as we know, it's safe. Now. The four of us who comprise the Secret Service protection unit—plus Judy--can cover you guys for the next forty-eight hours without a problem. So that's what we'll do. Judy checked with the White House and they—don't ask me how—checked with the Russkies and ascertained that a few days' delay shouldn't be a problem."

"What about in the UK?" I asked.

"We'll have a ton of help from the Brits," he said. "We'll fly back to CONUS from the UK courtesy of the eighty-ninth. That flight has been fragged already. You and the family will be totally safe once you get on that airplane."

Luke's words were sounding good. Things were starting to look up. I thought I might be able to cheer up Maria, Elizabeth and Esmé. Hell, I was feeling better about things myself.

"So what do you think about us going to dinner?" I asked.

"Go ahead. Stay with your regular routine. We'll be in your hip pockets, so don't worry," Luke said.

So Maria, Elizabeth, Esmé and I went to the Explorers' Lounge. Maria joined me for a Ketel One dry martini. The Russian girls' trio played. Tamara was her usual gracious self. While we waited, *Nordschiff* started to quietly slip away from the pier. After cocktails, we went below for dinner.

Our Canadian friends were there and we joined them. They had taken a tour of Hamburg that they had enjoyed. Maria and I listened to Priscilla and Charles telling us about their day trip, seeing the world-famous whorehouses on the *Herbertstrasse*. Esmé rolled her eyes at the mention of the infamous Hamburg houses of ill fame. Priscilla sported a fresh tattoo on her left ankle—a side view of *M.S. Nordschiff*.

"Drat! I was hoping to get a tattoo as well!" Esme snarled.

"Well, let's all thank the Lord that that

opportunity has come and gone," I said. "It would have been an absolute horror show for me to try to explain to your parents how I'd let their fourteen-year-old daughter get a tattoo in Hamburg!"

We bullshitted the Scotts about having to cancel our day trip due to a stomach bug from which we'd since miraculously recovered. The two teenagers snickered off and on as they chatted. Dinner was very German--thick, juicy pork chops with sauerkraut and beets. I washed it down with a dark beer; Maria and the Scotts used glasses of Riesling.

We were chatting while the wait staff bussed our table prior to bringing us Strudel and coffee when Ally stopped by, tapped me on the shoulder and nodded toward the exit. I stood up and followed her to the vestibule of the Pinnacle Grille.

"We got some news that may be troubling," she said. "Four Latvians boarded the ship this afternoon in Kiel. With tickets. Three men and a woman."

"I thought Latvians were the good guys," I said.

"They are," she said. "Except that almost thirty percent of them aren't Latvian at all. They're Russian. They speak Russian, eat Russian and drink Russian. And their politics are Russian. So we really don't know about these clowns that came aboard this afternoon."

"What do the Danes say?" I asked.

"They're suspicious. They were the ones who tipped us off. The guys and the gal have seemingly legitimate Latvian names and passports. But the Danes are still very suspicious. They seem convinced that these guys are Russians."

"What about us Americans? What do we know? What are we saying?"

"Nothing yet, except what I've just told you. We got pretty good copies of the first pages of their passports from the Danes and we've phoned them back to D. C. for analysis. My first concern is that these guys may be small fry and be pretty deep in the weeds to be known quantities," Ally said. "But we'll see what comes back."

"So meantime, what do we do? Hide?"

"No. We'll be all over you. You'll be safe. Stay all together and you should be fine."

"In that case, after we finish coffee and dessert, I think we'll go back to the Explorers' Lounge for a bit of music and an after-dinner drink. Then we'll crash till breakfast at sea tomorrow."

"Sounds fine to me. Luke and I will be on top of you, Maria, Elizabeth and Esmé. Mike and Emma will cover the Latvians. Or Russians. Whatever the hell they are."

I ambled back to the dinner table. The Strudel and coffee had been served and largely consumed. Except for mine. A situation that I remedied by wolfing down the Strudel between gulps of lukewarm coffee. That was helpful in preventing speech--unhelpful chatter about my little talk with Ally about the Latvians or Russians or whatever the hell they were. Finally, I wiped the last Strudel crumbs from my lips with a linen napkin and took a last sip of tepid coffee.

"Anyone up for an after-dinner drink?" I asked.

Maria arched her eyebrows and said, "Sure."

Our Canadian friends said, "No, thanks. We're bushed. Long day." The two stood up. We stood up as well and said our good nights.

There was a five-piece combo playing in the Explorer's Lounge in place of the Russian girls and three or four couples were dancing to the music, which seemed to lean toward seventies and eighties American pop stuff. *Do You Wanna Dance? Super Trouper* and the like. Tamara took our orders—cognacs for the three adults, Sprites for the two girls. We watched the dancing couples while we waited for our drinks. Tamara returned with them quickly; two twentyish-looking guys suddenly popped up out of nowhere and asked the girls to dance. They accepted. With alacrity, I noticed. I looked around and saw Luke seated at a side table. Everything seemed fine. After several songs, the band took a break and Elizabeth and Esmé returned to the table.

"That was fun!" Elizabeth said. "Yes," Esmé agreed. "They were fun. And funny."

"Do you know where they're from?" I asked, somewhat suspiciously.

"Scotland. Near Aberdeen," Elizabeth said.

I recalled a comrade from my Navy days, a Royal Marine major named Angus Davidson. From Aberdeen.

"Come visit us in Aberdeen," he'd said. "Come in the summertime for the fishing and the fornicating. Or come in the wintertime when it's too cold for the fishing."

I wasn't sure that I was all enthused about our girls frolicking with the "fun" lads from Aberdeen.

"How about their ages?" asked Maria. "Did they tell you how old they are?"

"They said they were twenty-one. Both of them," Esmé said.

"Arghh!" I muttered. "Dirt bags preying on young girls."

"Maybe they thought we're older than we actually are," Elizabeth said with a little smirk.

"Maybe so. But I still think they're dirt bags," I said. I would have said more except I didn't want to scandalize Esmé.

Chapter Sixty-Eight
Litvinov

The Embassy of the Russian Federation
Washington, D.C.
Mid-June

Colonel Litvinov approached the door to his office. His wristwatch—always on time—read 7:18 a.m. He was surprised to find the door unlocked. Usually the office staff arrived a few minutes before eight. He was even more surprised when he opened the door and stepped inside and Valeriya greeted him with a hug, a forceful kiss—full lips first followed by a firm tongue and finally by nibbling teeth--and a smile. Litvinov could feel a burgeoning hard-on. He backed away from Valeriya and wondered if she'd noticed. The exchange was pleasant enough, but there was a shitload of complications. He was married to the Ambassador's cousin. Valeriya seemed to be the Ambassador's main squeeze. Being nailed with his hand in her pants could cause a monstrous shitstorm.

"Good morning, Colonel," she said, still smiling.

"Good morning to you," Litvinov said. "Did I miss something? Or forget something? Is today my birthday?"

"*Nyet*, you ass. Your cousin, the Ambassador, needs to see you. Right away. Rock Creek Park. Just below Shoreham Drive. Wear running clothes."

"Well Valeriya, you gave a great start to my day. But now things are starting to go downhill. My running clothes are at home. If I go home and change and then run to Rock Creek Park, I won't be there in less than an hour."

"Then I suggest you forget the running clothes and head for the park right now," Valeriya said. "H. E. left five minutes ago."

"Can you get me a car this early?"

"Of course," she said, picking up a phone.

Twelve minutes later, Colonel Litvinov spotted Ambassador Malenkov jogging toward him along the trail in Rock Creek Park.

"Let me out here, Yuri," he muttered to the driver of the embassy vehicle. "Pick me up here in ten minutes."

"Yes sir," said the driver.

Colonel Litvinov climbed out of the vehicle just as Ambassador Malenkov approached.

"Where are your running clothes?" the Ambassador asked in Russian.

"At home," Litvinov said. "If I'd gone home to change, I'd have missed you."

"Very well. Let's walk for a few minutes."

Litvinov slipped out of his suit coat and loosened his tie. He estimated that the temperature was already well over eighty. Fahrenheit. He'd begun getting used to the American way of reciting outside temperatures in degrees Fahrenheit. The two men walked down the trail toward the Kennedy Center.

"Something's fucked up," the Ambassador said, "In Moscow."

"Tell me something I don't know. Something's always fucked up in Moscow."

"*Da*. But *this* 'something' has to do with us."

"Uh oh," Litvinov said.

"Do you still have a copy of that list?" Malenkov asked.

"List?" hissed Litvinov in a whisper. "You mean that list of American conspirators I gave you?"

"The same."

"*Nyet*. I put all the paper related to that situation through the shredder."

"So did I," the Ambassador muttered. "Through the goddamned shredder. I didn't want a trace of that information lying around the Embassy or the Residence or wherever. I shredded everything. Twice."

"I remember most of the names but probably not all of them. And I do still have a copy of the book. But why this sudden renewal of interest? What's going on?" Litvinov asked.

"Well, I don't know what's going on. But something is. I got a so-called 'secure' call at the Residence this morning. From Kirilinkov himself. Only God knows who else listened to that call. The Minister said that we need to get the list to Kehoe. Soonest! He also said that he had tried to get it to him through quote other channels unquote. But there was a problem, whatever that means. And now it was up to us. And—get this—any and all contact between the embassy and/or me and the White House and Kehoe was to be totally clandestine and off the record."

"Stalin's teeth! What the hell are we supposed to do? Tie the list around a brick and throw it over the White House fence at three a. m.? Even that way, we'd probably get caught and any and all confidentiality about the Embassy connection with the White House would go down the toilet!"

"Not to mention that the list might not be accurate or complete, given that it would be based on our memories of it," the ambassador mumbled. Colonel Litvinov looked at his watch. "We need to turn around in a minute or so. Yuri is picking me up where he dropped me off in six minutes."

"Okay. The only other thing I need to tell you is that whatever form our communications with the White House takes, you'll be part of it."

"Well, shit," muttered Litvinov. "That really makes my day."

"Go ahead and turn back to catch Yuri. I'll run to the Kennedy Center and turn around there. Keep your schedule open. We'll need to meet again soon. For more than a couple of minutes. Meantime, try to recall all the names on that list."

Ambassador Malenkov started to jog and Colonel Litvinov turned around and started hiking back up the hill towards Connecticut Avenue.

Chapter Sixty-Nine
Alan

"I have to go to the loo," Elizabeth announced, glancing at Esmé.

"I'll go with you," Esmé said. Both girls stood up.

I knew that the heads were right outside the doors of the Explorers' Lounge, which were right behind the bandstand, just vacated by the band. I didn't see any problem. The girls left. I glanced over at Luke. He watched the girls as they exited the Lounge and then looked at me with raised eyebrows for a second. Then he got to his feet and started after them. I stood up and began to go after him.

It probably took all of four or five seconds for Luke to exit the Lounge. Probably no more than one or two seconds more for me to follow him. When I reached the passageway where the heads were located, Luke was slamming on the door of the Ladies' loo with the palm of his hand.

"Elizabeth!" he shouted. "Esmé!" he shouted again. Apparently hearing nothing, he pulled the door open and went inside. I followed.

The bathroom was empty.

"Jesus Christ!" he hissed. "They're not here!"

A jolt of ice water squirted into my heart.

"Jesus," I whispered. "I can't believe Elizabeth would take off without telling us. I'm not so sure about Esmé though. And I think Elizabeth looks up to her. We'd better check the casino."

"I'm worried that they didn't take off for the casino on their own," Luke muttered. "But I hope I'm wrong and that's what they did."

Luke had pulled out his mobile and was punching keys while he checked the stalls.

"Do you have all four of our friends in sight?" he asked into the phone.

"Okay," he answered after a long pause. "We may have a major problem on our hands. Elizabeth and her girlfriend excused themselves to go to the head. But they're not there. Alan and I just checked it out.

We're heading for the casino now. Keep your eyes on the guys you can see. If we don't see the two girls in the casino, we'll double back to your stateroom."

"Jesus! What the hell is going on?" I asked.

"The four Latvians split up—four ways," Luke said. "Mike and Emma could only keep track of two of them—they stayed with two of the males. They don't know where the other male and the female are."

"So. I say again. What the hell?"

"We check the casino and hope for the best. We're almost there."

Seconds later, we hurried into the casino. There were several women of a certain age whaling away on the slots and a number of imbibers hunkering over the roulette wheel. A poker table was in full swing and another two tables hosted blackjack players. But no teenaged girls.

"Not here," I muttered through clenched teeth.

Chapter Seventy

Alan

Kieler Bucht
Mid-June

"I'm going back to the Explorers' Lounge to get Maria and get her back to our stateroom," I said. "Maybe Ally will join us. If not, I'm hoping to see *some* U.S. Secret Service Agent show up in our stateroom soonest. Otherwise, I'm striking out on my own to get my little girl back. Both my little girls, actually."

"Alan. This is a situation in which you'd be best off leaving things in the hands of the pros."

"That remains to be seen," I said, a bit testily. "Latvian—or Russian—scumbags, under the watching eyes of the so-called pros have apparently snatched two teenaged American girls—my daughter and daughter *pro tem*. So the idea of 'leaving things in the hands of the pros' gives me pause. To say the fucking least."

"I can't blame you for thinking or saying that, Alan," Luke said. "But getting them back ASAP would be best left to us—even with all our warts."

"We'll see," I said. "We'll see. Now I'm going to get Maria and barricade us in our stateroom whilst we try to figure things out."

I turned and headed back to the Explorers' Lounge. When I arrived back there, Maria was sitting at our table but had company. Ally had joined her. I leaned over Maria.

"Let's go back to the stateroom, Sweetheart," I said.

"Where's Elizabeth?" she asked.

"Let's go to the room," I repeated, taking her hand.

She looked me in the eye, her eyes narrowed slightly and I would have bet a thousand bucks that she knew something was terribly wrong. It wasn't hard to see that she wasn't liking this one damned bit. But she got to her feet.

Ally closed her phone and got to her feet as well.

"I'll go with you to your room," she said. "Luke will meet us there."

"Let's hope that the girls are in our room," I said. "Or theirs."

The four of us got in the elevator. Ally was doing her job, staying on top of us.

We got off the elevator on our deck and walked to our stateroom in silence. I banged the door of the girls' room first. Nothing. I used my key card and opened the door. Once again, nobody. I opened the door of the stateroom across the passageway. Ours. Nothing. Except there was a folded piece of paper on the deck. It had "USA" scrawled on it with a black marker. I started to reach for it.

"Hold it, Alan!" Ally said in a noisy whisper. "Allow me. I don't think we'll be able to get anything off it, but let's not take any chances of maybe losing a print or two!"

She took a silver pen and a matching pencil from her purse and used them like clumsy chopsticks. She picked up the folded sheet of paper, looked around and put it on the credenza next to the TV set. Maria closed the stateroom door. Ally used the two silver writing implements to spread open the folded paper.

Someone had used a Sharpie to scrawl:

THE RUSSIAN BOOK! NOW! ON PROMENADE DECK PORT SIDE OR GIRLS ARE OVERBOARD BY MIDNIGHT! LLEWELLYN NEEDS TO COME ALONE! WITH THE BOOK!

"Jesus Christ," I muttered. I glanced at my watch. Ten oh-two. A cell phone chimed.

"Luke is on his way, too," Ally said.

"My first instinct is to open the safe, get the god damned book and take it up to the Promenade Deck, port side," I said.

"Let's wait till everybody else gets here," Ally said. "It'll only be a few minutes. Remember, our first priority is getting the girls back safely."

"Jesus H. Christ! How could I not remember that?" I snarled.

Luke arrived a minute or so later. Everyone started talking at once.

"Sit down, everyone. Please," Luke said, making a 'be seated' gesture with his hands.

"Where are our girls?" demanded Maria.

"Please. Sit down. I'll tell you what we know but it will help if we all keep calm. Please."

Everybody seemed to settle down, more or less.

"First of all, we have notified *Nordschiff* security that the girls are missing," Luke said. "We've also advised them that we think the Latvians/ Russians are involved. They—Nordschiff—have notified Interpol, Latvian police, German authorities as well as the Russians. We—the United States Secret Service—have two of the four under observation. At least, that's what we told *Nordschiff* Security people. Actually, we have two of them in handcuffs. The other two, one Janis Vetra, a male, and one Inga Valters, a female, are unaccounted for. And we think the two of them are holding the girls. But at this point, we don't know where."

Luke paused and pulled out a three-by-five card from his shirt pocket.

"We've heard from Washington. Vetra is actually Lavrentii Skolnikov and Valters is actually Ludmilla Baranova, both Russians, both Mafiya. Both relatively low-level rats."

"Okay," I said. "Nobody knows where these two assholes are or where they might have our girls. Seems like we need to do something to smoke the bastards out. And get a lead on the girls' locations that way."

"My recommendation," Luke said. "Is to give *Nordschiff* security a chance to find them. They know the ship. They know all the hiding places. They're searching already."

"Okay," I said, reluctantly. "But time marches on."

I glanced at my watch.

"It's now ten-ten," I said. "According to that piece of paper, our girls go over the side in an hour and fifty minutes."

"I know, Alan," Luke said. "You're right. But let's give the ship's security another twenty minutes to find the girls. They know the ship."

"Fifteen," I said. "Like you said, they know the ship. They should find the girls within fifteen minutes. If they haven't, I'm going after them."

Everybody in the crowded stateroom looked at one another uneasily. I looked at the slight handgun bulge under Ally's blazer. I wondered if Luke would shoot me if I made a grab for her weapon. I looked at my watch. Ten-twelve. An hour and forty-eight minutes...

"I have an idea," I said. "It might buy us some time. I still have the plastic gift shop bag from Saint Petersburg. We can put another book in it and I can take it up to the Promenade Deck and hang out on the port side until one of these assholes shows up. I hold out the book in the bag and demand the return of the girls immediately."

"But, dollars to donuts, that won't work, Alan," Luke said. "These bastards won't show up with the girls. One or both of the Russians will be there. They'll demand the book. If you give them a fake, you'll just piss them off and the girls are toast."

"I won't give it to them if the girls aren't there. That's the way we can maybe buy some time."

"I still don't like it," Luke said. "If you seem to be holding out on them, they very well might shoot you and toss your dead ass over the side. And then do the same thing to the girls."

"I don't think they would," I responded. "They want the goddamned book too much. The real one. With a fake book and me and the girls dead, they'd never get it."

"I don't think that's a chance anyone wants to take," Luke said softly.

Suddenly another idea popped into my fevered brain.

"Wait a minute, Luke," I said. "Where are we with this situation? Russians have our girls. They want a book that's locked up in my safe. And which I've been charged by the President of the United States to deliver into his sweaty hands. The Russians are threatening to throw our girls over the side in less than two hours time if we don't give them the book. If I go to the Promenade Deck with a phony book, maybe we can buy some time for the girls that way."

"No way, Alan. You'd just be putting yourself in a confrontational situation."

"Well then," I said. "I just came up with a plan. You just shot it down. What's *your* plan?"

Silence ensued.

"That's what I thought," I said. "So your plan is 'Do nothing. Not a fucking thing.' Is that it?"

Silence.

"And, we're not in the U.S.," I continued. "We're on the high seas. If I can meet with the Russians for a couple of minutes, maybe we can get an idea of where they have the girls stashed. And then go get them."

"Alan, you are one stubborn bastard," Luke muttered.

I dove into the closet and opened the safe. I yanked out the plastic gift shop bag, which contained the *Poems of Anna Achmatova* book.

"Any one got a spare book? I don't want to give them the real thing. All of ours are on our Kindles," I said.

"Maybe a Kindle would stall them a little bit longer," Luke said. "They might take some time screwing around with it, trying to figure it out."

"Good thought," I said. I dropped my Kindle into the plastic bag. It looked like Maria and I would have to share a Kindle for the rest of the trip. I placed the actual Achmatova book back in the safe and spun the dial.

"I'm off to the Promenade Deck, port side," I said. I left the crowded stateroom carrying the gift bag.

The Promenade Deck appeared to be deserted when I let myself out of the after doors on the port side. The night was still cloudy and almost dark—no visible sky. The sea was calm with only a light chop. Nordschiff seemed to be knifing through the sea rapidly with almost zero resistance.

I walked forward almost to the bow where there was a bulkhead and a door separating the deck from the forecastle. I changed direction and headed aft on the port side. Shortly after I passed amidships, I heard a voice from behind me.

"You haff de book?"

I turned and faced a skinny guy in a raincoat.

"Yes. I do," I said, holding up the gift shop bag. "Where are the girls?"

"You vill see de girls after you hand over de book," the skinny guy said in heavily accented English.

"I need to see the girls. In front of me. Then I'll give you the book."

"That's not de way it works," he said. "You giff me de book. Den I go get de girls."

I handed the gift shop bag toward him and, as he reached for it with his right hand, I clamped onto his wrist.

"*Sukin sin*!" he snarled. "Son of a bitch!"

I pulled down and he fell halfway to the deck and groped under the raincoat. His left hand emerged, clumsily holding an ancient, black Makarov PM handgun. I used both hands to pull him further down and twist his wrist violently. The Makarov dropped to the steel deck with a *thunk*. I picked it up. My skinny companion stepped toward me and I squeezed off a round while the muzzle was still pointed at the deck. He went down.

"You cocksucker!" he howled. "You shot me! T'rough de fucking foot!"

"Next one will be about two and a half feet higher and closer to your midline, asshole!"

"I can't believe you shot me in de foot, you son of a bitch!" he screamed.

"Well, take a look at your bloody fucking foot and believe! Let me explain the score to you. You're lying here on the deck. Two of your asshole buddies are handcuffed to each other and to a bed in a stateroom with duct tape over their mouths. You're about to join them. Maybe we'll use some more duct tape to apply a couple of rags to the holes in your foot to slow the bleeding. But maybe not. Your girlfriend is holding our two girls somewhere. You need to tell us where. If you hesitate, we'll start pitching your worthless asses over the side, one at a time. And the book that you guys seem to want so desperately is safely stashed. You'll never get it."

I pulled out my cell and called Luke.

"Hey! I've got a Russian slime dog on the deck. Promenade Deck. I just blew a hole in his foot. With his own gun. I'd like to get him and his blood out of sight," I said.

"Jesus Christ!" Luke mumbled. "Can you stanch the bleeding?"

"Yeah, I think so. I'll try. But there's still a lot of cleaning up to do."

I wriggled out of my shirt and then pulled off my undershirt—a plain, white tee shirt. I ripped the shoe off the whining turd's foot and threw it over the side. Then I wrapped my undershirt around his profusely bleeding foot and tied it in a knot. I stood up.

Luke picked that moment to show up with an armload of towels. He looked at the Russian on the deck and the mess of blood around his foot. He tossed me a towel.

"Wrap this around the maggot's foot. To keep it from leaking. Then haul his worthless ass below. To Room four-dash-two-thirteen. That's where Mike has got the other two douche bags. Hook him up with his buds. I'll clean up here and be right down."

"Mutterfuckers!" hissed the dirt bag on the deck. Even though English was not his primary language, his knowledge of street-level obscenity was impressive.

"You're in no position to editorialize, asshole," muttered Luke. "You're in the cage and things are about to go south for you. Very quickly."

"Bastids," whined the shit bird.

I wrapped a towel around his bleeding foot, not any too gently. He inhaled sharply.

"Okay. Time to stand up," I said.

"I can't, mutterfucker. You shot a hole in my foot!"

"Stand up or my buddy and I will throw your sorry ass over the side. I'll be goddamned if I'll carry you below."

I parked the nine-millimeter in my waistband. Then I grabbed his right hand with my left and yanked. He got to his feet, haltingly. I jerked his right arm around my neck, leaned into him and dropped my left arm to grab his waist.

"Okay, my friend. We're off. You'll be able to join your buddies, for a little while, at least."

I used my right hand to shift the Makarov to the back of my waistband. We took a couple of steps and I stopped him and turned around to look behind us. Sure enough, he was leaving bloody mini-footprints.

"Luke. Throw a towel on the deck so dipshit here quits leaving footprints," I said.

"Will do," Luke said. "But get him below in a hurry. He'll start leakin' again pretty soon."

I walked our prisoner across the towel that Luke had spread on the deck. He left one tiny bloody mark. His next step was clean.

"Okay. We're off," I said.

"I'll get this mess cleaned up and join you below in four-two-thirteen in a couple of minutes."

Chapter Seventy-One
Litvinov

Embassy of the Russian Federation
Washington, D. C.
Mid-June

It was just after four-thirty a.m. when the ring tone on Colonel Litvinov's iPhone bored through his hangover and into his brain.

"Allo!" he half snapped, half croaked. While holding the phone to his ear, his eyes widened and he straightened up in bed.

"I'll be there in fifteen minutes," he said.

"I have to go to the embassy right now. Emergency," he muttered to his wife, who was now half-sitting up in bed.

"I'll fix tea," she said. "Emergencies" in the middle of the night were not all that uncommon at the Russian Embassy in Washington.

Colonel Litvinov splashed cold water on his face a few times and rubbed toothpaste around his gums before rinsing his mouth. Back in the bedroom, he donned a pair of tan gabardine slacks, a blue oxford shirt and loafers. Anna, his wife appeared with a steaming mug. A teabag string hung over the mug's rim.

"The sugar is already in," she told him.

"*Spasiba*, thanks," he told her, taking the mug and kissing the tip of her nose. "I'll call you when I find out what's going on."

A warm drizzle was falling as Colonel Litvinov pulled out of his driveway in Great Falls. He pushed the appropriate switch and the wipers clicked on. The George Washington Parkway was virtually deserted, but he stayed at the speed limit, taking an occasional sip of the hot, sweet tea. Thank God for Anna!

He noted with some alarm that His Excellency Malenkov's Mercedes Six-Hundred was parked in its space. The Ambassador usually kept the Mercedes at his residence overnight.

Good God, he thought. *The shit must really be in the fan for H.E. to be here at this hour.*

A glance at his watch told him that the time was four-fifty. His mobile chimed. He hit the Bluetooth button just as he nosed the Buick into a parking place.

"Litvinov," he mumbled.

"Where are you?" Valerya's sultry voice burbled from the speaker.

"In the parking lot," he answered.

"Come right up," she said.

It must be really bad shit, he thought. *Otherwise, Valerya wouldn't throw security considerations to the four winds like she just did. Probably at Malenkov's behest.*

He flashed his ID at the FSB security guard at the door and raced up the stairs directly to Malenkov's office suite which he entered without knocking. Valerya hooked a thumb over her sweatered shoulder toward the Ambassador's office.

"Go on in," she said, unsmiling. Not a good sign.

Ambassador Malenkov sat at his desk in shirtsleeves and no tie. He had reading glasses perched on the tip of his nose. It appeared that he had a copy of the book *Seven Days in May* on his desk. He looked up.

"Val. Have a seat. Thanks for coming in at this ungodly hour," the Ambassador said.

"What's up?" Litvinov asked.

"Remember 'the list'? The list of possible American conspirators in the plot against Kehoe?"

"*Da*. The one we both shredded," Litvinov answered.

"Wasn't Vice Admiral Donegan's name on the list?"

"Yes. For sure. That's one name I definitely remember. She's the Director of Naval Intelligence," Litvinov replied.

"'*Was*' the Director of Naval Intelligence," the Ambassador said. "Detachment Zed picked up some radio traffic from the Metropolitan Police. Apparently Admiral Donegan is dead. Shot to death whilst running on the C&O Canal Towpath this afternoon. Evidently shot by a sniper."

"Holy Christ," whispered Litvinov. "To say that the plot thickens would be a gross understatement."

"Detachment Zed" was the common abbreviation for "Special Intelligence Detachment Z," an undercover embassy office that used specialized antennas on the embassy roof to monitor various local D. C. radio networks. Including those of the Metropolitan Police Department.

"Apparently the MPD has no fucking idea about who the shooter is," Malenkov grumbled. "I cabled Moscow, requesting enhanced satellite coverage of any networks that may have any news of this—this assassination. And that's what it is. An assassination, pure and simple!"

"Do you think that Kehoe got wind of the plot and her involvement in it and had her taken down?" Litvinov asked.

"*Nyet*. I don't think that at all. If he found out about the plot, he'd most likely have her picked up. Or—worst case—make her mysteriously disappear--forever. But I doubt if James Kehoe would have her murdered in a popular jogging spot in the middle of the day. Hell, I run there myself once or twice a month!"

"Well, you know him better than I do, cousin."

"*Da*, maybe so. A little. But neither of us knows a fucking thing about how, why or by whom Admiral Donegan was assassinated," the Ambassador observed.

"Once eight o'clock in the a. m. rolls around, I'll start discreetly asking around," Litvinov said. "If you'll excuse me, I'll go and start working on a list of people to call,"

"Good," said the ambassador. "But be as unobtrusive as possible. 'Low-key,' as our American hosts say. We don't want people starting to think that we're somehow connected to Donegan. Much less her murder. And I'll drop some quiet inquiries myself a little later this morning."

"Got it. Definitely low-key," Litvinov said, getting up from his chair.

Chapter Seventy-Two

Alan

Kieler Bucht
Mid-June

I was leading the guy clumsily. His right arm was behind my neck and my left hand gripped his belt. He evidently couldn't put any weight on his left foot. We had made it almost to the forward ladder well—him doing a heavy hop—when he cracked a vicious left elbow into my forearm, causing me to lose the grip on his belt. He started scrabbling under my blazer trying to get the Makarov. It didn't take a lot of internal debate on my part—I turned toward him and re-grabbed his belt, dragged him two steps to the rail, lifted and threw his skinny ass overboard.

"Hey, Alan! Everything okay?" Luke hollered.

"Everything's fine," I replied. "Now."

"What's going on?"

"Nothing. Now," I said. "He elbowed me and went for my gun. We had a short fight. I won."

By this point in the conversation, I was back to where Luke was finishing up swabbing the blood off the deck. I was still breathing a bit heavily from the exertion of my short wrestling match as well as from the excitement.

"So where the hell is he?"

I pointed over the side.

"You threw him overboard?" Luke asked, incredulous.

"I told you. He attacked me. We fought. I won. He went over the side."

"Jesus H. Christ Almighty!" Luke hissed.

"Look! I may have helped us out. We no longer have an albatross leaking blood from a gunshot wound to the foot. That puts the Russians— or whoever the evildoers are—down one. You guys—the Secret Service--have two of the three remaining slime dogs in handcuffs. The third and lone remaining dirt bag probably has the two girls but has no back up. Now. And *Nordschiff* security is looking for her and the two girls. I'd be willing to bet they'll find them if they haven't done so already. So we should be okay on that score as long as no one saw our asshole friend go into the drink. And since we haven't heard the six blasts of the ship's whistle and *Nordschiff* isn't turning, it's safe to assume that his moonlight dip went unnoticed. Let's go back to our cabin and figure out where we go from here."

Just as I was inserting the key card in the lock on our door, I heard a semi-scream that sounded happy.

"Daddee!" Elizabeth was sprinting toward me down the passageway, followed closely by Esmé, who was followed not so closely by a smiling female Danish lieutenant.

My daughter jumped on me like a mountain lion jumping on a newborn jackrabbit and her buddy Esmé followed suit so I nearly toppled over right there in the passageway.

"Girls!" I semi-yelled. "So great to see you!" Talk about your understatements. They hugged me and I hugged them. I think I felt some hot tears on my neck.

"Let's go inside and see Mom," I said. I looked back at the Danish Merchant Marine Officer. She smiled.

"We've arrested the Latvian woman who was holding the girls. For abduction. She is in the ship's brig."

"*Nordschiff* has a brig?" I asked.

"Yes and no. We usually reserve two or three interior staterooms with special locks for "special situations," she said. "Thankfully we don't have to use them very often."

Luke had opened the cabin door and the girls squirted in and more squealing ensued. I turned back to the lieutenant.

"I'm Alan Llewellyn, Elizabeth's father," I explained. We shook hands. "Thank you so much for rescuing the girls from a bad situation."

"You're welcome. I'm Sofia Nielsen. We were glad to be able to help. Two of my colleagues are taking two other Latvians—or Russians—to the brig for involvement in the abduction. But there seems to be one Latvian—a male—still missing. Do you, by any chance, know anything about him?"

I make it a practice not to lie—ever.

"I think I saw him on the Promenade Deck about fifteen minutes ago," I said, hoping that Luke had done a good job with the blood clean-up and that the Danes wouldn't look too hard. I also felt a fairly severe conscience twinge about my prevarication. It wasn't a lie, *per se*, but it was something less than the whole truth. My good Guardian Angel was yanking furiously on my right ear. My evil angel was blowing in my left ear. When it suddenly started to pour rain furiously outside, I murmured a prayer of thanks to whichever angel was responsible for the downpour and the thorough, mother-nature cleanup of the bloodstains on the Promenade Deck.

Chapter Seventy-Three

Alan

```
The North Sea
Mid-June
```

"What I think we need pretty soon is a quick council of war, so to speak," I said. "We're due in Dover—which means leaving *Nordschiff*—Saturday morning. Which is the day after tomorrow.

"Right now, I'm pretty well shot and don't think I'm capable of making rational decisions. I think we all could do with a few hours sleep. So let's plan on meeting at ten a. m. tomorrow.

"The way I see it, we're relatively safe on board ship from now until we disembark in Dover. I think we should continue our recent precautions—staying together, locking doors and cooperating with our Secret Service friends. Then, we disembark and I have no idea what happens then. Inshallah, we'll be out of the woods."

"We're working on a plan for that with the embassy in London and headquarters in Washington," Mike said. "The embassy is coordinating with the Brits. We'll have an update brief for you guys tomorrow morning. So I second Alan's suggestion about getting some sleep. Hopefully we'll have the plan updated and ready to go by our ten o'clock meeting tomorrow."

"What happened to the other Latvian dude?" Esmé asked.

"He met with an unfortunate accident," I said.

Esmé rolled her eyes. And grinned a little.

We scattered to our staterooms. I ensured that the Secret Service had the girls' room covered before slipping into our cabin, stripping out of my raunchy clothes and visiting the loo for a quick whiz and teeth brushing. I jumped into my "nightwear," gave Maria a quick smooch as I dove into my side of the rack and was asleep in seconds. Having thrown the Russian asshole over the side a couple of hours before didn't interfere with my sleep at all. After all, he had kidnapped my daughter and daughter *pro tem*.

Next morning, for once, Maria was out of the rack before I was. I heard the FOOSH! Of the toilet flushing and realized the bathroom light was on. The flushing shipboard toilets sounded like the startup of jet engines. Must have had something to do with the performance of a modern sewage system on a large passenger vessel. A glance at my watch told me it was almost seven-thirty. My eyes were gritty and my back was stiff, but I climbed out of the rack anyway.

I threw on a pair of sweat pants, stepped across the passageway and tapped on the girls' door.

"What's up?" one of the girls croaked.

"Can you guys be ready to go up for breakfast in twenty minutes?" I asked.

The stateroom door made unlatching noises and suddenly Elizabeth was standing there with half-closed eyes wearing one of the Arsenal team jerseys she uses as pajamas.

"Give us a half hour, Dad," she mumbled.

"A half hour it is," I said, glancing at my watch.

The stress didn't impede our breakfast appetites. All girls loaded up on fresh fruit and omelets. Yours truly went with fruit juice, smoked salmon, creamed cheese and trimmings over a lightly toasted bagel. And, of course, coffee.

We got a leisurely three-mile walk in after breakfast as *Nordschiff* knifed through a calm North Sea. Before we knew it, it was time for our ten a. m. meeting.

At nine-fifty, there was a knock on our door. It was Mike.

"*Nordschiff* has given us the use of a conference room. Room six-one-thirteen. That'll give us a little extra space," he said.

"Okay. We'll be there in a few minutes," I said. I jotted down the room number on my little pocket notebook.

Once we were seated in the ship's Conference Room, Luke stood.

"Here's the plan as it stands now," he said. "Today we take care of shipboard money and paperwork loose ends. The Purser's office will let us know, by stateroom, what we owe and how to pay. We tie up at zero-six-hundred tomorrow. There will be an announcement to stage luggage in the passageway this evening. You'll get special tags today for all luggage and you need to attach them to any and all bags you want to see again in the near future. The tags will enable special handling—all our luggage will be put in a special van from the U. S. Embassy.

"There will be another announcement for 'the U.S. Contingent' to disembark and will give a station number. That announcement will be mixed in with some other names in a segment of the alphabet, so listen carefully. You'll need to hand in your room key cards as you disembark, so make sure you have them with you. Once ashore, British police and U. S. Marines—all in plain clothes—will escort us to a little caravan of SUV's. We hop aboard and then we're out of Dodge and bound for RAF Mildenhall, which is a little less than two-and-a-half hours away."

"What sort of security will we have en route Mildenhall?" I asked.

"Well, for starters you'll have us, the Secret Service. There will be Marines in the vehicles and British police escorting us," Luke said. "We should be fine."

He looked around the conference table. Esmé stuck her hand in the air.

"Yes Esmé?"

"Are we expecting any danger? Between Dover and Mildenhall?" she asked.

"We have no definite info on that. We're just playing it safe," Luke answered. "Anything else?"

Ten seconds later, we adjourned.

Chapter Seventy-Four
The DNI

Oxford, Maryland
Mid-June

The meeting had been scheduled for noon. The text message simply read CHASENOON and went out shortly after zero-eight-hundred. At eleven-forty, the "guests" began trickling in. About half of them were dressed for work in business suits and "formal" shoes. The other half had changed into cargo shorts or jeans topped by polo shirts and bottomed by flip-flops or topsiders.

Pablo and Carmen circulated among the arrivals, offering cocktails, bottled water and canapés. Sam Braxton circulated as well, greeting each guest as he or she arrived and stroking him or her for a few minutes afterwards. Madame Speaker DeWitt arrived at eleven-fifty-eight. Braxton welcomed her and made sure she had a drink and a super jumbo shrimp speared on a long palm toothpick. He backed away from the Speaker and announced to the room, "Let's grab a seat, everybody. Info time."

Braxton opened the meeting at two minutes after twelve o'clock.

"Okay. There's still a leak. And it seems to be directed to certain elements in the Russian government. Or from the Russian Government! Russian! Why the hell it's going there or coming from there I have no idea. But there are indications that at least one Russian faction is trying to let the White House know what is going on," he announced.

A number of growled epithets burbled to the surface in the warm Chesapeake air.

"I'm convinced we need to move things up on our little calendar," Braxton continued. "Way up."

"Uh, okay Sam. But I'm going to need a minimum of twenty-four hours lead time to get everything on line at *Algorithmics*," Ironsides said. "At a minimum."

"You'll get the time you need, Rob," Braxton replied. "But our plan is starting to come apart at the seams. I'm not sure why, but there's a fair bit of active sniffing around that's got me worried. We need to make some major adjustments and then execute. Like as soon as possible after your twenty-four hours! But, understand that we still definitely need a U. S. Government shutdown to kick things off."

"What the hell is the story with Donegan?" Nagle asked.

"I'm glad you asked. I think she was—has been—a major part of the problem. I'm guessing now—so there's no certainty here—but I think she was having second thoughts about the operation. And maybe even leaking info about the plan."

"So? Somebody decided to take her out? Hired a sniper to shoot her down like a mad dog while she was running during her lunch hour?"

"I don't know about that. It wasn't us," he lied. "A running dog? Maybe some of her Navy buddies got wind of what she was involved in. There has always been a dark side to Naval Intelligence. Hence the sniper?"

The latter phrase was framed as a question and inflected as such. Braxton let it hang in the humid air. Nagle narrowed his eyes a millimeter or less and then looked away.

A seventy-two-inch flat screen TV dominated the great room of Chase Cottage. Braxton fingered a remote. A list appeared on the screen.

The heading read *FINAL SCHEDULE*.

"You've all seen the original planning schedule that we all participated in producing. I'm going to flip through that for review purposes and then focus on the changes we've agreed to. I'll cycle through the updated schedule with changes highlighted. Then I'll go through the changes again and answer any questions. Here's the new E-Day," he said. "19 June" popped up on the screen.

"Kehoe's going to the Hamptons on Long Island. On eighteen June. Specifically, Hampton Bays. He and the First Lady, Franny, have a couple of old high school buddies who got married and own a summer "cottage" there. Chuck and Arlene McCall. Their primary residence is in Manhattan. The President's old buddy—Chuck—runs a successful headhunting group for high-level business recruiting. Mrs. McCall—Arlene—was a classmate—and roommate—of Franny's at Manhattanville College in Westchester. On the weekend of the eighteenth through the twentieth of June, the President and Franny plan on staying with their old friends.

"Even though the place is kind of small and unprepossessing, security will be tight. We'll have to make the snatch then and there. Even now, I'm convinced that we're starting to run out of time.

"Here are the rest of the changes:"

Braxton thumbed the remote and the next slide popped up on the huge screen. It and the following slides were as he'd predicted. The original schedule, followed by the updated plan with the same slides except that items to be changed were highlighted in green.

"Okay. Here's the new stuff," Braxton said. "E-Day is nineteen June. The ball will start rolling at zero-five-forty when Algorithmics will pull the plug on Government and some non-government C4I systems. We will have a five-man FBI team landing at zero-five-forty-three by helo in the back yard of the McCalls' summer place and they will use flash bang grenades to suppress security and apprehend Kehoe on the spot. They'll get him on board the chopper immediately and haul ass for Westchester Airport in White Plains. We'll transfer a mildly sedated President to an FBI-owned and operated Gulfstream-Four jet, which will be already cleared for takeoff for a flight to Leavenworth. He'll be held in the infirmary there for twenty-four to forty-eight hours, after which he'll be transferred to a private cell, pending trial by special commission. The rest of the stuff— public relations garbage mostly—will go off pretty much as we originally planned with modified dates and times."

He clicked the remote.

CHANGES TO DAY TWO (E-DAY):

- **0700: DELETE FOXNEWS.**

"After discussions with several of you, I've changed my mind about pulling Fox News off the air. After consultations, we decided to let the bastards stay alive and keep on broadcasting. They might screw things up so badly they could actually help us out. Besides if we pull their plug, it may cause needless suspicions about our motives," Braxton added.

- **0715: ADD NEWSCASTER MARK HALBSGUT TO CHRIS MARKS IN THE SPEAKER'S OFFICE.**

"Halbsgut has way more credibility and gravitas than that douche bag Marks," Braxton mumbled as heads nodded.

- **0729: CHANGE CHIEF JUSTICE'S TIME TO 0731.**
- **0729: CHANGE FORMAL ANNOUNCEMENT TO 0735.**

"I think those last two changes are self-explanatory," Braxton. "Just timing." He turned up the lights and shut down the huge TV.

"What about Girtler?" Nagle asked.

"I'm glad you asked. Again. We were all wrapped around our own axle because of the time when we were planning to grab Kehoe. The zero-five-forty-three time—give or take maybe five minutes, max, was carved in stone. Any other time of day or night would decrease our chances of success considerably. Also, we'd have to make the grab on Girtler pretty close to the same time. If we snatched him early, it'd be a definite dog whistle to the Secret Service for the snatch of Kehoe. If we waited for more than a couple of minutes after grabbing Kehoe, the cat would be out of the bag. A phalanx of secret service agents would descend on Girtler and start calling him 'Mister President.' His protection would suddenly be ironclad.

"Then we got lucky. Seems like Girtler flies home to Ohio every Friday evening. Except he doesn't. He *does* fly home on every Friday—except the third Friday of every month. He spends the third Friday of each month at the Georgetown flat of one Michelle McCants."

"Not Michelle McCants of Channel Ten News fame?" Nagle asked, disbelief dripping from his question.

"The same," Braxton said. "But it gets better. Guess what date the third Friday of June is this year?"

"Surely not the eighteenth?" mumbled General Smalls.

"Aha! Every once in a while, God comes down on the side of the good guys. We'll jump old Mister Hair Transplant while he's languishing in post-coital bliss after jumping the bones of Michelle McCants."

"And how the hell did you tumble onto that little nugget?" General Smalls asked.

"A leak from a leak," Braxton said. "Tell him, Roberto," he said, nodding at Ironsides.

Ironsides smiled shyly.

"WikiLeaks," he said. "But the leak wasn't intentional on their part."

"You mean you hacked WikiLeaks?"

"Something like that."

"There is one other thing. NSA has picked up additional exchanges of email between Kehoe and Alan Llewellyn. They spoke again of a 'Baltic Cruise.' I have no idea what that means, but where there's smoke, there's usually fire. And this definitely qualifies as 'smoke.' We'll have to monitor as much of that traffic as possible to learn as much as we can. Right now, all we know is that there may be 'something rotten in the State of Denmark' with that Russ-Llewellyn connection and the Russian leak of our plan.

"We'll just have to continue to monitor things. But I think we're done for now," he said, standing up.

The room exploded into noisy chatter. Braxton listened for several minutes and decided he had mixed feelings about what he heard. He continued to wander around the room, listening without comment to the conversations, which ended up lasting for forty more minutes. It was five-fifteen and the shadows were starting to lengthen on the Eastern Shore when the guests started trickling out of Chase Cottage.

Chapter Seventy-Five
Sammy and Ashleigh

Annapolis, Maryland
Mid-June

"Look. Look hard and see who's there. There'll be a crowd. So look hard. And keep your ears open, too. You probably won't hear much of anything. It's a funeral, after all. But listen anyway," Darps had coached them.

Sammy and Ashleigh had, as instructed, taken Darps' car with its DOD Sticker, allowing them entry to the Naval Academy Yard along with limited parking privileges. They entered the Yard at ten-twenty-three and showed the guard their White House ID's. The funeral was scheduled to start at eleven.

"That dome is the chapel," Sammy said. "We might as well park anywhere. It's only about a two-block walk from here." "And there's a parking space," Ashleigh said, turning the Saab convertible into a space alongside the Halsey Field House.

"We'll just have to walk nice and slowly. I don't want to walk into the chapel all sweaty," Ashleigh said.

"Slowly is good," Sammy said. "We get to see more that way. More people."

The Annapolis morning was sunny and sweltering with the temperature nudging ninety. Sammy carried the jacket of his dark gray suit; he wore a gleaming white long-sleeved shirt and a tie of muted red, gray and blue tones. Ashleigh wore a short-sleeved, sky-blue dress topped by a necklace of black pearls. She carried a small purse that matched her dress. Her medium heels were white. As agreed, they took their time walking to the chapel.

As they approached the chapel's gray stone steps, Ashleigh clutched Sammy's arm.

"Isn't that tall guy in the dark blue suit Sam Braxton, the DNI?" she whispered.

"Yup. For sure," Sammy whispered back.

He slipped into his suit jacket as they arrived at the foot of the steps.

"Makes sense for the Director of National Intelligence to be at the funeral of the Director of Naval Intelligence," Sammy muttered. "He was her boss, sort of. Or one of her bosses."

The two of them found their way to a pew in the rear of the nave.

A few minutes after the two were seated, a white-uniformed Midshipman escorted a woman in a dark blue suit and wearing large sunglasses down the middle aisle toward the altar. Sammy nudged Ashleigh.

"Speaker of the House. Congresswoman Helen DeWitt," he whispered.

Ashleigh nodded but didn't say anything.

Minutes later, a lone woman in a yellow dress and also wearing sunglasses, strode down the aisle and took a seat in a pew a few rows in front of Ashleigh and Sammy.

"Isn't that Suzanne Palmer? The ex-National Security Advisor to the President?" Sammy whispered. "The blonde in the yellow dress who just sat down."

"Yes. I'm sure I saw her at Union Station. It's Palmer," Ashleigh replied.

"Yeah. I'm pretty sure you're right," Sammy muttered.

Minutes later, a man in his mid-thirties slid into a pew across the aisle from Ashleigh and Sammy. His haircut looked like it could be military; he was wearing a slightly baggy brown suit.

Suddenly, they heard the drums outside. Solemn, faintly thunderous, faintly sinister, crescendoing. They heard barked military commands and the drums suddenly ceased. Then they heard the band outside play three verses of *Anchors Aweigh* and eight sailors bore the flag-draped coffin of Vice Admiral Donegan into the chapel and placed it on a gurney. The huge Naval Academy pipe organ boomed out the opening notes of *Nearer My God to Thee*. Lieutenant Commander Bobby Donegan, clad in the high-collared Service Dress White uniform, followed the casket. A priest, a cross bearer, a thurifer, boat bearer and two acolytes met the little procession, which stopped just inside the nave. The priest used incense and holy water to honor the Admiral's remains and then he and the acolytes turned to face the altar and began the procession down the center aisle, leading the coffin. Bobby Donegan, followed by a gaggle of what Sammy and Ashleigh assumed were Donegan family members plus a sizeable bunch of sailors, officers and Midshipmen, made up the remainder of the funeral procession through the chapel.

"Know that guy?" Ashleigh whispered. "The guy in the cheap suit?"

"No," Sammy whispered back. "Never laid eyes on him."

Chief of Naval Operations Admiral Sam Winston delivered the eulogy in which he cited Admiral Donegan's multiple major sacrifices for her country—the loss of her husband in the Afghanistan War and, ultimately, her own death at the hands of a "murderous, cowardly sniper."

Attendance at the graveside service was restricted to immediate family members, so Ashleigh and Sammy waited by Darps's car while the Navy band and color guard accompanied the horse-drawn gun carriage carrying the flag-draped coffin to the nearby Naval Academy Cemetery. The drums continued to beat solemnly. Suddenly, a four-plane formation of F/A-18 jet fighters roared over the Yard from the Chesapeake, with one of the jets breaking away as they flew over the cemetery.

"The 'missing man' formation," Sammy said. "I heard that the Admiral's late husband's squadron was flying."

They waited till they heard the funereal rifle salute and the band playing *The Navy Hymn*. Only then did Ashleigh head the Saab back to Virginia.

"Well. Any surprises there?" Sammy asked, once they were heading west on Route Fifty.

"Braxton, the DNI, was definitely *not* a surprise. Like you said, he was her boss. Sort of. But I *was* surprised to see Helen DeWitt, the Speaker of the House, there. I mean, maybe they were yoga buddies or something, but I can't see that their jobs threw them together all that much. If at all. And Madame Speaker can't have a helluva a lot of free time on her hands. Funeral time plus travel time today must add up to three and a half hours or more. Today! That's an anomaly. At least to me," Ashleigh said.

"I think I agree," Sammy replied. "Maybe they knew each other from Madame Speaker's time on the HPSCI."

"The more I think about the woman in the yellow dress, I'm sure it was Palmer. I'm sure we guessed right. The National Security advisor. Whom Kehoe fired. But then there was the guy with the short haircut and the cheap suit. I *know* I've seen him before. And not too long ago," Ashleigh muttered.

Chapter Seventy-Six

Alan

Dover, U.K.
Mid-June

They picked up our heavy bags at zero-six-forty-five. Luke, Mike and Ally hovered over us and Judy hovered over us as well, albeit in a smaller orbit.

Mike seemed to be talking incessantly on his mobile.

"They'll tell us that we're disembarking in twenty-two minutes," he announced. "There will be a five-vehicle convoy of black, lightly-armored SUV's. We'll just go directly to the vehicles—there will be a few Marines from the embassy in civilian clothes to usher us to the right vehicles. Then it's off to RAF Mildenhall. Luggage will be taken care of. There will be a C-20 from the Eighty-Ninth waiting to take us back to DC."

"Okay," I said. "I'll have 'The Poems of Anna Achmatova' strapped to my back. With its all-important piece of paper. Inshallah, they will be safe. As will the women. And me, of course."

Twenty-one minutes later, a male slightly Danish-accented voice, made an announcement: "Passengers, whose last names begin with the letters K as in Kaffé through N as in November, plus members of the U.S. Contingent, should disembark, pick up their luggage at station A-4 on the pier and proceed to customs and immigration.

"Hope your Baltic North voyage was pleasant and that we'll see you again in the near future," the voice said.

Mike stepped up and interjected, "Between the Secret Service, the Marines and the British cops, we should be able to keep you safe. There should be no risk to you, your family or the book."

We started the transfer to RAF Mildenhall quickly and without incident--initially. We disembarked from N*ordschiff* and pointed out our various pieces of luggage to officials who loaded them on carts. We handed in our shipboard tickets and climbed into a black Ford Expedition. My copy of *The Poems of Anna Achmatova* and its little piece of paper with all the numbers remained safely strapped to my now-damp back with a spare belt underneath my shirt. Our departure went smoothly. I assumed our luggage was in a trailing SUV.

About forty-five minutes later while I was semi-dozing, everything suddenly went south. I saw the white-hot flame of the SUV ahead of us exploding after, we learned later, passing over a prematurely detonated IED. Pieces of the vehicle—some of them still aflame—rained down around and on top of us.

"Don't stop!" Mike screamed over his mobile. "Bypass the wreck—go off road if you have to!"

We hauled ass. Our driver followed Mike's instructions. Mike was in the shotgun seat, left side, British style. Maria, Judy and I shared the middle bench seat and Elizabeth and Esmé were in the rear, scared shitless. Another SUV, bouncing wildly, pulled in front of us, filled with young guys with short haircuts and short shotguns—no doubt, U. S. Marines. I was worried about the two girls' anxiety panic. I reached around and grabbed Elizabeth's hand. Esmé's hand glommed onto mine as well.

"I need to hold someone's hand, too," she said.

"Keep your heads down," I whispered, without knowing why I was whispering. Our SUV had rocked and rolled over the craggy terrain alongside the road, accelerating the whole time. Now we were back on the main drag doing eighty-five miles an hour. There were no further comments for the next several seconds. Then Mike got back on the phone and started trying to make sense out of what had happened during the past few minutes. I think I had it figured out by the time another black SUV raced past us on the right side of the road.

One: Someone had detonated an IED underneath the vehicle in front of ours. The vehicle looked to be completely ruined. The vehicle was carrying British police.

Two: Our vehicle sustained only minor damage.

Three: Whoever detonated the IED had screwed up as our vehicle was the presumed intended target.

Four: We were at least partway out of the woods. British police and U. S. Marines were leading us toward RAF Mildenhall at a high rate of speed.

Five: *The Poems of Anna Achmatova* and its mysterious little piece of paper were still safely strapped to my back.

Six: The Russians—or, at least some Russians—really wanted that fucking book. And its little piece of paper with all the numbers.

Chapter Seventy-Seven
Sammy and Ashleigh

Chestertown, Virginia
Mid-June

"Where are you?" Darps asked into the phone.

"Just passing Quantico," Sammy replied.

"Good," Darps said. "See you here in twenty minutes or so."

Seventeen minutes later, Ashleigh pulled Darps's silver Saab convertible into its parking space outside Ripley Hall on the campus of Martha Washington University in Chestertown.

"Welcome back!" Darps said, meeting Ashleigh and Sammy at the front door as if they'd been gone for four months instead of four hours. "Take a few minutes to get refreshed. I'm guessing that you didn't have time to have lunch, so we've ordered sandwiches and drinks. Anastasya should be here with them momentarily."

"Sounds good. I'm starved," Ashleigh said. "I'm guessing that you're meeting us at the front door with sandwiches inbound means that you want to talk about the funeral and who attended."

"Oh yes! Right down to the slightest detail," Darps said. "And here's Anastasya with the sandwiches," he added, nodding toward a VW that was pulling into the parking lot. "Let's sit down in the SCIF when you're ready."

Five minutes later, after head calls all around, the small group sat down around the modest conference table in the SCIF. The meeting started with everyone unwrapping sandwiches.

"Okay," Darps said. "I'll kick things off, even though it doesn't have anything to do with the Donegan funeral. At least I don't think it does. Somebody tried to blow up Alan while he and his family were *en route* RAF Mildenhall from Dover earlier today. Llewellyns are all fine. Judy, Mike and Luke are all fine. Book is safe. Two British cops are dead. Two are WIA but in stable condition and are expected to make full recoveries. The Brits think it was Russians—but not official Russian Federation Russians. Russian Mafiya. How they arrived at that conclusion or supposition I have no idea. They're pretty sure that the Russians screwed up and blew up the wrong car.

"Alan and company are now airborne and are heading for Andrews. Their ETA is seventeen fifteen this evening. Local time."

Darps glanced at his watch.

"A little over two hours from now. Okay. Your turn."

"Ladies first," Sammy said, nodding at Ashleigh.

"Okay. Attendees," Ashleigh answered. "Congresswoman Helen DeWitt, Speaker of the House."

"Holy shit," Darps whispered. "She was actually *there?* At the funeral? What's her connection to Donegan?"

"We have no idea," Ashleigh said. "But she *was* on that train with that small bunch of intel people that came in from southwestern Virginia. I was struck by her attendance at the funeral. I had no idea that she and Admiral Donegan were friends. Nor that there was any sort of connection between the Speaker of the House and the Director of Naval Intelligence. So, my little 'anomaly warning bell' pinged in my head.

"Then, when I remembered that she got off the train at Union Station with those intel weasels, it made my little bell ring louder."

"I can see why," Darps said. "What else? Or who else?"

"Okay and this was no surprise. Sam Braxton, the DNI. He almost had to attend."

"Agreed," Darps responded. "Matter of protocol. No surprise there."

"Then there were a couple of more 'anomalies'," Ashleigh continued. "There was a blond woman that both Sammy and I thought we recognized but weren't sure of. At least, not at first.""

"So you've seen her before?"

"I'm pretty sure I saw her at Union Station," Ashleigh said, turning to Sammy. "But then things started to come together."

"Yep," Sammy said. "After a bit she came back in focus," Ashleigh muttered. "It's got to be Suzanne Palmer. Erstwhile National Security Advisor to the President. Fired by said President. For running her mouth too much."

"Just a second," Darps said, getting up. He walked over to a safe against the wall, which was already open. He pulled out a folder and returned to his seat.

"Remember this?" he asked, pulling out a sheet of paper festooned with various classified markings.

"Of course! The list! Her name is on it. It was definitely Palmer!" Sammy blurted.

"Of course!" echoed Ashleigh.

"Okay. We're starting to connect dots. But her presence wasn't really an anomaly. She *was* the President's National Security Advisor. She may well have had frequent contact with the Navy's Director of Intelligence. At least before she got fired. They could have been friends, even."

"Agreed," Ashleigh responded. She turned to Sammy. "What about the guy with the short haircut? The one in the baggy suit?"

"That's another puzzler," Sammy said. "I'm positive I've never laid eyes on the guy before. You think you might well have, Ashleigh."

"You know how you see someone and say to yourself, 'I *know* that guy,' but then can't remember where or when. Much less who," Ashleigh babbled.

"Let's see, said Darps. "Can either of you guys think of a place or circumstance where one of you—specifically you, Ashleigh—were there and Sammy was not?"

"Well, Union Station. I was running by myself when I saw those people come out. The intel people. But the guy in the cheap suit wasn't with them. I'm sure of that."

"Anyplace else?" prodded Darps

"Well, there was that reception at Fort McNair," Ashleigh answered. "You and your wife were there," she said.

"Yeah. I remember. But I don't remember any guy with short hair wearing a cheap suit," Darps responded.

"Ta dah!" Ashleigh exclaimed. "That's because he wasn't wearing a cheap suit! He was wearing a uniform! And it was Russian!"

"I'll be dipped in dung," Darps muttered, reaching for the mouse. He clicked through several entries until he settled on a photo of a Russian admiral.

"No, that's not him. Our guy was Army," Ashleigh said.

Darps clicked the mouse again.

"Bingo!" Ashleigh whispered.

LITVINOV, Valentin I., Colonel, Infantry. Military Attaché read the caption.

"Well, son of a bitch," muttered Darps. "What in God's name is a Russian military attaché—in civvies—doing at the funeral of the U. S. Director of Naval Intelligence?

"Well, get this," Darps snapped after clicking the mouse again. A photo showing Litvinov shaking hands with Michelle Hookes appeared. Litvinov was in uniform and held a highball glass in his left hand.

"I'm pretty sure that was at the Russian Independence Day reception," Ashleigh said. "I *know* Michelle Hookes was there. I saw her."

"The Naval Academy Chapel is well within the fifty-mile radius allowed for foreign attaché travel," Sammy said. "So he didn't need to request permission to go to the funeral."

"Maybe he was there for the same reason we were," Ashleigh mumbled. "To see who else was there."

Suddenly, the red phone pinged and its little red light flashed. Darps grabbed it. "BIAS Five, sir," he answered.

"Oh, good," he said. Then he nodded and listened.

Finally, he nodded some more and said, "Okay. We'll see you when we see you," and hung up the phone.

"That was Alan. They've landed. He's inbound. Should be here in about forty minutes."

"What's up with the book?" Sammy asked.

"It may be coming here," Darps answered. "There were three NSA dweebs on the plane and they couldn't break the code. It seems nobody can. They've scanned and emailed the original back from the airplane to NSA. Nobody there can make anything out of anything, either. They say it's all total gibberish."

"Good Lord," said Ashleigh. "How many lives did it cost to get that book here? And now nobody can make heads or tails out of it?"

"Stand by for some heavy rolls, Anastasya," Darps said. "That hairball may land in your lap."

Anastasya rolled her eyes.

"God help us," she croaked. "I'm certainly no cryptographer."

Thirty-five minutes later, Alan, Maria, Elizabeth and Esmé showed up at the BIAS front door. Alan was carrying the book.

Chapter Seventy-Eight

Alan

Chestertown, Virginia
Mid-June

had to admit that (a) I was whupped from the last leg of the trip. My PTSD was probably worse than it was when we left the States two weeks ago; and (b) I was mightily frustrated with the lack of any knowledge whatsoever about the contents of the book that I held in my grubby paws and risked my ass and those of my extended family to pick up and safeguard.

"Welcome home, Shipmate," Darps said as he opened up the door. "Congrats on still being in one piece. And same for your wonderful family. Umm, is that *THE* book? The source of so much angst?"

"That's it. And nobody has a clue what sort of info is contained therein. I told Kehoe he'd need to go back to his Russky sources and ask them what its message was and he looked at me like I'd suggested that I molest his sister. Crappy idea, I guess."

I looked at my little extended family. They didn't look nearly as bedraggled as I felt, but they *were* starting to show a bit of wear and tear around the edges. Then I looked at my watch. And then at Maria.

"Okay," I said. "I have a plan. Just hatched this very minute. The Air Force driver is still outside. With our luggage. Let's have her take Esmé and her luggage home, followed by our luggage and us. We'll unload and have the driver wait. I'll call China Wok for Chinese food delivered to the house and then have the Air Force gal drop me back here at *BIAS*. Maybe then we can come up with a plan for what to do with the effing book. I'll walk home in time to nuke the leftover Chinese."

That's what we did. I was kind of taken aback at Esmé's tears as we dropped her off at home. She gave each of us a huge teary hug.

"Thank you, thank you!" she gasped. "It was a wonderful cruise! A great adventure! But Mister El, don't forget the Oklahoma Anomaly!"

I had to wonder about the "Oklahoma Anomaly." The night when all the lights on Fort Sill went out for exactly two minutes. An anomaly that Esmé had brought somewhat forcefully to my attention.

I dropped the two Llewellyn women at 1506 Prince Henry along with our bags and made a quick call to China Wok with a delivery order for crab Rangoon, steamed dumplings, chicken wings and a large order of shrimp lo mein. Then I jumped back in the Air Force SUV for a quick trip back to BIAS.

The place was quiet as the grave till I got to the SCIF. There, pandemonium was reigning.

"I think we've got something, Shipmate!" Darps announced.

"From the book?" I asked.

"Yup. From the book," Darps answered. "Anastasya had it in her pretty little hands for less than thirty minutes when she noticed something. Tell him, Anastasya."

"My favorite Achmatova poem of all time is *We Don't Know How to Say Good-bye*. It's number thirteen in the book. I turned to it right away and then I noticed something almost immediately. The English version is on the right-hand page, right where it's supposed to be. But the Russian version is *not* on the left-hand page where it's supposed to be."

"What is there?" I asked.

"The Our Father. The prayer. In Russian."

"You're kidding," I said.

"No," she said. "There's more. If you include the Sign of the Cross—'In the name of the Father, et cetera,' Achmatova's poem and the Our Father have the same number of lines. So I numbered all the Cyrillic letters in the prayer—including those in the sign of the cross--and then tried to cross-reference those numbers with the numbers on the piece of paper that came with the book. That gave me gobbledygook. Gibberish! Nothing! Then I changed the prayer back to English and did the same thing. Garbage again! Then I went back to the Russian version of the prayer—the one in the book—and transliterated it. I changed the Cyrillic characters to Latin characters. The alphabet we use in English. But the language was still Russian. So the beginning of the Sign of the Cross became "Va imya otsa, I Sinya" and so forth. Then I tried matching that up with the numbers. 'Source XRay R Ironsides' is the first thing that dropped out."

"Holy shit! That's the name that the Russians gave to Kehoe. The MFIC of *Algorithmics, Inc*," I said.

"That must mean that "XRAY" who signed that email saying the Russians had the list is actually Roberto Ironsides. And I'm guessing that he—Ironsides—is one of the conspirators as well."

"That's not all," she said. "There are more names coming. 'Konspirators. Braxton, Sam. Donegan, VAdm USN.' That's as far as I've got."

"Holy Christ!" I muttered and reached for the red phone.

Chapter Seventy-Nine
Litvinov

Colonel Litvinov entered the Russian Embassy via a back door and glanced at his watch. IT was just a few minutes shy of eighteen hundred. The embassy was quiet. He wondered if his cousin, the Ambassador, was still aboard. The ambassador's Mercedes 600 was still in its parking spot—a good sign. He hurried to his own deserted office, punched in the security code, entered, reached for the phone and punched in more numbers. The ambassador's secretary, Valeriya, answered.

"It's me. Is he still there?" he asked.

"*Da*, but he's getting ready to leave."

"Tell him to wait. Stall him if you can. I'll be right up. It's important," he said.

"I'll try," she said.

Forty-five seconds later, Colonel Litvinov burst through the door of his Ambassador's office suite.

"The list of conspirators! I have it! I'm pretty sure it's all of it! If the White House is desperate to get it, here it is! At least all of it that I can remember and dig up. I just confirmed two final names twenty minutes ago. For a total of eight names!"

"Let me see it!" snapped the ambassador.

Litvinov handed him a folder. The ambassador opened it and pushed his eyeglasses up to the bridge of his nose.

"*Da*. This looks like what I remember. There may have been one or two more names on the original. Do you think your original source would be able to get this copy of the list to the White House? To Kehoe himself?"

"No fucking way! Not in a million years!"

"Why ever not?" asked the ambassador, irritated.

Litvinov dropped his voice to a hoarse whisper. "Because his—the source's—name is on the list. He sold it to us—the Russian Federation.

I'm sure he never dreamed that we'd be giving the list to the American White House. Much less anyone else in the U. S. Government. So there's no fucking way he'd agree to be complicit in divulging his name to the White House—or any other part of U. S. officialdom."

The ambassador flicked the list with his forefinger.

"Who is this bastard?" he asked.

"Ironsides," Litvinov answered in a croaked whisper.

"You've got to be shitting me!" the ambassador growled. "That's the name that Moscow told me to give to Kehoe when we first told him about the plot. But whatever the case, we need to figure out a way to get this list to the White House. Preferably without any Russian fingerprints on it. And, as you point out, Ironsides is totally out of the question as a messenger."

"Do you know Michelle Hookes?" Litvinov asked.

"*Nyet*. Who's he?"

"She. It's Michelle, not Michael. And she's some sort of special advisor to Kehoe. A wealthy, elderly widow. Who walks along the National Mall for exercise every evening. They—Hookes and Kehoe—are quite close. I understand they talk every day."

"Do you know her?" the ambassador asked. "More importantly, does she know you?"

"*Da* and *da*. At least a little bit. I met her here, of all places, at our embassy. At last year's National Day reception. We chatted a little. She's quite charming, actually. Afterwards, I read up on her background."

"Would she recognize you? If, if you 'ran into' her, as the Americans say?" asked the Ambassador.

"Maybe. If I were in uniform. I was in uniform the only time we met."

"Well, if you 'run into her' on the National Mall, you probably won't want to be wearing your uniform, you ass," snarled the ambassador.

"I think I'm beginning to see where this is going, Cousin," Litvinov responded, with a smirk. "I'll run along the Mall wearing running clothes—if I can nail down some parameters, like where she walks and when she walks—I'll 'bump into her' and pass her the list of conspirators. For delivery to Kehoe. And there will be Russian fingerprints all over the fucking thing. All mine."

"You're on the right track," the ambassador replied. "Except for the fucking fingerprints. Perhaps if you wore a t-shirt with 'RUSSIYA' in red letters on the front, she might realize that you two had met before. And then she'd take your little note seriously."

"I think that a shirt like that would make me stand out like the proverbial baboon's ass on the National Mall."

"Maybe so, maybe so," said the Ambassador. "But time is of the essence, so it's probably worth the risk."

"Good point. Not that I'm comfortable with it. I'll try and get some firm numbers from Detachment Zed on when and where she walks."

Chapter Eighty

Alan

Chestertown, Virginia
Mid-June

"Hey, Gunny!" I said when the other end of the red phone line picked up and Gunnery Sergeant McKinnon answered. "This is BIAS Six. Llewellyn. I need to speak to the man ASAP."

"Yes sir," the Gunny said. "Give me a minute to see what I can do."

Ninety seconds later, a new, female voice came on the line.

"Hello, Alan. It's Michelle. Our boss is meeting with the Crown Prince of Morocco. Then he's slated to host a state dinner for the Prime Minister of Japan," Michelle Hookes told me. "I can probably get him to call you back around twenty-three hundred if that works for you."

"Okay, Michelle. That would be a decent last resort. But if he steps out to take a leak or something, he should know that we have the 'the list'—I think you and he both know what I'm talking about."

"Mother of God," Michelle said. "I'll try and slip word to him one of these minutes."

"Darps is on his way to the White House with a decoded copy of the list. He should be at the southwest gate with it in less than an hour," I said.

"Okay," she said. "I'll tell the Marines and the staff to expect him. I'm heading home."

"Okay, Michelle. 'Bye," I said.

I had to wonder about how important "the list" really was at 1600 Pennsylvania Avenue. Since it contained the names of high-ranking members of the U.S. Government who were determined to oust the President of the United States from office by force, I would have thought that such a list would be deemed pretty fucking important. Hence the reason Darps was wrecking speed limits as he tried to race north on traffic-clogged I-95.

After we finally decoded the Russian book cipher, I said, "I wonder why those NSA weenies couldn't come up with the same stuff."

"Algorithms," Ashleigh said. "They're too hung up on algorithms and computer-based solutions when all it took was a little human ingenuity."

Anastasya was nodding her head in agreement and I was in total agreement with both of them. When the list was finished, here's what it looked like:

```
SOURCE XRAY ROBERTO IRONSIDES;
CONSPIRATORS IRONSIDES;
REP HELEN DEWITT, MC D-NY, SPEAKER;
SAM BRAXTON, DNI;
VADM DONEGAN USN, NAVAL INTEL;
DICK NAGEL, DDIR CIA;
STUART MC CONNELL, DDIR FBI;
LTG WILL SMALLS, ARMY ACSI;
SUZANNE PALMER, FORMER NS ADVISOR TO PRESIDENT
KEHOE.
```

Chapter Eighty-One
Litvinov

The George Washington Parkway
Mid-June

Colonel Litvinov took the stairs and checked in with Detachment Zed in the Embassy basement.

"Miss Hookes usually walks along both sides of the National Mall, along either side of the reflecting pool right after she returns home from her job at the White House," Milenka, a blond-headed technician with the detachment told him, after a few keystrokes on her computer.

"She normally returns home from work around five-thirty or five-forty-five. Then she walks right away. Usually about five-fifty. A personal, private bodyguard follows her. It could be a man with short, black hair and a moustache. Or a woman with frosted brown hair. Both bodyguards usually wear blue jeans and polo shirts. If it's cool, they wear Washington Nationals all-weather jackets. They carry handguns holstered under their shirts."

With a couple of flashes of lemon-yellow fingernails, Milenka put two Russian Embassy photos of the guards up on the screen.

"Ms. Hookes is usually back home by six-fifteen or six-twenty. Could be as late as seven-ten, depending on her start time."

"Okay. I'll try and catch her today around the reflecting pool between five-forty-five and six-oh-five. *Spasiba*, Milenka," he said.

He printed out a single copy of the list of conspirators, folded it in triplicate and put the page in an envelope that had an "Embassy of the Russian Federation" return address. He sealed the envelope, scrawled "For President Kehoe" in English on the front and crossed his fingers. He slipped the envelope into a plastic food storage bag. Then he changed out of his suit, donned running shorts, a pair of Adidas running shoes and an olive drab t-shirt with "RUSSIYA" in black Cyrillic capitals on the front. Then he called for an embassy car, which he had drop him off at the east side of the Lincoln Memorial. The time was seventeen-fifty.

He jogged around the side of the Lincoln Memorial and headed east on the mall. Keeping his pace modestly slow, he ran along the mall and eyeballed his fellow joggers. He noted that he had failed to ask Milenka at Detachment Zed whether Michelle Hookes normally walked clockwise or the reverse. He made it to the Washington Monument without seeing anyone he recognized. Glancing at his watch, he noticed that it was eighteen oh-five when he turned back towards the Lincoln Memorial. A few strides into his westward leg, he caught sight of a short, gray-haired woman walking towards him on the left side of the trail. Behind her left shoulder a broad-shouldered man with a mustache walked at the same pace. The bodyguard! He'd have to make the exchange quickly.

"Good evening, Ms Hookes," he said. "This is the list of conspirators, for President Kehoe."

He handed her the plastic bag. Thanks be to God, she took it.

"*Spasiba*, Colonel," she mumbled, getting his rank right. It was okay— she must have recognized him. She smiled at him as she took the list.

Litvinov stepped past the mustachioed bodyguard and dashed away toward Fourteenth Street. He glanced over his shoulder. The broad-shouldered bodyguard appeared to be examining the plastic bag holding the envelope. Litvinov crossed his fingers once again. He turned and headed north on Fifteenth Street.

"I've got to get back to the White House immediately. Faster than these old legs can get me there," Michelle Hookes told her bodyguard. The latter spoke into a handheld radio.

"Let's just get over to Constitution Avenue," he said. "There will be a ride there, in the right lane, momentarily."

No sooner had Michelle and her bodyguard turned left on Constitution when a black Escalade pulled in front of them, its tail lights flashing.

"This is ours, Ms. Hookes," the bodyguard said. "Please get in."

Four minutes later, the Escalade stopped a few meters short of the southwest gate of the White House.

"It'll take us ten or fifteen minutes to get the vehicle cleared through the gate. If you're okay with walking in, that'll probably be faster," the bodyguard said.

Michelle Hookes was already climbing out of the Escalade and freeing her White House pass from the inside of her blazer. There was no need as the uniformed Secret Service guards recognized her immediately.

"A car will be here in a second, Ms Hookes," said one of the guards. "Here it is," he said moments later as a navy-blue Lincoln pulled up at the inside of the gate. She climbed in and was dropped off seconds later. She entered the West Wing and went directly to her office.

Chapter Eighty-Two

Darps

```
The White House
Washington, D. C.
Mid-June
```

Darps pulled up to the Southwest gate at the White House. The guard recognized the vehicle and punched a few keys on a computer.

"Pull up and park on the left, Mister Taylor," he said. "Then go up to the door where the Marine is standing. She's expecting you."

Darps followed the gate guard's instructions. A Marine Sergeant stood beside the nearest door. Darps addressed her. "Good evening Sergeant. The guard at the gate told me to give you this. Don't let it disappear. It's red hot."

"Aye sir. We've been expecting it. I'll get it to where it needs to go."

"Okay, Sergeant Enright," he said, noting the Sergeant's nametag. "I'm depending on you."

"Thank you, sir," Sergeant Enright responded.

Not knowing what else to do, Darps turned back towards the silver Saab.

"Jesus H. Roosevelt Christ!" exploded the Leader of the Free World inside the West Wing.

"Two! Not one but two! Two lists of American conspirators who want to throw me out on my ass and presumably lock me up some place!"

The President stood in the Oval Office. He was clad in black tie. The State dinner for the Japanese Prime Minister was due to start in seven minutes.

"The lists are identical, Mister President," Michelle Hookes stated quietly. She was still clad in the warm-up suit from her walk. "Both of them came from the Russians. One directly. One of their military attaches handed it to me on the jogging trail on the Mall about halfway between the Monument and the Lincoln Memorial. About twenty-five minutes ago. The other one came via *BIAS* in the Baltic Sea. That was in a book Alan picked up in Saint Petersburg on Russian instructions. It was in code, but

275

BIAS was able to break the code. But both lists are identical. Both contain Admiral Donegan's name, God rest her soul. And she's dead. Apparently, she was prepared to sing, but someone got a sniper to her first. Now we've got to jump on someone else—or everybody else—on the list!"

The president glanced at his watch.

"Set up a meeting for nine tomorrow morning," he said. "In the Situation Room. Syd should be there. And Alan needs to be there too. In the background. Secret Service. Attorney General and FBI Director. You need to be there. I'll have you run the meeting. I don't think anything can happen between now and noon tomorrow. Probably not for a few days. First thing we need to do is nail down the timetable for this little scheme. And if we have to break some balls to do that, so be it. Go ahead and prepare an agenda for the meeting. I'll be outta the dinner by ten and I'll look at it then. Don't feel like you have to stay till after dinner. And take a staff car home."

"Yes, Mister President. Enjoy your dinner."

"Shall I have the mess fix you some dinner?"

"No thanks, Mister President. There's a pepperoni pizza in my freezer at home that is calling my name."

"Gotcha. Understand."

Chapter Eighty-Three
Michelle

The White House Situation Room
Mid-June

President Kehoe stepped into the Situation Room exactly at zero nine hundred. Everyone stood.

"Please sit down," he said. "Sorry for the short notice, but I feel we're facing a problem with which we can't afford to fool around, much less delay. Michelle, please tell everybody what's going on."

Michelle Hookes stood up and cleared her throat.

"About four weeks ago, the President had an extraordinary meeting with the Russian Ambassador. I say the meeting was extraordinary because it was unscheduled, impromptu and 'outside normal channels.' By that, I mean the Russian Presidency was out of the loop. At any rate, the Ambassador advised the President of a so-called plot, within the U.S. Government, aimed at ousting the President and Vice President from office. Presumably by force.

The breath intakes in the Situation Room were clearly audible.

"The ambassador named only one plotter or conspirator and he was not a Government employee or appointee. His name was-is-Roberto Ironsides, President and CEO of *Algorithmics, Incorporated*. *Algorithmics* is a small firm that specializes in solving knotty IT problems for cutting-edge technology firms.

"The president had the Secret Service take a look at Ironsides and they found nothing particularly sinister. His firm does do some pretty arcane stuff and solves high-tech problems that supposedly no one else can. Ironsides, himself, is highly respected as a skilled hacker amongst hacker circles, whatever that means. The firm, *Algorithmics*, has done some black-contract work for the Government—all of it for various parts of the U. S. intelligence establishment. Many of their people hold extremely high security clearances.

"The President tasked an element of our Intelligence Community to look into the issue. He lifted the restrictions on collecting intelligence inside CONUS and they went to work.

"The President subsequently received word from the Russians that they had additional information to pass. The trouble was that quote the Russians unquote apparently were not 'official' in the sense that they were speaking independently, without the knowledge or approval of the top levels of the Russian government. Hence we had to resort to clandestine means to obtain this 'additional information.' And, using these clandestine measures, after some time and effort, we were able to obtain a list of the conspirators' names. The list was encoded when we picked it up in Saint Petersburg. We broke the code for that list yesterday afternoon. Then, a bit later yesterday, we received a second, identical list—in plain text—from a different Russian source here in Washington.

"As I think I said, the two lists are identical."

She reached for a mouse, clicked it and the lists appeared side by side on the computer screen.

Murmurs of "Holy Christ," "Sweet Jesus," and "Son of a bitch," zoomed around the Situation Room.

"Obviously, one of the people whose name is on the list is dead. Admiral Donegan. But, before she was killed at the hands of a sniper, she had indicated, indirectly to us, that (a.) her name was probably on the list and (b.) she was willing to talk. We have to assume that some or all the plotters are behind her murder.

"Another very strange thing is that both lists name Ironsides as a conspirator and both lists name him as 'Source Xray'. And what makes it very curious indeed is that we—the U.S.—have received some spotty information directly from Source Xray."

"So, Ironsides was playing both ends against the middle," Jack Irving, the FBI Director muttered. "Plus my deputy is involved in this plot up to his ass."

"Exactly. The Russians have told us explicitly that Ironsides is their source as well as a co-conspirator. But, as I said, we have received some information from Source Xray himself.

"We are faced with a couple of knotty problems," Hookes continued. "We have no details about the plot. Nothing on timing, methods or place. Then, the alleged coup involves a major chunk of the U. S. Intelligence Community. Not to mention the U. S. House of Representatives. That makes it terribly difficult for us to task the Community to collect any more information on the plot details without showing our hand."

"Let's just arrest all of 'em on the list and sweat 'em. Separately, of course," suggested vice-President Girtler. "We could even haul their asses off to Gitmo."

"I don't think that will fly with this president," Hookes replied, nodding toward Kehoe, who nodded in apparent agreement.

"He really would prefer to snuff this out quietly and without fanfare. We start dragging a lot of U.S. citizens off to Gitmo, the fecal matter will really hit the fan. And that's the exact opposite of what the man wants."

"Okay. Makes sense," Girtler muttered. "Then I'd suggest inviting Braxton, the DNI, in for a chat. And probably putting a tap on Ironsides' phones and a team on him."

Hookes scrawled on her note pad. She turned to the president. He stood up.

"Thank you, everyone," he said. "We've noted everyone's observations and suggestions. Michelle is right. I'd just as soon strangle this baby in its cradle and do so without making any noise."

The meeting was over.

Chapter Eighty-Four
Alan

I had tried to be as unobtrusive as possible at the Situation Room meeting. And I was pretty sure I'd succeeded. I'd kept my mouth shut. The BIAS cat wasn't really that far out of the bag and I didn't want to do anything to change that. So I didn't. I sat in back and buttoned my lip. Michelle had said a lot of interesting, even provocative things. As I headed south on I-95 toward Chestertown, a semi-random thought niggled at my frontal lobes. Esmé! And her "Oklahoma anomaly."

Even with blue tooth steering wheel controls, I'm reluctant to use the phone while driving. I'm not the world's best multi-tasker, to say the least. But this was serious. I pressed the button on the steering wheel.

"Call home," I intoned.

After two rings, I heard Elizabeth pick up.

"Hi Dad," she said.

"Hi, Kiddo," I answered. "How's everything?"

"Fine. What's up?"

"I'm not sure," I said, feeling like an idiot. "I was wondering if Esmé was around. I have a couple of things that I'd like to ask her about."

"It's only ten-thirty. She's probably still asleep. Do you want me to call her and have her call you?"

"Um, yes. But only if she won't be highly pissed at either one of us for waking her up," I replied.

"No problem, Dad. I'll give her a call."

About five minutes later, my blue tooth ring tone jangled, startling the shit out of me. The little screen on the dashboard said "Esmé."

"Good morning, Esmé, "I said.

"Hi, Mister El. What's up?" she asked. She didn't sound at all sleepy.

"Um, it's about our little Oklahoma anomaly," I said carefully.

"You mean the Fort Sill blackout?" she asked.

"Yes, Ma'am. I have a couple of questions and I don't necessarily expect you to have the answers. But I do hope you have a thought or two about the questions."

"Shoot, Mister Ell. I'll try," she said.

"Okay. For starters, once upon a time you described a possible scenario for what happened at Fort Sill. If I remember correctly, you described one of the options as 'bad guys running some sort of test.' Do I have that right?"

"Yeah. That sounds about right," she said.

"Okay. Let's take that a step further," I said. "Let's assume you're right and evildoers were running some sort of test. Let's say the test worked. Do you think the next step might be a shutdown of *all* Army C4I stuff? Not just at Fort Sill, but nationwide? Or even worldwide?"

"Yes sir," she said, unhesitatingly. "If it was a test, then it was almost certainly a small-scale trial run in preparation for something bigger. I have no idea of how much bigger. But definitely something bigger."

"Okay, Esmé. That leads me directly to my next question. Do you think this possible electronic shutdown could be part of an even bigger plot against the Government?" The whole government? One going way beyond the Army?" I asked.

Silence ensued for what seemed like thirty seconds. I was about to ask if she was still on the line when she came back.

"That's a tough question, Mister El," she said in a small voice. "I mean, I guess it could be. But I don't think we have any, any—" She stopped, momentarily. "Any evidence. Proof. Or even any strong clues," she continued, after a short pause in our conversation.

She was definitely a sharp cookie.

"Good answer, Kiddo," I said. "Let me ask you this. Do you think this little mini-test at Fort Sill—if that's what it was--could have been a precursor to a serious try to take down the government?"

"Wow! I dunno, Mister El. That's a pretty open-ended question."

See what I mean about her being a sharp cookie?

"But," she continued. "Since you asked, I'd have to say that yes, I think it is *possible*. The precision of what whoever made that stuff happen at Fort Sill suggests to me that 'whoever' isn't a bunch of doofuses playing in someone's basement. So, yeah, I'd guess that 'whoever' is probably aiming pretty high."

"Okay, Esmé. Thanks a lot. That really helps me. I owe you one," I said.

"How 'bout a glass of *pro secco* next time I see you?" she asked, sweetly.

"Good-bye, you sly little vixen," I answered and pressed the hang-up button on the steering wheel. I was surprised that she even knew what *pro secco* was.

Chapter Eighty-Five

Alan

Chestertown, Virginia

Mid-June

As I was driving onto the Martha Washington campus in Chestertown, my blue tooth rang and jangled my nerves. The little touch screen read "Home." I punched the phone button.

"Hi!" I said.

"Hi, Dad!" Elizabeth said. "Did Esmé call you?"

"Yes, Sweetie, she did," I said. "Not only did she call me, but she helped me out quite a bit. So thanks for calling her."

"Well, goodie. I'm glad she helped you. Was it about the Fort Sill lights-out episode?"

"Yes. We can talk about it some when I get home. Right now, I'm pulling into my parking place at work," I said, hoping that I wasn't sounding like I was brushing her off.

"Okay, Dad. See you when you get home."

Everything sounded fine at the ranch. I climbed out of the Explorer and headed into Ripley Hall.

"Let's get together in the SCIF," I told Judy.

"The 'plot gang'?" she asked. "Now?"

"Yes and yes," I said.

"Okay," I said, to start the meeting off five minutes later. "This meeting is under the Thunder code-word. I think all of you know I've just come from a meeting in the White House Situation Room. The subject was the plot against the president. President Kehoe was there. He started things off but he had Michelle Hookes run the meeting. Here's what she had to say, more or less.

"As most of you know, this whole shebang started with an unscheduled meeting between the President and a Russian diplomat. In this meeting, the diplomat stated that there was a plot against the President quote somewhere in the U.S. Government Unquote. He named a non-government civilian, one Roberto Ironsides, as one of the conspirators. You all may know who Ironsides is, but neither Kehoe nor I did. Kehoe sicced the Secret Service on him and learned that he's the chairman and CEO of *Algorithmics, Incorporated*. The latter is a somewhat dark-side IT problem-solving outfit. They've had a few black contracts with elements of the U.S. Intelligence Community. Ironsides himself is somewhat notorious amongst hacker circles.

"The President responded by tasking 'elements of the U. S. Intelligence Community,' to take a look at the issue. As part of that, he tasked the FBI to 'keep an eye on things.' Syd Girtler was at the meeting and he suggested that the FBI should arrest Braxton and Ironsides and haul them off to Gitmo 'for a chat.'

"At some point, Kehoe—I'm not sure when--got more info from the Russians to the effect that they had more scoop to pass along, possibly identifying some or all of the other conspirators. It became apparent that the Russian info was coming to us from sources, ahem, independent of the top of the Russian government.

"After a few weeks, we ended up with not one, but two lists of conspirators. Both lists were identical. One we obtained through clandestine means in Russia; the other came to us from the Russian embassy here in Washington. Both lists contained the names of Ironsides and Vice Admiral Sheila Donegan. Not to mention Madame Speaker Helen DeWitt of the House of Representatives.

"We still lack critical details, such as timelines and plot methodology. That's basically what Ms. Hookes told us in the Situation Room meeting.

"On my way out of the White House, Michelle Hookes dragged me into the Oval Office where President Kehoe was waiting for me.

"'Loose, old horse!' he said. 'What thinkest thee about that?' Or words to that effect."

"'I kind of like the Vice President's idea,' I told him, referring to the Veep's idea of bringing Braxton in for a chat. 'But methinks that we don't have enough info. We have the lists, coming from the Russians as they do. We don't know the when, the where, or the how. Even if we rounded up every swinging dick on the list, plus the, ahem, others, we have nothing that would stand up in court. Unless one or two of them collapsed and confessed everything. So, I guess I'm saying we have to dig for more information. I guess that means more work for me. Not to mention my troops,' I said."

"Oh well, you know what they say. 'Life's a bitch and then you die,' the President of the United States told me."

"On my way back here, I recalled the Fort Sill 'incident,' which we discussed here a while back. Somebody shut down the entire Fort Sill Army C4I infrastructure for exactly two minutes a few weeks ago. I'm beginning to think that the two 'happenings' may be connected. That is, the Fort Sill blackout may be tied to the alleged, anti-government plot. That's a huge, logical leap as well as an important footnote to the summary of the Situation Room meeting."

I sat down.

Chapter Eighty-Six
Alan

Chestertown, Virginia
Mid-June

"I think you need to let the White House know of your—our--suspicion, Shipmate," Darps said back in my office. "And maybe recommend that they investigate Ironsides and *Algorithmics* and find out if they did in fact engineer that blackout at Fort Sill. And, if so, why didn't they coordinate it with the Army? For starters."

"'For starters' is right," I said. "I think any investigation by the White House—by the Secret Service or the FBI, or both—needs to look into where else this *Algorithmics* screwing around is going. Like, is it developing into part of an anti-government coup attempt?"

"That's way above my pay grade. But even if it weren't, I'd say hell yes, they need to look in that direction. The White House—or somebody up there—definitely should find out where this fuzzball is headed."

I agreed and nodded toward Luke and Mike who were seated together.

"Go ahead and close the loop with the Secret Service," I said. "They were at the meeting in the Situation Room. But they should know what we're thinking. I'm going to call *Cheetah* and tell him what we're thinking. Now."

I reached for the red phone.

"This is *BIAS* Six. Llewellyn. I need to speak to the man. ASAP," I said.

I waited for about a minute. Then Kehoe's voice came on the line.

"What's up, Loose?" he asked.

"*Algorithmics* and Fort Sill," I said.

"What the hell are you talking about?" he asked, sounding just a tiny bit testy.

"You'll see. And I'll make this quick," I said. "Roberto Ironsides is on both conspirator lists. It also sounds like he might be in the Russians' pocket. His firm, *Algorithmics, Incorporated* may have engineered that electronics blackout at Fort Sill a few weeks ago. That, in turn, may be a prelude to a larger, government-wide shutdown, which could well be a part of a coup attempt. I suggest you have him—Ironsides--picked up ASAP and milk him for whatever you can. Look at his phone records, his computers, trashcans, and burn bags, whatever. Grill him hard on the Fort Sill episode and see where that leads. And do it quickly. If he gets wind that you're nosing around, he could be running off to tan his buns in Curacao or enjoy some salmon fishing in Kamchatka and we'd be high and dry. Or, he could have seized control of the U. S. Government and have all our asses locked up someplace."

"Okay," he said. "I hear what you're saying. I'll run it by the Secret Service up here. I'm thinking of a quick visit to a safehouse."

"Don't forget. It looks like the conspirators are all from the U.S. Intelligence Community. That could well mean the FBI."

"I'll keep that in mind. Stay well."

He hung up. I wasn't sure what he was talking about.

I had no way of knowing if he took me seriously or not.

Chapter Eighty-Seven
President James Kehoe

```
The White House
Early September
```

"**A**llison. Would you please be so kind as to inform Speaker De Witt's office that I'd like to chat with her sometime this morning," President Kehoe said into the bitch box on his desk.

The tiny daytime indicator at the top of his computer screen showed 9:12 AM.

"Yes, sir. Right away."

Two minutes later, Allison's head popped into the Oval Office.

"Madame Speaker. On Line One," she said.

"Thanks, Allison," Kehoe said and reached for the phone.

"Good morning, Helen," he began. "How are you feeling this morning?"

He listened to her marginally non-committal reply and thought he detected a slight quaver of puzzlement in her voice.

"I'm calling to invite you to the White House for a private lunch. Today," he said.

"Well, this is quite a surprise," Speaker De Witt parried.

"I know. And I apologize for that," Kehoe said. "But it is a matter of high urgency. I wouldn't spring it on you so suddenly if it weren't."

"Should I call you back on the secure line, Mister President?" she asked. "Perhaps that way we could discuss what this is all about."

"No Ma'am. This is just between the two of us. Shouldn't take more than an hour, maybe an hour and a half at most."

"What time would you like me to be there, Mister President?" she asked, resignedly.

"Let's say twelve fifteen. And the lunch will be private. Just thee and me," Kehoe said.

"Okay, Sir. See you at twelve-fifteen," she said.

"Looking forward to it, Helen," he said, crossing his fingers.

The Speaker's limo arrived at the West Wing entrance at 12:13. A Marine Corps Corporal led Congresswoman DeWitt to a small, private dining room not far from the Oval Office. The President was already there.

"Would you care for a cocktail?" the President asked after they were seated.

"Are you having one, Mister President?" DeWitt asked.

"That's a tough call," Kehoe said with a nervous chuckle. "If I have a cocktail, then I won't allow myself to have wine with lunch. It'll be ice tea city all the way. But yes. I think, I'll have a Scotch and soda."

"I'll have the same," Speaker DeWitt said.

The drinks arrived quickly. Kehoe took a sip of his and put the glass down.

"Helen, you and I go way back. Once upon a time, we were both junior Congressmen from New York. We worked together on both the test ban treaty and the inheritance tax bill. We became pretty good friends in the bargain. That makes what I'm about to say terrifically difficult."

He stood up and retrieved a leather folder from a sideboard.

"I have here two lists—or two copies of the same list. They're identical. They contain the names of conspirators involved in a plot to throw me and Syd Girtler out on our asses and into a federal prison. Your name is on both lists."

"That's ridiculous, Mister President," Speaker DeWitt almost barked. "That's someone's fiction. Total Nonsense!"

"I don't think so, Helen," Kehoe answered quietly. "You'll notice that the first name on both lists is that of Sam Braxton, the DNI. We had Sam picked up by the Secret Service and transported to a safe house. He blew the whistle on a plot to temporarily shut down the U.S. Government's C4I infrastructure and, during the shutdown, lock Girtler and me up at Leavenworth Federal Prison. After which, you Madame Speaker, would be sworn in as President. After all, you, as Speaker of the House, would be second in line to succeed me. Since Syd was also to be arrested and jailed, you are the one."

Madame Speaker turned pale. And turned away.

"The list also contains the name of Roberto Ironsides, head honcho of *Algorithmics*. The Secret Service also picked up Ironsides and took him to a safe house as well. He confirmed Braxton's story, including your role in the plot. And your ultimate place in the plot's completion. I guess I should feel flattered.

"Finally, there's the matter of Admiral Donegan's murder. We're still nibbling around the edges of that, but I think everything points to Braxton, Ironsides, and company. And possibly DeWitt, by extension. I'm not at all sure how that might play out legally.

"I mentioned earlier that you and I go back a long way. I did not mention that we share the same party affiliation. But we do. And I don't think anything is to be gained by causing a self-imposed, self-destructive shitstorm within the Republican Party. I seem to remember hearing a couple of months ago that you had a granddaughter with some rare illness. AML?"

"Yes. 'Acute Mylogenous Leukemia.' It's not all that rare. Some twenty thousand people are diagnosed with AML in the U.S. every year. The bad news is that ten thousand people die from it every year. The good news is that Tammy, my granddaughter, is ten years old and young people seem to be much better at responding to treatment. Which is chemotherapy. Which she's getting now."

"Any thoughts?"

"Yes sir. A ton. But what are your thoughts?"

"Well, um, they are pretty random. From your bio, I see you're sixty-two. That tells me a couple of things. One, you're young enough and spry enough to be very helpful to Tammy's mom during Tammy's chemo treatment. Two, my guess is that both Tammy and her mom would be grateful for your help and support during a very challenging time. And three, at sixty-two, no one is likely to look twice at your retirement from the House of Representatives for compelling family reasons—a granddaughter with leukemia sounds pretty compelling to me."

"Mister President, you make a pretty convincing case."

"I think my scheming lies in the direction of what's best for the good guys and the country. And despite where you've been sitting in this nasty little cabal, I still consider you one of the good guys. Like I said, we go back a long way."

"Can I think about it some?" DeWitt asked.

"Of course, of course," Kehoe said. "But not for very long. The train is leaving the station and is starting to pick up speed. The farther away it gets, the less control I have over everything."

"I understand, Mister President," DeWitt said softly. "Now, if you'll excuse me, I've suddenly lost my appetite. And I do need some time to think."

She finished the dregs of her Scotch and stood up.

"Thank you, Mister President," she said. "You'll be hearing from me."

Chapter Eighty-Eight
President James Kehoe

The White House
Early September

The following letter arrived on the President's desk Wednesday morning.

Office of the Speaker
22445 Rayburn House Office Building
Washington, D. C. 2003

Office of the President of the United States
The White House
1600 Pennsylvania Avenue
Washington, D. C. 20500

Dear Mister President,

The purpose of this letter to request retirement from the House of Representatives and as Speaker, effective immediately. I have recently learned that my granddaughter—the daughter of my own daughter and her husband-has Acute Mylogenous Leukemia (AML), a potentially fatal illness. She has started a chemotherapy regime and my wish is to be able to help her and her parents through a very difficult time. Fortunately, Tammy, my granddaughter, is ten years old and, the younger a patient's age at the time of diagnosis, the better the prognosis. Nonetheless, I feel that my daughter, her husband and their daughter can use my help and support through a truly difficult and challenging time.

My plan is to leave Washington and relocate to the Minneapolis-Saint Paul area where my granddaughter will be receiving her treatment at the University of Minnesota University Hospital.

I thank you for your support and consideration.

Very respectfully,
Helen DeWitt

The President refolded DeWitt's letter carefully.

"Allyson, let's get a press release out that says we accept Speaker DeWitt's retirement with profound regret but we understand her extremely difficult family situation and our prayers are with her. Let's get it out on the street ASAP."

Chapter Eighty-Nine

Alan

Chestertown, Virginia
Early September

I wasn't sure where to go. I was sure I'd given the President everything germane that we'd collected. Plus some stuff that we hadn't—including suppositions that Esmé and I had conjured up. And I wasn't even sure that Kehoe took us seriously.

There was a mild rumble of late summer thunder outside when Maria announced that dinner was ready.

We Llewellyns had a delightful evening meal of grilled cube steaks with mozzarella served over angel hair pasta and under a mushroom-marinara sauce. The grated Parmesan cheese, combined with four-cheese Texas toast rounded things out nicely. Maria's insalata—-arugula, fresh tomatoes, sliced capicola and olives, topped with extra-virgin olive oil swirled with sherry vinegar--settled our stomachs perfectly.

I stifled a burp, just as rain started pounding on our windows like giant handfuls of gravel.

"Thank you for a fabulous meal, Sweetie," I said.

"You're welcome," she said. "What's the matter?"

"Matter?" I asked, querulously.

"With you," she said. "You're only partially here. Part of you is somewhere else."

"Yeah. You're right," I said. "Fortunately, my taste buds are with the part of me that's here. Dinner was great."

"You are a true snake in the grass, trying to deftly change the subject," she replied. "Now what about the part of you that went away? Where did *he* go?"

"Hell's bells. I don't really know. And even if I did know, it's all code-word protected, so it's off limits for discussion here. I feel like I'm in a tennis match, my opponent just served and the ball stopped in midair ten feet above the net."

"So, who's your opponent?" Maria asked.

"I'm not even sure," I said. "The Russians? The American conspirators? I just don't know."

Just then, my cell buzzed. It was silenced and lying on our kitchen counter. Instead of ringing, it vibrated and sounded like a rattlesnake on the counter. I jumped and looked at the little screen.

"LI Sound," it read. It was Kehoe and I snatched it up.

"Yes sir," I said.

"Okay. Here's what we're going to do," Kehoe said. "Secret Service agents are on the way to arrest Ironsides. Even as we speak. They say the two lists from two different sources plus his and Braxton's statements give them probable cause. They'll bring him to a safe house in Virginia and chat with him. They'll explore further *Algorithmics* connections with the Fort Sill blackout. If they nail down an *Algorithmics* tie-in with Fort Sill, they'll try to follow that up and we'll pick up Braxton again. And see what sort of additional light he might be able to shed on this operation."

"Okay. That sounds good," I replied. "I think it's vitally important that you put the fear of God into Ironsides. He should know that, if he goes to trial and they find him guilty, he and *Algorithmics* are out of business. We should start with cancelling all their security clearances. Maybe end up with an extended stay at some federal slammer.

"And please let's not forget Admiral Donegan, God rest her soul. I'd bet my ass, hat and overcoat that at least one of those two motherfuckers—Ironsides or Braxton—was behind her murder," I added.

"You may well be right about all that,' he said. "But I still want to keep this off the skyline. Incarcerating Ironsides' ass indefinitely at Gitmo or wherever might put everything in lights in the sky. And we sure as hell don't want that!"

"Well you've had his ass incarcerated in a safe house already," I said.

"Yeah. But we can't keep him there indefinitely," he said.

"Speaking of lights in the sky," I said, a bit hesitantly. "What about Madame Speaker? Congresswoman DeWitt? She's in this mess up to her eyeballs."

There was a short gap of silence.

"Yeah. I know. She's also the Speaker of the House of Representatives. That means, per the U.S. Constitution, she's next in line to succeed me after Syd. But she's not anymore because she's retired, effective yesterday. For "family reasons." She has a granddaughter who is ill and fighting acute myologenous leukemia or AML and she feels she needs to be there for her daughter and her granddaughter. And I can certainly understand that," he said. "There should be a White House press release about her retirement going out as we speak," he added.

I decided that saying nothing was my best option. So that's what I said. Nothing.

"For what it's worth, my guess is that the next Speaker will be Paul Winkler, Republican from California," Kehoe said.

"Well, I wish him well," I said lamely. I wouldn't know Representative Winkler if I'd run into him on Constitution Avenue. The important thing was that DeWitt was now out of the picture. Then a malignant thought popped into my mind.

"What about the Bobsey Twins? Braxton and Ironsides? I assume you can't keep them locked up forever. Won't one or the other or both spill the beans about DeWitt's role in the plot?" I asked.

"Yeah, I've thought about that. We're trying to make sure that doesn't happen," he said. "Talk to you soon."

Chapter Ninety

Alan

Chestertown, Virginia
Early September

I was still in limbo when I walked home from work. I let myself in the front door and Maria shouted, "The President's coming on!"

I stepped into the family room where, sure enough, the Press Secretary was announcing, "Ladies and Gentlemen, the President of the United States." I plumped my ass down on the sofa and watched as Kehoe stepped in front of the mikes and straightened his tie.

"Good afternoon, Ladies and Gentlemen. I'd like to bring you up to date on a situation that has surfaced within our government just recently and has been contained but which the American people should be aware of.

"Some elements within our Intelligence Community have been harboring policy positions which differ markedly from those held by this administration. These positions have prompted some members of the Intelligence Community to take actions that could ultimately render any and all official government action ineffective.

"Accordingly, I have relieved the Director of National Intelligence, Doctor Samuel Braxton, of his duties and revoked all his security clearances. I furthermore have revoked all security clearances of Mister Roberto Ironsides, Chairman and Chief Executive Officer of *Algorithmics*, Incorporated. All contractual efforts by *Algorithmics* on behalf of the U. S. Government have been suspended indefinitely. All U. S. sponsored security clearances for *Algorithmics* personnel have been terminated. Several of the latter are under investigation on a variety of charges. There are also a number of the members of the Intelligence Community who are under investigation as we speak.

"I have time for a few questions."

"Yes sir, Mr. President. Bill Key, New York Times. Is there any connection between what you just described and the death of Vice Admiral Donegan, the Director of Naval Intelligence?"

President Kehoe: "That issue is currently under investigation. As long

297

as the investigation is ongoing, we'll have no further comment. But, as soon as we get things clarified, I'll let you know."

"Mister President, Kathy Gore, CNN. Are any formal charges being brought up on Doctor Braxton or Mister Ironsides? Or any other Government personnel or *Algorithmics* employees?"

President Kehoe. "Not at this time. The whole matter is under investigation by the Secret Service and the FBI. I'm sure we'll have more for you as the investigation develops."

"Mister President. Jim Kelleher, Washington Post. There were some newspaper reports of a communications shutdown at Fort Sill, the Army's Field Artillery Center, several weeks ago. Is there any connection between that shutdown and this apparent anti-Government plot?

President Kehoe. "We are pretty sure there is. Our investigations are proceeding on the assumption that there is a connection between the Fort Sill communications anomaly and the anti-government plot. But the whole thing is under investigation. We'll have more for you on that as the investigation develops. Thank you."

President Kehoe left the podium and the TV channel faded to the duty talking head.

"Holy shit," I said.

"Amen," Maria said.

I wasn't sure what to do or whom to call. Kehoe had taken things into his own hands—as was certainly his right. *BIAS* was now out of the loop. The good thing was that *BIAS* had not emerged as a player in this shitstorm. We were still under the radar and I wanted to keep things that way. Hardly anyone knew who or what we are. I was confident that Kehoe would agree, in spades. I'd meet with Darps and Judy in the morning to take a look at hanging items on the *BIAS* to-do list. Seemed as if we suddenly went from zooming along at Mach Two to sloshing around at one or two knots.

Chapter Ninety-One
Alan

A few weeks later, I was glancing at the "Irish sports pages"—the Obituaries pages—of the Chestertown *Star,* where one particular obit caught my eye.

BRAXTON, Samuel Allen.

Doctor Samuel Allen Braxton, age 60, passed away suddenly of an apparent heart attack. Doctor Braxton was born in Ft Wayne, Indiana to Dale C. Braxton and Sharon Meadow (Carlson) Braxton. Sam graduated from the New Mexico Military Institute before attending Purdue University where he earned his degree in Aeronautical Engineering. Four years later, he received his Ph.D. in aeronautics from the California Institute of Technology. He loved his country and served proudly as an intelligence officer in the United States Air Force until retiring from active duty in 1998. After his retirement from the Air Force, Sam went to work for the National Security Agency at Fort Meade, Maryland. He subsequently transferred to the Intelligence Community Staff in Washington, D.C. before being appointed Director of National Intelligence by President Kehoe. In addition to his parents, he is survived by his former wife of twenty-eight years, Suzanne (Jordan) Braxton, children Taylor (Braxton) Weiss and Quentin Robert Braxton and grandchildren Robin and Nancy Sherman and Robert Braxton, Jr. A private memorial Mass was held on September 18. In lieu of flowers, memorial donations may be made to the American Heart Association.

Hmm, I thought.

"Maria," I said. Maria was up to her lovely ass in doing some sort of military-historical research. "Would you be kind enough to take a look at this?"

I handed her the newspaper where I had circled Brazton's obit with a yellow Sharpie.

"Sweet Mother," she mumbled.

"Read the whole thing," I suggested, which was exactly what she was doing.

When she finished, she looked up at me.

"I smell a rat," she said.

"More than one," I said. "Sixty-year old guy—who was an avid runner—he ran at least one Iron Man, for God's sake—drops dead. Of a quote apparent unquote heart attack. Quote private unquote funeral Mass. At undisclosed location. Presidential appointee, yet no mention of big shot attendees. A whole bunch of rats."

"So what are you thinking?" she asked.

"Probably the same thing you are. Thinking, that is," I said. "Plus I don't think I want to say what I'm thinking. Especially not out loud and indoors. But I do think I need to call Darps," I said.

"I agree," she said.

"Hello, Shipmate," I said, into the phone a few minutes later. "Do me a favor and get on line and find today's edition of the Chestertown *Star*. Go to the Obituaries and see what jumps up at you."

"Holy shit," he muttered, a couple of minutes later. "Braxton!"

"Let's have coffee at our favorite little farmhouse first thing tomorrow," I suggested.

"Eight o'clock?" he asked.

"Perfect," I said, ending the call.

I brought yesterday's copy of the Chestertown *Star* with me out to our Wilderness shack and arrived at zero-seven-fifty, courtesy of several lucky green lights. The coffee was starting to smell pretty good a few minutes later when Darps rolled in.

"Here it is in black and white, Sports Fans," I said as I handed the obit page of the *Star* to him and started to pour steaming mugs of coffee.

"Sweet Christ," he hissed. "If the Washington Fat Cats get a hold of this, they'll be howling for Kehoe's blood. This is damned near an accusation of murder!"

"That's how I read it," I said. "I showed the obit to Maria. She didn't say anything but her eyes said it all. She agrees with us. So what to do now?"

"I'd say not a fucking thing," Darps said. "Kehoe's a big boy. He's got the Secret Service looking after him. He gave the press conference about the coup attempt. And maybe Braxton did die of a heart attack. That obit wasn't written in the White House."

"At least not that we know of," I said. "But I agree with you. Let's leave this particular stone unturned. For the record, we take the obit on its face value. Sudden heart attack. Family wanted low profile, private funeral and burial. That's that."

Darps sucked down the last of his coffee and walked to the sink. He started rinsing out his mug. I unplugged the machine.

"See you back at the ranch," I said.

"Roger that," he said.

It wasn't more than nine or ten days later when I got a call from Darps. It was a Thursday evening.

"Do you read the Annapolis *Capital-Gazette*?" he asked.

"No," I said. "Why?"

"I'll show you tomorrow. How 'bout we meet at the farm first thing?"

"Uh-oh," I said.

They were hooking up a black horse to the old-fashioned hearse when I drove past the Gillis funeral home in the rain. That didn't seem like a good omen. I arrived at our dilapidated safe house near the Wilderness Battlefield around seven-forty-five. The day was chilly and rainy so I turned on the heat before I turned on the lights. Then I set up the coffee maker for a half pot—about enough for two mugs. I heard Darps' Saab roll in just as the air started to warm and the coffee aroma began to spread.

He was carrying a folded-up newspaper.

"Take a look at this," he said. "Here we go again, swapping newspapers. Smells like the coffee is just about ready."

He reached for a mug and handed me the folded paper. Someone had circled an article with a bright green highlighter.

Man Disappears on the Potomac

the headline shouted. The story continued:

A Virginia man, apparently sailing alone, disappeared from his sailboat yesterday near the east bank of the Potomac River in Charles County, Maryland. The missing man, identified from boating records and by his wife, Marion, was Roberto Ironsides, age 54, a Longtime resident of Stafford County, Virginia. Ironsides has been associated with Algorithmics, Inc., a cutting-edge, high-tech software development firm, for many years. He had retired as the Algorithmics CEO shortly before his death. Investigators do not believe foul play was involved at this point.

"That section of the Potomac is fairly shallow and can go from dead calm to pretty damned rough, very quickly, especially at this time of year," Sergeant Robert Abramowitz of the Maryland State Police stated. "We are treating this case as a tragic accident."

Ironsides' body was recovered from the Potomac yesterday. Two fishermen spotted his boat drifting with no one aboard and notified police shortly before noon. Coastguardsmen recovered his body about a mile downstream from the drifting boat an hour later.

"What do you think of that, Shipmate?" Darps asked.

"I'm not sure I want to tell you what I think of it," I said. "If you get my drift."

"I think I do. Get your drift, that is," he said. "When you put this together with that recent Braxton obit, one has to wonder about how lily-white the hands of your old high school running mate are."

"Let's not go there," I said. "I think that maybe our charter doesn't cover us waking up this particular sleeping dog."

"Yeah. I agree, Shipmate. Let's forget about it."

"Agree," I said. "Meantime there's a new code-word note from Cheetah sitting in the SCIF."

"Does it say anything about sleeping dogs?"

"No," I said. "It's a new dog. And very wide awake."

"Good," he said.

"Speaking of sleeping," I said. "That trip to Saint Petersburg must have blown something out of my system. Lately I've been sleeping like the proverbial dog."

Epilogue
Officer DiRienzo

Gerlach Community College
Gayles Ferry, Virginia
Late June

The lightning lit up the campus parking lot like instantaneous, extremely bright, ragged daylight. As Officer Gerry DiRienzo, the campus cop, alighted from the battered black Ford, a deafening clap of thunder slammed down on the campus. He flinched jerkily and nearly knocked his hat off on the top of the police car door. The VA shrink had told him that his "exaggerated startle reflex" was one of several symptoms of his PTSD, a souvenir from Viet Nam. He thought of a raggedy-ass tee shirt he had at home in a drawer that had a map of Vietnam on it and the words "I left Vietnam but Vietnam never left me."

The first raindrops started to fall. DiRienzo held his hat with one hand and steadied the Glock on his hip with the other while he jogged toward the door of Campbell Hall. It had been raining pretty hard that night back in March. A cold rain with no thunder. But it was a cold, hard rain. Not like this evening's summer rain.

He wasn't all that wet when he got to the door. *I've really gotta start thinking about retiring,* he thought. The rain caused him to think back to that March evening when Campbell Hall had erupted in a bloodbath caused by some fucked up kid with a vintage M-14 military rifle. Just thinking about that night made him break out in a sweat. The asshole had started coming down the stairs, waving the rifle and Gerry had fired his Glock and dropped him halfway down the stairs.

Upstairs had been a total charnel house. A ton of dead kids. And a dead professor. The kids who weren't dead were screaming and bleeding. The death toll was reported to be right at twenty, including a fifty-something-year-old professor and the punk with the rifle.

He walked up the stairs quietly. He could hear soft voices coming from the classrooms at the top of the stairs. Classroom voices. Low and calm, the way classroom voices were supposed to be.

This might be a good time to pull the ole plug, he thought. *Maybe now's the time.*

Another lengthy flash of lightning lit up the outdoors and flashed through the windows of Campbell Hall, followed immediately by another deafening crash of thunder.

That's it, thought DiRienzo. *My Guardian Angel is talking to me and trying to tell me something. Like "You're done here, Paisan'. Time to go fishing and play some golf in South Carolina." And she's right. I'm gonna write the goddam letter as soon as I get home.*

He glanced at his wristwatch. Two and a half more hours.

The End

Thank you for reading **Baltic Thunder.** I hope you enjoyed it. As an independently published author, I rely on you, the reader, to get out the word. So if you enjoyed **Baltic Thunder,** please tell your friends and family. I'd also greatly appreciate it if you'd **write** a brief review for Amazon.com. Thanks again and stay well.

Walt

ABOUT THE AUTHOR

Walt Breede was born in White Plains, New York. He graduated from Archbishop Stepinac High School and the United States Naval Academy at Annapolis. Commissioned in the Marine Corps, he served as an artillery officer, mathematician and intelligence officer. He served a combat tour in Vietnam, as a gunnery instructor at the Army Artillery School at Fort Sill, Oklahoma and as Assistant Naval Attache at the American Embassy in Ankara, Turkey. After retiring from the Marines, he became a high school math teacher and coached several sports. He and his wife Elizabeth have five children and seven grandchildren. Walt and Betty reside in Tarpon Springs, Florida.

Note from the Publisher

We had just about completed post-production work on *Baltic Thunder* when I received the sad news that Walt had suddenly passed away on July 24, 2020.

Walt was a great American – a patriot who served his country for 26 years as a commissioned officer in the United States Marine Corps with a variety of challenging assignments including two tours as the Naval attaché in Ankara, Turkey.

But beyond the success he had professionally, Walt was a kind and engaging person who cared deeply about his family, his students, and his country. I greatly enjoyed working with Walt on his two previous novels, *Sanity Check* and *Brainstorm*, and then finally on *Baltic Thunder*.

I will certainly miss Walt's approach to story-telling and the insight that he brought to national security affairs that made his novels authentic and exciting. But mostly, I will miss our conversations and his friendship.

John McClure
Signalman Publishing
September, 2020

Also by Walt Breede (and featuring Alan Llewellyn)

Snow On The Golden Horn
Altar Stone
Sanity Check
Brainstorm

www.ingramcontent.com/pod-product-compliance
Lightning Source LLC
Chambersburg PA
CBHW070834280626
47161CB00015B/590